He kissed her as though he would never let her go . . .

with a hunger that matched her own. The strange, exciting glow inside mounted higher and higher, and she let it take her where it would. Her whole body rejoiced in the pressure of his arms, forcing her ever closer to him. Her fingers explored his hair, the back of his neck, his earlobes, his cheeks. She wanted, somehow, to be engulfed by him.

His hands found their way under the velvet cloak and reached up to caress the bare skin above her low-necked gown in back. Then his mouth left her lips to travel over her face, her cheeks and eyes and forehead, and then downward, to her neck and the soft, cool hollow of her throat.

She was drowning in sensation, eyes closed, head back, when he broke his hold roughly and pushed her back into the chair. "No, Stephanie, no!" He kicked the little footstool out of the way and strode to the window.

"Alan!" she cried out in shock and hurt.

Silence settled, broken only by the crackle of flames in the fireplace.

"Why not? What's the matter?" she whispered.

"I'm not the man for you. I never was . . ."

A Duet For My Lady

A Duet For My Lady

MARJORIE DEBOER

WARNER BOOKS

A Warner Communications Company

WARNER BOOKS EDITION

This Warner Books Edition is published by arrangement with Wildstar
Books, a division of the Adele Leone Agency, Inc.

Cover design by Anthony Russo

Warner Books, Inc.
666 Fifth Avenue
New York, N.Y. 10103

 A Warner Communications Company

Printed in the United States of America

First Printing: October, 1987

10 9 8 7 6 5 4 3 2 1

FOR POLLY
Whose story has yet to be told

CHAPTER I

Alan Dunstable paused before the gravel walk that crossed the green rectangle of Berkeley Square. It had been six years since he had first come to this particular part of London's Mayfair. He was conscious, for a brief moment, of a vast difference between that time and this, but the difference was more his state of mind than anything else; the difference between an ambitious, naive young man from the country seeking patronage from London's *ton*, and the self-confident, widely traveled person he had become.

In appearance he was much the same. He had left his Soho flat gloveless and hatless, without the walking stick gentlemen usually relied on when they ventured forth. His brown frock coat was rumpled and travel-stained as usual, and his only concession to style was a fresh white neck cloth. He might have worn a black top hat—he owned one now—but he had forgotten it. That was another fashion that seemed as unnecessary to him as the wigs of the past generation. His thick, curly black hair was all the covering his head needed, and he didn't care if the wind blew it or the sun browned his already weathered face.

What the devil did Valeria want with him after all this time? It was five years since they had last met. The Lady Valeria Hammond he had known was now Lady Burleigh, Countess of Woodworth, envied for her success in landing

1

the prize bachelor who had eluded two generations of eager aristocratic womanhood. Was she happy with her aging earl? If she wasn't, what did she want him to do about it?

He resumed his stride, passing beds of July-bright marigolds and purple pansies, white-smocked nannies pushing prams, older boys playing tag around the pagoda-style pump house with its red roof in the middle of the square. The Chinese influence was everywhere, from the Scottish border south to George the Fourth's pavilion at Brighton, that incongruity so derided by his fellow journalists.

The houses across the square were, by contrast, dully, invincibly British, their look-alike stone or whitewashed brick facades adorned with similar pedimented doors and ironwork gates separating them from the walkway. The only distinction in the house he now approached was in the green hanging ferns and scarlet-and-white petunias cascading between the molded rungs of twin second-story balconies. Valeria's touch, he was sure.

Reaching deep into the pocket of his frock coat, Alan fingered again the note Valeria had written him, making sure it really existed. It did. He opened the iron gate and looked up briefly. Had she watched his approach across the square—a tradesman's approach, without horse or carriage?

He knocked the wolf's-head knocker sharply against the iron wreath beneath it and waited, looking about him. Except for the children in the square, the afternoon was quiet. Next door, a mobcapped maid in blue skirt and flat shoes carried a newspaper-wrapped parcel down the stairway to her mistress's kitchen. Farther along, a red-coated postman was chatting with a coachman waiting on his box for his passenger. The door before him opened. Alan felt the palms of his hands sweat.

Octavian, the black West Indian footman Valeria had hired some half dozen years ago to give her friends a bit of a start, looked at him inquiringly, without recognition. Standing six foot four, he was both resplendent and intimidating in his scarlet-and-gray livery.

"Good afternoon, Octavian. I believe I'm expected." He handed the footman a card that read, "Mr. Alan Pickering Dunstable. King's College, Cambridge."

The address belonged to his now-deceased father who had taught ancient and medieval history at the university. In the four years Alan had used it, he had never been questioned, and the aura of academic respectability the card gave him had often gotten him past doors that would have closed swiftly to a mere journalist.

Octavian's dark face lit up in tardy recognition. "Mr. Dunstable? Yes, sir. It's been a long time, sir. If you'll wait in the foyer, I'll announce you." Stepping aside, he bowed Alan in.

A few minutes later the footman returned to escort Alan upstairs to a sitting room whose mullioned windows were framed in blue silk. The room was dressed in varying shades of blue—dark in the thick Brussels carpet, pale in the brocaded upholstery of rosewood chairs and settees. Scarlet pillows cushioned the window seat, and potted red geraniums decorated the gray marble fireplace mantle.

Almost before he spotted her, Lady Burleigh had arisen from a kidney-shaped desk by the window and had come forward, her hand extended, a smile on her face. He was startled to see that the once slender, diminutive figure had taken on a plumpness that flowing sleeves and a high-waisted gown could not hide. Even her face was rounder and fuller. Self-indulgent middle age, he thought, with a twinge that was more relief than regret.

"Alan! How kind of you to come."

Her blue eyes met his with warmth. Her blond hair was knotted high at the back of her head in the same Grecian style he remembered, and her movements in the ivory muslin-and-lace gown were as graceful as ever. Added pounds had not entirely spoiled her appeal.

"It's been far too long," she said, her voice like honey. "Why do I never see you anymore, *mon cher ami*?"

He took her hand, nearly tongue-tied with old memories. Her touch was cold, the palm slightly damp. She was nervous, too, then. He relaxed a little.

"I never thought you would be particularly happy to see me," he said, releasing her hand. "And I'm away much of the time. Burleigh isn't here, then?"

"No, indeed, he rarely comes to London anymore. He prefers to rusticate at Enderlin Hall. But do be seated, Alan. I was about to order tea. Or would you prefer something else?"

He wanted to say he'd prefer a stiff brandy, but he just smiled back and nodded. "Tea would suit me excellent well, Countess."

"Ah, how formal you sound," she mourned. "We knew each other rather better at one time."

He met her blue eyes with amusement as he took a delicate chair near the tea table. "A short time, to be sure. And not one I should think you'd care to remember."

Her bow-shaped mouth went into a little pout as she turned toward the embroidered bellpull near the fireplace. "Then your memory is exceedingly faulty, sir. I have ever been unconventional, not unlike you. It was one of the burdens Lucien had to bear when he agreed to marry me. He handles it well, the dear. He hasn't an inkling about the exhibit, however, and I don't intend to tell him."

"What exhibit?"

She smiled as she seated herself on the Sheraton settee opposite him. "If you've attended the new art show at the Royal Academy, you would have seen the work of one Phoebus Rivington—who is myself."

She had clearly hoped to surprise him, and did. Alan leaned back in his chair with a shout of laughter. "You finally did it, then?"

"I did, indeed. Whether from talent or sheer persistence, I'm not sure. At any rate, I am now exhibited and judged, although it was only allowed on condition that I use a male pseudonym. It suited me to agree to that. Lucien would have been horrified to have his wife's name bandied about in public."

"So you're in London for the show?"

"Partly, yes." Valeria raised her dark arched brows—the product, Alan was sure, of art, not nature. Her manner, as he remembered well, was a bewildering mixture of the seductive and the candid. He could not quite believe she had asked him to come to renew their old, short-lived intimacy. Yet he had never been good at second-guessing either her motives or those of any woman. He realized that the mere idea of bedding her now was distasteful, although he was not sure why. She was still a handsome woman, despite the added pounds, and looked less than her thirty-six years. There was no reason why her seven years' seniority should mean any more to him now than it had five years ago, when they had both been lonely and each had, somehow, spurred the creative energies of the other.

A young maid in gray, with white apron and mobcap, wheeled in a small cart with the silver service and laid everything on the tea table between them—a plate of crumpets, the pot of tea with its matching bowls of milk and sugar, and two delicate gold-edged cups in their saucers.

"I'll take care of it now, thank you, Hortense," Valeria said. The girl bobbed a curtsey and withdrew. A slender frown line appeared between the countess's perfect brows as she began to pour the tea. "The other reason is Grey, Alan. That is why I asked you here."

"Grey?" Alan asked cautiously. "What about him?"

It always disturbed him to think of Grey Talbot, now Viscount Talbot and Valeria's nephew by marriage, or to encounter him, as he did infrequently, coming out of White's or watching a cricket game at Lord's. It brought back memories best left alone, even though it pleased him that Grey was no longer hostile to him. Indeed, Lord Burleigh's nephew invariably greeted Alan amiably and sometimes invited him to dine at his club. Alan as invariably declined the invitation, on the theory that the less said and remembered between them, the better. Now he realized he had not seen Grey for over a year.

Valeria handed him his cup—she had remembered his preference for cream and sugar despite the years and her preoccupation. An amazing woman, Valeria.

"You knew, certainly, that his wife had died," she said.

"Yes. A damned bloody shame. A fall from a horse, wasn't it?"

"Yes. Polly was always determined to ride to the hounds, even when she was the only woman in the hunt. She was a good rider, too; it was just one of those accidents one can't foresee. But it's been eight months now and . . . well, to be frank, Alan, Grey is still all to pieces."

She passed Alan the plate of crumpets, then took one herself, broke it open and began spreading a generous amount of butter on it. "Lucien is in a constant miff at his mooning about. He keeps reminding Grey he must get back in the saddle, so to speak. He even recommends that he find another wife. Then Grey goes into a sulk and they have words, and I have to mediate. It's all most tiresome."

"Yes, no doubt," Alan echoed, his voice carefully neutral.

"So I brought Grey to Town with me," she continued. "I persuaded him that I needed his services escorting me during the Academy showings."

Alan returned his teacup to the table so that he could concentrate on his crumpet. It was sweet, with tiny orange bits as well as currants in it. Delicious. He could eat the whole plateful. His breakfast had been sparse and his lunch nonexistent.

After a brief pause, which he didn't bother to acknowledge, Valeria continued. "At any rate, I do believe I've found a most marvelous solution to his doldrums, if I can only get him to see it, too. That's why I need your help."

Alan's head jerked up. "My help?"

"I've met this delightful girl. An American—don't look so amazed, Alan, I do meet Americans on occasion. She's quite attractive. One might even say she's cultured, in a . . . Western sort of way. And she's most fond of music and singing. Just the ticket for Grey. He and Polly used to sing together often; they had such merry times. I'm sure it's one of the things he misses most about her."

"I can't believe you'd matchmake, Countess. It never works out."

"*Au contraire*, I was practically responsible—no, I *was* responsible—for getting Polly and Grey together. And he needs someone desperately, Alan. Someone young and cheerful and sympathetic. I think Miss Endicott would be all of those things. She is here with her parents. Mr. Endicott is a shipowner and here to confer, unofficially, with London merchants and even some government people, I believe. Something about trade restrictions in the West Indies. He's a friend of the American Minister, Mr. Rush, and they've entrée into the very best circles. From what I've seen, he must be extremely well-off. There was some sort of to-do back in Philadelphia concerning their daughter, Stephanie. Mrs. Endicott has confided to me that she hopes the girl will be attracted to some lord and vice versa.''

''What sort of to-do?''

''I didn't ask. These matters are rather delicate, my dear, and we're not *that* well acquainted. All I can say is Mrs. Endicott has it in mind that her darling daughter's chances of finding a husband are much better here than in Philadelphia.''

''But—a *lord*?'' He asked the question between bites, wondering more and more what all these female concerns had to do with him.

Valeria laughed. ''I'm not sure, but I suspect these egalitarian Americans feel lords are the only Englishmen worth having.''

''So mother and aunt are both matchmaking. And what do the principal parties think of all this?''

''I believe there may be a spark of interest. At the affair I gave last week, I made sure it was Grey who handed Miss Endicott in to dinner. When he discovered she has a passion for music, like himself, he took the initiative to invite her and her parents to the Royal Opera to see *The Barber of Seville*.''

''Well, then.'' Alan lifted his hands in a shrug and slapped his knees. ''Why do you need me?''

Valeria pressed her rouged lips together and shook her head. ''It's not so simple. The Endicotts leave for Brighton next week. They don't expect to return to London before they sail for Philadelphia, in September at the latest. There is simply not enough time for anything serious to develop between Grey and Miss Endicott in a week. And so . . .''

She hesitated and took a sip of tea. Alan waited, quiet now—and wary.

''I understand you've been hired by the *Times* to do a series of pieces on the United States and democracy and that sort of thing, is that true?''

''Now how the devil did you learn *that*? It was supposed to be a secret.''

"Your editor, Mr. Baynes, and I are friends of a sort," Valeria said complacently. "You don't suppose I got to my advanced age without making certain I had some useful contacts, do you?"

Alan, still wary, only smiled.

"The long and short of it is . . . a suggestion . . . a request . . . No, not that, but I thought perhaps . . ." She broke off, shrugging a little, and finally said, "When do you hope to sail?"

"Probably late September. Early enough to avoid the worst weather on the Atlantic, and late enough so I can get some money together for my expenses. The *Times* will pay boat fare, and that's all. I hope to land in time to observe the presidential election, and stay until after the inauguration next March."

"Do you suppose, if I help with a loan, that you could move it up a little? Could you plan to go on the same ship as the Endicotts?"

"Why the devil should I?"

"And then persuade Grey he should go along with you, see new lands, new sights? And besides, you need the benefit of his particular viewpoint when you do your pieces on America," Valeria finished. She leaned back and awaited his response with bright, expectant eyes.

Alan stared at her for a long moment. When he spoke, his voice was gruff. "My dear lady, it's not as if we were old school friends or members of the same club, or any of those little things that hold gentlemen together. There was a time when Grey royally hated me."

"But not anymore, I think."

"He's civil enough on the surface, I grant you. But I have no idea how I could persuade him to accompany me to America."

"Then you must simply make cheese out of chalk. He's at such loose ends that I think he would find the proposal attractive, even though he might have to be pushed."

"If he's at all interested in Miss Enderby or whatever her name is, he might have thought to accompany her himself."

"I daresay it hasn't occurred to him—yet. As I said, he needs more time."

"It's the most woolly-crowned notion you've ever had," Alan said rudely.

"Only consider it a bit." Valeria smiled her most enticing smile. Though he was unaffected by her posing, he was reminded that he might, after all, owe her something for old times' sake.

"It's not as though I'm asking anything for myself," she said, as if she had read his mind. "But you might consider that you owe Grey something."

"Grey wouldn't thank me for interfering."

"No, but someone needs to, just the same. I've done all I can."

Alan rose hastily, although the plate of crumpets was still nearly full and he had calculated he might eat three or four without exceeding the bounds of good manners.

"Lady Burleigh," he began with deliberate formality. "I am not..."

She rose and walked to the desk, returning with a white slip which she handed him. "A ticket to the Royal Academy show Sunday afternoon. Grey and I will be there. I'll see that the two of you meet, and you can take it from there. Get him interested in your voyage last spring, as a start. To Greece, wasn't it?"

"Yes, Greece," he repeated, surprised at how well she had kept track of him.

"You might think of it as saving his life," Valeria said.

He shook his head, a little smile on his lips, his eyes withdrawn and cool. "I doubt I could ever be the instrument of Grey Talbot's salvation, my lady. Quite the contrary."

She continued to stare at him hopefully. He left as quickly as he could, feeling as trapped as a hare before the hounds.

CHAPTER
II

The Clarendon Hotel on Bond Street was among the most elegant hotels in London, its rooms boasting rich furnishings, comfortable beds, and amenities such as full-length looking glasses and handsome porcelain bathing tubs in which one could immerse nearly half one's body. The service was commendable, once the staff knew who was generous with tips. The dining room boasted the cuisine of the best French chef in town and charged accordingly—as much as four pounds per person for a lavish dinner.

Morton Endicott was fully aware of the hotel's extravagance, but it pleased him to be able to introduce his wife Dorothea and their daughter Stephanie to the finest accommodations to be had. Although he had not quite understood how bringing the two of them with him to England would solve the "crisis" Dorothea insisted Stephanie was facing, he had been delighted to have them accompany him on the long, uncertain voyage over the Atlantic, and during the equally uncertain course of his business discussions in various parts of England.

Crisis was a word Stephanie herself would not have used. The only crisis she faced, this hot July afternoon, was the total death of conversation between herself and Lord Talbot. After a long, tiring afternoon, Mrs. Endicott had left the two of them alone in their hotel suite to take tea. The move was embarrassingly obvious. Indeed, the whole outing that had preceded it had been an embarrassment. Stephanie only hoped Lord Talbot himself didn't recognize such a bold-faced attempt to bring the two of them together.

But of course he must recognize it. He might be passive, but he was not stupid.

"There's one sandwich left, Lord Talbot, do take it."

"Thank you. Perhaps I will." He reached for the sand-wich, probably for lack of an alternative activity.

"Shall I send for more tea?"

"Oh, no, thank you, this was quite sufficient."

Stephanie looked into the teapot again, but it was just as empty as the last time she had looked. She was a tall girl, with slender cheekbones, a straight, delicate nose, wide, lushly fringed green eyes, and hair the color of maple syrup. Her complexion, her mother often deplored, was a shade dark, almost tawny. Even creams and pearl powder couldn't reduce it to an acceptable ivory. Dorothea Endicott could not imagine where her eldest daughter had gotten such a complexion. Morton teased his wife that some renegade in her family's past had taken a squaw to wife. Dorothea Endicott did not appreciate this kind of humor, but when the artist who had painted Stephanie's portrait the previous year had raved about the color of his subject's cheeks, she ceased to complain.

Right now, Stephanie felt as if that complexion was about to melt completely away. She longed to push back a lock of hair from her perspiring temple, loosen the ruffle at the throat of her blue muslin walking dress, rub the ache from her neck. She also longed for Lord Talbot to be gone, but he must never know that.

He clearly felt the same way. His forehead glistened, and even as she watched, he pulled out an immaculate handker-chief and blotted it, with a slight smile that sought to assure her that *she* was not the cause of his discomfort. He was very good-looking. The boyish expression in his blue eyes and the gentle smile of his full, chiseled lips were endearing. He was tall enough to look down at her when they were side by side—a characteristic she always looked for, since too many gentlemen were no taller than she, and some were even shorter. He was fastidious in his dress, still in his twenties, and the heir to an earldom. According to her mother's criteria for men, she ought to be madly in love with him, but there it was—she was not.

There was really no reason, either, why they could not talk freely, as they had done on several occasions in the past two weeks. It was all because of that dreadful expedition. As usual, her mother had dominated the conversation. The uncouth insults the Thames boatmen shouted across the water to each other dismayed her, though she had heard them before. She had deplored the conditions of the lions and bears and the one gorilla of the Royal Menagerie at the Tower of London (truly, they *had* looked unhappy and bedraggled in their compounds). She was disappointed in the way the Royal Armour and Crown Jewels had been displayed—the latter stuck away in a vault dimly lit by two tallow candles.

Then Lord Talbot's servant met them with the viscount's phaeton and drove them toward St. Paul's. But the narrow, crooked streets had been so hot, the garbage-strewn gutters so malodorous, the beggars and hawkers so importunate, that they had abandoned their intention to visit the cathedral, climb to the Stone Gallery, and look out over the city—an idea that had caught Stephanie's fancy. Instead, returning with relief to the comparative cleanliness of the West End, they had stopped at the Royal Academy's exhibit and viewed the paintings. Stephanie was impressed by Lord Talbot's revelation that one large canvas, depicting a small boat threatened by stormy seas, had been painted by Lady Burleigh, not by someone named Phoebus Rivington. Her mother, frowning, said only that the sky was surely too strange a color to be real. Soon afterward she complained of sore feet, and Lord Talbot obligingly returned them to the Clarendon where Mrs. Endicott, regaining her good nature, invited him to take tea with them, pleaded fatigue, and vanished.

So here they were.

The art of keeping the conversation going was up to the lady, Stephanie knew. Her green eyes darted about the sitting room, looking for something she might comment on.

They finally alighted on the painting over the fireplace mantle: a red-coated rider jumping a magnificent black hunter over a rustic gate.

"Do you enjoy hunting, Lord Talbot?" Stephanie asked.

Lord Talbot looked up and smiled his relief. "I used to enjoy chasing fox." Then his smile died and so did his voice. His half-eaten sandwich suddenly drooped in his hand as his eyes sought a far corner of the room.

"Used to?" she asked. "I'm afraid I don't understand."

"My wife died in a fall from a horse," he said in a heavy monotone. "It was during a fox hunt. I don't expect to ever hunt again."

Stephanie wanted to die with humiliation. She had known about the unfortunate death of his young wife—indeed, had understood that this was the reason for the viscount's solemnity, and had agreed with her mother that he needed diversion. But she had not known the circumstances of the tragedy. And so, of course, she must put her foot in it. She felt a blush rise to her cheeks.

"I do beg pardon, Lord Talbot, for that thoughtless question."

"Not at all." He dismissed her apology with a wave of his hand. "You didn't know. And I should be able to speak of it easily by now. But somehow, I can't."

Unthinking, needing some kind of motion, she arose from her seat. "Perhaps you'd like some porter? Or ale? It is such a warm day."

He arose too. "No, thank you, I really must take myself off." He had considered her action a signal to end his visit—not at all what Mama wanted. She tried to think of a way to keep him longer.

"Um, I . . . understand we may see you tonight at the Rush's soiree."

"Ah . . . I believe I did receive an invitation," he said vaguely.

"Father is a friend of the Minister, and so I agreed to sing for the gathering tonight," she said, hoping to draw him into a discussion of the music.

But instead of asking what she would sing, he only said,

"Very courageous of you, Miss Endicott. In that case, I shall try most earnestly to be present."

He bowed, made his good-byes, and left her. Stephanie sighed, shrugged her shoulders, and unbuttoned her ruffle, letting her warm neck breathe again. She had taken only a few steps to retrieve the new novel she was reading—Scott's *The Bride of Lammamoor*—when her mother, in lace cap and flowered wrapper, entered the room. A small woman in her early forties, her trim figure and smooth complexion attested to a long-standing battle against the ravages of time.

"Lord Talbot is gone already?" Dorothea Endicott's hazel eyes were stern under her curled brown fringes, and her mouth was downturned in dismay. Having to look up to meet Stephanie's gaze did not deter her from reproof. "Stephanie, child, couldn't you have managed somehow..."

"What would you have me do, Mama, bar the door or fall on his neck? Neither seemed quite dignified."

"Really, Stephanie!" Dorothea did not approve of levity in young ladies, but she had been unable to curb this tendency in Stephanie.

"Your presence might have kept the conversation going, had you stayed." Stephanie's smile and reconciling tone turned the complaint into a compliment. It was a trick she had developed long ago to deflect criticism.

Her mother was somewhat mollified, but continued her scold. "Surely, Stephanie, you've learned by now how to converse with a gentleman without my presence."

Stephanie picked up *The Bride*. "I made a terrible faux pas. Why did no one tell me Lord Talbot's wife died in a fox-hunting accident?"

"How could we have known that? Why, what did you say or do that was so awful?"

Stephanie explained their exchange, and how quickly Lord Talbot had taken his leave afterward. Dorothea Endicott closed her eyes and clapped one hand to her forehead. "Oh, dear, what can we do? Why didn't you keep the conversation on music?"

"No matter how much we both approve that subject, one can't keep to it forever, Mama. But cheer up, he has promised to be at the soiree this evening. Perhaps I can make it up to him." She reseated herself on the settee and opened *The Bride of Lammamoor*. Dorothea followed and sat beside her. Hiding a sigh, Stephanie closed the book, one finger in her place.

"I must say you are cool enough about it," Dorothea said. "You don't seem to realize we leave for Brighton next week, and our viscount seems not at all in the way of declaring his interest."

"I'm not certain I care to have him do so."

"You said you like him."

"Oh, yes, I like him. He is pleasant and obliging, and we have some interests in common. But he seems to have no desire to *do* things. I believe he was in the army at one time, but he says he hated it, so he sold out. He seems to have no direction for his life."

"A man in Lord Talbot's circumstances, with his title and wealth, doesn't *have* to do anything. He loves music as you do. If it weren't tempting fate, I'd say he's made to order for you."

"It's just that he's a trifle tedious, Mama. I'm constantly seeking ways to cheer him up, find some lively spark in him. Sometimes he responds, but it never lasts. He sinks down into that passive politeness, and it all gets tremendously wearing."

"He's had a great loss."

"I'm sure he has. To hear Lady Burleigh talk of her, Lord Talbot's wife was without compare. I must say *that* is a little wearing, too. Can anyone really expect me to take her place?"

Her mother rose impatiently and flung out her hands. "Of course not, literally! But we made this trip for your sake, Stephanie, and the least you can do is cooperate."

"Yes, Mama," Stephanie agreed. This time she didn't bother to hide her sigh. It wouldn't do to contradict her mother, though she knew perfectly well her father had planned for a good year to take the trip to England alone, for business reasons. It was only after last Christmas's miserable confrontation that her mother announced that she and Stephanie were to accompany him. Dorothea was not long in reminding her of the reason.

"When you broke your engagement to young Harlow—and for the most frivolous of reasons—you ruined the best chance of your life for an advantageous marriage. Not only that, you gave the impression to all the other eligible males of Philadelphia that you are both difficult and flighty. Depend on it, they'll give you a wide berth from now on. If I'm not much mistaken, that little incident has confirmed you into spinsterhood, so far as your hometown is concerned."

"I'm not certain that would be so bad," Stephanie murmured, her head averted.

"What did you say?"

"Nothing." She shook her head and smoothed the cover of her book with gentle fingers. It never seemed to do any good to remind her mother that she had not loved Dick Harlow; that, even though he had money and good taste and a beautiful house on Walnut Street, he was a bore. The same might be said of Lord Talbot.

"I never dreamed finding the right husband would be such a rigamarole. And everyone is so dreadfully solemn and insistent about it."

Dorothea reseated herself next to her daughter and said, more calmly and very decisively, "It is the single most important step in a woman's life."

"Then why can't I decide who I want, and when I want him?"

"I'm not at all certain you know what you want."

"Something—someone . . . different." She couldn't explain who would be right. She only knew who was not right.

"How different?" Dorothea's voice was alarmed.

Stephanie broke into a peal of laughter. "Oh, Mama!" She put a consoling hand on her mother's arm. "I don't know, I'm sure."

"Living in England wouldn't be different? A man with a title, who will someday be an earl, would not be different from an American gentleman?"

Stephanie only shrugged her shoulders and looked down at her lap. What *did* she look for? Someone with enthusiasm, someone with ideas, someone with a certain *spark* . . . like her father. Morton Endicott might not be handsome or young, but when he walked into a room, people noticed.

And to Stephanie, he was the most exciting man she knew. Her mother ought to have understood that, but somehow she did not.

The idea of remaining always in England chilled her stomach, but saying so to her mother was out of the question. The Endicott family did not admit to the stronger emotions, and rarely expressed their affection for each other. If she sometimes felt, like now, that it would be heaven not to need to defer to her mother's wishes, other things—little things—held her back.

How could she forego, once and for all, nightly confidences with her sister Clarinda, cribbage games with her brother Hugh, or her father's hearty greeting at breakfast, "How's my princess today?" How could she put a whole stormy ocean between herself and her dear friend, Kate Hamlin, or Aunt Pru and her children, or even Uncle Perry, her confidant and musical mentor? How could she marry Lord Greycliff Talbot, no matter how good-looking and obliging and musically inclined; be sentenced to live in some drafty country house throughout the damp English winter; compete daily with his glorified memory of the first Lady Talbot; deal with either the supercilious servants she had encountered in London, or the broad-accented country ones, who might as well speak Chinese for all she could understand of their meaning?

"You read too many novels," her mother said severely, pointing to the book in her hand. "I know what you're waiting for. Some devastatingly handsome, exciting stranger who will sweep you off your feet. Let me tell you, Stephanie, it doesn't happen that way. Your father and I married because of family considerations. We were fond of each other, but not wildly in love. And it has worked out most satisfactorily. I have the kind of life I prefer and, best of all, I have three beautiful children. One has to look to the future and recognize that love is, after all, a momentary emotion. If you don't take other things into consideration, you may end up very unhappily, all the more so because you entered marriage with too many illusions."

Stephanie could stand it no longer. But being well-bred (too much so, she sometimes thought), she arose from the settee cooly, and did not throw *The Bride of Lammamoor* across the room.

"You are probably right, Mama, and I promise to do better with Lord Talbot, next time we meet. But right now, I feel a headache coming on..."

"I'll have Jenny bring you some of my lavender drops, dear. Do go lie down. You want to feel your best for the soiree this evening."

Stephanie nodded. She had taken a few steps toward the bedroom door when her mother added, "Of course we could stay longer in London. If it would be fruitful, I mean. We could always join your father later in Liverpool before our ship sails. I feel that if the two of you only had more time..."

"I wouldn't dream of altering our plans," Stephanie said. "And I truly look forward to Brighton and the sea after today's heat. As for Lord Talbot..." She hesitated. Her mother looked so dreadfully expectant. "I wouldn't put too much stock in his interest in me," she finished and escaped.

CHAPTER
III

It was time for Stephanie to sing, and, so far as she could determine, Lord Talbot had not shown up after all.

"We are pleased," her hostess, Mrs. Rush, said, "that my countrywoman, Miss Endicott of Philadelphia, has consented to favor us with a few songs this evening."

Stephanie rose and stood beside the Broadwood grand pianoforte while her accompanist, Mrs. Ashton-Jones, a small, gray-haired lady who taught music at a girl's academy, took her place at the lyre-backed chair before the keyboard. A second-floor ballroom built for entertaining many people, the room was adorned with red ceiling-to-floor damask draperies and a huge candlelit chandelier. Over fifty people who had been milling about the room, drinking punch and talking in small groups, now took seats or leaned against the long sideboard and turned their attention to Stephanie. She tried not to feel intimidated, though her mouth was dry and her throat raspy after talking to so many people.

She had consented to sing to please her mother, who had some idea that if Lord Talbot heard Stephanie's voice at its best, he would be smitten forever, throw off his lassitude, and sweep her off her feet in the best romantic tradition. Thus, both Stephanie and her mother would be satisfied. But Lord Talbot had not chosen to come.

She had a new gown for the occasion, made by a

dressmaker in Leicester Square at an outrageous cost and
delivered only that morning. It was made of white gauze
over green watered silk, the bodice and puffed sleeves
decorated with lace ruffles, the neckline daringly low. Three
full-quilled flounces finished off the skirt just above her
white satin slippers. Her brown hair, shining with amber
lights, was arranged in ringlets about her face, long curls
over one shoulder, and caught up behind either ear with
yellow-and-white daisies. She should have been gratified to
look her best; yet she somehow felt she had been put on
display—and for no good purpose.

Usually, Stephanie loved to sing. Dorothea Endicott declared her daughter had been born singing. At home in
Philadelphia, she sang spontaneously, effortlessly, with groups
of laughing, enthusiastic friends gathered about the keyboard. But tonight she felt on her the critical, supercilious
eyes of Lady Sefton, who had inspected her with an eye-
glass during introductions, and Lord Hertford, who had
commented sarcastically on "republican ladies" when she
had boldly declared she had no wish to meet His Majesty
while at Brighton. She had had little training. Would she
sing everything wrong for this sophisticated crowd of American dignitaries and English aristocrats?

Looking perfectly poised and calm, subduing by sheer
will the trembling in her knees, she surveyed the room one
more time. No, he was definitely not here. Not that it
mattered. But there was another young, dark-haired man
standing near the back of the room. Who was he? His curly
black hair, cropped short, his blue, brass-buttoned coat and
white stock, with none of the jeweled studs or waistcoat
fobs the other men wore, stood out in the crowd. Then she
ceased taking inventory of his clothes because their eyes
met and, in a strange, electric moment, held.

His were dark brown and gazed steadily from under
straight, jutting black brows. The corners crinkled and the
whites gleamed momentarily in a ray from the overhead
chandelier. The cheeks were broad, the jaw square and
stern. Suddenly his disinterested, faintly mocking expression softened into something akin to recognition, and the
straight, firm lips parted slightly. But even as she stared

back, unthinking, mesmerized, his gaze resumed its distance and he turned away.

Stephanie discovered she was trembling, even though for the past ten seconds (or maybe twice that long, she had no idea) she had not thought about her singing at all. Coming to herself, she nodded to Mrs. Ashton-Jones, who played the introductory chord for her first number.

> "Drink to me only with thine eyes,
> And I will pledge with mine.
> Or leave a kiss within the cup,
> And I'll not ask for wine."

She did not again look toward those intense brown eyes as she sang. It was an old, well-loved, well-known song, but to sing such words to such eyes seemed somehow dangerous. She sang, instead, to her father, who was seated beside her mother near the punch table. His ample chest strained his satin vest, his bald head shone in the light from the chandelier, and his ruddy face beamed with pride. *Someone with a certain spark. Someone like Father . . .*

She sang just for him.

The guests clapped politely, even enthusiastically. Encouraged, Stephanie continued with "Voi Che Sapete" (Tell me, fair ladies, Vers'd in love's art, O, is this love, then, Wakes in my heart?) and "Batti, Batti" (While united and delighted, All our days shall sweetly glide). Behind the protection of the Italian words, her eyes grew bolder, her body more relaxed. The applause was loud and prolonged. After she had sung Handel's "Where E'er You Walk," they would not let her retire.

"If you would kindly favor us with another . . ." Mrs. Rush suggested from the front sidelines.

Stephanie looked through her music, brought out a sheet and showed it to Mrs. Ashton-Jones, who looked through it and nodded. Then Stephanie turned back to the guests.

"Thank you all for being so kind to a rebel from across the sea," she said with a contagious smile that her audience quickly returned. "Now, I'd like to sing for you a song by a fellow Philadelphian. Mr. Francis Hopkinson wrote this way back in 1759. He continued to compose other musical pieces, but he was also a lawyer, a judge, and a public servant.''

She paused and glanced at her parents. Dorothea Endicott wore a warning frown; Morton, a broad grin. She decided to continue. ''Mr. Hopkinson was also one of the original rebels. He signed the Declaration of Independence in 1776.''

Hearty applause burst from the few Americans in the room, followed by scattered laughs from the English. She dared to glance again at the black-haired, brown-eyed young man and was surprised that he, too, was clapping enthusiastically, a broad smile on his lips. He was almost handsome when he smiled.

With a little curtsey for their response, she signaled to Mrs. Ashton-Jones, who played a short introduction.

> ''My days have been so wondrous free
> The little birds that fly
> With careless ease from tree to tree
> Were but as blest as I.''

Her voice floated effortlessly out to the audience, gathering momentum from its enthusiasm. She could have sung all night. Perhaps it was the words. Perhaps it was the encouragement in those steady brown eyes, the continuing smile on those firm lips. Her eyes flitted past his and away, but she was ever conscious of his gaze.

When she finished, everyone rose, clapping. She blushed at the ovation, her pulse beating with exhilaration. People crowded forward to offer congratulations. She could think of nothing to say except ''Thank you.''

''Did you see a young man with curly black hair, wearing a blue coat?'' she asked her hostess when she had a chance. ''Dressed rather informally?''

Mrs. Rush frowned at her for a moment, then her eyes brightened. ''Oh, you must mean Mr. Dunstable. He wasn't really a guest. He's a journalist and will be making a trip to the United States soon. He wanted to talk to Mr. Rush about it.''

''I'd like to meet him,'' Stephanie said.

"Oh, my dear, he's not really your sort. Besides, I believe he has left."

Mrs. Rush was evidently correct. Stephanie did not see Mr. Dunstable again. Lord Talbot never appeared at all. Despite her musical success, the evening turned out rather flat.

White's, on St. James's Street, had once been a Tory club, but the distinction between it and Brooks's, across the street, had blurred with the years. Lord Burleigh, a decided Whig, had long been a member of White's and so, of course, was his nephew, Lord Talbot. Alan Dunstable, who was not a member (nor would he have joined if asked) now entered that august male sanctum in Grey's company. He had been here before, always someone's guest, and was familiar with its tradition of good food, extravagant gaming, and the famous bow window from which Beau Brummell, before retiring to the continent to escape debtor's prison, used to view the passersby and make his astringent, inimitable comments for the amusement of his companions.

Grey had been an intimate of Beau Brummell's at one time, a dandy who cared more for manners and dress and cutting a dashing figure in his chariot and pair than anything else. He had spent his time gambling and drinking and thinking up outlandish midnight follies like the rest of his kind. That had been before he met Polly. Now, according to Valeria, Grey was again spending a disproportionate amount of time at White's, and she believed that if he weren't stopped soon, his decline and fall were imminent.

Believing it none of his business, Alan had intended to stay out of her scheme for rescuing Grey. He had deliberately destroyed the ticket to the Royal Academy show she had given him, and failed to appear on the previous Sunday. But since his glimpse of Miss Stephanie Endicott across the ballroom at the American Minister's rout, he had changed his mind, though he could not have explained why.

Then fate decreed that he and Grey practically collide in the doorway of the Booksellers' Coffee House on Paternoster Row, where Alan spent much of his time. Grey explained that Lady Burleigh had sent him there for the latest issue of

The London Magazine. Though he saw through the ruse, Alan impulsively invited Grey to sup at the coffeehouse. "White's food is better," Grey suggested. Alan was unable to deny that—and so here they were.

Escorted by a dignified butler, they were soon seated at a round, white-clothed table for two in the dining room. Grey, with the unassuming courtesy that was second nature to him, asked the waiter to bring them a bottle of porter, then told Alan to order whatever he liked. Taking advantage of this generosity—such offers were his only opportunity to dine really well—Alan ordered turtle soup, salmon, lamb cutlets, a green goose, and apple tart. Grey settled for soup and salmon. Alan thought his face was thinner, as though he had lost considerable weight.

But Grey seemed determined to be hospitable, giving in neither to melancholy nor to unhappy memories of the past. "I'm glad we met," he said as he poured the wine for both of them. "I've enjoyed reading your pieces on Greece in the *Times.* And the earlier ones, on Spain. You're making quite a name for yourself as a peripatetic journalist, aren't you?"

Alan shrugged, though he was secretly pleased with Grey's praise. "It's hardly work. I do pretty much what I like, travel where I like. It's rather a good way to see the world."

"Better than writing poetry?"

"I still do that, on occasion. But I no longer hope for the kind of celebrity Byron once enjoyed."

"Tell me about Greece. Tell me what you weren't able to put in those articles."

Alan told him about the Greece tourists didn't see: the dirt and crowding of Athens slums, the primitive ways of the peasants in the rocky northern mountains, the seething undercurrent of unrest under Turkish rule. He finished with his opinion that Greece was getting set for an uprising.

Grey listened and made intelligent comments. He did not seem at all the melancholy mourner Valeria had described. "It must be quite wonderful to have a goal in life, to have plans for the future," he said.

"You have no plans for the future?"

"None that I can seem to concentrate on."

"What about the boy—Kevin, isn't it? Surely you have plans for him."

"Oh, well—that's more or less settled. Uncle Lucien has taken over the details concerning his schooling, pretty much as he did with me, don't you know. Private tutors, Harrow, Cambridge. Kevin needn't take up a profession because he's assured the succession to the title. And Uncle Lucien will see that he keeps abreast of politics when his time comes to enter the Lords."

"And what does Kevin like to do?"

"What does any five-year-old like to do? Ride his pony and swim in the pond and play with his puppy. And, on occasion, give us all a scare when he decides to get lost."

Alan took a sip of his wine and reversed his thoughts about Grey's mental well-being. "You seem rather an uninterested father."

Grey sent him a sharp look, then turned away to twirl his wineglass. He took a leisurely drink, then said, his eyes averted, "Surely you knew that Kevin is really Uncle Lucien's son, not mine. He wouldn't acknowledge him, of course, since he was illegitimate. And when Polly . . . When Polly lived, it didn't seem to matter. We had a place in Suffolk, near Newmarket and my father. But when she . . . died, it seemed logical to close down the place there. My father had passed away by then, and I had no reason to stay. So Kevin and I moved to Enderlin Hall—a homecoming for me. Enderlin Hall had always been a retreat. It isn't any longer. Especially now that Uncle Lucien seems intent on making Kevin *his* son in all but name."

His eyes continued to rest on the edge of his plate after he finished speaking. Alan shifted his feet uncomfortably and played with the silver napkin holder.

"Sorry, old chap," he said after a lengthy silence. "I know Lord Burleigh has always been used to getting his way."

Grey looked up. "Except with Polly," he said, his eyes alight.

"Yes, except with Polly," Alan agreed with a grin, relieved her name had come out freely this time. Both returned to their drinks. Privately Alan tried to assess

Valeria's judgment. Was it true that all Grey needed was
some direction, a reason for living? Would Miss Endicott be
the one to supply it? Or was Valeria's interest in Grey's
well-being simply her way of smoothing out what had
become an irritating domestic situation? With Valeria, it was
sometimes hard to see the concern under the brittle, society
manners. Still, the woman had some emotional depth to her.
If nothing else, her paintings showed it. And he could not
help but agree with her judgment about Miss Endicott, just
from seeing her that one night.

"I understand from Lady Burleigh that you've been
seeing something of a young woman from America," Alan
said.

"Ah, yes, Miss Endicott. Enjoyable young lady. Likes
opera." Grey's eyes were vague, seeking the far corner of
the room where liveried waiters quietly and efficiently
moved from table to table, heavy trays balanced with perfect
grace on their outstretched palms.

"I saw her Friday last at the American Minister's soiree.
He'd been kind enough to invite me so I could ask him
some questions about the United States. That's where I'm
going next."

"Oh, really." Grey remained vague. His thoughts seemed
to have been arrested by that last mention of Polly's name.

"Yes, I heard her sing, as a matter of fact. Extraordinary
voice, quite extraordinary. She ought to sing opera."

"But will not, I am sure, because she is destined to
become the dutiful wife of some Philadelphia gentleman,
not a public performer."

"Quite," Alan admitted. "But I suspect social restrictions are not so immovable in America, else she wouldn't
have sung to such a crowd."

"My dear chap, her father and Richard Rush are old
friends. Rush is from Philadelphia, too. His father was a
famous physician, and the Minister and Mr. Endicott are
both members of the Philosophical Society. It was not at all
improper for Miss Endicott to sing for a private gathering at
the Rush residence, whether British or American."

Whenever Grey began defining what was proper conduct
and what was not, Alan was at a loss. It was an old

argument between them, one that the years did not seem to have softened.

"I only meant to comment on Miss Endicott. A beautiful girl, don't you think?"

"If you care for those tall, willowy types."

"What struck me was her complexion. Almost golden, tawny. Much nicer than the white-faced London ladies, who worry so about keeping the sun from their skin."

Grey laughed—a welcome sound, even though Alan suspected it was at, rather than with, him. "My dear chap, you have been too long in Greece. You've become used to those Mediterranean types."

Alan laughed, too. "Perhaps," he conceded.

The soup arrived, and he concentrated on sipping it. Excellent seasoning. He knew good food, now, when he tasted it. He wondered why he had not accepted Grey's invitations to dine before. Then he remembered his very good reasons and mentally shied from them.

Miss Endicott. His thoughts returned to her automatically. Grey seemed perfectly uninterested—or was he only pretending? Could there be a man alive who would not turn to take a second look at the golden Miss Endicott? If her appearance had struck him first, her grace and sense of repose had kept his eyes riveted on her as she waited to sing. Her voice had charmed him into a kind of dazzled wonderment. And, finally, her good-humored promotion of America and what it seemed to mean to her, as part of her encore, had shown a certain courage in that mostly aristocratic gathering, and, possibly, a developing sense of the ironic, which most females did not understand, much less enjoy. Alan had a great appreciation for the ironic.

The present moment was full of irony, he thought as he finished his soup. He had no sooner decided that Valeria was right, and he ought to invite Grey to go to America with him, than Grey showed so little appreciation for Miss Endicott's attributes, Alan believed he was not worthy of her. And in that case, he ought not be party to any scheme, however well intended, to bring Grey and the American miss together. Miss Endicott needed someone who would appreciate everything about her. She needed someone who could match the passion and power of her music, someone who . . .

"So you're going to America," Grey said. "Did you meet Miss Endicott or her family? That would give you an entrée, once you're there."

"Actually, I didn't. Just as Miss Endicott finished singing, Mr. Rush decided it was a good time to talk to me about my trip. We repaired to his library, and I didn't meet anyone. But there's still time, of course."

"Yes. How long will they be in London?"

"I have no idea. By the way, Grey . . ."

The waiter delivered the salmon, smothered in a white lemon sauce. Alan refilled his and Grey's wineglasses. *No, he told himself, I don't have to say this. I don't need anyone else's viewpoint for my articles about America.*

"I shall probably return to Enderlin Hall next week, once Valeria's exhibit is done," Grey said, his voice reverting to mechanical boredom.

"And do what?"

"That, my dear Alan, is the prime question."

"Actually, Grey, I have a proposition for you."

"Indeed?" Was there a spark of interest in Lord Talbot's blue eyes? Suddenly Alan found himself explaining his proposition, making a convincing case for an amiable companion, a person from the upper orders who would have a different view of the fledgling American democracy than his own. "I have always thoroughly admired the American experiment," he said. "I don't have the proper distance— most especially for the *Times* which, for all its vaunted independence, will want the pieces slanted in favor of England's ancient monarchy. Your opinion would be most valuable."

"My dear chap, I could not possibly . . ."

"Why not? You said yourself you have no reason to remain in London. You have nothing especial to take up when you return to Enderlin Hall. Kevin is being well looked after by your uncle, and it only frustrates you to share his home. Don't you think it might do you a bit of good to get away, see new places?"

There. He had done it. The devil with Valeria, anyway.

Not for coming up with the idea, but for making him the go-between. Forking a morsel of salmon from its bone, Alan gave Grey a surreptitious glance. The blue eyes were veiled again, staring vacantly toward the tall windows draped in heavy wine velvet. He had not started eating his fish, and his right hand—a long-fingered, slender hand, white as a lady's, with his Kings's College ring on the third finger and a ruby sparkling on the little one—played absently with the handle of his fork. His smooth good looks were troubled by two faint frown lines running between his brows. Alan saw that a gray streak was starting in his dark brown hair at one temple. Like his uncle, Grey would look distinguished, but middle-aged, by the time he reached thirty-five.

"Do you want time to think about it?" Alan asked. "There's no rush. I shan't sail before September."

Grey nodded that he had heard, but his eyes remained far away. "America," he said at last. "Polly was supposed to be from America, do you remember?"

Alan nodded, though Grey wasn't looking at him. He had never been sure where that story had come from. Grey answered his unspoken question. "It was a tale my uncle made up, to hide the fact that she was pure cockney. Back when . . . he'd taken her as his mistress."

"Against her will?" Alan ventured. Again, he had never quite known the truth about those tangled relationships.

"Not exactly. But she had nowhere to turn, no place to go. He took her in. It was, I suppose, the price a penniless woman often pays for protection and security." His eyes returned to Alan's. "You know, Polly always wanted to go to America."

Alan was not sure whether he had won or lost.

CHAPTER
IV

On the day the Endicotts left England, the sun bathed Georges Dock in Liverpool with a July-like warmth, although September was in its second week. It told Stephanie to rejoice in her departure, rejoice that her mother's goal of finding her a husband had not been achieved, that she would return home single—and single-hearted.

She had loved parts of England: street singers in London, concerts at Bath, the Royal Opera in the Haymarket. She had enjoyed green countryside, colorful, orderly gardens, shopping for exotic treasures on London's busy streets, the walks along the sea at Brighton, and the sight of the King's strange, wonderful pavilion, where he hid from his Queen and plotted divorce.

She would remember with warmth the hospitality at old country estates, and the pensive courtesy of Lord Talbot in London. The importunities of prospective suitors in other places had already blurred, easily forgettable. She would remember in particular—and for no discernible reason—the warm, interested, appreciative gaze of a black-haired stranger seen across a glittering London ballroom. What would he have been like, that unknown journalist who was "not really her sort," according to Mrs. Rush? No matter. She would never see him again. As time went on, he would be only another of those strange, one-time encounters that lingered on in memory—people unmet but speculated on. What if . . .? How strange the turns of fate that guided one's future.

Even before they reached Liverpool, it was obvious that Dorothea had given up her quest. This past week she had not even tried to pair Stephanie with the eligible son of the American Chamber of Commerce man, an acquaintance of Morton's, when she gave a small dinner at their hotel. Mostly, Stephanie was relieved. Occasionally she wondered why her mother had seemed to surrender to fate. It was not at all like her.

Their ship was Morton's own—*The Good News*. It was to be the first of several ships he intended for a new venture—a regularly scheduled mail and passenger service connecting the United States and England. During the past week, *The Good News* had been in dry dock, being copper-bottomed by Liverpool metalworkers, but now she was tied at the dock, loaded and ready to sail, her hull gleaming with a fresh coat of white paint above the waterline.

Seeing her for the first time—tall masts and yards silhouetted against the September sun, the bowsprit thrust out over the dock—Stephanie felt a thrill of awe and delight. Atop her mainmast a white pennant waved, bearing the green silhouette of a tulip tree's leaf. The line had been named for their country place north of Philadelphia, Tulip Hill. The figurehead at the ship's prow was a bold carving of a bare-bosomed, strong-faced female with flowing yellow hair, holding a trumpet to her lips with both hands. The sort of symbol seafaring men loved, Stephanie guessed, but her mother would ignore.

Good News. Morton had been warned that it was foolhardy to start such an enterprise in the midst of an economic depression. But he had always done such things by instinct rather than by the accepted wisdom of the day and he had always, thus far, succeeded.

"What do you think of her, my dears?" he asked as they walked toward the ship, Morton and Dorothea first, Stephanie behind with Jenny, who carried newly bought winter bonnets for the ladies in two large bandboxes.

"She's beautiful," Stephanie said. Although she was

overly warm in her leghorn bonnet with its wide bow under
her chin, and the high-collared, long-sleeved green mantle,
she felt that everything was beautiful today, or exciting, or
marvelously interesting.

"She's not very big," Dorothea said. She had become
accustomed to the imposing girth of the frigate on which
they had taken passage last March, and clung to the notion
that bigger meant safer.

"Four hundred and thirty ton, two hundred forty feet
long," Morton said. "True, she's small, but she's stout-
hulled, and carries plenty of canvas for speed."

Dorothea shivered. "Whenever I board a ship, I remember all the wrecks I ever heard about."

He patted her shoulder. "Hard to believe this pile of
timber and canvas can survive all the Atlantic can throw at
it, isn't it? But I vouchsafe it's stout as any ship I've sent all
the way to China."

Around them the dock traffic swarmed. Stephanie took it
all in with avid eyes, ignoring her mother's rule that, in
public, young ladies should look neither to right nor left,
but only where they were heading. Another ship along the
pier was just being loaded. Gruff orders sounded from
shipboard and dock through megaphones. Men rolled hogs-
heads and barrels up a planked incline to the lower deck.
Two-wheeled carts groaned under precarious loads as mules
plodded to and from unloading sheds. Men smoked cigars
as they checked shipments and added up long columns in
their ledgers. Glass and fine china, woolens and cottons and
delicate linens, iron, coal, and salt, all going west, to the
Americas.

Across the way a constant stream of people moved in and
out of the taverns and lodging houses. A common sort, to be
sure—sailors on leave, stevedores, barmaids, river "rats"
as her father called them, and loafers, but all investing the
scene with a marvelous energy that Stephanie longed, somehow, to share. Tall warehouses half-blocked her view of a
church, but its spire soared above the obstacles, piercing a
low-flying white cloud. As far along Georges Pier as she
could see, a veritable forest of ship's masts lifted her eyes
and her spirits to the sky. Nearby, a large derrick hoisted a

cow into the air and onto the ship. The cow, its legs hanging helplessly, mooed in consternation. Stephanie laughed and pointed it out to her mother, hoping to coax a smile.

"Yes," Dorothea said grimly. "I know just how she feels."

"Oh, Mama, don't, I pray you. We shall be quite safe."

But she knew it did no good to say anything. Since they were small, Morton had taken his three children on boats up and down the Delaware and the Schuylkill. Stephanie had ridden coastal packets to New York and Wilmington and learned to row a small boat across the Schuylkill near their country home before she was ten. When she was twelve, she had accompanied her father on the first steamboat to navigate the Delaware as far as Trenton. Having failed to protect her children from such recklessness, Dorothea would watch, tight-lipped, from shore whenever Morton initiated the children to the hazards of water-borne travel. It did not appease her to know they had grown up to respect but not fear the sea, nor to hear Morton tease Stephanie that she was sure to be the first woman to sail on one of his ships around the world.

The sea had been a bone of contention between Morton and his wife before Stephanie was born. It had started early in their marriage when Morton was still supercargo, in charge of the merchandise aboard his father's ships. The year before Stephanie was born, Dorothea learned, second-hand, that his ship had been boarded by pirates in the Mediterranean. Morton returned safely and laughed off the danger. On the next voyage, they had done battle with a French frigate in the West Indies, and Morton came home with a gunshot wound in his shoulder. This time his wife, holding their infant daughter, unsympathetically presented him with an ultimatum: it was either her or the sea. Morton chose Dorothea and retired from adventure. Stephanie, learning his history over the years, sometimes suspected the choice had been hard for him.

Captain Turnbull, a tall, hearty man in his early thirties, greeted them as they boarded. He had been introduced to Stephanie and her mother by Morton the previous week as a good friend. Stephanie's passing thought at the time was

that he was her mother's next candidate for a prospective
suitor, but it turned out he was married. Anyway, Dorothea
would never have furthered her daughter's acquaintance
with a seafaring man.

As other passengers boarded, Captain Turnbull turned to
greet them. Mr. Bates of Virginia, tobacco planter, and his
wife. They were a handsome couple, elegantly dressed and
self-assured, with soft Southern accents. Everyone exchanged
how-do-you-do's. As her parents made small talk, Stephanie
watched the seamen out of the corner of her eye. How
efficiently they responded to the orders bawled out by the
second mate, scrambling up the masts and along the yard-
arms to make last-minute adjustments of the canvas, straining
at the winches to wind the heavy, tarred ropes. Their
sun-weathered skin and muscles rippling under dark, striped
jerseys fascinated her. Their eyes, in lean hard faces below
black kerchiefs that hid their hair, never met hers.

"Stephanie," her mother said, recalling her to propriety.
"Mr. Wells will show us to the ladies' cabin now."

She had wanted to take the tour of the ship Morton had
promised them. But Dorothea said, "We must get out of the
crew's way until we're at sea," and Stephanie realized she
was worried about the seamen, looking at them.

"Get settled in, then I'll stop by and show you around,"
Morton told Stephanie with a sympathetic wink. She had to
be content with that.

Mr. Wells, the first mate, guided them down a narrow,
steep stair and aft, to the ladies' 'tween-decks cabin. Jenny
brought up the rear with the bandboxes. Watching her
mother's straight, slender, indomitable back in the faultlessly
fitted poplin pelisse, Stephanie's irritation at being bustled
off the deck was mixed with sadness. The tension between
her parents, the frequent differences of opinion, seemed to
have hardened over the years rather than mellowed. *We
were not wildly in love,* her mother had said, *and yet it has
worked out most satisfactorily.* But had it? Given her mother's frequent annoyance with Morton, was her advice on
choosing a man dependable?

Stephanie found the boudoir-sitting room in the ladies'
cabin delightful. Even Dorothea approved the cushioned

sofas and rosewood card tables, the mirrors and landscape (not seascape) paintings on the satinwood-paneled walls, the tallow candles enclosed in glass chimneys in the wall sconces. Off this common room were six little cubicles for sleeping and personal toilettes. Taking the one next to her mother's, Stephanie laid her reticule atop the upper of the two berths fastened to the wall, and looked around. The space was crowded. A low-boy stood in one corner, its glass drawer handles glowing in the shaft of light coming from the single porthole. A long, narrow shelf ran along one side to a washstand and commode, over which a mirror had been installed. Under the washstand sat a water jug and a covered bucket for waste water. Every night, Morton had told them, the steward would bring a fresh jug of water for their washing and drinking needs, and take out the bucket of waste. The water would be strictly rationed, as it had been on the trip over.

Stephanie's valise and trunk had been placed next to the lowboy. She knelt to open it and unpack some necessaries. She could hear her mother talking to Jenny on the other side of the thin partition.

"The mattresses are good enough, I see—I was particularly insistent about that little detail to Mr. Endicott. Jenny, you may put the bandboxes in that corner. I shall take the lower bunk. My, there's not much head room, is there? The quilts are already clammy. You must be sure to warm them before we come to bed at night. Stephanie, dear," she called out, "are you quite sure you'll be all right alone?"

"Quite sure, Mama," Stephanie called back. She spread a little rug out beside her berth and began arranging her handkerchief box, her comb and brush, and some jars of creams and scent in the top drawer of the chest. There seemed very little room to put anything.

Her mother appeared in the doorway of her room. "Mrs. Bates seemed very nice, didn't she? I wonder how many other women will be aboard." She looked around the boudoir again and rearranged the little pillows on the sofa. "Yes, they really did quite well, didn't they? Did your father say whether we're to have a steward or a stewardess? I much prefer a woman looking after me."

"He didn't say," Stephanie replied. She was relieved when a knock on the cabin door told her Morton had come for her.

"Certainly not," Dorothea said, when Morton asked if she wanted to join them to see the ship. "I believe I shall try to take a nap. I'm feeling a little uneasy already, and we haven't even left the dock. But you two go ahead." She didn't mention being pleased with the cabin's arrangements, and Stephanie thought her father looked disappointed.

Beams of light danced off the green-painted bulwarks and blinded Stephanie for a moment as they returned to the deck. "I've a surprise for you," Morton said, leading her toward the gangway. "Guess who's aboard?" He pointed to a tall, slim, immaculate figure who stood at the rail, his back to them, his attention on the activity on the wharf. Stephanie immediately recognized Lord Talbot and was amazed. Then, remembering her mother's complacency these past few weeks, she understood. Surely there was some kind of plot.

"How very strange!" she said in a low voice. "He never mentioned going to America to me. Did you know he would be sailing with us?"

Smiling, Morton avoided answering her by calling out, "Lord Talbot!" The viscount turned to greet them with a smile.

"A last-minute decision," he explained. "A friend of mine is going to America and asked me to come along. Thought it might be just the ticket for me. Sea air and change, don't you know."

She reclaimed her hand, which he had held longer than necessary. "I'm delighted to see you, Lord Talbot," she said. "And who is your friend?"

"Alan Dunstable. He's a journalist. The *Times* has commissioned some articles about the United States from him. It looks as if we'll be there for six months or so, traveling about."

Dunstable, Dunstable . . . *Oh*, came Mrs. Rush's voice in her head, *You must mean Mr. Dunstable*. A vision of warm brown eyes enfolded by eyelids that crinkled when he smiled, of curly black hair and an independent turn of the head . . .

Lord Talbot was speaking to Morton, but for a few seconds she did not hear what he said. More people climbed aboard, in two's and three's. Her eyes followed their progress absently. When she forced herself to listen, Morton was saying, "He'll have to ask Captain Turnbull. It's quite possible he could use someone to look after the livestock. It's always a problem finding a sailor willing to take on the task, unless he's off the farm. A man and his son, you say?"

"Yes, Irish. He was all set to sail on another ship for America last week, and was robbed of the passage money. Been here ever since, destitute, with no way to get back to Ireland, and no reason to, for that matter—he's leaving some dreadful situation, like they all want to do. Alan is always getting into conversation with unlikely people. He discovered this man in the tavern last evening, and promised to say a word, if it would help."

"Well, why not?" Morton asked warmly. "I'll say a few words myself. We're not taking steerage passengers, but if he can work his way . . ."

"Where is Mr. Dunstable, then?" Stephanie asked.

Grey Talbot turned to her with a slight shrug. "Traveling with Mr. Dunstable is a bit like trying to accompany a will-o'-the-wisp. I've no idea, at the moment. Either aboard, arguing with your captain, or . . ." He broke off and pointed to the foot of the gangplank. "I do believe that's him, now."

Stephanie's eyes followed his gesture. First she saw a tall man in a short, faded jacket and soft floppy-brimmed hat, carrying a large bundle on his shoulders. Behind him a shorter man led a small boy up the gangplank. It took her a moment to recognize the second person. The black curls were hidden under a top hat, and the firm, square chin was nearly lost under the high collar and black cravat. His tight, gray trowsers and dark blue frock coat outlined a broad, powerful build. As his face came more clearly into view, it was the dark eyes, narrowed against the sun, that confirmed his identity.

Seeing Lord Talbot, he waved a greeting and hurried his small charge forward. Seeing Stephanie beside her father, he hesitated ever so slightly, and his expression seemed to alter. By the time he had beckoned the countryman to them, his eyes regarded her with bland disinterest. Unexpectedly, a pulse beat in her throat. She was grateful for the shielding shadow of her leghorn bonnet as Grey introduced them.

"How d'you do, ma'am?" Mr. Dunstable's voice was deep and slightly hoarse, as if he had been shouting or singing too much. He bowed with a perfunctory air, clearly uncomfortable with the custom. "Miss Endicott. We are fortunate, indeed, to meet the owner of the line and his daughter as well." He turned to Morton. "These are Mr. O'Brien and Eddie. Your captain has kindly given Mr. O'Brien permission to work his passage. I trust this meets with your approval."

"As a matter of fact, we were discussing that very thing," Lord Talbot said. Morton assured Mr. O'Brien that he was welcome. The boy looked up at them with shy, worried eyes. His clothes seemed either too large or too small.

Mr. O'Brien shifted his bundle to his feet. His shoulders were stooped, his eyes weary. "I'm sure I don't know what I'd done without the gentleman's sayin' a word for me, sir," he said. Compassion flooded Stephanie. She looked to Mr. Dunstable with mute appreciation for what he had done. He was pointing out some feature of the rigging to the boy.

Because of the chance encounter, Morton guided the two Englishmen as well as Stephanie on a tour of the ship. Their first goal became to establish Mr. O'Brien and Eddie with the livestock, settled atop the hatches near the forecastle. A seaman who was doing battle with a recalcitrant pig that did not want to be fenced gladly turned the task over to Mr. O'Brien, and went off to get buckets so the newcomer could milk the cow, which was advertising its distress at missing the morning milking with loud periodic moos. The sheep were bleating, and the hens and ducks, perched in the long boats, cackled and fluttered their wings worriedly. Over the din, Stephanie found it hard to hear what her father was saying. Something about plenty of fresh meat, milk, and eggs, no doubt. They had had enough of dried beans and molasses on the voyage coming over.

As they continued the tour, Stephanie had to be content to walk alongside Lord Talbot while the journalist preempted her place at Morton's side and asked about the ship's proportions, the amount of sail they carried, the size of the crew, and the kind of cargo in the hold.

"Twenty-six seamen, including able and ordinary," Morton explained. "Two mates, a carpenter, cook, two stewards, and two cabin boys. Mostly American, a few limejuicers and one Italian. Hope there's no trouble between 'em. We got all colors—black, brown, white, towheads, redheads, freckles. It doesn't matter, so long's a man does his work. They'll get fresh meat twice a week, soft bread, potatoes, molasses, and pickles. Better'n any British merchant vessel, I'd warrant."

Later she heard him say, "There'll be more mail in future, when the schedule gets established. More passengers, too. Since we don't carry steerage passengers, we can load the tween-decks with linens and other textiles, worth more per pound than anything else. Got salt in the holds, too. In the future, I hope it'll be strictly passengers and mail, mail and passengers."

They had just finished inspecting the galley where the food was prepared when Stephanie felt the ship shift and start to move out.

"They're backing her out from the pier and into the Mersey," Morton judged. "Easiest way to do it, if the wind serves, and it shifted favorable about an hour ago. I call that a good omen." He pulled a big watch out of his vest pocket. "Eleven thirty—not so bad. Should get a good start into the Irish Sea before dark."

"Can we go up on the poop deck and watch, Papa?" Stephanie asked eagerly.

"Don't see why not, so long as you stay with me and don't get in anyone's way," Morton replied, and led the way.

Returning to the ladies' cabin some time later, Stephanie found her mother, already affected by the rolling motion underneath her, sitting as quietly as she could on a sofa,

embroidery lying listlessly in her lap. Mrs. Bates, apparently unaffected, was talking animatedly to a large young
woman whom she introduced as Miss Taylor of Albany,
New York. Both stopped to listen as Stephanie relayed her
surprise at meeting the two Englishmen, and went on to
describe the inhabitants of the manger, the appetizing smells
already emanating from the galley, and the way the captain
had gotten the ship into the river, with the yards braced
around as the lines were eased off, letting the ship go out of
the dock stern first. She also remembered to tell about Mr.
O'Brien and Eddie, and how Mr. Dunstable had helped
them.

Dorothea was less impressed than Stephanie with Mr.
Dunstable's benevolence. "A gentleman who condescends
to become involved in the problems of poor strangers seems
to me a very undependable sort of acquaintance. Of course,
he's a journalist, isn't he?" As though that explained the
aberration.

"But Mama," Stephanie protested. "What about your
own work at home with orphans and distressed widows?"

"That is altogether different, Stephanie. That is Philadelphia." Then she grew thoughtful and added, "It is marvelous, however, to find Lord Talbot aboard. I hope you'll
make proper use of this voyage, Stephanie."

Stephanie shook her head and smiled. "You never give
up, do you, Mother."

"I always try to do the best I can to lead my children in
the right direction." She glanced toward Mrs. Bates and
Miss Taylor who, although somewhat mystified, nodded
their approval.

"And what time is dinner?" asked Miss Taylor, whose
figure suggested that food was usually her first consideration. "Has that been determined? I've been told that it is
best to have a little in one's stomach to counteract seasickness."

"Dinner isn't until four," Stephanie said. "Tea at eight
this evening. But bread and cheese are available in the
dining room now, if you wish, and a steward will bring a
lunch here if you ring."

"I couldn't possibly eat anything," Dorothea said. "My

stomach is queasy, even now. Although I'm sure your father won't understand how this is possible."

"Do we dress for dinner?" Stephanie asked.

"Certainly. Morton assured me the Green Tulip Line is to be run by gentlemen. What would Lord Talbot think if we did not?"

By dinnertime, *The Good News* had sea room and a clear course, and the ship was trimming away for the Irish Sea, helped by a southwest wind. Dorothea had agreed valiantly to go to dinner, though she declared she would not eat much. It seemed to help her to dress up, and she expressed pleasure to Stephanie, sotto voce, when she saw that the other passengers had done so, too. Lord Talbot surely would have no reason to be offended. The ladies, in their high-waisted muslin or silk gowns, had adorned their bare necks with jewels and dressed their hair with filagreed combs or feathers. The men sported cutaway coats, satin waistcoats, silk cravats, and jeweled studs. Except for Mr. Dunstable, whose waistcoat, Stephanie noted, was plain linen and quite unadorned.

Once they had gone through the pretentious arched doorway to the dining saloon, which was announced with marbled columns, she saw the pianoforte Morton had promised her sitting in a small alcove. Armchairs and small tea tables were arranged on either side, providing a cozy corner for people to chat over drinks, play cards, or show off their musical skill.

"Do you like the arrangement?" Morton asked, looking at her slyly.

"It's perfect, Papa," she said. "I doubted you would really be able to put a pianoforte on board."

"It remains to be learned what the sea air will do to its innards," he warned her, "but we'll see how well the instrument holds up."

The cherrywood-paneled room held a long mahogany table and padded horsehair chairs for twenty people. When the ten men and six women, as well as the captain and first mate, found their seats, it was nearly full. Introductions were made amid pleasantries about learning to eat and walk aboard a moving ship. The men made jovial bets on who would make it down to dinner the following day if they encountered high seas. Glancing toward her mother, Stephanie saw that she was trying to ignore such crude remarks.

The Endicotts gravitated toward the captain's end of the table, along with Mr. and Mrs. Bates, Lord Talbot, and Mr. Dunstable. Even before the soup arrived, Morton began to discuss the irksome British trade laws with Mr. Bates—this despite Dorothea's silent eyebrow signals that tried to remind him of her long-standing rule: talking either business or politics at a dinner table where ladies were present was quite out of line. As usual, Morton became so involved in his topic, he forgot to heed her.

By the time the white-coated stewards brought the soup, the discussion had grown heated. Morton, carelessly dipping into his bowl, enthusiastically defended his contention that the British were softening, little by little. English merchants in Manchester and London had agreed with him that the old Navigation Laws were obsolete. Even the Prime Minister, in his speech in Parliament the previous May, had implied as much.

Mr. Bates, the planter from Virginia, contended that Morton was much too optimistic. The British monopolistic laws would continue to stifle free trade all the way from the Bahamas to Newfoundland, and Mr. Endicott surely had misinterpreted that old-guard Prime Minister, Lord Liverpool.

Morton waved his soup spoon in protest. A large, greasy spatter landed on his satin vest. "I admit," he acknowledged, "that he didn't come right out and say 'damn the Navigation Laws.' But Parliament would've skinned him alive if he had . . ."

"Morton, I beg you," Dorothea said in hushed, shocked tones. "There are ladies . . ."

"Beg pardon, my dear."

The old battle stemming from her mother's ladylike rearing and her father's rough-and-tumble education aboard a merchantman privateer was in full swing. At home, Stephanie and Hugh and Clarinda joked with their father when he strayed from "Mama's rules," and even Dorothea didn't seem to mind so much. In public, in the company of people she did not know, she was invariably hostile and mortified. Stephanie, in turn, became critical of her mother and defensive of her father. Why couldn't she see that his easy, affable friendliness was more important than spilled soup? That his colorful language was part of his vast, all-encompassing enthusiasm?

"The first time I set eyes on your mother, I knew she was the one for me," Morton was fond of telling his children. Dorothea, if she were present, would respond, "Oh, pshaw, Morton, you know full well that it was a good year after we met before you so much as asked to partner me in a dance."

But Morton had insisted on his version. He had adored her from afar, never dreaming he had a chance with this gently bred, educated, vivacious daughter of a respected Philadelphia judge. *His* father, Josiah Endicott, had not thought his eldest son needed any but the most rudimentary education, even after he had become rich in the China trade and could have afforded to send him anywhere to school.

Stephanie never knew precisely how this wide gulf had been bridged. When Great-Aunt Tabitha Fletcher came to visit (which was very rarely), her acerbic tongue excused her nephew's lack of polish to strangers by saying that the marriage had saved the Fletchers from financial ruin and had given the Endicotts a hefty nudge up the social ladder. But if her mother had not been "wildly in love" with her father, Stephanie suspected she had been very much attracted to his vitality and enthusiasm, as well as to the money he was sure to inherit.

"I heard Lord Liverpool's speech," Alan Dunstable was saying. "I, too, was surprised to hear him admit that America's prosperity would be to Britain's advantage." He handled a knife as he spoke. His fingers were not white and long-tapered like Lord Talbot's, but sturdy and brown, and the index finger was stained with ink. "But may I caution you, sir, about being too sanguine of a quick change in trading policy. In England, the political power still lies with the landed aristocracy. And their notions are about as easy to alter as the habits of the three-toed sloth."

Morton, the captain, and Mr. Bates laughed heartily. Mr. Dunstable seemed surprised that he had said anything comical. Stephanie laughed, too, more loudly than she ought to have, to relieve the tension she had absorbed from her mother. Mrs. Bates's glance showed surprise that Stephanie had been following the men's conversation, not the ladies' discussion of Paris versus London fashions. Dorothea frowned at her daughter. Mr. Dunstable turned an inquiring smile toward her.

"You made a very apt simile, sir," Stephanie said, still choking with laughter. She put her napkin to her lips to stifle further merriment.

"You sound very knowledgeable, sir," Captain Turnbull said to Mr. Dunstable. "Although I must confess surprise at hearing such sentiments from one of your class."

Mr. Dunstable shrugged slightly. "Perhaps you mistake my class, Captain. I am only the younger son of a Cambridge don. My older brother practices medicine. He is the respectable one—and the one who inherited a living. For myself, I only scribble for various rags."

"He is being too modest," Lord Talbot interjected. "Actually, Mr. Dunstable has earned a considerable reputation for covering stories of international moment, ever since Napoleon's defeat at Waterloo. He has observed and written about the recent uprisings in Italy and Spain. To have this present assignment from the *Times* of London is no small achievement. I fear, however, that the United States, without war or revolution, will seem tame to him by comparison."

The undercurrent of sarcasm in his voice surprised Stephanie, who had supposed that this friend of Lord Talbot's was her definition of "friend"—a long-standing relationship such as hers with Kate Hamlin, whom she had known since she was eight years old. She would never have said a slighting word to anyone about Kate.

Mr. Dunstable smiled and shrugged his shoulders. "A better living than writing poetry, certainly."

"Indeed, Mr. Dunstable, do you write poetry as well?" Mrs. Bates asked. "How very interesting. I do so adore the poetry of Mr. Wordsworth and Mr. Scott. His 'Lady of the Lake' is so romantic."

"I used to, ma'am. I find I no longer have the time," Mr. Dunstable returned. "My poetry, I fear, was never anything like Scott's."

"What was it like, then, Mr. Dunstable?" Stephanie asked.

"Different, madam," he said curtly.

She was taken aback by his manner and could not refrain from a tart reply. "Oh! Forgive my asking, sir."

He softened. "The fault is mine, Miss Endicott. As for the poetry, perhaps I lacked a proper subject."

Mrs. Bates suggested that a voyage might be a good time to resurrect such talent—at the least, there would be no lack of *time*. Mr. Bates, bored with talk of poetry, asked Captain Turnbull the likelihood of rough seas. The captain said wryly that smooth sailing all the way was an act of providence he did not foresee, but the present good weather should hold for several days. Stephanie, remembering belatedly to be well-bred, returned her eyes to the stewed chicken the steward had placed before her.

CHAPTER
V

Traveling with Morton Endicott, one was expected to rise early, soon after the crew had holystoned the white decks, and take at least one turn about the ship. Stephanie enjoyed this, once she had gotten used to keeping her balance on a moving vessel. One felt the tug of the wind on one's bonnet, the brightness of the sun in one's face, and smelled the tangy, salt-laden air. If one were lucky, one spotted porpoises at play. As the ship passed the Isle of Man and entered the North Channel between Scotland and Ireland, numerous schooners and fishing smacks with gulls wheeling and crying after them were in view. Their captains called to one another for news. Encountering a vessel with a good catch, Captain Turnbull sent for his cook, and they bought enough fresh fish for the passengers' dinner. As Stephanie well knew, no self-respecting seaman would eat fish, except out of dire necessity.

Dorothea, invariably the most seasick late in the evening, slept mornings and didn't share her husband's and daughter's exercising. At night Stephanie would hear her through the thin partition that separated their sleeping quarters, retching and groaning, and Jenny's footsteps and soft voice as she ministered to her mistress. At lunchtime, Dorothea would only take tea and a few bites of biscuit, but her need for social intercourse drove her to the dining saloon for dinner. She felt at her best then, but if she ate too much, driven by hunger, the whole cycle started again about teatime.

Nights were uncomfortable for Stephanie as well, but for different reasons. If her mother's distress awoke her, she would become aware of the calls of the crew, the bell clanging the change of watch, the rattle and clatter of shifting sails. The berth seemed very hard, despite the thick mattress, and whenever she turned over, it creaked unmercifully. If she got up to get a drink of water, the night air was cold and dank, even though, in daylight, the weather remained pleasant.

Four more weeks, four long weeks at least. It was only at night that it seemed much too long. Going west took longer, the wind would be against them most of the way, and they must take care to stay north of the gulf stream, which drove ships east, to Europe. Traveling west, the average crossing was forty days. What would happen in forty days? Caught between her mother's aspirations for her future and the presence of Lord Talbot aboard, that length of time seemed fraught with possibilities—or danger.

When Morton, donning an old soft-brimmed hat from his seafaring days to protect his balding head, climbed the port ladder onto the poop deck to talk to Captain Turnbull, Stephanie often went with him. She wore her warmest mantle and snug-fitting satin bonnet to protect herself from the brisk wind that blew freer over the poop deck. Here, one was closer to the rigging, to the constant squeak of yard, mast, and spar, and the flap of the sail, deflecting the wind or yielding to it. The roll of the ship was more pronounced at this height, but she had always been a good sailor. Standing to starboard, she enjoyed the motion as she looked out to sea, across the miles of waves, to an awe-inspiring horizon of white clouds and blue sky. The helmsman, standing behind the wheel at the stern, his eyes upon the compass in its binnacle, paid no attention to her. Captain Turnbull and Morton exchanged stories of the sea or argued about the advantages of steam versus sail.

"Someday we'll have steam-powered packets and won't be so dependent on wind and canvas," Morton said confidently.

"Ridiculous idea," Captain Turnbull snorted, chewing on his cigar. "Steam power may be all right for inland rivers and lakes, but you'll never cross an ocean with it. Why, just the coal needed for such a voyage would take up all the space in the ship's hold. And what about the expense of both fuel and engines? The wind is free."

"I was considering trying it next year," Morton said offhandedly, his eyes twinkling. "Some engineering fellows I know are eager to give it a try. The *Savannah* made it to Liverpool last year..."

"Using sail most of the way," the captain pointed out.

"Still, they tried steam, and it worked. It'd be nice to have the option if you get becalmed or off course."

"Morton, you're a dreamer. Wooden ships aren't heavy enough to carry the weight of the engines."

And so the argument, good-natured but vehement, ran between the two. Not expected to take part, Stephanie's mind wandered elsewhere. Almost invariably, it returned, sooner or later, to the two Englishmen aboard.

They were so very different—Lord Talbot and Mr. Dunstable. Lord Talbot moved with gentle grace and spoke softly, never making unnecessary gestures or nervous movements. He was affable, yet so melancholy. His smiles were half-smiles, soon gone, and his thoughts seemed to be elsewhere even as one spoke to him. Mr. Dunstable's every move was energetic, his brown-eyed gaze intense, his hands restless, his voice husky and abrupt. Something about him was very intriguing. Stephanie liked people and wanted to be friends with them. Too bad there had to be such a gulf between males and females, so that mere friendship between unattached men and women seemed to be impossible. Why, for instance, did Mr. Dunstable talk freely to her father when they met him and Lord Talbot during their promenades on deck, but when she tried to engage him in conversation, he backed off, almost visibly? If she persisted, intrigued by his colorful profession, he would soon excuse himself and leave them, and she would wonder if she had said something wrong.

The friendship between the two Englishmen intrigued her as well. The quips they exchanged at dinner or during those brief interchanges on deck gave her an impression that their differing habits sometimes warred with that friendship. Lord Talbot was precise and fastidious; Mr. Dunstable was careless and preoccupied. Mr. Dunstable teased Lord Talbot about his lifelong dependence on his manservant, from whom he was now separated. The valet, having just married, had declined to accompany his master. Lord Talbot, knowing his friend had no servant, had decided he could do without, too. He was managing it, but not without difficulties and regrets. Lucky for him, Alan Dunstable declared, there were stewards aboard for the express purpose of seeing to the needs of passengers like Lord Talbot.

When Mr. Dunstable made such comments, Stephanie caught flashes of anger in Lord Talbot's eyes, quickly covered. It made her wonder what had led him to accept Mr. Dunstable's invitation—and why that invitation had been given.

If the chance to know Mr. Dunstable seemed remote, the chances to become better acquainted with Lord Talbot increased each day. When Stephanie and Mrs. Bates and Miss Taylor, discovering a mutual love of music, gathered about the pianoforte before dinner, Lord Talbot soon got in the habit of joining them. Sometimes he sang or hummed along, but more often he just listened as the two younger ladies sang and Mrs. Bates played. Toward mid-afternoon, when Dorothea usually felt better, she would accompany her husband and daughter in a walk on the deck. If they happened to meet Lord Talbot, Stephanie's parents quickly found excuses to leave her alone with him. After a few days of this sort of thing, she and the viscount needed no prompting to take strolls on the deck together or challenge each other to a game of cribbage at one of the small tables in the alcove off the dining saloon.

The idea that everything was proceeding according to some well-laid plan grew in Stephanie's mind. The presence of Lord Talbot was too convenient to be pure coincidence. She found herself wondering how it had been accomplished. Did Lord Talbot himself have an inkling of the "plot," as she privately called it?

"I'm very curious," she confessed as they walked the

deck together on a gray afternoon, muffled and gauntleted against a brisk wind. "Pray tell me how you happened to choose my father's packet for your trip to America."

She felt safe in bringing up the topic, since the other passengers had deserted the deck for the protection of their respective cabins and would not interrupt them. Lord Talbot adjusted his scarf higher about his ears as a gust from the northeast struck their faces. Stephanie held on to the deep brim of her leghorn with both hands. Its ribbon ends flapped against her chin.

"Alan planned the trip," he said. "He had heard about this new Green Tulip Line and wanted to try it. I rather imagine it's something else he can write about."

"Did he know this was my father's line?"

"I haven't the least notion. *I* never told him, although it is possible someone told me. I don't really recall when I first heard . . ." His voice trailed away with his familiar vagueness. It was quite obvious he did not share her suspicions, nor was he a party to the plot.

They turned back from the stern of the ship, Lord Talbot discreetly guiding her by the elbow. She was relieved to feel the wind shift to their backs. *The Good News*, taking advantage of a rare northeast wind, was galloping full sail through the rough seas at an exhilarating rate. The air smelled of salt and approaching rain, but the prospect of a storm did not intimidate Stephanie. Her father, she knew, was up on the poop deck with Captain Turnbull and the two mates, doubtless keeping an occasional eye on her and Lord Talbot as they strolled along the starboard side of the main deck.

The crew were not much in evidence. Two lookouts in the crow's nests, straining their eyes on horizons fore and aft, were invisible to her unless she tilted her head back and stared up the rigging—a decidedly unladylike stance. One man checked the fastness of the shrouds amidships (strolling beside the bulwarks, they had to walk around him), and another mended a brace near the prow.

"One more question, Lord Talbot," Stephanie said, taking his arm in a confiding manner. "Have I done something to offend Mr. Dunstable?"

He looked down at her with raised eyebrows and a faintly sardonic expression. "Why would you imagine such a thing, Miss Endicott?"

"Because he seems to avoid me so pointedly."

"Oh, no indeed." His slight smile appeared. "I believe he admires you most wholeheartedly. He's doing a good bit of writing, however, and when he's not writing, he talks to the off-duty sailors, the mates, and, who knows, perhaps even the cook."

"Does he indeed!" She marveled at the vision of Mr. Dunstable in the galley, interviewing the cook during the bustle of meal preparation. It sounded exactly like something her father might have done.

Lord Talbot's gaze swung out onto the horizon, where the gray sea churned against the overcast sky. "Alan always wants to know everything about everything," he said.

Stephanie, half-turning to follow his gaze, felt the wind sting her cheeks again. Ahead, the waves swelled and broke high against the ship's prow. She knew she ought to go below, but the conversation had become too interesting. A few more minutes wouldn't hurt.

She stopped, leaned against the bulwark, and turned to him, away from the sight of the sea. "How long have you known him?"

He didn't answer at once, and she wondered if she ought to apologize for even asking the question. Then he settled his beaver more firmly on his head and turned to meet her eyes. She was surprised at the pain clouding his own.

"Seven years. I've known Alan Dunstable just seven years, come October." His posture had turned to stone, as if he were reliving something with his whole being, not just remembering it. He seemed unconscious of the bluster of wind and waves about them. She questioned him with a raising of her eyebrows.

"I had taken Polly to Newmarket to meet my father and sister." His eyes wandered from hers again, back out to sea, and his gloved hands ran along the top of the smoothly painted green bulwark. "Uncle Lucien had given me a new racehorse for my twenty-first birthday, and he was to run in the First October—that's one of the Newmarket races. The

day we arrived, Father was at the public house, toasting my
horse's victory in advance, he said. He'd drunk a bit too
much and . . . and it was Alan helped me get him home.''

After a pause he added, "I didn't like him much." He
grabbed onto the brim of his hat in time to save it from the
wind.

"Why not?"

He made a gesture like an apologetic shrug. "He didn't
seem a gentleman to me. And then, I thought he was
making up to Stella, my sister, and she was growing too
fond of him."

"Oh. And was he . . . making up to her?"

Again a mischievous wind threatened to steal his hat. He
frowned at the sea, then at her. "It's getting rather choppy.
Shall we go below?"

The words were not quite out of his mouth when she
heard the second mate shout from the poop deck, "Hands
by the halyards! In top-gallant sails!"

They glanced toward the voice, lost behind canvas. Seamen
appeared out of nowhere to attack the windlasses. The
machinery creaked, and the sails crackled and flapped as
they collapsed onto the yards.

"A moment longer," Stephanie detained him. "Unless
you'd rather not answer my question."

"Your question?" His eyes returned from the sailors'
labors to her.

"About your sister and Mr. Dunstable."

"Ah, yes. Well, he wasn't really, I suppose. Not then.
But they both wrote poetry and Stell thought he was
wonderful. I thought he was the wrong sort for her to fall in
love with and I told her so."

The wrong sort. Just the phrase Mrs. Rush had used to
describe Mr. Dunstable.

"And was he the wrong sort?" Stephanie persisted, even
though her companion was looking out to sea again with a
worried frown.

"Stand by to reef topsails!" came the call from the poop
deck.

"I say, Miss Endicott, I do think we should move below."
This time Lord Talbot took a firm grip on her arm. "We've

a way to the ladder, and it looks like a bit of a squall over there."

A gust of wind whipped his words away. Spray frosted her face as she turned to the horizon. The clouds overhead seemed more ominous than before and were moving across the sky at an alarming pace. Even as she watched, the dark clouds shuddered with distant lightning, and a rumble echoed across the waves.

"All passengers to their cabins! All passengers to their cabins! We're in for a blow!" came Mr. Wells's stentorian voice through the megaphone. It was clear he meant her and Lord Talbot.

She let him hurry her toward the stairway now but was not ready to abandon the topic. "About Mr. Dunstable," she resumed, holding her hat against what had become a gale.

"Are you interested in him, Miss Endicott?" His voice was sharp.

"Certainly not, I only wondered . . ."

He stopped her at the entrance to the ladder, where they were protected by the wall of the poop deck. "I rather think I ought to tell you what I told Stella, way back then." He still had a peremptory hold on her arm, and his face had grown very solemn. "Alan Dunstable is ambitious and . . . and unique, in a way. One can't put him in a category. He goes his own way. He always has, and I doubt he'd change for any woman."

She started to protest that he had no need to tell her such things. He interrupted by saying, "He wasn't ready to marry seven years ago, and it's unlikely he's ready to marry now, or ever. So I would suggest you be on your guard, Miss Endicott." His warning delivered, he dropped his hold on her arm as if he had just realized what he was doing.

She gazed at him in astonishment. Raindrops splattered in her face, stopping any retort she might have uttered. The deck was now alive with frantic activity. The second mate bawled orders, the men grunted and swore amid the squeaks and rattle and flap of the rigging, whipped by an increasingly ferocious wind. They scrambled with amazing agility up and down the ratlins and out over the yards, fastening the upper and lower topsails.

Lord Talbot smiled at Stephanie, a mute apology for speaking so severely to her. They said no more as he helped her step over the high coaming that protected the opening in case a wave washed over the deck—a prospect that now seemed more than likely as the second mate shouted hoarsely, "All hands! All hands on deck!"

With a thrill of foreboding, Stephanie scurried down the ladder, holding her skirts with one hand and the rail with the other. Lord Talbot's hand slid down the wooden rail just behind hers. She nodded a good-bye to him at the foot, and turned toward the ladies' cabin. At its door she nearly bumped into Jenny, who was leaving it.

"Oh, Miss Stephanie, I'm glad you're here. Madam is in a state. You better go to her right away. I'm s'posed to take a message to Mr. Endicott."

Stephanie nodded, forgetting to warn the maid that the last she had seen of Morton, he had been on the poop deck. She went through the empty boudoir to her mother's cubicle. Dorothea, very pale, was lying on her berth amid pillows and quilts.

"Thank heaven you're here, Stephanie. I was afraid you'd be swept overboard if you didn't come back soon. No, no, you mustn't stay with me. I expect to be miserably sick, and you won't want to be here. Jenny will be back directly and do whatever needs doing."

"I'll just stay till she returns," Stephanie said. The ship's pitch and roll had become more violent. She grabbed for the edge of the upper berth to keep her balance. "Can I get you anything, Mama?"

Dorothea, turning her face into her pillows, said weakly, "Just that basin over there, dear."

Stephanie brought the basin and fell into the chair. From her own room came the sound of small items crashing to the floor, of the wastewater pail banging against the commode. She had neglected to put away her toilet articles before leaving the room earlier.

"Oh, dear, I hope my scent bottle didn't break," she said.

"What's keeping Jenny" Dorothea moaned. "Will you see if you can find her, Stephanie? I—I'll manage somehow until she returns."

Stephanie arose, wondering if her mother meant she would manage not to throw up until Jenny returned. Strong, faithful Jenny. How unpleasant the crossing must be for her as well.

In the sitting room, the candles in the wall sconces flickered alarmingly at each pitch and roll of the ship. The cabin door opened, and Mrs. Bates and Miss Taylor staggered in.

"Have you seen Jenny?" Stephanie asked. Both ladies shook their heads and lurched toward their rooms, handkerchiefs over their mouths. Stephanie, balancing herself against the furniture, which was nailed to the floor, found her way to the passageway, where she braced against one bulkhead, then the opposite one, as the deck kept falling away from her feet. Even her strong stomach was beginning to feel queasy.

She reached the men's cabin and knocked on the door. After a long moment Mr. Dunstable opened it. He frowned in surprise. Her hand went involuntarily to her throat, even as she wondered why the sight of him startled her so. "M-my father?" she asked, holding fast to the door frame.

"He's not here, Miss Endicott. Can I do anything for you?"

"My mother needs Jenny, our maid. Did she stop by?"

"She did, indeed. I suspected your father was topside, with the captain, and told her so, but I didn't expect her to go looking for him."

"Thank you." She turned away, not knowing what to do next. With the ship's violent rise and fall, she could not even walk in a straight line, nor was she dressed to withstand the harsh rain that now pelted the decks.

"You're surely not going after her yourself, are you?" he called after her. She heard the door close and looked back to see that he had come into the narrow passageway after her. "I'll find her for you."

"Oh, no, I wouldn't dream of imposing . . ."

"No trouble at all," he said. "You must want to return to your mother."

Just then the outside door swung open and Jenny careened through it as if performing a half-circle dance, one hand on the door, the other pulling a small boy after her. Her frantic effort to close the door against the driving wind and rain succeeded only after Mr. Dunstable forced his powerful shoulder against it.

"Jenny!" Stephanie exclaimed.

The maid's hair and cap were dripping, and her soaked mantle clung to her shoulders and arms. The boy began to sob. After a moment's wonderment, Stephanie recognized Eddie O'Brien, the little Irish boy.

"I found him wanderin' the deck, miss," Jenny said. "Lost from his papa. I don't know what to do with him."

"I'll see to him," Stephanie said. "Mama needs you, Jenny."

"I'm sure she does, miss." Jenny wiped a wet strand of hair away from her forehead with the inside of her sleeve. Her normally amiable expression was aggrieved. "You know, Miss Stephanie, there's some things a lady's maid just shouldn't be expected to do. I hope your mama will understand that."

She staggered into the ladies' cabin. Stephanie bent toward the boy, who had fallen into a forlorn huddle at her feet. He looked up at her warily, tears coursing down his dirty cheeks. Her queasy stomach turned over at the strong barnyard odor coming from his wet clothes. She swallowed, braced herself against the ship's roll, and managed a smile. "My, you got wet, didn't you?" She held out her hand. "Can you get up? Come with me, and we'll get you dried off."

But Eddie shook his head. "I want my papa. Where's my papa?" he wailed.

"Let me take him," Mr. Dunstable said. "You know me, don't you, Eddie?" As he knelt beside the boy another violent pitch of the ship sent his right arm against Stephanie's thigh. Startled, she backed away. Mr. Dunstable didn't seem to notice. "Listen, your papa's all right," he told the boy, "but you need some dry clothes. How about coming along with me for now?"

Eddie stopped wailing and regarded him with his thumb in his mouth. When Mr. Dunstable picked him up and set him on one shoulder, he did not object.

Stephanie edged away from them. "Well, if you're sure," she said, sounding more reluctant than she felt.

Mr. Dunstable spread his legs wide for balance, one hand around Eddie's leg, the other on the door frame. "Of course I'm sure, Miss Endicott. You'll have enough to do, tending your mother until her maid has got herself dried off." He smiled and nodded at her.

"Thank you, then," she said, a little stiffly. She turned and groped her way back to the sitting room, to her mother.

CHAPTER
VI

The mizzen backstays gave way about midnight and pitched their topmast into the hungry waves. The jibboom broke soon after. The prolonged crackle of splintering wood, sounding as if the ship's very hull was being ripped apart, marked the storm's climax.

By then Stephanie had long since given way to nausea. Even as the storm began to abate, she could do nothing but cling to her mattress or hang her head weakly over her basin. She did not attempt to call Jenny. There was very little the maid could do, and Stephanie did not want to deprive her mother, who found Jenny's very presence a kind of comfort. Once the wind ceased wailing in the rigging and the waves stopped slamming against the ship's hull, she fell asleep. By then the night was nearly spent.

When she awoke, the first thing she noticed was the stifling, disagreeable smell. In a few minutes, despite her groggy head, it became unbearable. With a groan she arose and padded to the porthole, shivering as her bare feet met the cold planks of the deck beyond her little rug. But the porthole was stuck. After several minutes of futile tugging on the latch, she returned to the bed, shivering, and donned her wrapper that lay at its foot. Her head still spun, and there was a faint ache in her temples. Her throat was raw and her stomach sore. She stared balefully at the pan she had thrown up in but seemed helpless to do anything about it.

She was just wondering if she dare call to Jenny and risk waking her mother when a knock sounded and the maid appeared in the doorway, looking as if the storm had not affected her at all. Her comfortably stout figure in its neat blue-striped dress and gingham apron was, at that moment, the most welcome sight in the world.

"How're you feelin', Miss Stephanie?"

"Dreadful. Can you bring me some water?"

Jenny moved to the water jug and poured some into a tin mug. Sitting on the edge of the berth, Stephanie drank it gratefully while the maid emptied the offending pan into the waste bucket and rinsed it out. "I'll get rid of this soon's I can, Miss Stephanie. Sorry I didn't come earlier, but your mama . . ."

"How is Mama?"

"She's sleepin' now, but she had a real bad night, as you can imagine."

Stephanie rubbed the ache in her forehead, then huddled into her wrapper and wondered if she ought to go back to bed.

"D'you think you'll be ready for a visitor soon?" Jenny asked. "'Cause there's been a gentleman to see you."

"A . . . who?" Stephanie raised her head sharply, narrowly missing the frame of the berth above her.

"Mr. Dunstable. He asked how you did at about nine; then again at ten and eleven. It's near noon, now. He might come round again."

All thoughts of returning to bed vanished. Stephanie reached up and pushed her disheveled hair back from her face. "I'm sure I'll be all right, soon as I wash and have some tea. Will you find my green cotton twill? And if Mr. Dunstable returns, say I'll see him in about half an hour."

"I'll come back right away," Jenny promised, heading for the door with the waste bucket. "An' I'll ask the steward to send tea. Anything else you'll be wantin'?"

"Not for now. Perhaps—you'd better ask for a pot of tea. Is anyone else up and around?"

"Mrs. Bates got up and went out a while ago. That slave

girl of hers is cleanin' up her room. Miss Taylor and Mrs. Wynett are still abed, so the sittin' room's empty now. Your papa stopped about an hour ago to see how everyone did.''

"I'm sure *he* was fine," Stephanie said, a little resentfully.

Jenny nodded with a smile, promised to be back soon, and disappeared.

By the time Mr. Dunstable returned, Stephanie had donned her warm green dress, put a white cashmere shawl over her shoulders, brushed out her brown curls and tied them back with a green ribbon. She had tried to pinch some life into her cheeks but was not sure she had succeeded. Jennie had burned sandalwood incense in the room, and the atmosphere was now tolerable. The porthole remained firmly shut.

Her head still felt a little strange when Jenny announced Mr. Dunstable in the sitting room. She patted her hair before the mirror. "Do I look all right, Jenny?"

"Fine, miss."

Stephanie grimaced. "You always say that. Will you see what's keeping the tea? I do believe that would help a great deal."

She followed Jenny into the boudoir, not quite sure she was up to facing Mr. Dunstable, wondering why she was so nervous. He stood only a few feet into the room, as if unsure of his welcome. His blue jacket was well pressed, his ivory waistcoat was starched and spotless, his stock was neatly folded with a black silk cravat tied over it, and his black boots shone. He carried a package wrapped in newspaper.

His brown eyes softened in concern at her appearance. "I was sorry to hear from Mr. Endicott that the storm made you ill, madam," he said, bowing.

"I'm much recovered, Mr. Dunstable," she said. "But thank you, anyway. How is little Eddie?"

"He is doing well, and is now restored to his papa."

"It was kind of you to take him in."

"And of you, to offer," he returned. Still they stood—awkwardly, it seemed to Stephanie.

"Do sit down," she suggested. "Jenny has gone to fetch us tea."

As he hesitated, seeming both tongue-tied and frozen to

the spot, she took a seat on the nearest sofa. "My mother is still indisposed, although Papa is well enough. You seem to be of an equally strong constitution, sir."

Alan finally took the chair she had indicated. "I hope that isn't a crime, Miss Endicott. I confess to not succumbing to the storm, but it was a worthy enough opponent. You need not feel ashamed. Some came out of it even worse."

"I'm sorry to hear that. In what way?"

"Two seamen were injured by falling spars when the mizzenmast broke, and another was swept overboard by a breaking wave while they were trying to pay out a cable—something they do to keep the ship headed into the waves, as I understand it."

She gasped and clasped her hands together. "I had no idea! Is the poor man all right?"

"I'm sorry to say he was lost at sea. Captain Turnbull held a service for him this morning."

"Oh, how dreadful!"

Alan sprang to his feet. "Damme, I shouldn't have said such a thing. Do forgive me, Miss Endicott, I have little acquaintance with polite conversation." He stood over her, his strong face dark with concern. "Is there anything I can do?"

"No—no. Do take a seat, I pray you." She smiled up at him wanly and took a deep breath. When he did as she bid, she asked, "And to what do I owe this visit, sir?"

For a moment his deep-set eyes remained on her, and he did not respond. Sunshine eyes, she thought, for they were perpetually narrowed, as though against a blazing sun. She knew by now that they could twinkle with laughter or glow with concern, as they had just a moment ago. Whenever that happened, his stern mouth and jaw softened remarkably.

"I came on Lord Talbot's behalf," he said, squaring his shoulders and leaning back in his chair. His expression relaxed. So did Stephanie. "He heard from Mr. Endicott that you were ill. He wanted me to give you this—to help you through the day."

He handed her the slender package he carried. She took it gravely, glad of an excuse to look away from his gaze.

"I—thank you. But why didn't Lord Talbot come himself?"

"Because he is indisposed as well, madam."

Stephanie could not stop her spontaneous laugh. Alan smiled and waited. "I'm sorry," she said. "It really isn't a bit comical, as I well know. Tell him I do thank him. Well, I shall thank him myself, of course, when we both feel better. I appreciate your bringing it."

As she spoke, her fingers untied the string and tore open the newspaper wrapping, revealing a small book bound in white leather. *Poems*, the gold-embossed Gothic script read on the cover, "by A Gentlewoman." She looked at Alan inquiringly.

"They're by Lord Talbot's sister," he explained. "All sonnets. Very well done, in my opinion."

"How nice of him," she said warmly. "I'm sure the book means a great deal to him, and . . ." She stopped suddenly, wondering if the gift itself meant a great deal. Lord Talbot had not given her a gift before. Did this one mean he had become interested in her after all? And if so, how was she to respond?

She frowned unconsciously.

"You don't seem pleased," Alan noted.

"Oh, it's nothing. I just thought . . . of something."

"Perhaps I should go." He half-rose in his chair.

"Oh, no, do stay. Tea is coming, I assure you, and I should like your company, if it does not bore you too much."

He settled back in the chair willingly enough, but now she was not sure how to proceed. She took refuge in the book, turning its smooth pages. The poetry was on the right side of each page, with accompanying engravings on the left that apparently illustrated each verse.

"I should like to meet Lord Talbot's sister," she said. "Of course, it's too late now."

"Yes, I'm afraid it is."

Something in his voice made her look up quickly, to see the same flicker of pain in his brown eyes that she had seen in Lord Talbot's blue ones the day before.

"She died very young," he explained gravely. "Six years ago."

"What a shame! Lord Talbot has had a lot of sorrow in

his life, hasn't he? I knew about his wife, of course. I had no idea he lost a sister, too."

"His only sister," Alan said. "I don't know how devoted he was to her. They had lived apart ever since their mother died a dozen or so years earlier. Lord Burleigh took Grey into his home and educated him. Stella stayed with her father in Newmarket. He was a squire who had lost his lands to debt and ran a bookstore. That's where I met her."

"Lord Talbot's father was in trade? How surprising! I thought the English aristocracy never engaged in trade. Some of them were positively rude to Papa because they considered that he was 'engaged in trade.' "

"That's only too true. But, you see, Lord Talbot's father was only gentry. Besides, he was desperate for a living. Even Grey's title is only courtesy, because he's Lord Burleigh's heir. Of course his mother was aristocracy. She married 'beneath her' as they say."

Stephanie wondered if her parents, especially her mother, knew all this. She looked back at the book, trying to hide her surprise at all this new information about Lord Talbot who, she had supposed, had lived the life of an aristocrat from the time he was born. Then she remembered Lord Talbot's assessment, just the day before, of Mr. Dunstable. He had "made up to" Lord Talbot's sister. Had he, perhaps, been in love with her?

"How old was his sister?" she asked. "When she died, I mean."

"Eighteen."

The single word sat there like a little drop of doom. She looked up to see a scowl on his face. "What a pity," she said faintly. She shifted her feet and moved the conversation to safer ground, hoping for the arrival of the tea.

"Tell me about your travels, Mr. Dunstable. Obviously you're a seasoned sailor to have survived last night's storm."

His eyes suddenly mocked her, and she wondered if he recognized her retreat from uncomfortable things. "I don't think you really care about my travels, Miss Endicott. But I should like to know your reactions to England, as an American. Perhaps I can use your perspective for some sort of comparison when I write my articles."

"My perspective?" She was suddenly adrift, more uncomfortable than ever. Why wouldn't he stick to the safe, acceptable topics?

Jenny arrived at last with the tea tray.

"Sorry it took so long, miss. The galley's all disorganized, cause o' the storm. Between puttin' things to rights and answerin' calls for special food from the passengers, it's a wonder you got took care of at all."

She set the tray on the little table between Stephanie and Alan. Besides tea, there were breakfast biscuits, cutlery, white napkins, and a small tub of butter. By the time Jenny had left them to find out how Dorothea fared, Stephanie had decided she could answer Mr. Dunstable's question frankly. Perhaps it would make him as uncomfortable as he had made her.

She poured a cup of tea and handed it to him. "You may as well know, Mr. Dunstable, that I went to England prepared to despise it heartily. It is part of the national attitude, you know—despising the country we fought twice in the last fifty years. My father is more broad-minded. He believes trade will bring nations to understand each other."

To her surprise, he was grinning. "And did you despise us?"

"No," she admitted. "Oh, there are parts of it I despise. Your fat, playboy king, for one. Your tedious restrictions on women, for another. I thought Philadelphia society had enough rules. They are nothing as compared to London rules!"

"I'm sure you're right, Miss Endicott. If you haven't already guessed it, I have little use for the rules myself. I'm eager to visit the United States, where 'all men are created equal.' "

"Well, it's not quite like that, yet," she cautioned him.

"No. There are the slaves."

"Oh. Yes . . . that, too." How easily he managed to disconcert her!

"Every society has its skeletons," Alan said, his strong lips curving in a smile. "I realize that quotation is only an ideal. But I greatly admire the American experiment, the ideal. What I should most like to do is visit the author of the Declaration of Independence.''

"Mr. Jefferson?''

"Yes, indeed. 'The Sage of Monticello,' I hear he is called. Do you suppose he would receive me?''

"I don't see why not,'' Stephanie reflected. "But I hope you realize that many people will be prejudiced against you for the same reason I was prejudiced against England.''

"But not anymore?'' His eyes flashed, making the rapid-fire question much more personal than its words implied. She flushed.

"Not anymore,'' she said, looking away.

Suddenly he was all business. He drained his cup in a swift movement and leaped to his feet. "I really must leave now. Thank you for the tea. Our conversation has been most . . . interesting.''

"I thank *you*,'' she managed to reply, holding out her hand. She felt caught off guard by his quick movements, even more so when he hesitated a lengthy moment before giving her hand a quick shake, then dropped it. Lord Talbot, she was sure, would have responded to her gesture with grace and good taste. "I haven't finished giving you my views of England,'' she said playfully.

"Another time,'' he promised. "I really cannot stay longer.'' He departed swiftly as though he had an appointment to keep. But what appointment could it be, here on a ship in the middle of the Atlantic, a place from which he could not escape?

CHAPTER
VII

"It's a lovely book," Dorothea Endicott agreed, paging through *Poems* by A Gentlewoman. "How thoughtful of Lord Talbot." Her gaze at Stephanie as she returned the book suggested that the gift was, indeed, significant.

Stephanie received it silently, grateful that this piece of news had diverted her mother's mind from her anger at Morton, who had not been in the men's cabin as she had supposed during the storm last night. Instead, he had spent the first hour of bad weather on the poop deck with Captain Turnbull, "reliving his youth, no doubt," Dorothea had guessed, scornfully.

Now she lounged in the ladies' boudoir, still wearing her velvet wrapper, her hair concealed by a white muslin-and-lace cap, and sipped mint tea. It was nearly time for dinner, which had been delayed an hour, and the sea was perfectly calm. Dorothea declared, however, that she had not yet recovered from the effects of her sickness and would be unable to leave the boudoir.

"I shall certainly cherish the book," Stephanie said. "But it is curious, don't you think, that Lord Talbot didn't wait to present it to me himself?"

"As Mr. Dunstable said, he was not feeling well. Indeed, I believe everyone, save for a few hardy souls like your father, suffered dreadfully."

"And Mr. Dunstable," Stephanie said thoughtfully, running a finger over the gold lettering on the little volume.

"I do hope nothing untoward happened during his visit, Stephanie. I was quite shocked when Jenny told me he was here with you alone, once you'd sent her out for tea."

Stephanie glanced at her mother out of the corner of her eye to see if she was, perhaps, joking. No, of course she wasn't, she was perfectly serious. Stephanie could not subdue a little tilt at the corner of her mouth as she said, "Nothing untoward happened, Mama. On the contrary, Mr. Dunstable was almost . . . shy. At any rate, he seemed very anxious to leave. I really think he does not like me very much."

"Oh, fiddlesticks!" Dorothea said, but she looked relieved. She sat up and put her teacup in its saucer decisively. "Now, Stephanie, I was thinking. You should find a duet you and Lord Talbot could sing for the ship's concert that is being planned. Do you have anything in your trunk that would be suitable?"

"I might. Whose idea was that, by the way, yours or the captain's?"

Her mother looked momentarily disconcerted. "Why, I . . . I believe, actually, it was Lord Talbot who mentioned what a very fine voice you have. And that there were several people with enough musical knowledge to contribute to an entertainment. It's just like family, you know, here on ship. We've met a number of lovely people."

"You don't need to persuade me to sing, Mother!"

"But . . . a duet with Lord Talbot?"

"I'll look over my music. Do you suppose he ever does opera? There's a delightful duet from *Don Giovanni* that I bought in London last summer: *"La ci darem la mano."* It's for tenor, and I think Lord Talbot is a baritone, but perhaps the range isn't extreme, and he could do it."

Lord Talbot appeared in the dining saloon for supper about the time Stephanie and her father did. Like many of the passengers, he still looked pale and walked unsteadily. Stephanie was quick to say to him, "I've read some of the poems from the book you asked Mr. Dunstable to give me. They're lovely. I do thank you for them.''

He frowned at her as though trying to focus his attention. ''Book? Oh, yes, quite. Well, I'm happy if it pleased you.''

''It was particularly kind of you to share your sister's poetry with me.''

''Oh, that. Well as I said . . .'' He really did look as if he weren't quite recovered. Then the blankness in his eyes disappeared, and he smiled a little. ''Forgive me. A bit of a headache yet, I'm afraid. What I meant to say was, Alan really appreciates Stell's poetry more than I do, since he's written the stuff himself.''

''Still, you must be glad to have that memory of her. I didn't know, until he told me, that she had died so young.''

A strange, almost hostile look passed over his face. ''Oh. He told you that, did he?'' And then, as other diners came between them and settled into their places at the table, he said, ''Shall I seat you, Miss Endicott?''

It was obvious he didn't want to pursue the subject of Stella Talbot's death. Stephanie did not bring it up again.

The Good News ''limped along,'' in Morton's phrase, for several days under cloudy skies while repairs were made on the damaged rigging. A new jibboom was fashioned and installed by the ship's carpenter, a new mizzenmast was raised amid cheers from crew and passengers, and damaged sail was replaced from the extra canvas carried aboard.

Dorothea, having survived what she believed was the worst the Atlantic could throw at her, was feeling better all around. She began to walk the deck regularly for short periods, either with Morton or with Mrs. Bates and Miss Taylor. When the musical group gathered about the pianoforte between the end of dinner and teatime, she was invariably present, seated near a candelabrum on one of the horsehair chairs, embroidery hoop in hand and sewing box at her feet, basking in the reflected glory of her daughter's pure, sweet voice.

The musical group had grown from three to seven. Mrs. Wynett, a retired music teacher at a Boston girls' school, turned out to be an accomplished keyboard player. A slight, balding lawyer from Le Havre, Monsieur Entremont, sang a passable tenor and played the violin. Miss Taylor, in addition to possessing a pleasing contralto, played the flute. Colonel Rathburn, who had joined the group when he heard them sing a military air, sang with great gusto, but he was invariably off-key.

At first they had played and sung spontaneously, each person suggesting a favorite song or air, bringing music if they had it along. If they didn't, Mrs. Bates could usually pick up the air after a few hearings and find the chords for it. Mrs. Wynett, despite her own proficiency, expressed amazement at her Southern friend's ability to play by ear.

Their theme song became "High Barbary." It was Colonel Rathburn who had introduced them to it.

"Look ahead, look astern, look the weather in the lee.
Blow high! Blow low! And so sailed we
Down all the coasts of High Barbary."

The rollicking tune got everyone in the right mood. After surviving the storm, they felt a special kinship to its unknown composer. But most of the songs had a romantic turn. Indeed, it sometimes seemed to Stephanie that almost every song anyone suggested hinted of romance. There was, for instance, the old English air Lord Talbot had proposed:

"Gather your rosebuds while you may
Old time is still a-flying
And that same flower that smiles today
Tomorrow will be dying."

While the four ladies and three gentlemen sang, played, and laughed, other passengers often gathered about the rosewood card tables, drinking Madeira or port or ale, betting on hands of whist or loo or vingt-et-un. If Mr. Dunstable was present, he sat at the dining table, sometimes with Stephanie's parents, sometimes with another male passenger, more often by himself. And Stephanie would feel his eyes on her even though, whenever she glanced his way,

they were on his drink, or he was writing something down
in the black-bound notebook he always carried with him.

> "Then be not coy, but use your time;
> And while you may, go marry
> For having once but lost your prime
> You may forever tarry."

Stephanie always finished this song with her color high,
even though Lord Talbot never caught her eye to show he
found any significance in the words. Instead, she would be
conscious of Alan Dunstable's presence, even across the
room. What was it about the gaze of those brown "sunshine
eyes" that disturbed her?

The idea of a more formal "concert" had caught everyone's fancy. All in the "musical set," as Dorothea called
them, agreed to contribute some sort of presentation—even
Colonel Rathburn. Fully aware that his voice was more fit
for calling cadence than for singing, he volunteered to
perform sleight-of-hand tricks instead, and intersperse them
with one or two stories of his exploits with General Jackson,
on the trail of Seminoles and Spaniards in Florida. Everyone
pretended to be pleased with this, although his stories were
already notorious in the gentlemen's cabin for their tedium.

Stephanie brought out "*La ci darem la mano*," and
persuaded Lord Talbot he could sing it with her. They
prepared "The Bluebells of Scotland" as an encore, and
joined Miss Taylor and Monsieur Entremont in a quartet.

Stephanie knew she possessed a voice people enjoyed
hearing, so she usually sang without much self-consciousness.
But as she and Lord Talbot practiced together, she realized
that it was possible to become mixed up by her partner's
mistakes, and to get flustered when her attempts to cover
them did not succeed. The problem seemed to be his
concentration. He would forget to come in at the right time,
or he would forget the words. When the melody altered on
repetition, he often forgot the alteration. With two days
remaining before the concert, Stephanie suggested they
rehearse more often. Lord Talbot agreed, sheepishly ac-
knowledging his slowness.

"It's quite all right," Stephanie said. "We've nothing much else to do, have we?"

Thanks to those special practices, some social barriers began to crumble. Stephanie, growing tired of his repeated use of "Miss Endicott" during the rehearsals, suggested he call her Stephanie. "If you will call me Grey," he returned.

"Of course." She added impulsively, "It seems an unusual name."

"It's really Kevin Greycliff Talbot. My father, whose mother was Irish, named me for his Irish Grandfather O'Hara. The Greycliff comes from my mother's side of the family. To my father, I was Kevin to his dying day. To my uncle, after he took me in to educate me, my Irish heritage was quite unacceptable. So he started calling me Grey before I was twelve. I answer to either."

She laughed at the face he made. It seemed that Lord Talbot—Grey—was coming out of his melancholy.

Putting their acquaintance on a first-name basis seemed very comfortable at that point, and Stephanie thought little of it. Dorothea, hearing the new way they addressed one another, raised her eyebrows at Morton and smiled at Stephanie. Clearly, everything was proceeding according to plan (or plot).

Grey himself did not take advantage of the new familiarity, or of his role as Don Giovanni, trying to seduce Zerlina as he sang "Give me your hand." Stephanie, too, held back from any realistic interpretation of Zerlina's words, which admitted that love must have its way. Concentrating on the music alone, they finally performed it flawlessly, and with much self-congratulation, during their final rehearsal with Mrs. Bates.

"I believe we should ask Lord Talbot to stay with us when he comes to Philadelphia," Dorothea Endicott suggested to her husband on the morning of the concert. "Doubtless he will come to our city sometime before returning to England. I'm sure Stephanie agrees with me that we do not want to terminate our friendship with so charming a person when we dock in New York."

Stephanie pricked up her ears at her mother's suggestion,

even while she felt a familiar irritation at her mother's habit
of attributing to Stephanie a thought she had never expressed.
They were seated in chairs on the deck, making the most of
a bright October sun, yet swathed in quilts against the wind.
Dorothea's and Stephanie's eyes were shaded from sea glare
by wide-brimmed leghorn bonnets, Morton's by a broad-
brimmed hat.

Morton nodded. "I quite agree, my dear."

"And what of Mr. Dunstable?" Stephanie asked. "I
assume the two of them will continue to travel together."

"Well, of course," her mother said after a pause and a
frown. After a moment she added, "You seem particularly
anxious on Mr. Dunstable's part, Stephanie."

"Not at all. I only thought it would be awkward to invite
one without the other."

"True enough. I had nearly forgotten Mr. Dunstable. It's
been several days since I've seen him."

Stephanie had noticed this herself, but she had not remarked
to anyone how much she had wondered at his absence, even
from the dining room.

"I've seen him," Morton said. "He's been interviewing
one of the older seamen who, according to Turnbull, is
making his last voyage. Mr. Dunstable said he's thinking of
writing a book about the man. He has some mighty interesting stories to tell of his seafaring days."

"He interviews him during meals, too?" Stephanie asked
incredulously.

"I'd guess that's the only time he can, so he's even been
eating in the mess with the crew."

"How like Mr. Dunstable," Dorothea said with a meaningful frown.

Stephanie nearly bit her lip to avoid retorting, "How do
you know what Mr. Dunstable is like, Mama?" Then she
felt a vague disappointment, as though she had been slighted.
Mr. Dunstable had preferred his seaman to her as a source
of information. But then, how could she ever have stories to
match those of a world-weary old salt?

"I rather like Mr. Dunstable," her father said. "He's
done a great deal in his young life. He speaks of going on to
South America, after his tour of the United States."

"Where the inhabitants are fighting against Spanish rule?" Dorothea asked in surprise.

"Yes. Revolutions seem to interest him. Danged dangerous way to make a living, of course. But I hope you do invite them both. I'd like to see more of Mr. Dunstable as well as Lord Talbot."

As if on cue, Mr. Dunstable himself appeared on the deck. Stephanie decided he must be taking his exercise, for he walked rapidly along the bulwark, looking out to sea. His neck was swathed in a muffler, but his black curls were without a hat. Impulsively she called out his name.

He halted and turned, then came toward them more slowly. "Good morning, madam, good morning, sir," he said, bowing. "Miss Endicott."

His bow to her was a half-bow and his brown eyes, squinting against the sun's brilliance, moved quickly back to her father, who asked, "Happy the long voyage is almost over?"

"In a way," Alan Dunstable replied. "It has been most interesting however."

"We've seen little of you lately, sir," Stephanie said. "My father tells me you're gathering material for a book on some seaman's life."

Alan, looking a little abashed, ran his gloved fingers through his hair. "Well, Miss Endicott, it's a possibility, of course. I'm always collecting stories. But to sit down and make a book out of them—that would be quite another thing."

"Morton, I believe I've had enough of the sea air," Dorothea said, pushing aside her quilt and planting her feet firmly on the boards. "Stephanie, child, you ought to come in, too. It's really too cold."

Stephanie rose obediently and folded her quilt. Mr. Dunstable, only a few steps from her chair, backstepped to give her room. Impulsively, Stephanie laid the quilt down and said, "No, Mama, I think I'd prefer a brisk walk about the deck. Would you be kind enough to accompany me, Mr. Dunstable?"

His eyes flickered in surprise, although he could not have been more surprised than she was herself. He stepped back two more steps, but he could hardly get out of it—she had him trapped.

"It will be my pleasure, Miss Endicott," he said, bowing.

Stephanie knew she would be scolded for her boldness. Abashed by her own actions, she said nothing. But as the import of what she had done and the reason she had done it began to seep into her brain, the fingers that rested lightly on his arm began to tremble. She feared he could feel the trembling, even under the sleeve of his coat. Yet to take her hand away would call attention to her state, so she left it there in some discomfort.

She looked out to sea and tried to think of something to say. "We shall probably dock in two or three days, according to Captain Turnbull."

"Yes, so I understand."

"Will you stay long in New York, Mr. Dunstable?"

"I have no idea right now."

"Will you be at our little concert this evening?"

"I wouldn't miss it for the world," he told her gravely.

She looked at him then. "We hope you'll come to Philadelphia during your travels in the United States, Mr. Dunstable."

"I undoubtedly shall. I understand it is one of your most important cities."

"And the most beautiful," Stephanie said with some pride. "It has been called 'the Athens of America.' My parents will be most pleased to have you stay with us, whenever you decide to come."

"That is very kind of your parents," Alan said, his eyes on the horizon. "No doubt Lord Talbot is invited, too, else I would not be so fortunate."

"Yes, indeed, Lord Talbot, too," Stephanie agreed with a sense of defeat. It was quite obvious that Mr. Dunstable was not going to unbend. She said good-bye to him soon afterward.

About mid-afternoon Stephanie again climbed to the poop deck with her father. A haze had settled in the air about noon, reminding Captain Turnbull of the fogs they usually encountered as they approached the entrance to New York

Harbor. As he reminisced to Morton about incidents he had been involved in or heard of, Stephanie gathered that fogs in the area had sent many a vessel to its doom. A heavy fog could draw an impenetrable curtain about the many islands and inlets that guarded the approach to Manhattan, and a ship, wandering off course and foundering on the Jersey coast, might well meet with plundering wreckers as well as destructive rocks.

Morton, frowning and jerking his head toward Stephanie, led the conversation into more cheerful channels, but it was too late. Though she stood apart from them, Stephanie had heard every word. An eerie sense of unreality seized her. The ship was riding high in a sea so calm that it seemed to be suspended, not moving at all. The sun, starting its descent in the western sky, sifted pale light through the white atmosphere. The reflecting ocean was a blank expanse, blending with the sky.

No porpoises playfully flashed their tails now; no whales spouted in the distance. No bold, large-winged birds had been seen since leaving Ireland behind. The carved figurehead of *The Good News* strained with her trumpet toward an invisible horizon. Stephanie fancied that, if the ship ever reached the hidden line between sea and sky, it would slip through a crack and disappear into an endless void, the way sailors had once feared falling off the edge of the world.

She shivered and wrapped her arms about her. "Papa," she called out. "I'm going back to prepare for the concert." He nodded and waved.

Back in the ladies' boudoir, Dorothea scolded her daughter for exposing herself unnecessarily to the elements when she wanted her voice to be as clear as glass for the next few hours. Stephanie sang a scale to high C to prove that her performance would not bring disgrace to either of them. The exercise helped return her to reality.

The concert hour arrived and passed with high expectation, nervous participants, blushes for small mistakes, pleased smiles for the uncritical applause, and congratulations from the entertainment-starved audience. Stephanie sang in the quartet near the beginning of the program, midway with Grey, and as a soloist at the end. She had spotted Alan

Dunstable immediately, sitting in his usual remote corner at the dining table. His eyes did not meet hers, and she tried to put out of her mind her impulsive invitation of the morning and her unsettling reactions as they walked the deck.

When she and Grey sang "*La ci darem la mano*," she was not thinking of the journalist at all. For the first time, they caught the spirit of the duet—he, ardent, she, flirtatious and, finally, love-struck. The audience was delighted and wanted an encore. They complied with "The Bluebells of Scotland."

But when she began her solo at the program's end, Alan Dunstable, moving his chair closer, caught her attention. After that she could not forget him, and her eyes kept returning to him as she sang. The lights in the room cast shadows on the listeners so that she could not see his expression, but she felt his gaze on her as she sang Tom Moore's mocking words, set to an old, spritely melody.

> "When love is kind, cheerful and free,
> Love's sure to find welcome from me.
> But when love brings heartache and pang;
> Tears and such things,
> Love may go hang."

Once more, the applause was overwhelming. Mrs. Bates, accompanying her, whispered from behind, "They want an encore, dear."

Stephanie shook her head. "I don't have anything prepared."

"Surely you know this one." And Mrs. Bates began the first few bars of "Drink to me only with thine eyes . . ."

Stephanie wanted to say no, in a gracious way, but Mrs. Bates just continued to smile and nod, and went on with the song, playing it by ear. Finally Stephanie faced her audience and sang it. Right away, her eyes found those of Alan Dunstable and nestled there, unable to turn away. When she finished, he was the only one in the room who didn't clap or rise to his feet.

She saw him like that—too bemused to move—and the floor dropped away. Like the void she had imagined that afternoon, the future became, in one moment, a horizonless abyss, and she was falling, falling . . .

The ship and its passengers reached lower New York Bay off Long Island mid-afternoon on the seventeenth of October. A harbor pilot, meeting them that morning, maneuvered *The Good News* through the foggy Narrows. By the time it passed Governor's Island, the sky had cleared and the water was shot with the deepening orange and gold and magenta of a brilliant sunset. Stephanie and her parents stood on deck, watching the wharves on Long Island slip by and those on Manhattan grow nearer. They would stay aboard *The Good News* overnight and board a coastal vessel tomorrow to take them to Philadelphia.

Lord Talbot soon joined them, expressed his pleasure at having had their company aboard, and promised that he would surely plan to visit Philadelphia, although he didn't yet know when.

"Alan hasn't settled on his itinerary," he explained.

"And where is Alan?" Morton asked. It gave Stephanie a little start to hear his name spoken so familiarly by her father. She listened hard for the answer.

"He went ashore yesterday with a news schooner," Grey said with a smile, "so I asked him to find us rooms. But his major purpose seemed to be getting acquainted with the New York newspapermen."

Stephanie's heart sank, yet she was relieved. She could hope the pledge her eyes had sent him as she sang had been less obvious to him than it had been to her. She had seen him only once since the recital, and the meeting had seemed to her strained and unnatural. Saying good-bye to him might have revealed too much of her feelings, which were peculiar and contradictory, even to herself, while his feelings remained a mystery to her. Suddenly chickenhearted, she wanted to leave it at that. His refusal to say good-bye had rescued her from the brink of her void. If she could stay far away from it for a while, the sun would surely come out and the safe landmarks would reappear.

CHAPTER
VIII

New York was brawling, mercenary, bustling with energy, cosmopolitan along its busy wharves but still a village as one traveled north on Manhattan Island. Ordinarily Alan would have been eager to investigate its streets, observing, listening, tasting, and feeling its unique flavor. Instead, he stayed in his hotel room on the Battery, pretending to arrange and rewrite the notes he had taken on board ship. He had successfully managed to avoid any last-minute farewells to the Endicotts, but once he knew they had irrevocably left New York Harbor, he could not seem to concentrate on what lay ahead. Without the limitations of space imposed by the boat, he and Grey had agreed to take adjoining rooms, rather than share one, which made it easier for Alan not to confide the reason for his uncharacteristic retreat. He didn't care what Grey thought, so long as he didn't bother him with questions.

Instead it was Grey who went out to walk the streets of New York, carrying his stick, wearing his top hat and high boots over dark stockinet trowsers that soon became dirtied in the muddy streets that were also home to pigs and chickens. When he and Alan ate supper together, Grey was full of tales of his day's excursion.

While he was gone, Alan sat at a small desk overlooking the green, absently watched the self-important strut of pigeons looking for a handout, of boys playing marbles, of bonneted women and frock-coated men hurrying past. He did not see any of it; he saw only a tall girl with honeyed skin and molasses-brown hair and wide greenish eyes. Her habit of looking sideways at him, a slight inquiring smile lifting the corners of her lovely mouth, had crumpled his heart as if it were paper.

He was a fool.

He did not intend ever to marry. Life was too varied, too interesting to spend it tied down to one woman.

He had caused enough grief to a number of women in his arrogant quest for both pleasure and freedom from responsibility. He would not make such mistakes again.

He said all these things to himself several times a day, but they did not improve matters. Nor did they vanquish the image of Stephanie and Grey during the shipboard recital, singing "*La ci darem la mano*" together as if they meant it. He had studied Italian in his brief stint at Cambridge, and had traveled to Italy several times, so the language was no barrier to his understanding. A thousand darts had pricked him during the performance. He began to appreciate certain analogies about love and arrows that he had long ridiculed. He remembered again how he had agreed to speed Grey's recovery from melancholia against his better judgment; how he had hesitated to present the pseudo-plan to Grey; how he had been momentarily dismayed to receive Grey's note, two days later, that he was pleased to accept Alan's invitation, provided he still extended it. As though he had known.

But Alan Dunstable, student of the Enlightenment, did not believe in prescience or tricks of fate. The world was the way it appeared, and a man held his own future securely in his own hands, provided he knew how to respond to certain situations. The best way to respond to an impossible attraction was to work hard, find exciting new surroundings, and stay away from the attraction until its luster had faded. The heart always mended, given time and providing the other steps were diligently followed.

But this time he seemed immobilized. Over and over, he reviewed the events aboard ship that had brought him to such a sorry state: Stephanie's shining presence across the

dining table that first night (her laughter, his curt response
to her impertinent question); her heartbreakingly clear soprano, leading the others in song. Her compassion for a
smelly herdsman's child in the midst of a raging storm. Most
disastrous of all, he recalled his muddleheaded decision to take
Stella's book of poems to her. He had pulled the book out as
a reminder to himself of what he must *not* consider. The
inspiration of presenting it to Miss Endicott on Grey's
behalf had come after. By actively promoting Grey's interests, he thought to squelch his own. He hadn't expected the
tête-à-tête. He had thought Miss Endicott's mother or some
of the other ladies or the maid, at least, would be present.

He tried twice to write the letter he had promised Valeria
on docking in New York, but was so struck with distaste for
the project that he gave it up. Instead, he found himself
composing a love poem. He had never written a love poem
before. Without finishing it, he tore the paper into small
pieces and put it in the fireplace, making sure a glowing
coal quickly consumed it. He watched as the flames browned,
then blackened, then obliterated the lines: "Constant green-
eyed apparition, too lovely to be real. Green eyes that
sought my own one magic eye. . ."

He tried writing a dispatch to the *Times*, based on his
impressions as he had disembarked from the news schooner
with the *Journal of Commerce* reporters, then realized he
had too few impressions or facts to make a decent article.
He tried to write about the voyage over, but it was too
cluttered with those memories he must expunge. He finally
completed a letter to Lady Burleigh. In it he tried to
convince himself as well as her that the purpose for which
she had invested five hundred guineas was still foremost in
his mind.

> October 22, 1820
> My lady:
>   The Good News *docked day before yesterday,
> after a forty days' journey which was not hazard-
> ous. Grey seems much improved in spirits, and he
> and Miss Endicott have become rather good friends,
> calling each other by their first names. They spent*

*a good deal of time together on the voyage,
singing, playing games, walking the deck. They
sang a duet for the ship's concert which was well
received.*

*I must say candidly that I have no notion
whether or not a romance is developing. We have
a firm invitation from the Endicotts to visit them
whenever we are able. Before going to Philadelphia, however, I hope to travel north while the
mild autumn weather persists. I shall certainly
keep you informed of future developments, but
Grey's own letters may prove more revealing than
anything I can tell you secondhand.*

*Give my kind regards to Lord Burleigh, and
know that I remain*

> *Your humble and obedient servant,
> Alan Dunstable*

He signed it as he had always signed letters to her,
ignoring the brief passionate liaison of six years past that
now seemed to him no more than an irrational dream.

Grey had noticed the blue funk Alan had gotten himself
into, although he was too polite to say anything about it. His
only suggestive remark, made two days after the Endicotts
had departed, was, "The harlots along the Bowery are quite
brazen. I was surprised."

This was not the sort of talk Grey was addicted to, nor
the sort of company he had ever sought, even before Polly.
Alan did not reply.

"Just thought you might be interested," Grey pursued in
an offhand way. "I recall you used to be."

"No longer," Alan said. "An infantile habit, no more
than that."

"Oh, well, that's all to the good then, isn't it?"

Grey had no way of knowing how amazed Alan was by
his own disinterest.

His response wasn't much more lively when it came to
local affairs. "Everyone knows that President Monroe will
be reelected," Grey said. "The old Federalist party is dead,

and there is no other real candidate. Do you suppose the
great republican experiment is about to collapse? In, say,
five years, maybe ten, they'll revert to a heredity monarchy
like ours?''

Alan had no theories to advance. It surprised him that
Grey, who was a devotee of the English gentleman's sense
of privacy, had broken with it enough to get into a political
discussion with a garrulous tavern keeper and a Scots-Irish
grocer.

"I could hardly avoid it," Grey said. "Things are a bit
different here, aren't they? People are . . . friendlier, more
open, especially when they recognize that you're a stranger."

They had letters of introduction from Lord Burleigh to his
solicitor's New York contact, and from Richard Rush to
various acquaintances in the medical and legal professions.
By the third day, shaking himself mentally, Alan was ready
to take advantage of them. He talked the situation over with
Grey, and they decided to present themselves simply as two
English friends traveling together, interested in seeing the
new country, ready for experiences and congeniality, ready,
at the raising of an eyebrow or the extending of a cordial
hand, to eat, drink, and talk. Alan would not capitalize on
his connection to the *Times*, which might put some people
off, and Grey would drop his courtesy title of viscount.

It soon became apparent, however, that although Grey
Talbot preferred to do his eating and talking in the private
dining or drawing rooms of cultured men, Alan, though
accepting such invitations readily enough, believed the only
true pulse of the nation was to be found in the taverns along
the East River wharves, at the market at the end of the
Albany Pier, in the coffeehouses of lower Broadway, or at
the Exchange between East and West Dock. By mutual
accord they went their separate ways, Grey finding cordial
hospitality in the homes of Richard Rush's friends, and
Alan, a more uncertain welcome in the haunts of black-
smiths, printers, cabinetmakers, shoemakers, and coppersmiths.

If he met surliness, he soon realized it was because the
poor from England had been flooding the shores of America,
competing for the jobs that were scarce enough to the native
born. Once they learned he was only a visitor, not an

immigrant, attitudes changed, drinks were ordered, and opinions exchanged. Even the meanest citizen had his opinions, and the discussions went on far into the night. The dispatch to the *Times* began to take form.

During the first week in November, a letter arrived from Philadelphia, addressed to both men. Grey showed it to Alan at supper, and Alan raised his eyebrows at the signature. It was from Mrs. Endicott.

She would be delighted to have them as houseguests for Christmas, she wrote. It was a particularly pleasant time of year, not too cold to enjoy skating and sleighing and, of course, it was an important time for everyone to partake of a convivial family atmosphere. Morton and Stephanie seconded her invitation most urgently, and their daughter Clarinda and son Hugh looked forward to meeting them. They could stay as long as they liked, and plan to return after other necessary travels. They should look on Philadelphia as their home away from home.

Grey enthusiastically seconded Mrs. Endicott's invitation.

"I thought we'd go to Boston after the elections," Alan said. He didn't add that two months was scarcely long enough to rid himself of Stephanie Endicott's image.

"That's a chuckleheaded idea. Everyone tells me it snows more here than in England, and the roads could well become impassable. One should go south, with winter coming on."

"Philadelphia isn't exactly south."

"No, but it's on the way. We could take in Philadelphia, then go on to Baltimore, Richmond, Charleston—whatever points of interest there are down there, during January and February, then back to Washington for the inauguration in March."

"What about Boston?"

"Boston after the inauguration."

"Thanks for the travel schedule. Whose trip is this, anyway, yours or mine?"

"You seemed to need a bit of direction," Grey said with a grin.

"And you're anxious to renew your acquaintance with Miss Endicott," Alan returned.

Grey gazed back at him, a hard gleam in his eyes. "No," he said, "not particularly. But it would be devilish hard to spend Christmas all alone in a strange place."

Of course. Alan recognized, with his ever present sense of irony, that if he didn't agree, Grey's melancholia might return. Christmas would be difficult enough for Grey, away from Enderlin Hall, recalling the anniversary of Polly's death, without spending it in a lonely hotel room in a foreign country with no better company than Alan Dunstable. Grey was his responsibility and he owed it to him to take that responsibility seriously. He nodded almost grudgingly and left it to Grey to write their acceptance.

CHAPTER
IX

The white stone, three-story Endicott house on Tenth and Locust Streets had been built by Morton's father in 1790, a year after his ship's first trip to China had returned and made him rich. At that time, the location was considered practically in the country. The house and grounds took up a quarter of the square.

Josiah Endicott had spared no expense. Rosewood paneling, marble fireplaces (using the local blue-toned marble), parquet floors, expensive silk wall hangings and Aubusson carpets imported from France, Chippendale settees, and chairs and desks from England filled the rooms. The third floor boasted unusually spacious quarters for the servants, solid oak flooring, and thick walls for coolness in the summer.

When Josiah Endicott was struck down with yellow fever in 1810, Morton inherited the house, his mercantile business, and his ships. His younger brother Percival, whom everyone called Perry, and his sister Prudence inherited smaller bequests in proportion to their father's lack of confidence in their judgment. Josiah had always considered Perry an idler and a spendthrift because he preferred books and music to more practical matters, and Prudence had married George Sanford without his permission. When Sanford died in the fifth year of their marriage (only two months before Josiah himself, as it turned out), he only said his son-in-law had always been sickly.

Though Stephanie had fond memories of her first childhood house on Walnut Street, she had been delighted, at age eleven, to move into Grandfather's mansion, where she and Clarinda could have separate bedchambers. Her mother had a sewing and "meditation" room and no longer needed to entertain friends in her own chamber when Morton had business associates in the parlor. Replete with sewing table, and dressmaker's dummy, the sewing room also had a couch to which Dorothea repaired when she wished to be alone.

One of Stephanie's favorite spots in the house was the sunroom in the southeast corner. Furnished with wicker chairs, a small breakfast table, flowered chintz cushions, and potted plants, the room's many triple-paned windows encouraged the sun to warm it in winter and revealed the garden's splendors in summer. It was an especial favorite with her sister Clarinda, who was devoted to growing things. It was Clarinda who had persuaded her mother to install venetian blinds at the windows to regulate the amount of sunshine, and who had added so many new plants, for which she took full responsibility, that Morton referred to the room as the "greenhouse."

On this December morning, Stephanie and Clarinda sat across the table from each other in the "greenhouse," eating a late breakfast and watching the gentle fall of snow outside, a reminder that Christmas was only a week away.

"Kate's home," Clarinda said as she broke open her soft-boiled egg. "Sally heard it from their maid. She and her father returned from Washington last evening, rather late."

"That's good," Stephanie acknowledged absently. She spread strawberry jam on her toast.

"That means she and the senator will be able to come to dinner tonight. Mama is planning to send over an invitation."

Taking a bite, Stephanie only nodded.

"I thought you'd be excited, Steph. Kate is your best friend."

"I am excited."

Clarinda glowered at her. "You certainly don't seem so.

What I intended to say is, Hugh won't like her being here. Kate makes him nervous. But maybe it won't matter so much tonight, since the Englishmen will be coming, too.''

This time Stephanie gave her younger sister her full attention. "Kate makes him nervous! Whatever for?''

"I never told you—I guess I forgot to, because Kate and her father have been away, and with Hugh away at school as well . . .''

"Tell me what?''

"That Kate is in love with Hugh. Not only that, but she told him so—last summer, before he left for fall term at Princeton. And poor Hugh doesn't know what to do, because he doesn't feel that way about her at all.''

Stephanie abandoned eating to stare at her sister in amazement, Clare's hazel eyes returned her gaze and her slender-bowed mouth was curved up, anticipating Stephanie's reaction. Her face was rounder than Stephanie's and her dark curls, cropped very short during an illness the previous winter, made her look younger than her eighteen years. But more than her hairstyle had changed in the past year. It appeared that the girl who had scorned affairs of the heart and "squandered'' her time (in Dorothea's words) with history books and flower cultivation was now taking a genuine interest in love—at least the love affairs of others.

"That's dreadful,'' Stephanie said. "Poor Kate. What can we do?''

"I don't see how we can do anything, except hope that Hugh will change his mind. Or that Kate will abandon her hopeless passion and turn to another.'' Clarinda's voice turned melodramatic as she mimicked the lines of a play they had attended the week before.

Stephanie laughed but sobered quickly. "It's no laughing matter, is it, if she's truly in love with him.'' She shook her head in dismay. "I can just imagine what led up to it. Kate has never been one to sit around and let things happen to her; she's determined to make them happen, or die in the attempt. I can't see her trying to get Hugh's attention by all the acceptable little flirtatious devices girls are supposed to use, either. So she had to come right out and tell him.''

"Exactly,'' Clarinda agreed. "Oh, maybe last summer

she was waiting for him to come around. But when it became obvious he would go back to Princeton without a word said between them, she just told him.''

"How did you find out?"

"Hugh told me. I came home one afternoon, after going to that new wax museum on Market Street with Aunt Pru and the children, and here he was, walking up and down in the parlor in a most distracted way. He said Kate had just walked over, all alone, asked to see him, and explained quite frankly how she felt about him.''

"And how did he respond—did he tell you that?"

"Oh, he was shocked. He said he appreciated knowing her feelings, and—and he had always been fond of her, of course, but he wouldn't be ready to marry for a long, long time.''

"I should think not. He's only twenty."

"And Kate is nearly a year older. *That* bothered him, too. But mostly, he told me, he has never thought of her in that way, and doesn't see how he could begin doing so.''

"Now that they've been separated three months..." Stephanie said speculatively.

"It hasn't made any difference with Hugh. I don't know about Kate. Well, perhaps she'll get interested in one of these Englishmen.''

"Perhaps.'' Stephanie turned her gaze to her plate and took another bite of her toast. The boiled egg in its little dish was probably cold and looked less appetizing than before. She reached for an orange from the bowl in the center of the table and began to peel it, hoping it would moisten a tongue gone suddenly dry.

The door from the kitchen flew open to admit Sally with a steaming pot of freshly brewed coffee and a pitcher of hot milk, which she set between the two of them. She was a broad-hipped, square-faced woman of thirty. With her mother, Mrs. Buxton, she ran the kitchen and kept the house in order.

"Anything else I can get you young ladies?"

"No, thank you, Sally,'' Stephanie returned. Sally sent a disapproving glance toward her egg dish.

"Ma won't be happy you left that good egg. She'll think you don't like the way she cooked it."

"She always cooks it very nicely. I'm not very hungry, that's all."

Sally turned her attention to Clarinda. "An' Miss Clare, I'm to see that you put enough milk in with your coffee."

"I will, Sally, I will."

"Do it now, if you don't mind, Miss Clare." Sally took a stand at Clarinda's elbow and waited.

Clare sighed and rolled her eyes at Stephanie in mock exasperation, then performed the ritual of pouring hot milk and coffee into her cup together, the only way Dorothea allowed her to take coffee. Satisfied, Sally left them alone.

"You'd think I was still a baby," Clare fumed. "That's the way she was all the time you were gone. Between her mothering and Aunt Pru's constant alarms, it's a wonder I didn't come down with a case of nerves."

"We often drank café au lait in England," Stephanie said, trying to soothe her. "The coffee was terrible and the milk quite good, so it sort of evened things out. I rather like it." She poured her own, the same way.

"For heaven's sake, don't you mother me, too!"

"Oh, sorry," Stephanie said sarcastically.

A short silence followed. Stephanie concentrated on peeling her orange. Clare stirred sugar into her coffee, shifted her feet several times, and tried to catch Stephanie's gaze. She finally said, "Which one of them are you in love with?"

"Which one of who?" Stephanie asked, her head jerking up.

"Of the Englishmen. I'm pretty sure you're in love with one of them, and I know Mama hopes it's Lord Talbot. Is it?"

"No, I'm not in love with Lord Talbot," Stephanie said.

"That's a shame. I'd hoped you'd marry him, and then I'd have an excuse to travel to England. Is it the other one, then?"

"Why should you think I'm in love with anyone?"

"Oh, I don't know. Except you've been pretty irritable since you came home."

"Irritable! In what way?"

"Oh, just . . . you get upset over little things. Like that cape of yours I borrowed . . ."

"You got a big rip in it!"

"Mrs. Buxton mended it. It looks as good as new."

"It will never look as good as new, and you know it."

"There—you see? You're upset. And you're also very distracted. I almost never hear you practicing your voice lately, but you go around humming under your breath, which, by the way, is very annoying. I'm sure it's because of a man."

"Well it's not. It's just—being back home and having to get used to things . . . and people, again." She finished the sentence lamely, shrugging her shoulders, and returned to separating the orange sections. "Anyway, what do you know of love, besides what you've seen in the theater?"

Clare smiled in a knowing way that Stephanie found maddening. "Oh, I've been making a study of love—and the effect it has on people."

"Since when?"

"Since you and Dick Harlow."

"Good heavens, Clare!"

"I know you didn't love him, and I thought you were right to break off the engagement, no matter what Mama says, but he did love you, you know."

"*I* was never convinced of it. I would have been just another adornment for his fancy house."

"He must have loved you, because—well, because of the way he's been acting ever since."

"What do you mean? Mama said he doesn't go to parties anymore, but what does that signify? He always preferred his business affairs to such frivolities. Anyway, he went to visit relatives in Boston last winter after—after . . ."

"Yes, but as soon as you'd gone to England, he returned. And ever since, he won't go anywhere. He turns down dinner invitations; he doesn't even attend the Library Company meetings, and that used to be one of his passions. Remember how he collected subscriptions for the new library?"

Stephanie frowned and looked away from Clare's eyes.

"It couldn't be because I broke our engagement. Any number of girls would answer to his concept of a wife—and with all that money he's inherited, any number of them would be happy to accept."

"Well, he'll never ask them now."

"Are you trying to make me feel guilty, Clarinda Sue? Because if you are, I refuse . . ."

"No, not at all. I thought he was a stick, too. I could never imagine him as my brother-in-law. But that's what got me interested in studying how people react when they're in love. I thought it would be a good theme for study, in case it ever happens to me."

"Silly child!"

"For instance, I'll wager that by the time we go to bed tonight, I'll know one way or the other, just by the way you behave at dinner, if you're in love with one of these Englishmen who'll be visiting."

"Absolute rot!"

"Is it a bet? I'll give you my silver fox muff if I'm wrong."

"And what do you want in return?"

"Umm—let's see. That dear little bonnet you brought back from London with the blue velvet ribbons."

"That's not fair, Clare."

"Why not? It wasn't fair that you got to go to England and I didn't."

"It's ridiculous to wager on a matter of opinion. There is no sure way to prove which of us is right."

"Well, then . . ." Clare thought a moment. "I know. According to my recent—and *extensive*—studies of the subject, there are three inevitable reactions if a lady is in the same room as the man she loves: One, she blushes whenever he speaks to her; two, she looks at him whenever she knows he's looking elsewhere; three, she either talks too much, or very little. Now if you exhibit two out of three of these reactions, I think it will be fair to say you're in love. If you only exhibit one, I'll give you the benefit of the doubt, and we won't call our bets. Not only that, but I'll tell you exactly when you exhibited these symptoms, so you'll know I'm not just making them up. If I don't detect any of

these symptoms, you win. Now, what could be fairer than
that?''

"What if I refuse to acknowledge them?''

"You won't.'' Clare stared at Stephanie frankly. "You're
too honest, Steph.'' As Stephanie hesitated, she added,
"You've always loved my silver fox muff. And I noticed it
goes beautifully with the fur on that woolen cloak you
brought back from England. It will be just the thing for
walking on cold winter afternoons.'' Her eyes went to the
window, where light snow still fell.

Stephanie's head went up defiantly. "This is almost too
easy, but I'll do it. We'll see how much you've studied the
subject.''

"More than you may think, Big Sister,'' Clare warned.
Her hazel eyes narrowed, and her lips took on a teasing
curl.

Hugh had arrived from Princeton, where he was in his
third year, the day before. Tall like Stephanie and their
father, with Morton's expressive face and light hair and his
mother's hazel eyes, he was exactly between Stephanie and
Clare in age. He had angered Morton two years ago by
declaring a preference for politics and law over the shipping
business, but once Morton had adjusted to this change in his
dreams, he had agreed to send his son to Princeton and did
not refer to his disappointment again.

When Hugh learned at the noon meal that Kate Hamlin
and her father would be their guests at supper he said, "My
God, Mama, couldn't you have given them a day to relax at
home after their trip?''

"I'm sure I don't know what God has to do with it,
Hugh,'' Dorothea said with a frown. "Why are you being
profane?''

"He doesn't want to see Kate,'' Clarinda explained
knowingly, and so the whole story came out again. Hugh
looked both shamefaced and a little proud.

"Kate's a wonderful girl,'' Dorothea said pointedly. Usually she would have said "lovely,'' but even Dorothea
recognized that Kate Hamlin could never be accused of
being beautiful. She was rather long-faced with a thin nose,

her father's commanding chin, and unmanageable straw-colored hair. She was even taller than Stephanie, and possessed very little bosom.

"I thought Senator Hamlin had invited you to work for him when Congress convenes in January," Morton put in. "Isn't that what you wanted?"

"Yes, sir, he has, and I do want it. That has nothing to do with Kate and me."

"I don't see what you're so worried about," Stephanie said. "It sounds to me as if the whole thing has been laid out on the table. Kate knows how you feel, and you know how she feels. I doubt she'd ever behave like a lovesick female; you needn't worry about that."

"It's just deucedly uncomfortable now, seeing her."

"I don't understand any of you," Dorothea said. "Here I have three grown-up children, and not one of you seems even remotely interested in finding a mate. At your ages, I'd call that very peculiar."

No one bothered to answer her. Sally came in to clear the table, and Morton rose to return to his offices on Front Street. Dorothea left to inspect the rooms that their newest servant, the German immigrant girl, Elsa, had readied for the two Englishmen. Clarinda prepared to go shopping with Hugh to buy Christmas trinkets for Aunt Pru's children. Stephanie toyed with the idea of running over to the Hamlins, only half a square away, then decided to stay home in case their guests came. She went upstairs with the vague idea of changing into a different dress, but, confronted with the variety in her wardrobe, could not make up her mind what to wear. Her own aimlessness amazed her.

Uncle Perry saved her by arriving from Endicott Shipping, where he was in charge of the books. Grandfather Josiah's younger son might have been a spendthrift in his youth, but with middle age he had turned himself into a precise accountant. Morton paid him a generous salary, but his household in Camden was small and spartan, with only a couple to look after his needs. It did not seem to matter to Perry that he could have afforded a more ostentatious establishment. He was comfortable and liked to keep things simple. Because he had never married, no one tried to argue the point with him.

He was a competent performer at the pianoforte, and had been the first to recognize Stephanie's unusual voice and encourage her to use it. He had determined what teachers she should have and what visiting artists were worth hearing. Whenever she was asked to sing at people's homes, Uncle Perry accompanied her.

"I'm planning a little entertainment," he told Stephanie, discovering her in the upstairs hall. "Sometime between Christmas and New Year's Day. I thought perhaps you might have some suitable music in that pile you brought back from England. Mind if we go over it?"

"Not at all," Stephanie said, happy to have something purposeful to do. She led him down the stairs to the music room, located at the rear of the house off the formal drawing room. Rosewood cabinets and glazed bookcases lined two walls, and two chintz-covered wingback chairs stood on either side of the fireplace. The four-legged pianoforte, with its lyre-shaped pedal extension and brass rosette insets in the sides, purchased by Morton ten years before in New York, sat opposite the fireplace. The harp Dorothea had inherited from her mother but rarely played stood by the far window.

Stephanie went to the cabinet that held her special collection and found the music. She had purchased popular songs, operatic arias, and folk songs, as well as pianoforte solos for Clare and harp pieces for Dorothea. Soon Uncle Perry was settled at the pianoforte, playing through selections he considered promising, his tall frame bent concave over the keyboard, his sparse brown hair going seven directions, his bespectacled eyes peering single-mindedly at the music. Today, as usual, he wore an old (and therefore comfortable) black coat over the new, embroidered waistcoat Dorothea had given him for his birthday—a combination sure to call forth acid comment from her after he had left. Fashion was not Perry's strong point.

Music was, however, and he was not shy about voicing his opinion of her selections. "I don't care for that one. The melody has no originality." Or, "Ridiculous poetry, but what can you expect nowadays?" And he tossed them disdainfully to one side. Others met with his approval. "Aah, very nice. The words are from *Twelfth Night*, aren't they? Come sing this along with me, Stephanie. Very nice, indeed!"

They were in the middle of an Irish folk song—and Stephanie had lost track of the time—when Dorothea entered the room.

"I do believe our guests are here, Stephanie. A carriage just stopped in front of the gate." Her voice held suppressed excitement.

Stephanie felt herself go hot and then cold. She straightened from her position behind Uncle Perry, where she had been looking over his shoulder at the music, and clasped her hands tightly before her. Turning, she saw that her mother had taken particular care with her hair and wore an afternoon dress usually reserved for calling on important ladies. Stephanie still wore her morning gown, and her hair was probably a mess.

"Well," Uncle Perry said, abandoning his chair, "I ought to freshen up a bit. I'll leave the greeting to you ladies, and meet these young Englishmen later, after Morton gets here."

Dorothea looked her daughter over critically. "You'd better change that gown, dear," she said sharply. "I'm surprised you didn't do so earlier. Run upstairs now, before they get in the house. I'll send Jenny to you. And do hurry."

Stephanie hurried. With Jenny's help, it was only ten minutes later when she descended the stairs into the front hall, wearing a gown of rose muslin with lace ruching at the high neck, long corded sleeves, and four rows of embroidery set into the skirt. Her hair had been brushed back smoothly and simply and fastened with a matching velvet ribbon. Jack Buxton passed her on the stairs with a portmanteau in each hand.

She heard voices below but couldn't distinguish what was being said. As she reached the bottom of the stairs, the first things she saw were two tall black beaver hats and a pair of long carricks sprinkled with melting snow, hanging on the large brass coatrack. Near the marble-topped table where two silver salvers received the day's mail or a visitor's calling card, Dorothea was talking to Lord Talbot, laughing a little, one hand toying with a jeweled pendant at her throat. He smiled at her with his usual attentive courtesy, and did not immediately look up.

Alan stood a few feet from them, looking as if he were preparing to bolt in either direction. As she reached the bottom stair, he turned toward her and their eyes met.

She stopped as if a barrier had slammed down before her. His gaze, softening in recognition, shouted at her all the things she had not wanted to know. His frown acknowledged an uneasiness that matched hers. For a moment he didn't move an inch. Then he jammed the fist of one hand into the pocket of his frock coat.

Her sense of courtesy came to the rescue. He looked so uncomfortable there, standing apart and silent. She moved forward with a smile, her right hand extended.

"We're delighted to see you again, Mr. Dunstable," she said warmly.

His face lit up with an eager smile, crinkling the corners of his eyes. "I'm delighted to be here, Miss Endicott." His large hand smothered hers. Tiny shocks like pinpricks leaped from his hand to hers and shot up her arm. Startled, she nearly withdrew her hand. How fortunate that Clarinda was not here to witness it.

She untied her tongue with an effort. "I-it's a blessing the snow didn't interfere with your journey."

"Yes, we were fortunate. We only got into it the last hour or so, and by then we were on your good paved turnpike, so the horses weren't slowed down much."

"How fortunate, indeed," she echoed. She was conscious of a vast silence. Tardily she reclaimed her hand and turned to greet Grey Talbot. She avoided her mother's eyes.

CHAPTER X

Stephanie won her wager. The blue-ribboned bonnet remained hers, and Clarinda reluctantly handed over to her the silver fox muff that very night, before they went to their respective rooms to bed. This did not make it any easier for Stephanie to sleep.

So far as Dorothea's standards were concerned, the evening had been a success. Conviviality, shared laughter, incessant talk, and music filled the hours. Everyone seemed to get along with everyone else. If there were undercurrents of tension, none of them erupted into anything obvious. But for Stephanie, snuggling into the featherbed of her four-poster, the evening had become a jangled cacophony of impressions, with too many themes played at once. Chief among them was her dismay and wonder that Alan Dunstable had so swiftly and completely invaded and upset her cosy world. The electric moment when their eyes had met and their hands had touched could not be undone, even though they had kept their distance from each other, pretending.

Alan, questioning Senator Hamlin about American politics, amusing Clarinda by reciting comical verse, talking seriously to Kate Hamlin under a buzz of interfering voices that Stephanie's ears vainly tried to penetrate. (Independent, bold Kate, who scorned frivolous chatter and girls who flirted, had been completely engrossed in their conversation.) Alan, joking and laughing with her father, asking Uncle Perry about his collection of medieval manuscripts, comparing his experiences at Cambridge to Hugh's at Princeton. But she could have counted the sentences he directed to *her* on the fingers of one hand. Lying there, wide-eyed in the dark, she did count them; said them jealously over and over to herself.

"Good evening, Miss Endicott," he'd said in the drawing room when they gathered for dinner. (Sentence Number One—hardly intimate, hardly worth remembering, his smile cold, as though he had deliberately quenched it.) Anything she might have used to start a conversation was interrupted as her father introduced him to Kate and the senator, to Clarinda and Hugh and Uncle Perry, while her mother did the same for Lord Talbot.

Then, on the way to the dining room: "See what you can do for Grey. It's the anniversary of his wife's death." (Sentence Number Two, to be interpreted either as "Be kind to my friend; he's in a bad way," or "Stay away from me; find someone else.") The concern was valid. Grey had reverted to the absentminded politeness that had so irritated her in London. Uncle Perry and her mother kept him talking when she couldn't, but she sensed his lack of enthusiasm, the periods when his mind was elsewhere. And she noticed, more than once, the way he looked across the table at Clare, as if the younger, petite Endicott daughter in her yellow gown and cloud of dark curls somehow disturbed him.

Stephanie and Alan were not close enough to speak conveniently at the supper table. Once, during a lull in the conversation at her end, she heard her name on his lips and looked his way. He smiled at her in a jovial, impersonal way and raised his voice. "Isn't that right, Miss Endicott? We had three storms at sea, but only one that was truly severe?"

She acknowledged that this was true, and heard her father continue speaking of their voyage to the Hamlins, while Dorothea, at her end of the table, suggested that Stephanie and Lord Talbot sing the duet they had done on board ship, later in the evening. So much for Sentence Number Three. Mr. Dunstable had used her as one might a dictionary, to find the correct spelling of a word.

Sentence Number Four came after she and Grey had sung, as requested, with Uncle Perry accompanying them. Grey agreed to the duet with a well-founded reluctance. Although he made an effort to act the great seducer and Stephanie, encouraging him, played up her own part, he made all his old, absentminded mistakes, even with the music in front of him. At one point, they had to stop and start a section again, spoiling the aria's effectiveness.

Clarinda's eyes were on them both throughout the song, but Alan's gaze never met Stephanie's. Afterward, his passing comment was merely, "As lovely as ever, Miss Endicott." He might have joked about the less-than-perfect performance—he seemed to have joked with everyone else—but he did not. Hugh had stopped her answer by asking Alan another question about Cambridge.

His final sentence had not been much different from the first one: "Good night, Miss Endicott," along with a formal bow, as the party broke up.

"If you would," she said as he started to turn away, "call me Stephanie. We mustn't be so formal, now that you're a guest in our home."

He raised his eyebrows as though surprised by her boldness, but if he was about to answer, the words never came, for Senator Hamlin interrupted, a large genial hand on Alan's shoulder. "Come over anytime, Dunstable. I'll be happy to discuss with you the chief provisions of the Maine-Missouri Bill."

And then Grey came up and thanked her for something or other—helping him through a passage in the duet, probably—and the next thing she knew, Alan Dunstable had left the room.

Which one are you in love with? If she had been as honest as Clarinda thought her, she would have returned the silver fox muff as soon as it was offered, and given up the new English bonnet. But even then she hadn't faced the truth. Now, staring upward at the dark shadows of her frilled canopy, body taut between featherbed and quilts, hands clasped over her breasts, she said aloud, "I am in love with Alan Dunstable of London, England." A blanket of heat washed over her. She almost pushed the covers away, despite the chill of the winter night. Then it passed and she turned on her side, snuggling more deeply into her pillow.

Just before she went to sleep, she uttered a sarcastic little chuckle. Mama's little scheme had gone awry. She had fallen in love with the wrong man.

At mid-morning the next day, Stephanie left the house wearing her fur-trimmed woolen mantle with the attached hood and soft kid boots. Yesterday's gentle snowfall fell away from her rapid, determined footsteps as she turned up Tenth Street to Chestnut and beyond, to where the Hamlin's brick house sat in the middle of a fenced-in acre of garden and lawn.

Betsy, the colored maid, let her in with a welcoming smile. Miss Kate was upstairs in her sitting room, dealing with the senator's correspondence. After she had handed the maid her mantle and gloves, Stephanie climbed the wide stairway and went down the hall to the large room overlooking the street.

Kate's back was to the door, her pale head bent over a pile of papers on her father's desk.

"Hello," Stephanie said softly in the doorway.

Kate turned and sprang up with a welcoming smile. "Stephanie! Thank goodness you came. You've saved me from a morning of absolute boredom. Look what Father left with me!"

They embraced warmly. "We really didn't have time to talk last evening," Stephanie said. "I hoped you wouldn't mind my coming today."

"Have I ever minded your company? Come in and sit down. Are you cold? There's a nice fire here. Shall we have some hot chocolate?"

Stephanie said yes to both questions and let Kate lead her to one of the two big armchairs before the fire. Kate tugged on the bellpull, then plopped into a chair opposite Stephanie and leaned forward, her hands clasped, arms across her knees, her pale blue eyes alight.

"Well! How are you, Steph? Never mind, I can see you're fine—more beautiful than ever since your trip to England. You can't imagine how angry I was with Father for keeping me in Washington until Congress adjourned, separating us two months longer than necessary.''

"I was, too—if anyone can be angry with your father. Here I'd been storing up things to tell you for ages . . ."

"And then last evening there was simply no chance, without being rude."

"Yes. I do hope you had a good time, though."

"I had a lovely time. It's rather exciting having those two guests from England visiting, isn't it? How long will they stay?"

"At least until after the New Year. What did you think of them?"

Kate cocked her head to one side, considering. Her straw-colored hair, which had had some semblance of curl in it last evening, was again lank and straight, and carelessly tied back with a ribbon. She pushed back some stray hairs from her temple as she spoke. "Mr. Dunstable is interesting and Lord Talbot is handsome, but very quiet. Do you like him a lot?"

"Not as much as Mama wants me to."

Kate grinned. "Do these things ever work out as smoothly as parents want? Of course not. That's what makes them so fascinating."

"What about you, Kate? Clarinda said . . ." She hesitated, wondering now if Clare had made it all up.

"She told you about my infamous blunder of last summer, did she?"

Stephanie nodded. "She didn't exactly call it that."

"She ought to have. Hugh was probably mad as a fighting cock, but he behaved like a gentleman, as always. We got through last evening fairly well, don't you think?"

"Then you still feel the same way?"

Kate eyed her steadily for a moment, then flung out her hands in resignation. "I've been in love with your brother for . . . at least three years. I don't know, it just sort of grew on me. Last summer I got . . . desperate, I suppose." She stood up, hands clasped before her. "When you pass your twenty-first birthday, and no one has proposed—you know what I mean. Well, maybe you don't . . ."

"It's the same thing if the one who proposes isn't the right one."

"Anyway, I thought maybe all he needed was a little prod in the right direction. We've been friends for so many years, it should have been easy. It wasn't, of course. Not only that, I offended him. Men want to be the pursuers, don't they? They positively resent it if a woman speaks first. So I've probably ruined my chances forever and shall be an old maid, known only for being the first woman secretary to her father, the senator." She flung her hands toward the paper-strewn desk, walked around her chair, and sat down to it again. "Still, that's something, isn't it!"

Stephanie couldn't help smiling. Restless, energetic Kate, who had never hidden either her intelligence or her skepticism before the young men she was supposed to attract. Dorothea had more than once mourned Kate's fate—a girl without a mother (Mrs. Hamlin had died when Kate was six) who had no one to tell her how to behave socially. Stephanie doubted that Kate would have heeded such teachings. It was one of the things she loved about her friend, one of the ways she wished she could be like her. But, alas, Stephanie had been born not only to sing, but also to be conciliatory and to obey the rules.

"So you don't recommend telling a man you love him, even if it's true?"

"Not until he's convinced he's been the one to pursue *you* and win your heart, despite all sorts of obstacles. That's the game women are supposed to play, isn't it?"

Stephanie sighed. Somehow she couldn't bring herself to answer. Kate's glance turned sharp. "Don't tell me you were thinking of following my shining example?"

"Not . . . really."

"Are you worried about being an 'old maid'?"

"No. But Mama is."

"You won't be, you know. You're like a queen. You sail through social occasions with all the right gestures and the right words. You're beautiful and you always will be. Men will always be interested in you, Stephanie, and someday you'll say yes to one of them, if only to end the suspense."

Stephanie made a face. "Not I! I refuse to be pulled into

that 'marriage for the sake of convenience' idea ever again.
I shall settle for nothing less than love: wild, incredible,
irresistible love! Like—like Juliet. Or Lucia di Lammamoor.
Or Cleopatra and Marc Antony . . ." She jumped up enthusi-
astically, her arms embracing the world. It was only with
Kate that she engaged in such histrionics.

Kate laughed but sobered quickly. "Stephanie, all those
women either died or went mad for the sake of love."

Stephanie lowered her arms and stared at her friend. "It
doesn't have to be like that."

"No—that's just romantic literature."

"There *are* happy endings."

"Of course there are."

Stephanie sat back in her seat. "Is it Mr. Dunstable?"
Kate asked in a quiet voice. Then Betsy appeared with a
pitcherful of hot chocolate and two generous mugs.

When she had left and Kate was pouring their drinks,
Stephanie said, "How did you guess?"

"He was the only one you didn't exchange a dozen words
with last evening. I'd say you both pointedly avoided each
other. Hugh and I were doing the same thing, of course.
Thank God for crowds!"

"Does that mean you believe he might feel the—the
same . . . about me?"

"He might. I don't know. He's very unsentimental, isn't
he?"

"But he might very well never say anything."

"Why not?"

"Be-because . . . I catch his eye sometimes and I'm sure
there is some emotion there. But then he backs off, deliberately. As if some great barrier exists between us."

"He may not realize how he feels. He may need some
kind of push. But make it subtle, Stephanie, don't make my
mistake."

Stephanie sipped her drink slowly and gazed into the
fireplace. "I wonder what that might be."

If one dare not be bold in pursuit of a man, and the idea
of coy flirtation was distasteful, there was only one way to
go about it, Stephanie decided on her way home. Guile and

subterfuge. She was not used to considering such tactics, and wrestled with her conscience all the way. She did not decide on her course of action until she had arrived at home and discovered Clare in the sunroom, watering her sweet violets and camelias, and pruning her ferns. Clare told her that Hugh had taken Mr. Dunstable and Lord Talbot down to the Endicott Shipping office on Front Street. Papa was taking them to dine at the Green House, then they would tour the dock area, the Market, and some of the newer and most impressive buildings on Chestnut Street.

As Clare disappeared with her watering pot behind a large hanging philodendron, she added, "I think we settled up too quickly on our little wager, Steph."

Stephanie had been about to leave the room. Now she turned back. "What on earth do you mean?"

"I was thinking it over last night in bed. There was something about the way you and Lord Talbot sang that aria together . . ."

"We were just playacting."

"And then, you call him 'Grey.'"

"And he calls me 'Stephanie.' I asked him to, on the ship. We're quite good friends now."

"Well, that's the first step, isn't it?" Clare emerged from behind the hanging plant. "Despite what you said, I believe he's the one."

"If he is, you didn't see me exhibit any of your famous three symptoms, did you?"

"No-o-o," Clare conceded.

"Well, then. That's what the wager was all about—if you saw me doing any of those things. I still won. Agreed?"

Clare put the watering pot on the table and shrugged. "Agreed. I was too hasty. And I didn't have a real chance to keep an eye on you as I ought to have."

"No excuses," Stephanie laughed. "Before you know it, *you'll* be the one with the symptoms."

"Not likely."

"Why not? Wouldn't you agree Lord Talbot is very handsome?"

"Very," Clare admitted. "But I'm not sure I like him. A

couple of times I asked him questions, and he never answered, as if the question was beneath him."

"He's not haughty," Stephanie said. "Just—absentminded. Mr. Dunstable told me it was just a year ago yesterday that his wife died."

"But that isn't all. When we first met—and then several times during the evening, he gave me such *looks*. They made me shiver."

"Well, as I said, his mind was probably elsewhere."

"It was more than that." Clare felt the soil beneath her orchid cactus and wiped her fingers on an old rag. She came toward Stephanie. "If you and he are as good friends as you say, perhaps you could find out why."

Stephanie could not imagine Grey giving anyone looks to make them shiver, but she agreed to investigate the matter. Her mind was more occupied with another idea. Clare thought she loved Grey Talbot. What would happen if Alan Dunstable thought so, too?

"If you want to learn what Philadelphians enjoy, you ought to take in Peale's Museum."

"What is Peale's Museum?"

The questioner was Alan Dunstable, responding to Hugh's suggestion. Stephanie overheard their voices from the entrance hall as she descended the stairs late that afternoon. They had just returned from their day's activities. Morton, returning with them, continued down the hall to the kitchen, calling to Sally that they would have some mulled wine before the fire in the library.

The others greeted Stephanie as they hung their hats and greatcoats on the rack, laid gloves on the hall table, and stamped snow from their boots. The fresh cold scent of winter had followed them into the house. She breathed it in appreciatively. There was no doubt in her mind that Alan, although the shortest of the three, stood out from both Hugh and Grey. There was something about his energy, the way his eyes flashed as he glanced about the hall. Or was it simply because she admitted to herself that she loved him? How would it be—would it ever be—that she would have the right to run to him, be swallowed up in his embrace, and feel his lips on hers, the way she longed to right now?

She answered him before Hugh had a chance. "Peale's Museum has all sorts of fascinating things. A restored mammoth's skeleton, some great sea serpent that was caught off the coast of Massachusetts, displays of various stuffed animals. Some of it is scientific and some merely interesting or amusing. Mr. Peale often brings in people who do unusual things, for lectures or performances, as well."

Alan smiled. "I do believe you would like to join us."

Her eyes avoided his and leaped quickly to Grey's face. "Would you be interested in it, Grey? Mr. Peale also has an adjoining art gallery. He and two of his sons are rather famous artists."

"Of course," Grey said, amiable as always. He took the hand Stephanie had extended to him in greeting. "Are you to be our guide, then?"

"If you wish. What about tomorrow?" She glanced at Alan, as if she included him belatedly, for politeness' sake only.

"Perhaps I'll be in the way," he said, an eyebrow raised inquisitively.

"Not at all. Clarinda wants to go, too." (She had no idea whether or not Clarinda wanted to go.) "Neither of us has been there for ever so long, and new exhibits are constantly being added. And I know brother Hugh has other plans." She sent Hugh a meaningful glance.

He caught on right away. "Uh, yes. As a matter of fact, I do," he admitted. "I've a prior engagement tomorrow down at Southwark. Besides, I find Peale's rather a bore. But what can you expect of a man who named his children Rembrandt, Raphael, Titian, and—what are the others?"

Laughing, Stephanie slipped her hand under Grey's arm. "Never mind, Hugh. May I join you in the library? Mama is out visiting. You must tell me about your day." Unobtrusively she led him into the parlor. But she was less aware of Grey's arm or his tall presence by her side than of Alan Dunstable's gaze, piercing her shoulder blades like a knife.

CHAPTER
XI

The Endicott sisters and their male guests decided to walk to the Peale Museum the next afternoon. The day was crisp and fine and the sun brilliant, its glare compacting the fresh snow that lay across the raised brick walkways and pebbled streets. Sleighs with tinkling harness bells had replaced carriages. Small boys threw snowballs at each other and sent their sleds skimming down snowy slopes. Other children skated on a pond in a vacant lot. Two terriers chased each other in and out of a grove of trees.

The frolicsome spirit on the streets was catching. Stephanie began humming, then sang "Adeste Fideles," and Grey soon joined her. Alan scooped up some snow, formed it into a ball and threw it at a lamppost, where it landed with a neat splat. Clare, imitating him, missed, sighed disconsolately, and said, "I wish I had been a boy."

"Never!" Alan cried in mock horror.

Clare waved at the skaters. "They're all boys. It isn't proper for girls to skate. But Stephanie and I persuaded Mama years ago that we could skate in private where the river runs by our farm. Do you suppose we can go there after Christmas, Steph?"

"We always do," Stephanie called back over her shoulder. She was walking ahead with Grey. Clare and Alan were just behind on the narrow walkways—Stephanie had planned it this way.

"Tulip Hill is our farm," she explained to Grey. "It's about five miles north of town, on the Schuylkill. If the weather stays this cold, it will be perfect for skating."

"I'm sure Polly would have skated, too," Grey said, "if she had ever had the chance. I used to, once in a while, but it doesn't often get cold enough in England for a good cover of ice to form in the rivers."

Alan was asking Clare about the Quakers who had first established the city. "Their influence is still strong, isn't it?" Alan asked. "Hugh was deploring some of the strict rules laid down by the city council—no horse racing, no gambling—all due to the Quakers."

"Society of Friends," Clare corrected. "Don't blame them entirely. The Presbyterians are just as opposed to such things. And people can always go to Germantown for horseracing. But Friends don't celebrate Christmas, and I think *that's* a shame."

"And how do you celebrate it?" Grey asked, turning to Clare.

"Oh, we're very English—you'll see," Stephanie said, answering for her sister. "Mama claims descent from a Fletcher who was royal governor here, so we observe all the English traditions, as a lot of others do."

"Yes," Clare chimed in, "whenever Mama wants to put the cap on an argument with Papa about what is proper, she'll say, 'After all, I'm descended from a royal governor, and we need to uphold certain standards.' "

"Benjamin Fletcher was his name," Stephanie added. "But then Papa reminds her he was recalled to England under a cloud. Embezzlement or consorting with pirates, or something like that."

Alan hooted with laughter. Stephanie turned sideways to glance at his face and was rewarded by a youthful, vulnerable look she had not seen before. Her heart jumped and she turned away quickly.

"Papa also says we have Indian blood through Mama's ancestors," Clare put in. She and Alan came abreast of the others as they crossed a street. "That's where Steph got her complexion . . ."

"That's not true!" Stephanie interrupted.

Clare sent her a derisive grin. "You're getting just like Mama about our 'Indian connection,' Steph!"

Stephanie wanted to say, "Nonsense," but Grey, between her and Clare, had slowed suddenly. She glanced at his face in surprise and saw he had turned toward Clare as she spoke with a frown that seemed to have frozen on his face. His blue eyes were both hostile and blank. *Such a look.* Clare had spoken truly.

Clare responded in kind, staring back rudely at Grey. "Did I say something wrong?" she asked.

He seemed to come out of a momentary trance, shook his head, and said, "Oh, no, sorry, I . . ." But Clare had already turned away from him. "Here's the museum," she called over her shoulder, and started up the steps of the red brick building.

"The State House?" Alan asked in surprise.

"Mr. Peale's Museum is on the second floor," Stephanie explained. "He was allowed to use it after Congress moved to Washington."

Upstairs they were greeted by the skeleton of the giant mammoth whose bones had been discovered near the Hudson River twenty years before. Other exhibits combined natural science with artistic curiosities. Stephanie, hoping to further her plan in the most natural and unobtrusive manner possible, pretended boredom when Grey and Clare became fascinated by a tank full of sea creatures. She beckoned Alan over to a series of displays along a wall, separated from each other by screens. "What do you think of these, Mr. Dunstable?"

"The poet and the painter," Alan read on the printed placard. He frowned a little as he gazed at a stuffed chimpanzee wearing an artist's smock, standing before an easel with his brush and palette. The chimp's eye was on another chimp dressed in extravagant muslin and lace. A third monkey in a kimono and cap sat at a table, bent industriously over a piece of paper, pen in leathery hand, inkwell at his elbow.

He gazed at her in surprise, then back to the exhibit again.

"Do you like it?" Stephanie asked. "People seem either to love it or despise it."

"What do you think?" he countered.

"I've always detested anything stuffed because it's no longer alive. But I must admit some of these scenes are comical—almost endearing. Just the idea of that chimpanzee painting another chimp as if she were a famous beauty, or a member of royalty—and then contrast the idea with their serious monkey faces—I suppose it's funny and clever."

"I prefer the mastodon. With a skeleton, there's no ambiguity about dead or alive, human or animal."

"Yes," Stephanie admitted. "You're right about that." And she thought how careful they were, testing out each other's opinion, and wondered if he cared what she thought as much as she cared to know his viewpoint.

They moved on to the next display—a learned monkey in spectacles reading a scientific paper before an audience of gentleman monkeys. Stephanie broke into a laugh. "The Philosophical Society," she said. "See the medallion on the podium? That's their symbol."

"Oh, do you belong?"

"Oh, no, it's not for women. But Papa is a member. He's on the Trade and Commerce Committee, of course. There are five or six different areas, I believe. Mr. Jefferson was president of it until a few years ago. Papa could write a letter of introduction for you, if you still want to meet him."

"Thank you for remembering," he said. His voice was uncommonly gentle. She glanced away quickly. She had reined in her feelings to a remarkable degree, but she needed to be constantly on guard. Too many times the way he spoke or looked at her, as he did now, moved her deeply.

They turned to the next display, but she only glanced at it. "I must ask you something," she said, her fingers clasping the iron rail that stood between them and the exhibits.

"Yes?"

She looked up at him. "Clare says that Grey gives her odd looks at times. I didn't notice it until today, just before we got here."

"Yes," Alan said thoughtfully. "Grey has difficulty hiding his feelings."

"What feelings?"

"You see, your sister looks a great deal like Polly."

"Polly? Oh, his *wife*?"

Alan nodded. "Oh, not her features exactly. But she's the same stature, her hair is dark and she wears it much the same way Polly did when Grey first met her. I noticed that her eyes are even a similar color. And when she spoke in jest about the Indian ancestry, the way she lifted her chin . . . I noticed the resemblance, too."

"You did? How very strange!"

"I believe he'll get used to it," Alan said. "But meeting your sister on the anniversary of Polly's death must have been . . ."

"Like seeing a ghost," Stephanie finished when he hesitated.

"Yes, rather."

"Would you tell me something about her?"

"What has Grey told you?" he parried.

"Almost nothing. I understand from Lady Burleigh that she was something of a paragon."

Alan gave a short laugh. "Nothing of the sort!"

She frowned at him. "Really? Then why the everlasting mourning?" He shook his head, firming his straight, stern mouth as though he had no intention of answering. "I thought perhaps I have a right to know," she pursued.

"He loved her, that's all."

"That's *all*?"

"And had a devil of a time winning her. Then they had less than five years of happiness before she died."

"Yes, but . . ."

"But nothing!" Alan almost shouted the words. Another couple at the next exhibit glanced their way, startled and disapproving. He lowered his voice. "Do you suppose that just because he's a man her loss won't leave a permanent scar? If you can't understand that, I do, and perfectly well."

She was amazed at his vehemence. "I—I'm sorry. I realize Grey is an unusually sensitive man . . ."

"Not so unusual." Alan's voice was gruff but now subdued. "Some of us just don't show it."

They looked up to see Clare and Grey returning to them. "What are you two arguing about?" Clare asked with her infectious grin. "Grey wants to see the Art Gallery now. Are you coming with us?"

"*I* look like the former Lady Talbot?" Clarinda repeated in amazement as Stephanie gave her the information. It was nearly five o'clock. They had been resting after their return home, and now Stephanie sat on Clare's daybed at the foot of her four-poster as her sister dressed for dinner. Clare drew on her second quilted, lace-edged petticoat. Her face had turned from startled to solemn to skeptical. "I don't believe it."

"I'm sure it's true. Alan—Mr. Dunstable said he even noticed it himself. And, of course, it must explain why Grey looks at you so strangely at times."

"Well." Clare sat in a chair to draw on her stockings. "I hope he gets over it. It could get rather tiresome." She fastened garters around the stockings.

"Oh, he will, just give him time."

Clare heaved a sigh of exasperation.

"Don't you like him?" Stephanie asked.

"I'm not sure yet. He can be quite charming at times, but too often he seems rather . . . wrapped up in himself."

"He'll do better. We must help him."

"Yes, I suppose so." Clare sighed again as she stood up. "Help me with my dress?"

Stephanie picked up the pink dress Jenny had laid out on the bed and helped Clare get it over her head, then began fastening the hooks in back. Clare was several inches shorter than Stephanie was, more like their mother, with a tiny waist and narrow hips and small, firm breasts. Polly's stature, Alan had said.

"Perhaps I could find out more about her—Grey's Polly," Stephanie offered. "Would you like to know more?"

"Oh!" Clare seemed startled by the prospect. She waited until Stephanie had finished the hooks, then turned to face her. "I doubt you should ask Lord Talbot such a question."

"No, I won't, of course. But I might ask Mr. Dunstable."

Late that afternoon the Endicotts and their guests were all together in the family parlor, except for Hugh who hadn't returned from his visit to Germantown where, he had said, he was supping with his roommate from Princeton and his family. The parlor, just to the left of the big front hall, was cozily heated by a Franklin fireplace and decorated with blue velvet curtains, a Turkey carpet in dark wine, blue, and ivory, and two sofas covered in satin damask of pale blue and rose. Clare, having decided to be gracious and forbearing, was playing cribbage with Grey, and Stephanie and her mother were embroidering new pillow covers for the sofas. Alan was listening intently as Morton told him about the Philosophical Society, founded by Benjamin Franklin back in 1743. Stephanie had seated herself so that she could not see Alan without turning her head, and therefore would not be tempted to glance at him every few minutes.

Jack came into the room and announced that Mr. Endicott was wanted at the door. Morton rose, hurried to the front hall, and returned a few minutes later. "Saul is here with a message from Pru," he told Dorothea. "I think I ought to go over. Don't wait supper for me, my dear." He turned to Alan. "Sorry to run off. It's my sister, Mrs. Sanford. She's a widow and sometimes needs my help."

"Of course, sir, I understand."

Stephanie, turning to see her father leave, looked at Alan out of the corner of her eye. He was glancing about the room as if uncertain what to do next. An idea came to her in an inspired flash. She put her sewing on the nearby table before she could lose her courage, and stood up.

"Mr. Dunstable, I just recalled something I think you'll be interested in," she said. Everyone looked at her in surprise. She endured their inquisitive glances without flinching. "It's a-a book," she continued. "Would you care to accompany me?"

"Certainly." He rose and bowed in her mother's direction. "Excuse me, ma'am?"

Dorothea frowned, and for a moment Stephanie thought

her mother was about to object. But then she nodded to acknowledge his departure. Stephanie sailed out of the room ahead of him with a confidence she did not feel.

"It's in the music room," she explained to him as they went down the hall. "I keep my little store of books there, too. I had thought of it before you came, and now would be as good a time as any to show it to you." She stopped at the hall table and picked up a candle lamp glowing under a glass chimney.

"What sort of book?"

"Do you know much of Lord Byron's poetry?"

"Quite a bit." She heard amusement in his voice and turned to glance at him.

"I met him in London several years ago," he explained as they resumed their passage toward the drawing room. "When I thought I was a poet. In fact, he introduced me at a soiree at Lady Jersey's, where I was allowed to read some of my verse."

She waited for him to continue. He did not. As they reached the door of the music room she turned and said, "That was generous of him. How was it received?"

"Not very well." His smile mocked his failure. "But, to answer your first question, I know Byron's poetry quite well."

The room was in darkness. She set the small glow on a cabinet before a mirror, lit a three-tiered candelabrum from it, and set it on the back of the pianoforte. "He's no longer in England, is he?"

"No. He's in exile—forced into it by public opinion, they say. His wife got a legal separation. There was some sort of scandal."

"Do you like his work?" She moved to the bookcase and began searching for the book.

"I like it well enough. I doubt his earlier pieces reveal much of what he's really like."

"Is that what poetry is supposed to do? Oh, here it is . . ."

"It's what I think it should do," he supplemented gently, then took the volume she handed him. "Ah, yes, *The Prisoner of Chillon*. One of his more recent works, written in Italy, I believe."

"Mr. Mordecai Lewis, a local printer, published it last year. Hugh gave it to me for my birthday. I thought you might like to see the kind of work a Philadelphia printer can do. I could introduce you, if you're interested."

He took the slim Moroccan-leather-bound volume closer to the candlelight and began glancing through it. Now that she had handed him the bait, Stephanie was not sure what to do next. Her heart was beating too fast (surely he must hear it) and her cheeks were flushed, even though no fire had been laid in the music room today, and it was distinctly chilly.

To calm herself she sat on the harp stool near the window. "What do you think?" she asked at last.

"It's nicely put together. Engravings, too. Are they locally done?"

"I believe so. And the paper comes from the Gilpin mill—that's Pennsylvanian, too."

"You're quite a booster for home manufactures." The look in his eyes was lost in shadow. She suspected he was laughing at her. "Why do you think I'd be interested, Miss Endicott?"

"You're a poet. Don't all writers want to be published?"

"I am published—in newspapers and journals. I've abandoned my poetry."

"Why did you? Or is that an impertinent question?"

He shrugged. "I had to earn a living. I was trying to make poetry out of the suffering of unfortunates and it wasn't—acceptable. Byron said I was ahead of my time five years ago. Public taste hasn't changed much since."

"What a pity. Would you return to it if you didn't have to be a journalist?"

"Yes, probably." He came to her and handed her the book. "Thank you for showing it to me. Now, perhaps we ought to join the others."

She stood up. She felt less vulnerable, standing. Their fingers touched as she took the book, and the sensation zipped up her arm like lightning.

"What do you really want of me?" he asked softly. His brown eyes gleamed in the candlelight. The play of light and shadow had turned the harsh lines of his face gentle. Her heartbeat choked her throat and stopped her voice.

She moved away from him with a little evasive motion, as though she were escaping capture, and replaced the book on its shelf. When she turned back to him, she was in control again.

"Only one more thing. I want you to tell me . . . what you know of Grey's wife."

He stared at her and his eyes went hard. "Is that all?"

"What do you mean?" She groped for the piano chair, found it, and sank onto it as if she'd just completed an exhausting exercise.

"Why do you ask *me*?"

"I . . . dare not ask him."

"Why is it important to you?"

She looked down at her hands. Where were her reasons? Where, by the Lord God, was her skill at playacting? Why didn't she just come out with the truth?

But that was what Kate had done, and now she bitterly regretted it.

"Mr. Dunstable," she began in her best company voice.

"Alan," he interrupted sharply.

"Wh-what?"

"If you can call him Grey, you can call me Alan by now. Didn't you suggest it yourself, evening before last?"

"A-Alan," she acknowledged. "Yes, I did. Alan, I think you'll agree that if a woman is considering marrying a widower, she should know everything she can discover about his first wife."

Her voice grew stronger at the end, and she was able to look him in the eye again.

He walked back to stand before her. His face was unreadable. "You are seriously considering marriage to Talbot?"

"My mother has wanted it ever since London."

"And you?"

"Is there anything we should know?"

She saw his shoulders relax just slightly, saw the tense lines disappear from around his mouth, but his expression looked defeated rather than sympathetic to her request. He turned away and reseated himself near the door, across the room from her.

"I suppose, in your parents' view, yes," he said slowly.

"Will you tell me what it is?"

"I'll tell you what I know." His voice was resigned.

The mantel clock chimed the hour. Seven o'clock. She started up. "Oh, dear, we'll have to go to supper. I didn't realize how late it is. Mama will wonder..."

"If she doesn't already."

"But I still need to know. Promise you'll tell me."

"What clandestine meeting can we arrange, so I may deliver this important information?" His smile was sarcastic, tight-lipped.

She started toward the door. "I might take you to the printer's shop tomorrow. It's not far."

As she passed him he stood up abruptly and gripped her arm.

"Why, Mr. Dun—"

"If we're to be suspected of an indiscretion, anyway...," he said, and pulled her into his arms.

She had no further chance to speak. His lips on hers were fierce and burning. She was engulfed, smothered, invaded, her mouth bruised, her beasts crushed against him. He released her as suddenly as he had embraced her and was as quickly gone.

She heard her mother's worried voice. "Stephanie, where have you gotten to?" She put her hand to her mouth, still enveloped in the foreign sensation of his hard, strong body against hers, his mouth on hers.

"Oh, there you are, Mr. Dunstable." Her mother was at the door of the drawing room. "Is Stephanie...?"

"She's on her way, ma'am. Just putting away some books, I believe." His voice was controlled, casual. She started to follow—slowly, for she felt a bit tipsy. No, not tipsy, but alive—alive and awakened and tremendously hungry.

CHAPTER
XII

Unable to sleep, Alan arose at five o'clock the next morning and donned his old quilted robe and woolen slippers, both of which he had inherited from a father who had not seen fit to bequeath any real property to his errant younger son. He groped his way in the dark to the Franklin fireplace, coaxed to life some embers with old newspapers, added kindling and then more coals until a healthy blaze was established. From this he lit the candle lamp on the table with a long taper.

His purposeful movements were more precise than was usual this early in the morning. It was a relief to move about and concentrate on simple tasks after a night of mental agony, interspersed with brief, tantalizing dreams that only compounded the problem.

The little room was simply furnished. Mrs. Endicott had apologized for this, but Alan liked it. Located on the second floor, rear, it overlooked the kitchen and tradesman's entrance from Tenth Street, and the stables. Especially now, in winter, he found the view more interesting than the snow-covered garden on the other side of the house. From his window he could see the activities of the servants, the people who kept the household functioning. But now, all was still and dark.

He drew out his leather writing case, which was divided

into neat compartments containing paper, quill pens, extra quills, an inkwell, sand for drying the ink, and sealing wax. He would write a letter to Lady Burleigh. His second letter was long overdue, and, if left to his inclination, would remain unwritten. But he owed her that much, for she had been generous with money, enlarging the possibilities of his original plan.

> *Philadelphia, Pennsylvania*
> *December 21, 1820*

> *My lady:* (he finally wrote)
> *We have been three days in Philadelphia, staying with Mr. and Mrs. Endicott. At their kind invitation, we shall doubtless be here through the New Year. After leaving New York, we traveled to Boston, whose inhabitants call it 'the cradle of liberty,' a title that could be safely adopted by Philadelphia, too, I should think. I was able to obtain an interview with the ex-President, John Adams, at his simple home in Quincy. His mind remains as sharp as ever, and he asked me a number of questions about Great Britain that convinced me he still has no great love for the mother country. His son, the present Secretary of State, unfortunately shares his views.*

> *From Boston, we traveled west as far as Albany, where they are building a new canal to facilitate travel and transport between east and west. The weather remained favorable until the day we journeyed here. Philadelphia has had considerable snow, and is much colder than I had anticipated.*

> *But you are probably not interested in any of this. Grey was an amiable and interested companion the whole way, until the day before we arrived here. Then he confided in me that the next day was the anniversary of Polly's death. Memories seemed to take hold of him again, because he became absentminded and morose. Now I am counting on the holiday activities and the liveli-*

*ness of the household—and, of course, Miss
Endicott's presence—to bring him back to normal.*

*Miss Endicott herself is showing marked inter-
est in Grey, and may bring this union off, despite
his indifference. She has been pestering me with
questions about Polly, saying that if a woman is
considering marrying a widower, she should know
something about his first wife. My dilemma at this
point, on which you cannot counsel me, is how
much I really ought to tell her. Will it alienate
Miss Endicott—and her parents—to know what
Grey had to contend with when he married Polly?
How would they take her former liaison with Lord
Burleigh, and what might it say to them of Grey's
willingness to overlook 'immorality'?*

*Though the Endicotts are not Quakers, that
influence is strong in Philadelphia. I suspect they
will not look lightly on the human follies which
seem all too commonplace, and therefore for-
giveable, to you and me. I wish I had the advantage of your good sense in this matter.*

After his usual formal closing, he laid the letter aside,
pondering. How long could the charade that he was promoting Grey's union to Stephanie last? Even to write such
dispassionate prose to Valeria seemed the height of hypocrit-
ical mumbo jumbo. All he really wanted to consider was his
own imprudent actions of the previous evening. What had
been Stephanie's reaction to that damnable kiss? Would she
cancel today's expedition because of it? Did she, perhaps,
think of him as beyond the bounds of polite society because
of that kiss? He almost hoped so.

And wouldn't Valeria laugh if she knew he had gotten
himself so emotionally entangled with the very woman she
had picked out for her nephew!

He folded and sealed the letter, impressing the hot wax
with his ring, another memento of his father. Going to the
dresser to lay out his small clothes and cravat, he caught
sight of his face in the mirror. Pausing, he gave himself a
good look. Did his eyes express the cynicism he often felt?

Had he really placed himself beyond the reach of a good woman who was also marvelously desirable? Weakening in his resolve, he reminded himself of Stella. *Never again. Keep a tight rein, old chap. If she was made for either of us, it's Grey, not you.*

By now it was nearly six-thirty. A commotion in the yard below drew Alan to the window. A faint haze through the treetops indicated approaching dawn. Lights from the kitchen now reflected on the snow and lit the area. A mule-drawn wagon had turned in at the gate and was squeakily approaching the service entrance. When the driver, bundled in scarves, rang his bell, Sally Buxton came out the door with two large pitchers. The milkman jumped down and filled the pitchers from one of the large tin cans in the wagon.

Voices drifted upward. "How's it goin' with them two English fellows stayin'? You need more milk? I hears they're always wantin' milk in their tea." Alan couldn't hear Sally's softer reply.

So he and Grey were the talk of the neighborhood, even of the milkman. Would his outing to the printer's with Stephanie be equally conspicuous? The evening before it was he who had deflected Mrs. Endicott's suspicions when they had remained too long in the music room. Today, it would have to be up to Stephanie. Withdrawing from the window, he began to dress.

Morton Endicott was the only person seated at the dining room table. He seemed surprised and pleased to see Alan abroad so early.

"Sit down, sit down, it's good to have company. Since the children no longer attend school, I'm usually alone this time of day."

Alan took the chair next to his host with a smile. "Apparently you take seriously the adage of one of your most illustrious citizens: 'Early to bed, early to rise . . .'"

"Ah, yes, old Ben Franklin. Of course. All Philadelphians do. He's been dead these thirty years, and I vow he's in a fair way to becoming the city's patron saint." Morton rang the bell that sat next to his plate, which still lacked food.

"And what excuse do you have to be up and about before seven, my friend?"

Alan showed him the letter. "I awoke early and thought it a good time to write an overdue letter to England. What would be the quickest way I could send it off?"

"The mail coach office opposite Judd's Hotel on South Third sends out an early stage to New York. Today's mail has already left, but tomorrow's will be in New York by tomorrow evening. With luck, it'll be on the next ship leaving for London, maybe in a couple of days if the weather is good in New York. There won't be any more ships out of Philadelphia for at least three months because of the early freeze."

"Is that office anywhere near Mordecai Lewis's print shop? Your daughter has offered to take me there this morning."

"Has she? Stephanie?"

"Yes. She thought I'd be interested in what a Philadelphia printer does."

"Well, it's not far—just a couple blocks from Lewis's shop. Anyone can direct you. So, you're interested in printing?"

"As a writer, of course," Alan explained. Morton nodded as if assessing the import of this information or, perhaps, his daughter's reasons for taking Alan there. He gazed toward the door leading to the kitchen. "Sally's slow this morning," he complained and rang the bell again. "Well, Mordecai Lewis does excellent work. Puts out a weekly paper, too. Isn't afraid of stepping on toes. Believes 'Freedom of the Press' is the greatest of the amendments to the Constitution. He was jailed during Adams's administration for criticizing the government. He's older now, but no more prudent."

"He sounds very interesting," Alan said with a grin.

Then Sally entered, bearing a tureen of hot biscuits and gravy and a steaming bowl of scrambled eggs. She eyed Alan as she placed the dishes on the table before Morton. "I'll have your place set in a moment, sir," she told him.

"Have we enough food here to feed Mr. Dunstable, too?" Morton asked, peering into the tureen.

"I'm sure we do, sir. And coffee'll be here in a minute."

"Your servants seem efficient and cheerful," Alan said, once she had left them.

"Yes, we're fortunate. Sally's ma and pa were with my father, and stayed on after he died. Sally's past thirty and unlikely to marry now, so I expect we'll keep her on, too. And Harry Fry, my stable man, is a retired seaman, used to be on one of my father's ships. In fact, he was with the first ship I ever sailed. We went to China in '85, and he was thirty-five then. He's surprisingly spry for his age. The only one we have problems with is Elsa. Have you noticed her? The little German maid?"

"Oh, yes, I believe she does my room."

"I got her off a ship from Hamburg, soon after we returned from England. Doubtless she'll turn out all right, once she learns our ways."

"Indentured servant?"

"Yes. I paid her passage, and she promised to work for us for three years in exchange for her keep and English lessons. Mrs. Endicott is teaching her."

Sally returned and placed stoneware and cutlery before Alan. He helped himself to biscuits and gravy. "Grey has been wondering about servants. I've always done without. If one needs an errand run, one can always find a boy willing to earn a copper or two. But Grey thinks it'd be convenient to have someone along when we go on our next trip. He left his man back in England and misses him."

"There's a domestic service agency down on Market Street. But word of mouth may be a better way to find someone. I'll ask around. The Irish are pretty good domestics, if you're looking at immigrants. At least they speak the language. Those that were born here don't usually stay with it. They're looking for ways to better themselves. I don't hire Negroes because then people assume they're slaves, and I never held with trafficking in human flesh. Most Philadelphians would agree with me, but a few people have 'em." He ate at full speed, yet still managed to talk between mouthfuls, stopping only to cut up a biscuit or put jam on the fresh hot toast Sally had brought them.

"Is that something that could divide the country?" Alan asked as Sally poured his coffee. "Slavery, I mean."

"Seemed like it for a while. Now we got this big compromise Senator Clay engineered, admitting Maine free, Missouri, slave. It just puts the question off, to my mind."

Alan added milk to his coffee and took a cautious sip. "What should have been done, in your opinion?"

"Damned if I know. Slavery's a pernicious practice, no doubt about it. Trouble is, soon as you point this out to a Southerner, like Mr. Bates on the ship, he'll instinctively defend it. The final argument is always, 'How could the Southern economy survive without it?' "

"I intend to go south after we leave here," Alan said. "I'm also interested in going west, maybe as far as Pittsburgh. I'm beginning to believe six months isn't nearly a long enough time."

"You're probably right," Morton said. "I would suggest you get a taste of the Western farming communities in this state before you go south. You'll find some vast contrasts."

He finished his coffee in a gulp, wiped his mouth with a napkin, and arose from the table. "Don't hurry yourself, Alan. Two of my partners in the Green Tulip company are here from New York. We have a long morning ahead of us, looking over the books and making plans for expansion. I hope to have four ships running the packet service eventually. Give Mr. Lewis my regards, if you visit him."

"I'll do that, sir. One more thing, if I may." At Morton's nod, he continued, "I take it you've no problem with my escorting your daughter to the print shop?"

Morton's blue eyes were piercing under his bushy, graying brows. "If Stephanie has offered to take you there, I think I may trust her judgment," he said. The steely gaze turned genial and twinkly. Then Morton bid him good-bye again and left the room.

Hugh, learning that Grey had been a captain under Wellington in England's long struggle against Napoleon, had asked him if he wanted to watch the City Troop drill that morning. They had already left by the time Stephanie appeared in her father's library, where Alan had become engrossed in Philadelphia's foremost newspaper, *The Aurora*. He looked up as her shadow crossed the threshold and found it difficult to restrain a gasp of admiration. She was already dressed for the outdoors in a gray bonnet with blue velvet ruching and rosettes and white plumes, ankle-length mantle trimmed with silver fox fur, and a matching muff in her gloved hand. She was as tall and graceful as a Grecian statue, as lovely as one of Gainsborough's aristocratic ladies. Her color was high, but there was no other indication that she was embarrassed to address him.

"Can you be ready to visit Mr. Lewis's printing shop soon?" she asked. "I can walk with you there and introduce you before I go on to Washington Hall. The Handelian Society is having its final rehearsal this morning at ten."

He tossed the newspaper aside and leaped to his feet. "I'm ready as soon as I get my hat and coat. You don't intend to drive, then?"

"It is much simpler to walk than to go to all the trouble of having Harry hitch up the gig. Besides, everyone is busy, getting the house ready for Christmas. And I love to walk, as you may have gathered."

She stepped back into the hall as he approached and said, "I'll just tell Mama we're leaving, and meet you in the entry."

A few minutes later they were on their way. It was colder today, the air crisp and refreshing. Still, the sun shone, dazzling their eyes. Stephanie's embroidered cloth bag, which held her music, hung from one arm by its strings, and both her hands were inside her muff. Her attitude was polite but distant, as if nothing had happened between them last night. He pondered again, as he had all night, whether or not she had deliberately provoked his kiss.

Next door the Negro sweep and his small assistant were preparing to clean the chimneys, bringing in large cloths to cover the furniture. "Chimneys are cleaned once a month, winter or summer," Stephanie said in answer to Alan's questioning look. "And always just before the New Year. It's a city ordinance, to cut down on fires. Isn't there one in London?"

"I have no idea," Alan said. "I have never been a householder, in London or anywhere else."

She gave him one of those sidelong glances that always constricted his heart. "In a way, that's a bit sad," she said.

He didn't know why she should think so and, to divert her, pointed to the chimneysweep and asked, "Is he a slave?"

"Oh, no, he has his own business," Stephanie said. He marveled at her cool friendliness. Obviously the kiss had meant nothing to her. He recalled her behavior at the supper table last evening—as now, quiet and composed. Was she always so composed? Was there no way to break through that beautiful shell? He stopped himself, remembering he must not even try.

The brick walkway was dry in places where householders had brushed or shoveled away the snow, or icy where many feet had trod it. She walked over everything with surefooted grace in her fur-trimmed boots, greeting the people they passed. "Good morning, Mrs. Coxe. How is Grace? I haven't seen her for weeks. This is Mr. Dunstable from England." And a block later, "How are you, Mr. Lloyd? Did your wife recover from her cold? I should like you to meet Mr. Dunstable." And so on. She waved to a man on horseback and a couple in a carriage, as though Philadelphia were a village, not a city of over sixty thousand residents, and she knew everyone in it. Her smile brought wide smiles in return, and cordial welcomes for him, the fortunate visitor.

"Shall I escort you home after your rehearsal?" he asked her.

"Oh, no, there's no need for you to wait. I shall simply walk home by myself."

"Alone?"

"Why not?" She turned and smiled. "This isn't London."

"I keep forgetting," he said, smiling back. "No wonder you disliked it there."

"If I always needed an escort, it would limit me terribly. Will you tell me, now, Alan, about Lord Talbot's wife?" Her first spontaneous use of his given name seemed deliberate, intended to show that he was a friend—but no more.

"Yes, if you like." He looked down at the walk, hands in his carrick's pockets, as he picked his way gingerly through memory. "I'll tell you what I know. I don't pretend to know everything. Much of it comes secondhand, through Lady Burleigh." He glanced up at her. "Perhaps you're a mind reader. Did you suspect Polly wasn't a 'lady,' in the accepted sense of the word?"

"She was of the merchant class, then?" Stephanie asked. "So are we, of course, but in England . . ."

"Not even that," he interrupted. "She was a cockney, raised a servant in a tavern, without education. Her mother died when she was born, and she never knew who her father was."

"Oh, I see." Stephanie's voice was subdued, hesitant. She stepped carefully over a gutter as they crossed a street. He retreated to the strategy he had intended to use.

"Let me tell you my first memory of her. It was in Newmarket. She came with Grey for the races. Grey had a new racehorse, the first one he'd owned, a gift of Lord Burleigh. They stayed with Grey's father and sister, with whom I was acquainted. Grey's horse won, and he threw a big celebration. Somehow, I was invited. Grey said Polly was a distant cousin of Lord Burleigh's, brought over from America when the earl learned she had been orphaned and was destitute. He'd made her his ward. She was only sixteen—a lively, uninhibited girl, with a direct, cheerful manner. Naive, yet somehow knowing. Her accent bothered me right away. It was too much like the East London streets. Of course, I'd never met any Americans then, and had no way of knowing if Yankees spoke that way, too. It wasn't until much later—a year, I guess—that I learned it was all a hoax, that Lord Burleigh had invented the story of an American relation to hide the fact that he'd taken her as his mistress."

He glanced at Stephanie's face. She was frowning, and her features had gone rigid. She continued to stare straight ahead as she said, "Go on."

"Grey was fooled, too. He fell in love with her, thinking she was no more than his uncle's ward. When Lord Burleigh saw how his feelings were running, he goaded Grey into joining the army. He was in the Peninsular campaign, as you know. When he returned—it was Victory Summer, and we didn't know then that we didn't have Napoleon put away for good—Polly realized she loved him, too. But she couldn't let him know, couldn't do anything about it, because she owed everything she had to Lord Burleigh. He had educated her, taught her how to be a lady. She'd even learned to speak properly.''

Stephanie shook her head a little but said nothing. Alan was fully aware that his decision to tell her the whole truth was just the least bit self-serving. If he believed she deserved to know it, he also hoped it would offend her.

"The long and short of it," he went on, "is that she finally told Grey the truth. At first he was terribly disillusioned. Then he realized he loved her anyway, and he persuaded her to run away with him. This in spite of the fact that Lord Burleigh had threatened to disown him—both of them—if that happened. And in spite of the fact that Polly was pregnant with Lord Burleigh's child."

Again he stopped. Again, Stephanie would not respond, only walked a little faster, her chin high.

"I don't know how it was resolved," he said. "I was in Europe myself, then—Napoleon had escaped from Elba and taken over Paris, and the Allies were gearing up to confront him. But after Waterloo—after it was all over—I came back and learned that Lord Burleigh had relented, somehow, and Polly and Grey were married. She had borne a son before they were married, and Grey officially acknowledged Kevin as his son, but he isn't; he's Lord Burleigh's. And the earl eventually married Lady Hammond, who is now Lady Burleigh."

"Lord Burleigh wasn't married before?"

"No, he had never married. I think he would have married Polly at the end, but she wouldn't have him. She wanted Grey." After a short silence he added, "I have never seen two people more in love." Stephanie was quiet. "You're wishing I hadn't told you," he guessed.

"I—I suppose so," Stephanie said. "I won't say I'm not shocked. I am."

"I—hope it won't make you think less of Grey," he said, as a salve to his conscience.

She drew herself up as if manning all her defenses. "No-o-o. I shall think what I have always thought of him." She favored him again with her devastating sidelong glance and smile. "I appreciate your telling me, anyway."

He was depressed and exalted at the same time. She stopped and pointed to a shop across the street. "Here we are."

Mordecai Lewis was a tall man, long of face and nose, with sunken cheeks and a receding hairline over which his black hair, shiny with Macassar oil, was carefully combed. His eyes were deep-set under stern brows, but their gaze was mild and friendly as Stephanie introduced Alan to him.

"Delighted, I'm sure, Mr. Dunstable." Lewis shook his hand and bowed them into the shop. It was, Alan saw immediately, a larger than average bookstore. "My printing setup is in the back," he said. "That's where the money goes out. Here is where it comes in."

Floor-to-ceiling bookshelves covered two walls of the room, and larger books were displayed on tables scattered about the center. At the other end, large printed signs advertised the latest popular offerings, mostly products of American authors.

Alan was suddenly assailed with memories of another bookstore, a world away from this: the front room of the Talbot house on the edge of Newmarket, the stacks of dusty books, both new and secondhand, on tables and on the floor, the pigeonhole desk where Nigel Talbot was forever misplacing receipts. And his first sight of Stella, with her angel-spun hair and eager, naive face. . . .

". . . some beautiful engravings of famous scenes, done by Mr. Hill," Mr. Lewis was saying, more to Stephanie than to him. "A shipment just arrived. I must show you a copy."

Stephanie, looking pleased, followed the printer to the table where several copies of the new book were propped against small easels for better visibility.

Following them, Alan was surprised when a man who had been browsing at nearby shelves turned toward them. He was about thirty, with a high brow and overlarge mouth that visibly quivered at the sight of Stephanie. She stopped abruptly a couple of feet away from him, tension immediately evident in her stiff back.

"Hello, Dick," she said after a long moment.

"Hello, Stephanie." The words seemed forced. His pale

blue eyes held the vacant, dazed look of soldiers Alan had encountered after a battle. His shoulders were weighted by a dejected slump, his hair disheveled, his cravat carelessly tied. He looked over Stephanie's shoulder to Alan. "You have a new friend," he noted. His tone was bitter.

Stephanie stepped back and turned to include Alan. "Yes, I'd like you to meet . . ." she began.

The book Dick held slammed to the floor in the midst of her words. He grabbed the bowler and gloves he had laid on an adjacent table and strode up the aisle and out the shop without another word.

"Oh, dear," Stephanie whispered. She looked at Alan. "I'm sorry," she said as though she needed to apologize for the man's impoliteness. Then she seemed to dismiss the encounter with a toss of her head. "I don't believe I've time to look at the book right now, Mr. Lewis, but I'll surely do so soon. I must go on to my rehearsal. But do acquaint Mr. Dunstable with your establishment."

"I'll be pleased to, Miss Endicott."

She turned and gave Alan her gloved hand. "Until later, then?"

"Until later, ma'am," Alan said with a slight bow. The next minute she was out the door.

"A sad situation, that," Mr. Lewis said, shaking his head. "Not that I put all the blame on Miss Endicott, but Mr. Harlow has not taken her refusal well."

Alan was not above taking advantage of Mr. Lewis's willingness to gossip. "Who is he?"

"Dick Harlow. He and Miss Endicott were betrothed for about a year. They had intended to marry summer before last, but then his mother died, so they postponed the date. Would've taken place last January, if I recall correctly. Then she called it off." He shook his head again, his long face mournful. "A woman's privilege, I've heard said. But it changed an up-and-coming young businessman into that sad shell of a man. I've heard folks call Miss Endicott heartless, but, on the other hand, not one in a hundred would've predicted he'd take it so hard."

"There are a few women," Alan said after a moment, "who can do that to a man."

CHAPTER
XIII

On her return from England, Stephanie had first heard about the change in Dick Harlow from Aunt Pru. Hints from Clare and others still had not prepared her for the man who confronted her in Lewis's bookshop. Stephanie didn't realize how shaken she was until she was out of the shop and nearly to Washington Hall two blocks away. Even after the rehearsal was in progress, she had difficulty losing herself in Handel's glorious music, thanks to the persistent image of the vacant-eyed, bitter-tongued, beaten man Dick had become.

Clare had said only that he had become something of a hermit. Aunt Pru's warning had been more alarming, but Stephanie had not taken it seriously for Aunt Pru had a way of exaggerating things. If her thirteen-year-old son Tim caught a cold, it was pneumonia. If ten-year-old Annie showed symptoms of a fever, she predicted a resurgence of yellow fever. Last night's emergency had probably been a similar alarm, even though her father hadn't returned from Aunt Pru's house on Market Street until late. Sometimes, Morton explained, Pru simply needed the reassurances of male companionship. It was difficult for a woman to be widowed so young, and Pru was only thirty-five. He had more than once suggested that Pru and Perry combine households for both their sakes, but Perry always wriggled

out of it, claiming that Pru's constant alarms as well as her
excessive neatness would drive him to distraction.

So Stephanie had not taken seriously Aunt Pru's solemn
declaration that Dick Harlow was going mad. But now, after
encountering him, it seemed quite possible.

They were rehearsing *Messiah.* "Once more," Mr. Carr,
the director, said, breaking into her thoughts. "We'll have
to have more volume from the altos. This is the first chorus,
and the entrance is all yours. You must make it exciting."

They began again, a chorus of fifty mixed voices, some
very good, some indifferent, all in earnest. Stephanie found
it possible to have her mind in two places at once. As she
sang, her thoughts were far from "And the Glory of the
Lord."

Alan's kiss, then Grey's startling past, and now Dick's
puzzling condition. It was all, somehow, dreadful—except
the kiss. Dick's tentative goodnight pecks, polite and brief,
had been her only rehearsals for a touch that had burned to
the very soles of her feet. What had ensued after Alan left
her so hastily was almost worse. A warm sweetness had
filled the lower part of her abdomen, then spread in exciting
little ripples through her legs and back up her torso. The
sensation returned each time she looked at him at supper, so
she did not look at him very much, out of sheer embarrassment. Thank God the chatter of Hugh and Clare and her
parents made it unnecessary for her to contribute much to
the conversation. Her outrage the instant Alan had seized
her arm had vanished. Instead she only longed for another
kiss, a development on that first theme, a moment unhur-
ried, uninterrupted, that would allow her to respond and
bring her some sort of satisfaction. . . .

What this might be, she could not imagine.

" 'Oh, Thou that tellest,' " Mr. Carr announced. "Mrs.
Ramsey, are you ready? Chorus, be prepared to come in."

Stephanie switched her weight from one foot to the other
and turned her pages to the chorus part. Mrs. Ramsey began
her long contralto solo.

It was frightening to have one's emotions break down so,
even in front of other people. She dare not let it show. She
refused to let *him* know it had made a difference, so she had

kept their little appointment this morning. But that sweet excitement had returned as she walked beside him, even when she stopped to talk to neighbors.

A gentleman would have apologized for that kiss and said something about being carried away by her beauty. It would have been the start of a courtship. Alan Dunstable had not apologized, so where did that leave them? She had planned to answer an apology in a way her mother would surely have approved, by saying, "Just see that it does not happen again." She might have added some warning, such as "Or I shall be forced to tell my father." But Alan had not apologized. Besides, he probably realized her father was unlikely to act the heavy-handed protector of his daughter's virtue. Logic would suggest that she avoid him now, and bring him to heel, so to speak. If he loved her . . . But there was Grey's warning, of two months past. "He goes his own way, he always has, and I can't see he'd change for a woman." With Alan Dunstable, a kiss did not necessarily mean love. And even love might not mean marriage.

"Miss Endicott, are you ready with your recitatives?"

She heard her name with a shock. "Y-yes, Mr. Carr," she quavered. Only one chord sounded from the pianoforte to prepare her. She forced herself to concentrate. " 'There were shepherds, abiding in the fields . . .'

" 'Praising God, and saying . . .' " she finished, drawing out her clear high A.

" 'Glory to God, Glory to God,' " the chorus responded. Following the other sopranos in the chorus was now a simple matter. Once more, as Stephanie sang, her mind wrapped itself about a new revelation. Grey's Polly—a cockney servant girl, without parents. Born one of the "unfortunates," as Dorothea called them. Mistress to an earl, then wooed, in ignorance, by his nephew, by Grey. How unlike him it seemed. How strange, too, that he had never mentioned Polly's son, the child he had adopted. She could almost laugh, remembering how concerned her mother had often been about offending Lord Talbot's sense of propriety.

Polly, she could not imagine. Mistresses were tarts, beyond the pale, never spoken about in polite company. She had heard about them, not from her mother but from girlfriends

during her days at Poor's Academy for Young Ladies—
whispered information accompanied by shocked smirks. She
had never, so far as she knew, set eyes on one. Yet Clare
reminded Grey of Polly. And Alan had been quite obviously
sympathetic. In the museum, he had defended Grey's right
to mourn. "He loved her, that's all." That was all that
needed saying. Love was irrational. Alan seemed to understand that. What else had he said in the museum—something
about not showing his emotions? If only she knew what they
were!

It had never been so difficult to concentrate on a rehearsal. Chatting to friends afterward was, somehow, an irritating
intrusion. She wanted to be alone with her thoughts. Looking
forward to the walk home, alone, she turned down two
offers to share friends' carriages, from Mary Foster, now
happily married to Abe Coxe, and from Andrew Bingham,
who had been her first beau. Andrew was married now, too.

As she left the auditorium, the first person she saw was
Alan Dunstable, standing near a marble pillar in the entrance hall. He carried an armload of books fastened with a
leather strap.

"Having nothing else to do," he explained, "I thought
I'd return with you. If you have no objection."

His crinkly, sunshine eyes were gleaming, ready to smile,
and she could not halt her own smile even as her heart
leaped into her throat. "Your company is most welcome,"
she said. Her eyes fastened on the books, a safer place than
his face.

"You didn't know, did you, that you confronted me with
my greatest weakness," he said. "I cannot resist books or
bookstores."

"Philadelphia has a number of them."

"Then I shall surely be out of pocket before I leave
here."

"We'll have to keep you otherwise occupied, I can see
that." Their exchange was accomplished with mock solemnity, a good way to hide the excitement within her. He
shifted his burden to his other arm and opened the heavy
oak door to the outside, keeping it ajar for her.

"How did your rehearsal go?"

"Oh, well enough. We're only singing part of the Christmas portion, and two of us are doing solos. Then we'll sing some carols. Choral singing hasn't become an institution here, as it is in parts of England. How did you get on with Mr. Lewis?"

"Exceedingly well, thank you. Doubtless you know he prints pamphlets, too, on all sorts of subjects, and a weekly paper, *The Sentinel of Freedom*. He asked me to contribute to an issue."

"And will you?"

"I may."

"On what topic?"

"I haven't decided. How about 'Christmas in the New World?' " he asked, his eyes twinkling.

Pru's children, shouting greetings, ran down the steps from the front entryway of the Endicott house as Stephanie and Alan opened the gate. Annie reached them first, her brown curls streaming down her back from under her close-fitting bonnet, her red coat and dark skirts no impediment to her quicksilver movements.

"Hello, Stephanie! We've come for lunch. Are we going to hear you sing tonight?"

"I certainly hope so," Stephanie replied, leaning down to give her cousin a hug. "What would the Handelian Society do without its friends and family to sing to?"

Blond, freckled Tim, three years Annie's elder but not much taller, added, "Will it be very long? I don't like long concerts."

"Not very," Stephanie promised. "Now greet Mr. Dunstable. He's our guest from England. Alan, this is Tim, and Annie."

They shook hands with him in grown-up fashion, pleased that Alan greeted them as equals.

"What do you have there?" Tim asked.

"Books. Do you want to see what they are?"

"Of course!" they shouted together, and followed him eagerly into the house.

"Is your mother here?" Stephanie asked as she shut the door on the cold air.

"She's with Aunt Dorothea in the sewing room," said Tim. "May I see your books now, sir?"

At Alan's nod, they went with him into the library, across the front hall from the parlor. After hanging up her coat, Stephanie followed. Alan was laying his books out on a large table before the front window. *Travels in the United States*, *Geographical Description of the United States*, *Information for Emigrants*, and *A History of England* for schoolchildren.

"What a bore," Tim said with a groan. "They look just like schoolbooks. Are you really going to read them?"

"Certainly," Alan said. He looked at Stephanie as he laid out the rest: *The Hermit in Philadelphia*, which she knew was a satire, and *New England and Other Poems*. The next two titles were more unusual: *An Account of the Languages, History, Manners and Customs of the Indian Nations of Pennsylvania* and *A Portraiture of Domestic Slavery in the United States*. "According to your Mr. Lewis, every book here is by a Philadelphian," Alan said. "I thought that was quite extraordinary."

"Background for your articles?" she asked.

"Yes, they may be just the thing."

"And what about this?" She held up a slim volume entitled *How to Try a Lover*, a farce in three acts.

"I was curious," he said blandly. "Do you suppose the author meant 'how to test a lover' or 'how to be a trial to a lover?' Or are they, perhaps, one and the same?"

"Perhaps," she said, blushing unexpectedly. "Excuse me, I had better go and greet Aunt Pru."

In the sewing room, Dorothea and Pru had their heads together over a new gown Pru had made. She had intended to wear it to a dinner at Senator Hamlin's, but now she was having second thoughts.

"I'm afraid the neck is really too low," Pru said. "I shouldn't like to be thought loose. After all, I am a widow, and . . ."

"My dear, you've been widowed ten years, and you still don't look a day over twenty-five," Dorothea said warmly. "You don't need to act as if you're in mourning anymore, you know."

She did, indeed, look like a girl, Stephanie thought, admiring her pretty aunt from the doorway. She had been widowed when she was only twenty-five and had often declared she was too heartbroken to marry again. Had she decided, at last, that it was time to look for a second husband?

"Aunt Pru," Stephanie called from the doorway, then hurried over to receive her aunt's warm hug. "I didn't realize we would see you today."

"Morton asked me to come. I'm dreadfully concerned about Tim."

"What's the matter with Tim? He seems fine to me."

"He doesn't want to go to school anymore. He wants to go to sea, like Morton did. He was only fifteen when he went on his first voyage, you know."

"But Tim's only thirteen."

"Yes, but he says he's fifteen in spirit." Pru sighed in exasperation. "And Morton has always encouraged him about going to sea. Of course I realize Tim is his last hope for another generation of seamen in our family, since Hugh wants to study law, but even so . . ."

"But even Morton must realize he's too young," Dorothea said.

"Yes, he does, of course, but he made the mistake of telling Tim one time about twelve-year-old cabin boys, and now Tim has taken it into his head that he must be a cabin boy."

Pru's worries dominated the conversation until dinnertime when Morton joined everyone in the dining room. Despite his busy schedule with his visiting partners, he had promised to take Tim aboard one of his ships that was in dry dock that afternoon. Dorothea said, accusingly, that he would only make matters worse. Only the presence of Grey and Alan at the table prevented the argument from becoming a quarrel.

"If you don't mind," Alan said to Morton, "you can show me the ship, too."

"I'd be delighted," Morton said.

Tim and Morton returned from their expedition just as the sun set. Tim declared a new—and, to his mother, astounding—

resolution: to return to school willingly and attend to his studies, especially mathematics and geography, so that he would have a good basis to study navigation. After his sister and her children had gone home, Morton told them that during their tour of the ship, Tim had begun to understand the seafaring life better. Alan Dunstable had given him a shockingly realistic picture of the ordinary seaman's life, one he himself would probably have softened out of concern for his nephew's sensibilities. Alan had spared nothing. He pointed out the continuous hard work, the hazing from the mates, the drunken fights among the crew, the punishment with the lash if you didn't tow the mark, the poor food, the daily hazards of the sea, and the few pleasures. Coming from a stranger, it probably had more impact, Morton pointed out. Then, when disillusion had set in, he himself had suggested that with education, Tim could aspire to be a first mate and eventually captain—goals cabin boys rarely achieved. Captains were gentlemen, learned and respected by all, and in complete command of their ships. That was really what he wanted, wasn't it?

Dorothea said she was happy the issue was settled. She did not admit that she had had the wrong idea of what her husband hoped to accomplish with the expedition.

Alan had not returned with them. He had decided, Morton said, to stay down on Front and Water Streets, look around, and eat at a tavern that evening, to gain some local color for his article on Philadelphia. When he did not show up in time to go with them to the concert that evening, Stephanie became snappish to Jenny, who was trying to help her dress. The maid assumed it was nervousness and tried to soothe her. "You just calm down, Miss Stephanie. You know you always sing beautifully."

She tried to calm down. Maybe he would meet them there, or arrive late. But in a hall that held six thousand, would she even see him? She smiled at Jenny and apologized, and tried not to let Alan Dunstable unsettle her.

He never came. The concert went as well as it could and, as usual, Stephanie was bombarded with praise afterward, but it meant little to her. When the Endicotts returned home, he was not there, either. He did not return before she retired to her bedchamber, weary, disheartened and upset, both at Alan and at herself, for minding his absence.

The delectable odors of gingerbread, fruitcake, and sugar cookies began to permeate the house as Christmas approached. Stephanie discovered Clare hanging the mistletoe, which she had brought home the day before, with Elsa's help. Dorothea allowed this, but she did not quite approve. There was no reason, she said, that celebrating the birth of the Christ child should be an excuse for licentiousness.

"What do you think, Steph?" Clare asked, handing up a sprig to Elsa who stood precariously on a ladder under the entrance to the library. "Here, and the parlor, and the hall, at the foot of the stairs. Where else?"

"The drawing room," Stephanie said. "That's where we'll be on Christmas Eve."

"And over the entrance to the music room? Maybe you can trap Grey there."

"I have no intention of trapping anyone."

"Of course you do."

"What about Geoffrey Coxe?" Stephanie countered. "Isn't this just the least bit for your sake, too?"

"He's Mama's choice, not mine."

"Anyone else?"

"Oh, well, we shall see," Clare conceded. "It's for Kate and Hugh, too, of course. He can't possibly dislike her as much as he pretends to."

And did Alan Dunstable dislike Stephanie as much as he pretended? This morning he had already been out of the house when she went down to breakfast. If he had been at the concert, she had no way of knowing.

The mistletoe as well as the season reminded her again of Dick Harlow. It was just a year ago, on Christmas Eve, that the final rift had occurred. She could not help comparing yesterday's haggard appearance to his self-assured manner last year.

The feeling had been growing in her for some time that she could not marry him, but she had not let the thought materialize until they attended a party at the home of friends. Their wedding date was a month off then. It had

already been postponed six months earlier, when his mother,
long an invalid, had died. She should have recognized the
problem at that point, for the postponement had been a
relief. But it was the mistletoe that finally told her what
was wrong.

The Coxes' house had been filled with mistletoe. Several
unsuspecting females were caught under it and duly kissed,
but Dick did not take advantage of the custom. Then
Stephanie saw Mary Foster, newly engaged to Geoffrey
Coxe's older brother, Abe, caught in her fiancé's embrace
when they thought no one was looking. She had been
unable to take her eyes from their long, passionate kiss.
When they separated, with much reluctance, Mary's face
was flushed, adoring, beatific. It struck Stephanie like a
dash of ice water: *I'll never feel that way about Dick, never*!
She was seized by a passionate longing, stronger than she
had ever experienced, to know that kind of love.

All during the next dance with Dick, her head whirled
with the thought, *I can't marry him, I can't*. Finally, while
they danced, she told him so. He thought she was jesting or,
taken with some girlish whim, was trying to upset his
complacency. He attempted to cajole her. She only became
adamant, and asked him to take her home.

That night, in bed, she had thought of all the little things
about Dick Harlow that irritated her: his slow, didactic way
of speaking, his habit of pressing a finger against his lips as
he thought through a sentence, his inability to enter into
witty, lighthearted conversation, his overriding concern for
small details. When he met strangers, he always mentioned
the Germantown cotton mill he had inherited from his
father, his house on Walnut Street with its antiques, and his
grandfather's illustrious exploits in the Revolution.

She knew she would never again be able to overlook
these little irritations, that they would only grow as she was
forced to hear and see them again and again, over the years.
When, the next day, he insisted on taking her to his house
and tried to win her back by pointing out all the advantages
to their match, her irritation turned to anger. She shouted at
him that he didn't know the meaning of love, and marriage
to him would be like wedding a mummy in a museum.

His face had gone stiff and his eyes cold. "Very well," he'd said, "I'll ask the coachman to take you home." He did not say another word to her, and she could not take back her own hurtful phrases. The next day she learned he had gone to visit relatives in Boston. He had not returned when she left for England in March.

Had Mr. Lewis told Alan the story of her broken engagement, or as much of it as everyone knew? Was that why he was avoiding her?

He did return late that afternoon to go to dinner with them at the Hamlins. Stephanie took special care with her dress and hair, but Alan seemed bent on ignoring her most of the evening. She could not help noticing that he was showing a marked interest in Kate. In retaliation, she made an effort to be charming to Grey, but she came away from the evening thoroughly vexed. She was also hurt because Kate seemed to enjoy Alan's company immensely, as if Stephanie had never confessed her own interest in Mr. Alan Dunstable.

The tree was for Tim and Annie, who had gotten the idea two years before from friends among the German community. Dorothea was not convinced of its appropriateness to Christmas, either, but allowed it for the sake of Pru's children. She was very fond of her sister-in-law and the two children, who seemed like her own family.

Grey and Hugh helped Jack Buxton fasten the tapers on the fragrant branches the afternoon before Christmas, while Dorothea and her daughters looked on. Grey said he had heard of the custom in England, but it was not widespread, and they had not introduced it at Enderlin Hall. Stephanie wanted to ask him if his son might not enjoy it. Would Grey admit, then, that he had a son, or a child he acknowledged as his? What a stir it would cause everyone else, too much of a stir for a festive time like Christmas Eve. So she buried the question and soon forgot about it.

Alan was not there when they trimmed the tree. He appeared just before supper, without explanation or apology. More research for his articles, she supposed, but she refused to give him the satisfaction of asking about them. Though he gave no sign he had drunk too much, she smelled liquor on his breath when she passed in front of him to take her place at the supper table.

Besides Alan and Grey, Perry and Pru and her children were the only guests at the Christmas Eve supper. The center of attraction was the Yule cake, flavored with nutmeg, and filled with raisins, currants, and lemon peel. The rest of the light meal consisted of soup, cold meats, biscuits, dried fruit and nuts, out of respect for the prodigious feasting that would come after the church service on Christmas day. Afterward, they retired to the drawing room where the children discovered the tree. Annie danced delightedly about it several times, but Tim was more interested in ferreting out his gifts, hidden in its branches.

When Dorothea announced it was time for blindman's buff, Grey said that he was again reminded of Christmas Eve in England. "But I don't imagine you have mummers, too, do you?" he finished a little wistfully.

"Indeed we do!" Annie replied, her eyes shining. "That's the best part."

"There are some differences between English and American mummers, however," Morton put in. "For instance, instead of St. George, *our* hero is George Washington."

Blindman's buff had barely begun when Jack Buxton announced that the mummers had arrived. Morton went to the front hall to greet them, while everyone else found places in the drawing room. Tim sat on the floor, next to the tree, and Alan sat beside him. Annie found a place next to Stephanie on a settee and bounced up and down in anticipation.

"Really, Annie," Pru said with a frown. "You'll positively ruin Aunt Dorothea's cushions. Now do be still."

Annie tucked her hands under her skirts and held her legs still with an effort, but when the mummers filed in, she gripped Stephanie's arm in excitement.

There were five of them, fantastically dressed. All were masked and ranged from short to tall—the usual collection of neighborhood boys, the sons of laborers and tradesmen. Beelzebub wore a red suit and black boots and sported a beard. The Prince of Egypt was elegant in a gilded coat and paper crown. George Washington, in powdered wig and the buff and blue of the Continental Army, towered over the others. Old Cooney Cracker wore green-and-yellow motley and a ruff about his neck. The Lord of Misrule, wearing medieval doublet and hose, was hidden behind a full papier-mâché mask of laughing wickedness. He seemed to be older, and something about his walk and hand gestures were familiar to Stephanie. But tradition forbade anyone from trying to recognize the true identity of a mummer, so she put it out of her mind during the performance.

They formed a row before their audience, then stepped forward, one by one, to bow and identify themselves with centuries-old verses, the originals all but lost through countless local renditions. When it came to ''Old Cooney Cracker,'' an American invention, the verse lost any reference to the Christmas season that it might have once possessed:

> "Here comes I, old Cooney Cracker.
> I want some money to buy tobacco;
> Tobacco's good; cigars are better;
> Give me some money, or I'll marry your daughter."

At this juncture, the boy in green-and-yellow motley pretended to leap at Annie, who clapped her hands over her mouth and giggled.

After George Washington, in true patriotic style, had informed them about his gun and his good fight against John Bull (Alan and Grey exchanged glances and grinned), the Lord of Misrule waved his scepter and declared a battle between the forces of mischief and the forces of order. Stephanie did not think he made a good Lord of Misrule. He was not very agile, and his arm movements were clumsy. She wondered if he was substituting for someone who was ill.

The battle began. The Prince of Egypt and George Washington, representing order, fought Beelzebub and the Lord of Misrule with wooden swords while Cooney Cracker jumped about and reported the fray in singsong verse. At the end only General Washington remained on his feet to proclaim the victory of joy, love, and peace.

Tim and Annie led the cheers and clapping as the mummers jumped to their feet and marched about the room, doffing their caps and extending them for "a dole, kind sir; a dole, kind lady." Everyone was ready with pennies. Then Mrs. Buxton brought in the huge, fragrant wassail bowl, followed by Sally with roasted apples and poppy-seed cakes, which they placed on a large table that had been installed for the occasion against one wall.

"Our bounty is yours this Christmastide," Morton proclaimed, and the mummers flocked around the table.

Her curiosity rearoused, Stephanie watched to see the Lord of Misrule take off his headdress in order to eat and drink. Now she would find out who he was. But instead of joining the others at the table, he came to stand before her, trapping her in her seat.

She looked up at him with an inquiring smile. "Our bounty is yours," she repeated. "Pray, my lord, partake."

The Lord of Misrule shook his large papier-mâché head from side to side. "I shall not eat food nor drink wine," came a hollow voice from behind the fantastic face, "until you are once more mine. Remember what I say, Miss Stephanie Endicott."

Stephanie started back, one hand going to her mouth. A pair of ravaged eyes peered out through the mask's slits and pierced hers for an instant. Then he turned on his heel and left the room.

"Where's he going? Who was that?" Hugh asked in surprise.

Aunt Pru noticed the shock on Stephanie's face, and went over to her. "What is it? What happened to our Lord of Misrule?"

"I-it was . . . Dick," Stephanie managed. Taking a big breath, she tried to throw off a terrible sense of uneasiness. "He's never shown any interest in mumming before. Why, just a year ago, it would have been beneath his dignity."

"I told you he has gone mad," Pru said, shaking her head. She leaned over and patted Stephanie's shoulder. "Never mind, darling, he's gone now."

In a while, the other mummers left as well. Stephanie doubted anyone else in the family had even noticed the exchange.

CHAPTER
XIV

Snow fell on Christmas Day. In the Endicott house the fires were warm, the candlelight bright, the turkey and plum pudding succulent. Friends and neighbors came and went. Huge quantities of food and drink were consumed, and Stephanie at least paid lip service to joviality, although Alan continued to keep his distance, avoiding her eyes even when both were taking part in games with the others.

The next day the wind picked up, and gray clouds deposited more snow; but the following day the sun returned and it was calm. The weather remained cold, as Clarinda had hoped—perfect for their sleigh ride up the Schuylkill valley to Tulip Hill, where they could ice skate without upsetting Mama.

Dorothea, who believed the only proper place to be when the temperature was below freezing was by the fire, had no intention of participating in such an expedition. Morton was occupied with numerous matters at his office. In their stead, Uncle Perry and Aunt Pru were to act as chaperons to the six unmarried young people. Kate would go with them, as she had done for years. Pru's children were going, too. Tim was especially eager to show off his recently acquired ability to skate "high Dutch," cutting his name in ice and doing figure eights.

The girls donned woolen knickers and two pairs of

stockings under their skirts. On their heads they wore close-fitting bonnets of dark beaver fur, which tied under their chins. Skates and warm clothing were found for Alan and Grey, although both protested they had not been on skates for years and would cut sorry figures. It was nearly noon when they set out in two large sleighs, bells jingling and blankets piled high, to travel west to the Schuylkill and north through the Fairmount area and past the Falls.

Stephanie was both nettled and relieved that Hugh, avoiding Kate, filled his sleigh with Pru and Annie and suggested she get in beside Grey. Everyone assumed it was Grey she wanted to be with. Uncle Perry handed Kate and Clare into the second sleigh, and Tim declared he would sit by no one except Alan, so any crosscurrents that might have erupted were neatly solved. Jack Buxton and his wife had gone up to the farm early to start fires and alert Ned and Emma Nickerson, the couple who lived on the farm year-round, to the imminent invasion. Mrs. Buxton would prepare a hot meal for them when the skating was done.

"Papa bought Tulip Hill the year after he retired from the sea," Stephanie told Grey on the way. "I think it was a kind of peace offering to Mama. But there was a practical reason, too. The only way to avoid yellow fever every summer was to get out of town and go to the country."

"There are still some cases each year," Pru said when Grey expressed dismay. "August and September are the worst. By mid-October, it's safe to go back to town."

"The place has changed a lot, of course," Hugh put in. "It was just an ordinary farmhouse when Papa bought it. Now there are flower gardens, and grape-arbor walks, and promenades and terraces and bridle paths. I'm trying to interest Father in raising racehorses there."

"Don't forget the summer house," Annie put in, her eyes shining. "It's all by itself on a little hill. There's trees all around and you can see the whole valley and the river from there."

"Yes," Pru said dryly. "When we thought you were lost last year, that's where we found you, playing house with your dolls. I thought sure the Indians had stolen you away."

The road climbed and dipped, sometimes giving them a

breath-catching view of the valley. The white-clad country-side was dotted with farm buildings, and wisps of smoke curled up lazily from red-brick chimneys. On their left the river lay silent under its layer of ice and snow. The clear cold air bit their noses and seemed to amplify sound, so that Hugh, on the driver's box, could talk to those sitting behind him without raising his voice or turning around. For a while Grey and Pru dominated the conversation while Stephanie and Hugh grew silent and thoughtful. Hugh gave a clue to his thoughts when he said, "I think you might have managed to arrange this outing without including Kate, Stephanie."

"We always invite Kate. It's an annual affair."

"But this year, if you'd thought to accommodate me . . ."

"Does she pester you?"

"No-o-o, but . . ."

"Then relax and enjoy yourself, brother dear. You'll have to get used to having her around if you go to work in Washington for the senator. Kate's acting as his secretary now, you know."

"Oh, the deuce! Maybe I'll just go back to Princeton this term."

"Surely you don't detest her so much."

"No, but it's damned awkward—beg your pardon, Aunt Pru."

"You'll get used to being with her. You might even fall in love with her," Stephanie said with a little smile. "Or . . . maybe Kate will fall in love with someone else." She indicated the other sleigh, which Uncle Perry had decided to spur on to pass them. Kate and Alan, seated next to each other in the rear, were both laughing heartily. Stephanie felt an unpleasant jab to her middle, as if someone had struck her.

The sensation returned when she saw Alan kneel before Kate, as they sat on the boat dock, and help her tie the frame of the long, curved iron blades tightly onto her boots. She looked down at Grey, who was doing the same for her. His handsome head was bent intently over her boot. Not for the first time, she wondered why she did not love him. It would make everything so much simpler. She had told Alan that knowing the story of Grey's first marriage had not changed the way she thought of him, but that was not quite true. It had made her appreciate him more, for it showed him capable of a great love, one for which he had been willing to sacrifice money and position. On the other hand, she doubted he would ever love anyone quite like that again.

The boating dock, from which they canoed and swam in the summer, was located along the mouth of a little inlet formed by two natural fingers of land that jutted out into the Schuylkill. On a map, the outline of the shore would have looked like the profile of a long, comic nose and a jutting chin, with a short indentation in the space between to show the mouth. Local inhabitants called the projections Lender's Nose and Arnold's Chin. Stephanie had no idea why or when the names had come into use. Just beyond the chin sat Pine Island, named for the single tall pine tree that dominated its northeastern approach. This was the recognized boundary of their private strip of the river. Beyond it the current was swift, and river craft and barges were busy from late February to December.

Jack and Ned had worked hard that morning to shovel a path from the road down to the river, and had cleared snow off the little ice-covered inlet. The children were already on the ice, Tim demonstrating his figure eights to his admiring mother, Uncle Perry guiding Annie on hers until she got her balance. Kate and Alan were skating side by side, not touching. Hugh, who belonged to the Philadelphia Skating Club, was further out, casually showing off his skill at skating backward, and Clare was still on the dock beside Stephanie and Grey. Stephanie caught her sister watching her, but as their glances met, Clare looked away and slid off the dock and onto the ice. She took a few, surefooted strokes toward Hugh.

Grey said, "Well, shall we take a turn, or would you rather go by yourself? I shall probably fall flat in about two seconds."

Stephanie gave him one mittened hand. "Maybe if we skate together, it will be easier for you. Is the ice smooth enough?"

Little by little they grew bolder. Grey did not fall but instead displayed the same grace that dominated all his movements. Stephanie suspected he danced equally well. He told about skating on the Serpentine when he was in London, and on the pond at Enderlin Hall in Bedfordshire. Alan recalled skating as a child along "the backs" of the River Cam, where he had tried to copy the antics of the more skilled university students.

"How about some races?" Tim suggested.

"Where to?" Hugh asked.

Tim looked up and down the inlet. "Well, from Lender's Nose, past the Chin, to the big pine on the island."

"That's quite a long way," Perry said with a frown.

"Too far for Annie or me," Pru declared. "We'll just skate around here."

"I'll check it out and make sure the ice is safe," Hugh said, and dashed off, while Tim carried his idea to the others.

At first it was racing for males only. Then Kate, who was a swift, surefooted skater, challenged Hugh. "I wouldn't dream of taking advantage of you that way," Hugh said. "You'd get all tangled up in your skirts."

"Oh, you men think you're so great," Kate retorted, her eyes flashing. "Don't you think I know how to handle my skirts?"

It was Clare who initiated the idea of a relay race, one man teamed up with one girl to even out whatever advantage the men had. More discussion ensued when it was pointed out they needed a judge to declare the winner, and Annie was too uncertain of her balance to join in. Perry offered to be the judge and stay at the finish line with his niece, and Pru agreed to make up the fourth mixed couple.

"Two opponents go to Pine Island," Clare said, "and be ready to start back when the first opponents touch their partner's shoulders. We'll have two rounds each, two by two. Then the winning team from the first round will race the winning team from the second."

"How confusing," Pru said. "Why don't we just go up to the house and have a nice cup of hot chocolate?"

But no one paid any attention to her. "You choose your partner first," Clare told her aunt.

"Oh, very well," Pru agreed, and chose Hugh.

In the end, Stephanie and Grey, having beaten Clare and Tim in their race, were set against Kate and Alan, who had beaten Hugh and his Aunt Pru by a close margin. Kate and Grey skated to the island to prepare themselves for the dash back to the finishing line, while Stephanie lined up against Alan.

Uncle Perry redrew the starting line with the heel of his skate. Stephanie eyed Alan, who grinned at her. "A fight to the finish," he promised. She tried not to mind the way her heart plopped at his grin.

"All right, children," Uncle Perry called out. "Get ready. One, two, three—go!"

They went. Stephanie moved forward in smooth, easy strokes, having learned from childhood how to control her skirts by holding them tightly against one thigh and away from her other leg. Her feet were numb, and her cheeks felt frosted, but a glow had settled within. At first Alan shot ahead of her, but she saw that he was not really a skillful skater, for he'd never had much practice. It should be easy to pass him. *Girls don't beat boys in games*, came Dorothea's voice from the distant past. *Let the boy win, Stephanie, even if you think you can.*

Not this time, she wouldn't. She bent her tall frame into the wind and concentrated on making each stroke count. As they rounded Arnold's chin, she caught him, sent him a triumphant grin, and sped on.

"Oh, no you don't!" she heard him call. Refusing to look back, she increased her speed, but gradually she heard his breath just behind her.

"Come on, come on, Steph!" Grey shouted in encouragement. She reached him, touched his hand, and rammed into the pile of snow at the foot of the pine tree with such force she fell forward on her hands and knees.

"Too bad, Steph!" Kate sang out, then disappeared as Alan came in just behind her. He landed the same way, within inches of her. Stephanie rose to her knees and righted herself, breathing heavily.

"Oof!" She reached up to wipe away a blob of snow from her forehead. But her mitten was cold and snowy, and only left more on her face.

"Allow me," Alan said. He took off his glove, reached out and brushed away the snow with his bare fingers. She smiled at him in surprise. Suddenly his eyes crinkled with a warmth that startled then frightened her. In a senseless panic, she rose to her feet, called out, "Race you back," and skated off. A few seconds later she heard him close in on her.

She was winded and gasping—and knew it was more from his glance, his touch, than from her exertions. In another moment he caught her arm and whirled her around to face him. She was amazed at the strength that had stopped her forward momentum and turned her, as if she were a doll.

"What's your rush?" he breathed. "Our part of the race is over."

No one else was in sight. She realized then that in her eagerness to escape (from what?), she had lost her sense of direction. Arnold's Chin was just to her left instead of her right, and they couldn't see the finishing line, nor the racers, nor the cheering spectators. Her breath seemed to be choked off by her beating heart. She couldn't talk. She could only face him, wide-eyed.

His gaze softened, turning his whole face tender. The internal blaze he had started in her the week before invaded her. His hand, still bare, went to her forehead, boldly touching the curls that had escaped from her fur bonnet.

They came together gradually, inevitably, like two magnets. By the time his lips touched hers she was oblivious to labored breathing, numb toes, and stinging cheeks. His lips were so warm, so soft, so marvelously sweet, without the harshness that sometimes seemed to be an integral part of him. Gently, yet more and more insistently, as though they were of one mind, their two separate bodies came together. Without knowing how it had happened, she discovered her arms around his neck, her hands touching the hair below his cap. His hold on her was satisfyingly hard, drawing her ever closer, and his hand caressed her back slowly, in a deep circle, as if it wanted to delve through all those layers of mantle, dress, corset, and chemise. But still their lips held, and still she did not want it to end.

But when it did—for the realities of breathlessness and cold descended at last—his arms continued to hold her tightly against him, and his cold cheek pressed against hers. She didn't want to break the magic with words.

"You're not in love with Grey," he said.

"No," she admitted. "I never was."

The world intruded. Shouts echoed on the still air, distant, then closer. "Steph! Alan! Where have you two gotten to? The race is over. Kate and Alan won."

They separated slowly, joined hands, smiled at each other, and skated back to the others.

Did it show? Did her face look like Mary Foster's had under the mistletoe? No one remarked on it. Pru and Perry were anxious to get to the house to get warm. Annie was shivering and Tim, trying a cartwheel, had turned his ankle. They climbed the bank two by two, Perry half-carrying Tim, Alan with a supporting hand at Stephanie's elbow. Mrs. Buxton was awaiting them with hot meat pies, warm muffins, tea, and hot chocolate.

As they ate, they sat before a blazing fire in the oak-paneled study. Stephanie sat beside Alan on a small leather couch, laughing, joking, talking with the others. They did not touch. Right now, it was not necessary. The current that ran between them was disembodied but very real.

Stephanie studied the faces of the others surreptitiously: Hugh paying more than ordinary attention to Tim to avoid Kate, who was talking to Pru but kept glancing his way; Grey, absentminded as usual, smiling vaguely as the rest laughed, occasionally watching Clare with a speculative look (was he remembering Polly, again?); Clare trying not to mind Annie's pestering her to look for her old dolls when they got back to town; Perry recalling earlier times at Tulip Hill to whoever would listen; and she and Alan, behaving as if nothing had happened when, in fact, her world had changed forever. Even more than on the night she had acknowledged to herself that she loved this man, she realized she would never be the same again.

CHAPTER
XV

Alan spent much of the next three days away from the Endicott house. When pressed, he confessed to "snooping around" Philadelphia, talking to everyone, from immigrant German grocers to wealthy Quaker merchants, from the unemployed who waited around the Delaware docks or the marketplace for work to the doctors at the Pennsylvania Hospital. More than once he returned to Mordecai Lewis's Printing Shop and Bookstore, observed the process of typesetting, and got into long discussions with the owner on books, politics, and the general state of humanity.

He also told them he had attended a meeting of the Society of Free People of Color with a minister of the African Methodist Episcopal Church, and had spoken with the black owner of a sail loft, who used his money to buy freedom for other black people.

Dorothea said nothing when Alan's place at the supper table remained empty, but she could not be quiet about his forays into the black neighborhood. These she saw as somehow reflecting negatively on her own hospitality. She was much more tolerant of Hugh's invitation to Grey to attend a horserace at the Germantown track and, afterward, have supper with him at Richmond Point Hotel where he met friends whose talk was dominated by fishing and fox hunting. Only Stephanie knew why Grey returned from that outing sad-eyed and more absentminded than ever. Clarinda, finding that her witticisms failed to make Grey laugh, said melancholia was one thing, but the poor man was absolutely hopeless.

No matter how occupied she was, Stephanie found herself living for encounters with Alan. They were always brief, usually unexpected, and nearly always disappointing. Each time she sought some sign from him that the intimate moment on the frozen river had meant something special to him. Each time she was completely deflated. Did he take advantage of every girl who struck his fancy? The only indication that he now regarded her with any special favor was an offhand request, the morning after their trip to Tulip Hill, to escort her to the New Year's ball he understood they were attending. Then he asked her help in planning a costume, and she wondered if he had invited her only for that purpose.

Dorothea was surprised and concerned at the way they had paired off for the ball. "Is it true that Lord Talbot is escorting Clare to the New Year's Eve ball, and you're going in the company of Mr. Dunstable?"

"Yes," Stephanie replied, her eyes on the final stitches she was making in her pillow cover.

"I must say I don't understand your purpose."

Stephanie looked up. "Don't be alarmed, Mama. We're all really going together, so it doesn't matter, does it? I'm sure I'll dance as much with Grey as anyone else."

"I do hope Clare isn't falling in love with him."

"Clare? Oh, surely not. But . . . come to think of it, why would you object?"

"To have both of you interested in the same man?"

"But, Mama, we're not."

The ball was a Philadelphia Event. Everyone was talking about how Joseph Bonaparte, brother of the exiled Napoleon and ex-King of Spain, who had lived in Philadelphia for nearly five years, was giving a New Year's Eve costume ball, the largest of the season. Even people who sent their regrets—either because New Year's Eve fell on a Sunday and they considered dancing on the Sabbath a desecration, or because they were uneasy about such an obviously Gallic affair as a costume ball—discussed it. Whether they were excited, censorious, or just plain curious, all who received an invitation made sure their neighbors knew about it.

Morton had met Monsieur Bonaparte and rather liked him but was surprised to receive an invitation for his whole family. He did not seem to mind when Alan teased him about democratic America's taste for deposed European royalty.

As they left for the ball, Stephanie intended to match Alan's apparent indifference of the past few days by being cool and distant, and by dancing with a great many other men. But then Alan, sitting beside her in the secret dark of the carriage, opposite her parents, reached for her gloved hand. She allowed it to rest in his and was completely undone.

The four-storied, white stone Dunlap house, which the ex-King had leased, was one of the most imposing in the city, its grounds taking up nearly the whole square from Market to Chestnut, and from Eleventh to Twelfth Streets. The Endicott party arrived about nine o'clock in two carriages driven by Harry and Jack. Even without the livery worn by the coachmen of more pretentious families, they were stiff and proper enough to please even Dorothea, who had brought back from England some decided views on the proper conduct of servants that were sometimes difficult to put in practice.

The carriages turned off the street up a drive that led to a covered entrance on the side of the house. A length of carpet had been unrolled over the snow to prevent the ladies' delicate dancing slippers from becoming ruined, and lanterns lit their way.

Alan helped Stephanie alight and briefly enveloped each velvet-cloaked shoulder with a gentle, caressing hand. Chills shot through her. She glanced up at him but could not see his face in the night shadows. She walked slightly ahead of him, careful of the hoop of her Watteau gown, a copy of one her great-great-great grandmother had worn one hundred years ago. She wore ivory satin and gold lace over two quilted petticoats and a hoop near its hem to hold the skirt out. The back was fashioned in a long wide pleat of satin brocade from low neck to floor, the front shaped by sewed-in whalebone that pushed her bosom high. On her hair, which floated long and free down her back, sat a close-fitting lawn cap, trimmed with gold lace.

Alan was a highwayman, complete with high black riding boots, red cape, open-necked white shirt, wide-brimmed hat, and an old dueling pistol in his belt. With his weathered complexion and black curls, he looked the part completely, but she hadn't told him that.

"Aha, you're an Englishman," Joseph Napoleon said, greeting Alan. "I perceive it, by your speech." His eyes twinkled as if he also perceived some huge joke but could not divulge what it was. The joke, perhaps, was on him, for entertaining countrymen who had been his brother's deadly foes for so many years.

The ballroom at the top of a wide polished staircase was lavishly decorated with potted palms and bouquets of fra-grant hothouse flowers. An orchestra of six pieces was tuning up in the corner. Long mirrors on two of the opposing walls reflected the candlelight and crowd back to each other and created a dizzying infinity of rooms. Indian warriors, Roman emperors, Turkish harem brides, Arcadian shepherdesses—all were reproduced as far as one could see.

"May I have the first dance?" Alan whispered as they left the receiving line. His head was very close to hers, his breath in her ear. She nodded, unable to speak, while the fireworks he had set in motion shot through her.

During the Scottish reel, as they met and skipped in line with five other couples, bowed or curtseyed and joined hands, she was constantly aware of his eyes on her. When he took her arm for the allemande, she could not refrain from a piercing, questioning look. His intense brown eyes smiled back with a promise and a challenge that took her breath away. But when the dance ended, he only bowed and took her to Grey, her next partner.

This dance was a waltz. Grey, in a curled black wig and false mustache, lace at his throat and wrists as Charles II, waltzed beautifully but with a distracted air, looking over her shoulder into the crowd of dancers in a way that did not encourage conversation. He had seemed cool to the idea of the ball all week. Stephanie supposed he had probably attended many such events with his wife and was plagued with bittersweet memories.

"I—hope we aren't too dull for you," she said at last.

He looked back at her, his blue eyes startled out of their glaze. "Oh—forgive me, Stephanie. I was only . . ."

"Remembering?" she suggested softly.

"Yes. A bad habit."

"A sad time of year for you."

"I suppose it always will be. But the kindness of your family has helped a great deal." He was looking at her with his full attention now. "May I ask you something . . . rather personal?"

"I—I suppose you may."

"About Alan . . ."

"Not fair," she broke in, nearly missing a step in the waltz.

He didn't take her hint. "Do you remember something I said aboard ship?"

She glanced at him and didn't try to hide the pain in her eyes. "I think of it constantly."

"I've thought I ought to . . . make it even stronger. I've grown to like Alan very much. There's more to him than I once believed. But I cannot ignore the fact that he has broken more than one lady's heart in the past. I doubt yours is exempt."

His blue eyes were kind and sympathetic. *Oh, why,* she wanted to cry out, *couldn't it be you?*

"Does he think a-a wife would hamper his work?" she asked after a moment.

"I don't know. We've never discussed it."

The dance ended. He drew away from her and bowed. She could not pursue the conversation once he had returned her to her mother.

Between dances she was surrounded. Several gentlemen from Europe clamored to meet and dance with her. Friends wanted to meet and greet the English visitors, but only Grey seemed available. Clarinda, in flowing pink gown and gauze veil, a crown of flowers fashioned from her greenhouse, was Shakespeare's Titania, and surrounded by admirers. Hugh,

in a Revolutonary War uniform that had been Grandfather
Fletcher's, seemed enamored of a blond young miss she
didn't know. Kate came late with her father. When Stephanie
saw her, she was talking to Alan.

At the beginning, while he pretended to talk with Hugh,
Alan watched Stephanie waltz with Grey. Grey's right hand
was about her slim satin waist, his left held her ivory-gloved
hand, her rich brown locks catching gold light from the
glittering chandeliers. Had he been dancing with her, he
could not have refrained from stroking it. Her contact with
Grey was continuous during the dance. They could talk in
more than the disconnected sentences one might manage
during a reel. Alan envied Grey for this, as well as for other
things. Grey was an elegant dancer, tall and slim, with
natural grace. Alan himself was never quite sure if he were
keeping a steady rhythm with his feet. His was a different
sort of agility—a clumsy, oafish kind, he thought now, not
fit for polite society. Grey was the privileged one, the titled
one, the one with money. He was the preferred suitor and
Stephanie liked him. But, Alan knew now, she did not love
him, and that was really all that mattered.

All he need do to have her was say the word. She would
fall into his arms like a ripe plum into the harvester's hand.
All week he had been on the verge of some overt move,
then had drawn back. Evenings when she entered the music
room to sing for company, she would hesitate under the
mistletoe and look at him. When he had encountered her in
the upstairs hall the morning after the ice skating party—she
en negligee, with her hair clouding her shoulders—her
questioning green eyes had forced him to ask if he might
escort her to the ball. Her disappointment had been obvious,
later in the day, when she had invited him to accompany her
to the book seller's and he had mumbled something about
an interview he had set up.

She was his, so far as she herself was concerned, and yet
he had not acted. It was very unlike him.

Asking to be her escort had been a mistake. Asking her to
dance, if only holding her hands, had already created a nearly
irresistible temptation for him. He did not dare ask for a

waltz. Only during the cotillion would he again be her partner.

By now Hugh had deserted him for a young miss with blond curls and laughing, coquettish ways. The music changed twice, but he made no attempt to find a new dancing partner. Instead, he drank punch, walked around the periphery of the ballroom, and engaged in desultory conversation with unattached males like himself. Two were friends of Hugh's that he had met the previous week at the tavern. Like Alan they seemed more interested in watching than dancing.

"We're planning a private card party for Tuesday next, Mr. Dunstable, if you care for that sort of thing," Henry Wood said cordially.

"Naturally, since all gambling is illegal in this fair city, it's word of mouth only," Ted Groton cautioned him. "Your friend, Lord Talbot, told me he gambled a lot in London."

"Yes, he did at one time," Alan said. "I'm much obliged, but we are leaving Tuesday for Pittsburgh." He did not add that he had always preferred spending what little money he had at places other than gaming tables.

His eyes searched the ballroom floor and he finally sorted out the mirrored maze of dancers to find Stephanie again. She had a new partner, another tall man. At times he detested tall men. Whenever he stood beside Stephanie he was aware that her eyes were nearly on a level with his and privately cursed the wisdom that had ordained that men should always tower over their female partners. But what the devil! He had worse problems than that.

He looked briefly toward the large double doors through which they had entered the ballroom. Kate Hamlin stood there on her father's arm.

"If you will excuse me, gentlemen," Alan said, bowing. He made his way toward her. Kate smiled and waved before he reached them. The senator, his bushy hair tucked under a powdered wig, gave him a warm handshake and complimented him on his costume.

"To tell the truth, it's my real nature," Alan said with a laugh. "Would you condescend, Miss Hamlin, to be captured by a highwayman for the length of a dance?"

Her blue eyes searched his face frankly. He realized she was probably taller than he, even without her Maid Marian peaked hat and veil. She smiled, however, and said, "I should like that, Mr. Dunstable." She gazed out over the crowd. "How gaudy it all is, compared to our staid Philadelphia cotillions. I had no idea this room was so large. Oh, I see, it's the mirrors, isn't it?"

"A veritable maze," Alan agreed. "And a trifle dizzying until you get used to it. Perhaps Monsieur Bonaparte wants us to believe all of Philadelphia is here."

"Since you're in good hands, my dear, I see someone I need to speak with," her father said.

"Of course, Papa," Kate said. As the senator left them, she added, "I doubt he ever thinks of anything but politics. Will you be visiting us in Washington later in January?"

"I'm counting on it," Alan said. "But I'm going south first. I probably shan't be in Washington until they count the election ballots."

"Oh, that will be fairly dull—a formality only."

"The process interests me, nevertheless. By the way, do you know who is dancing with Miss Endicott?"

"Which Miss Endicott do you mean, Mr. Dunstable?" Her smile was sarcastic. She knew he used Stephanie's first name now.

"Stephanie," he said flatly, frowning.

"Where?"

"Over there, near that door."

"Oh, let's see . . . the man in harlequin dress?"

"Yes."

"I believe . . . why, it's Dick Harlow!"

"The one she was betrothed to?"

"Why, yes. How odd. He hasn't attended a ball or party since . . ." She dropped her sentence reflectively.

He watched them through narrowed eyes but had difficulty, in the crowd, following their movements. "Would you mind very much if we danced their way?"

"Very well," she agreed. "It's a waltz, so we can begin anytime. Do you think there is something wrong?"

He told her, as they began to dance, about the incident of the mummers on Christmas Eve. "She doesn't know I overheard her talk about it to her aunt. Mrs. Sanford thinks Harlow is mad.''

"Perhaps he is only recovered from his unhappiness.''

"Why should he be dancing with the one who caused it, then?''

"Why should he not? My, Mr. Dunstable, you seem positively proprietary toward Steph.''

He was, of course, but he did not bother to explain himself. With a good deal of maneuvering, he danced Kate to within good viewing distance of Stephanie and Harlow. They were scarcely dancing; rather, they were arguing vehemently, and Stephanie's expression was angry. He wanted to break in on them.

"I think you should leave them alone,'' Kate cautioned. "Stephanie can handle him.''

"How the devil did you know I . . .''

"It's all over your face that you want to interfere, my friend. But she might not welcome you. After all, this is between the two of them, and she's the one who must convince him his suit is hopeless.''

"You're right, of course.'' He turned them so he no longer saw Stephanie and Harlow. "You don't think he might be dangerous? Mrs. Sanford said . . .''

Kate laughed. "Dick Harlow dangerous? He's the mildest of creatures. That may have been the problem.''

"Why did Stephanie break the engagement?''

Kate looked after them thoughtfully for a moment. "She realized she didn't love him.'' After another silence she added, "No, that's not quite right. She had never loved him. She just believed he would do. Her mother kept after her to find—to accept—*someone*. But I think she had some experience—I don't know what—that decided her that—that love was too important; she mustn't settle for less.''

She gazed at him steadfastly, like a seeress about to predict his future. "I think now she's glad she waited.''

Alan stared back at her. Then he shook his head. "I believe I know what you have in mind, Miss Hamlin. But the whole idea is quite preposterous.''

The waltz ended, and he delivered Kate to Grey before he tried to look for Stephanie again. A cotillion was

announced. The whole company was expected to pair off
and participate. Surely he might be allowed, by his conscience as well as by any rules of decorum Mrs. Endicott
might have in mind, to return to Stephanie.

But he could not find her.

The mirrors made it difficult, but as people lined up, two
by two, for the sedate French promenade, he was able to
size up the company and conclude that Stephanie was not
among them. Neither was a tall man in a harlequin's suit.
Despite Kate's reassurance, an alarm bell sounded in Alan's
head.

He cornered a footman standing motionless by the ornate
double doors.

"Have a young lady with long brown hair, dressed in
cream satin, and a man dressed as a harlequin, come this
way?"

The servant assured him they had not, and suggested he
inspect the two anterooms leading off the ballroom, where
games of whist were in progress and the buffet had been
spread.

"Are there any more exits?" Alan demanded.

One stairway, the servant said, at the rear of the room
with the buffet. It led to the servant's hall and kitchen
below. But no lady or gentleman would go down there.

"Thank you," Alan said and turned on his heel.

The card room was empty. The buffet lay invitingly on a
long table—a center fountain with champagne, pickled or
smoked meats and little biscuits, nuts and fruit and cheese,
and a vast array of confections piled in artistic mounds on
silver platters. But the buffet, too, was deserted, save for
two liveried waiters who eyed him inquiringly.

Ignoring them, he opened the little door in the rear of the
room and clattered down the narrow stairs, his right hand
going unconsciously to the long-nosed dueling pistol at his
belt, a part of his costume. Not loaded, of course, and
totally useless except, perhaps, as a threat.

At the foot of the stairs, the narrow corridor was intersected
by two doors, to right and left. At the end, another door
probably led to the back of the house. The corridor was

empty, and Alan began to think he was on a fool's errand when he heard a scream.

He plunged down the hall and through the end door, which was slightly ajar. Off the few steps that led from a stone stoop, two dark figures—one tall and lean, the other in wide skirt—were locked in silent struggle.

Alan had never tackled anyone since his rugby days at public school, but he did so now, unmindful of his cape or the pistol in his belt. The descent of three steps gave his leap unusual impetus. He landed on Dick's back and both of them fell to the ground. Despite the unexpected attack, Dick struggled at once to get away. Alan dealt a blow to the back of his head and he dropped limply on his face.

Breathing hard, Alan crawled off the prone figure and rose to his feet. He was conscious of a bruised knee and elbow. "Oh, Alan!" Stephanie cried out.

She ran to him as light flickered from the open door. An anxious voice called out, "What's goin' on out there?"

She laid eager hands on his arm. He saw, by the newly escaped light from the doorway, that her hair lay in long disheveled strands about her shoulders, and the lace-trimmed cap was missing. Her eyes and cheeks glistened with tears.

Laying a hand over hers, he called out, "Nothing! A fellow just fell on the ice."

There *was* ice—and Stephanie was shivering beside him. He put an arm around her shoulders and drew her close. "Dick . . ." she whispered.

Alan looked down at the still figure at his feet. He had thought him unconscious, but as a servant hurried down the steps, holding a lantern aloft, Harlow turned over and raised himself on one elbow. He glared malignantly at Stephanie and Alan. "You damned Englishman," he breathed.

Alan turned to the servant. "Perhaps you can get some help for this gentleman," he suggested. "I hope he hasn't broken any bones. I'll tend to the lady."

She moved eagerly with him up the stairs and into the house. A housemaid, forehead sweating under her mobcap, appeared from the steaming, brilliantly lit kitchen and said, "D'you need help, ma'am? Are you hurt?"

"A place for the lady to sit down," Alan suggested.

"No, I don't want to s-sit down," Stephanie said, "I-I'm all r-right." Her voice wobbled. She closed her eyes and drew a shuddering sigh, then looked behind them toward the still-open door. "Don't let him see me again, Alan, I pray you. Just . . . take me home."

CHAPTER
XVI

Alan and Stephanie sat side by side on a padded bench in the cool, dimly lit foyer of Mr. Bonaparte's house. Stephanie was still shivering from her ordeal, and was grateful for Alan's arm on her shoulders. She felt as if they had sat there forever, but it was only a few minutes before Morton, summoned by a servant, came running down the wide, mahogany-banistered stair, the servant following with her hooded cape and fur muff.

She flung herself into her father's arms, and the tears started again. Morton patted her back. "There, there, Princess, what is all this?" He looked over her shoulder at Alan, who had risen as he arrived.

"Apparently . . ." Alan began.

Stephanie raised her head and burst out, "D-Dick Harlow tried to kidnap me!"

"Kidnap you!" Morton's scowl was fierce. "Dick Harlow?" Clearly, he could not believe his ears.

She back away. "He did, he did! Ask Alan—he caught him just in time. He had dragged me down the back stairs and out into the yard. We—we were at the buffet table, drinking punch, and he asked me to come to look at something out the window, by the rear door." She sniffed and felt the tears coming again. Morton, now listening in concern, automatically felt for his handkerchief, but because he was wearing his father's old sea captain outfit, could not find it immediately.

"Dratted costume," he muttered, then found the deep coat pocket and handed her his big linen cloth.

"Everyone was getting ready for the cotillion." She blew her nose. Somehow the homely action helped calm her. "Even the servants were gone, and there wasn't a soul in the room. I told him we should get in line. He said, 'Come look at this first.' I didn't know what he was talking about—he was acting strange, excited...I don't know. While we danced, he had talked about our being engaged again, as if it were a year ago and nothing had happened. I couldn't seem to make him understand...."

The tears started again. She blotted them away with the handkerchief and sank back on the settle. "I—I want to go home, Papa."

"Of course you do, darlin'. I'll have a servant go for the carriage right away. Otherwise it wouldn't be back for another hour."

"No, let me just go. I'll walk. It's only two streets away. I'm afraid he'll come back and see me..."

Morton turned and looked down the long corridor that led to the rear of the house. "I don't see a soul, my dear."

"He'll come back," she insisted. "He—I went to the door, the window, like he wanted, and he—he grabbed me and stuffed his handkerchief in my mouth—I think it was his handkerchief—and twisted my arms behind me and made me go down those stairs..." She hid her head in her hands, remembering the nasty sensation of cloth invading her mouth, the desperate strength with which Dick forced her to do his bidding, the pain in her arm.

Alan, taking the cloak from the servant, laid it over her shoulder. Its soft warmth soothed her. She looked up at them. "I just want to go home, now."

"I'll take her, sir," Alan offered. "Just let me get my carrick." He left them before she or her father could respond.

"I'll tell your mother you're going," Morton began.

"No, no, don't tell Mama, don't tell anyone."

He looked perplexed. "Now, Stephanie, darling..."

"Why spoil their evening?" she asked. She took a deep breath, trying to subdue the panic, the irrational panic that insisted she must run, run from this house . . .

"You can't walk in this weather, my dear. You need stout boots. Perhaps our host has a carriage . . ."

"No, no, it will all take too long!" The panic surfaced again. She jumped to her feet, fumbling with the jeweled clasp of her cape. "I'm going! I'll go alone if you won't . . ."

As she spoke, Alan returned, throwing on his big caped coat. He seemed to take in her state of mind in a glance. "Don't worry, sir, I'll see her safely home."

Morton looked from Stephanie to Alan and scratched his head, knocking his wig askew. "Very well, then, have it your way. My thanks, Alan."

The servant, seeing everything was settled, hurried to open the door. Stephanie hugged her father briefly. "Just tell Mama I—wasn't feeling well. Only that."

"Very well," Morton agreed. Relieved, she hurried out the door and was halfway to the street before Alan caught up with her.

"I say," he called softly, "can't you wait for an old man?" She turned and reached for his arm. "It's cold."

"We'll fly," he promised her.

The way was treacherous with ice, and her satin dancing slippers were useless to keep the chill from numbing her feet. The shadows, despite an occasional street lamp, suggested frightening precipices beyond each step. She clung to Alan's arm, still caught in the terror of her struggle with Dick.

"Why would he do such a thing, why?" she muttered, breathing hard as she walked her fastest. Her legs were long, and she had no trouble keeping up with Alan, but the swaying hoop that held the hem of her skirts out stiffly was a hindrance. It seemed to catch the wind, and the cold air went right up her legs. The velvet cloak, despite its fur trim, was not much use either. She began to realize how irrational her flight was. Dick Harlow couldn't have hurt her or threatened her further once her father and Alan were there.

She gave him a glance full of gratitude and unabashed love. He caught it and pressed her closer to his side, covering her hand with his.

"Are you all right?"

"My feet are freezing, but—yes."

"I can solve that."

"How?"

He stopped her and, without warning, picked her up in his arms, cloak, hooped skirt, and all.

"Alan! You can't . . . !"

"Sshh! Put your arms around my neck—that will make it easier."

"Put me down. I'm too heavy."

"You're light as a feather," he insisted, and walked even more rapidly to prove it.

After a moment she settled into his arms, feeling very foolish, yet light-headed with joy. Her feet hung free. Though they still stung with cold, they no longer seemed to have daggers of ice piercing them.

"I shall die of embarrassment if a watchman comes by," she said, her voice muffled against his shoulder.

"No one will come by," he promised her.

And though they passed houses where lights shone through the shutters and an occasional dog barked at them, no one saw them. They turned in at the service gate, and he put her down carefully, as if she were Dresden china. She took his hand and led him through the dark yard to the rear door, which was rarely locked. It wasn't now.

The warmth of the hall next to the kitchen enveloped them. Alan closed the door behind him as softly as possible, but it still squeaked and clicked. She could hear his breathing in the dark but could not see his face. She groped for the wall. "This way," she whispered, hoping no one would hear.

The door from the pantry and kitchen opened, and Mrs. Buxton appeared in nightcap and slippers. The candle she held outlined her portly frame and intensified the alarm in her face. "Who's there?" she called out in a formidable voice.

Stephanie laughed in relief. "Only I, Mrs. Buxton, with Mr. Dunstable. We returned early." The nightmare had evaporated in Alan's arms and now, back in her own home, she felt secure once more.

Mrs. Buxton's eyes went wide, and her round, chubby cheeks quivered in surprise. "Miss Stephanie! And Mr. Dunstable! Jack hasn't even got the carriage out yet, to pick you folks up."

"He can still go for the others. You see, we came . . ." She came to a complete stop, not knowing how to explain.

"Miss Endicott suffered an unhappy experience and wanted to come home, so we walked," Alan said. "We're cold but unharmed. May we have something hot to drink?"

"For sure ye may. You go on to the parlor. Elsa was there only a few minutes ago, puttin' more coals on the fire. I'll bring you some tea, straight off."

Mrs. Buxton disappeared, and they moved down the corridor to the parlor, which beckoned them with rays of light from its open door. In the room, a single lamp burned on a table before the blue velvet draperies, which were closed against the cold. Alan discarded his caped carrick, hat, and pistol, pulled Morton's big wing chair closer to the fire and beckoned to her. She pushed back her hood but drew the velvet cloak closer about her neck and shivered as she sat down. He picked up the footstool and set it next to the fender, then knelt and began to untie one of her satin dancing slippers.

Startled and embarrassed, she withdrew her foot. "Oh! You needn't."

He looked at her, his hands warm on her other ankle. "Do allow me," he said, his voice low and unusually husky. "If I rub them, they'll get warm more quickly." His eyes were solemn and filled with little lights. She nodded assent. As he returned to his task, her heart went into her throat and began to flutter violently. He removed both slippers, brought each stockinged foot onto the footstool toward the fire, and began rubbing them both with his large, capable hands.

She allowed his ministrations without a word. Embarrassment gradually changed to a warm glow that spread through her whole being. When Mrs. Buxton entered with the tea tray, Stephanie did not care that the housekeeper saw what he was doing.

Mrs. Buxton only said, "Well, I'll set it here," as she placed the tray, with its earthenware pot and two cups, on the tea table by the sofa. Stephanie thought she averted her eyes from them. "Anything else?"

They assured her in unison that there was nothing else, and she left. Alan resumed his massaging, and now she didn't want him to stop. The idea of drinking tea had become an intrusion. The warmth from his hands was creating a steady throbbing in her groin. His big hat lay discarded on the floor a few feet away, and the firelight cast silver lights into his black curls. They grew down the back of his neck in a most endearing fashion.

She reached out tentatively but didn't quite dare to touch him. He kept on massaging her feet, one after the other, not looking up.

"Alan, I . . . I love you."

His hands—his whole body—went still. He did not look up nor answer. Then he resumed his massaging. She drew back her hand, pulled her feet away and planted them on the rug before her. "Oh, Alan, what am I to do with you? I said I *love* you."

He looked up, leaning his arms across one raised knee. "I know." His eyes delved into her, and his straight stern lips trembled slightly.

"You know, you know! Then why don't you do something about it?" Distraction gave an angry edge to her voice. She stretched out her hands to him impulsively. He took them with a kind of fatalistic reluctance and rose to his feet, his gaze still on her. She searched those warm, brown sunshine eyes, and saw in them all she had ever seen and dreamed about—from across a crowded ballroom in London, in the ladies' cabin of *The Good News*, as he greeted her in her own front hall for the first time. . . .

"And I know you love me," she said. "You do, don't you?"

The silence seemed endless. "Yes," he said. "My God, yes I do." He pulled her up, into his arms. She closed her eyes as he met her waiting lips with his.

And now he kissed her as though he would never let her go, with a hunger that matched her own. The strange, exciting glow inside her mounted higher and higher, and she let it take her where it would. Her whole body rejoiced in the pressure of his arms, forcing her ever closer to him. Her fingers explored his hair, the back of his neck, his earlobes, his cheeks. She wanted, somehow, to be engulfed by him.

His hands had found their way under the velvet cloak and reached to caress the bare skin above her low-necked gown in back. Then his mouth left her lips to travel over her face, her cheeks and eyes and forehead, and then downward, to her neck and the soft, cool hollow of her throat.

She was drowning in sensation, eyes closed, head back, when he broke her hold roughly and pushed her back into the chair. "No, Stephanie, no!" He kicked the little footstool out of the way and strode to the window.

"Alan!" she cried out in shock.

Silence settled, broken only by the crackle of flames in the fireplace.

"Why not? What's the matter?" she whispered.

"I'm not the man for you. I never was. Ask your mother. Ask anyone."

"Can't I be the one to decide that?"

"No!" He whirled around, returned to her, restored the footstool to its proper position and sat on it, at her feet. "I never meant to fall in love with you."

"Nor I with you. But it happened."

"You were supposed to love Grey."

She stared at him in angry amazement. "Supposed to! What does that mean? Did you—are you involved in that— that *plot*? Oh, Alan!"

She began to laugh. Once she had started, she could not seem to stop. The irony of it was so rich, so marvelous. She had suspected a plot all along, but she had never dreamed it was Alan Dunstable's plot.

"Stop it," he said in a harsh whisper. But she did not, for she could not. She was helpless with an angry, despairing laughter. Tears began to roll down her cheeks. He stood up and grabbed her hands. "Damme, Stephanie, leave off!"

The oath and his harsh voice brought her to her senses. She looked up at him, gulped down a sob, and was silent.

His stern face turned tender. He sank to the stool, still holding her hands. "Hear me out, Stephanie. We need to be reasonable."

She stared back at him, wanting to laugh again at such a word. But instead she waited for his reasons, his logic for the contradictory behavior that had so plagued her.

"I . . . Lady Burleigh and I are old friends," he began. "She—how can I tell you this? She was concerned for Grey, for his extreme melancholy. She learned that I was going to America, so she approached me with this idea. She had met you and believed you would be ideal for him. There wasn't time for the normal courtship; you were leaving too soon for that. She hoped that if you and Grey had a chance to get really well acquainted—if you two were aboard the same ship for a month . . ."

He stopped, halted by the scorn in her eyes. "Yes, it was a foolish idea," he agreed. "I had no intention of going along with her at first. Then I heard you sing, saw you, at the Rushes' . . ."

"And agreed with her, then and there, that I'd be perfect for Grey." Sarcasm nearly choked her.

He dropped her hands and rose again, turning away. "That's what I told myself. I think now that I . . . wanted to sail on that ship with you myself." He whirled around to face her. "I've been at war with myself for months."

"But what is the battle about?" Stephanie cried out in bewilderment. "You know by now I don't love Grey, and he doesn't love me. It won't destroy him if you and I . . ."

"I took money from Lady Burleigh . . ."

"You promised her a happy ending, is that it?" Stephanie narrowed her eyes, trying to rein her emotions into the reasonableness he asked of her.

"No, I knew I dare not promise anything like that."

"Then what is it?" she cried out. "You kiss me—and then you ignore me. You're kind and thoughtful—and then you're cold. Don't you see you've been tearing me apart? I can't bear it any longer. Now you say you love me, but for some reason I can't fathom, we must not allow it. Why not?"

"I told you . . ."

"That's no reason at all. It's simply an excuse."

He shrugged, turned away, picked up the fireplace poker

and, for want of something better to do, moved some coals about.

"Are you secretly married?" Stephanie asked in a low voice.

"Certainly not."

"You—you think my way of life has been too different from yours? That I would be unable to adjust to being a journalist's wife? Or have you, perhaps, decided never to marry?"

He stood erect again, replacing the poker in its stand. "I'll admit to that," he said. "Everyone will say we're not suited." He turned back to her. "You were brought up to marry—what would an American say? Not an aristocrat, exactly, but a—a patrician."

"My grandfather, Josiah Endicott, started out as a common seaman. My father, although I believe him to be a *true* gentleman, hasn't the polished manners of a patrician, surely you've seen that. My mother taught me to be a lady. But I've always *felt* . . . more in touch with my father."

He allowed a smile to play on his lips. "You're offering me hope."

"I'm offering *us* hope. I'm . . ." She hesitated, remembering Kate's advice, then went ahead and said it anyway. "I'm offering you myself. To—to have . . . in any way you want."

He stared back at her. "Not so long ago, I might have accepted such an offer. Without reservations, without a word to you of marriage."

"Any way you want," she repeated, her chin going up defiantly.

"I will not shame you."

"Then . . . ?"

The room grew very quiet again. A flush started in her cheeks. She was pushing him for a proposal. She hadn't intended to, but it was happening. The shameless hussy and the reluctant bridegroom . . .

Stephanie lowered her head and covered her burning cheeks with both hands, then looked straight at him again. "You seemed to admire Grey's and Polly's marriage, their love for each other. They were worlds apart, too," she said.

"That was different. He was the one with position, with money."

"It doesn't matter." She shook her head, facing his gaze candidly, a brave smile on her face. "Oh, my darling, it really does not matter."

Another silence. Alan took a step toward her slowly. She rose and met him. He placed his hands on her bare shoulders and caressed the flesh of her neck and throat, as though testing whether what she said was true and he was, indeed, allowed such liberties. She covered both his hands with hers in a solemn invitation, her lips parted. He leaned forward and touched her lips lightly with his, then laid his cheek hard against hers. She felt his heart beat against her own, and the strong yearning blazed up within her and she knew she would go wherever he wanted to take her.

Somewhere, in the back of her mind, a door opened and footsteps sounded, but she ignored them, caught up in the message of her senses. But then Alan backed away, and she saw his mood had changed. At the same time she became aware of someone in the doorway, and looked up.

Grey stood there, an unreadable expression on his face. No one said a word for what seemed an age. Grey looked from one to the other, then at the tea things, untouched, the tea growing cold in its pot. His jaw hardened in a way Stephanie had never seen before.

"We're all home now," he said at last. "The ladies will be coming in directly—and your father, Stephanie."

His glance at her was reproachful. Then he turned on his heel and disappeared, even as Sally hurried by in the hall with a lamp for the front entry table. They heard the big door open again, this time with the sound of accompanying voices. She turned toward Alan. His hand returned to her shoulder.

"We must talk about this before you say anything to your parents."

"Must we?"

He smiled and kissed her quickly on the forehead. "You look neither sick nor the victim of a terrible experience. How do you expect to explain that to your mother?"

"I'm sure I don't know."

But Dorothea didn't even notice Stephanie's radiance as she burst into the room. "My poor baby!" she cried, as she gathered her tall daughter in her arms. It was clear that Morton had told her everything.

New Year's Day was filled, as always, with feasting and visiting. The Endicotts were receiving, and a steady flow of visitors came all afternoon. They warmed themselves before the drawing room fire, ate cheese and smoked oysters and lobster pâté with biscuits, and drank hot apple cider, ale, or mulled wine. They chatted for a half hour or so, and then went out to their waiting carriages to be driven to the next house. Morton's special friends settled in for games of whist in the library, and the young people who knew Clare, Stephanie, and Hugh drifted into the drawing room where the pianoforte had been moved. Clare and Uncle Perry took turns playing one old favorite after another, and Stephanie and Grey led everyone in singing along.

And all the time everyone thought she was being unusually charming and witty, Stephanie's mind was crying, *No time, no time! He's leaving tomorrow, and still he hasn't spoken.*

She longed to tell someone—even her mother—but Alan had asked her to wait, and so she waited, feeding on the inadequate diet of his long-distance smiles and the warmth of his occasional glances.

Dorothea was full of Stephanie's terrible ordeal of the night before. She must endure endless commiserations concerning it, and everyone's horrified speculations about Dick Harlow's mental state. My, how grateful they all were to Mr. Dunstable for intervening, Dorothea exclaimed wholeheartedly. It would have been an ideal time to announce their engagement, Stephanie thought. Her mother could hardly have objected while overwhelmed with such gratitude. But Alan had not proposed, after all.

No one knew what had become of Dick Harlow. According to the servants Morton had spoken to after Stephanie and Alan left the house, he had spurned offers of help, declared he was unharmed, rose and dusted the snow off his costume, and stomped off into the night without explanation. Stephanie, shivering, said, "He wasn't very warmly

dressed in that costume." But everyone reminded her that
he lived on Tenth and Walnut, even closer to the Bonaparte
residence than she. He had probably gone home and locked
himself in, as he had been doing all fall. Given his past
actions, that explanation was the most logical one. Stephanie
agreed. She did not want to insist that Dick had not been
logical last night. She did not want to think or talk about
him at all.

Senator Hamlin and Kate came for a late supper. With
Uncle Perry and Pru and the children, as well as two of
Morton's widower friends, the dining room was full, and
the meal went on forever. Stephanie hoped for an opportunity to see Alan alone and could not find one. He did not
help, being full of plans for the continuation of his travels,
asking advice, jotting down in his black notebook everyone's ideas on what he should look for, receiving addresses
of relatives or friends in Baltimore, Wilmington, Pittsburgh.

When the meal was finally over, it was Alan himself who
said, "Perhaps Stephanie will favor us with a song or two."
She could not refuse him.

With Uncle Perry accompanying her, she sang, " '*Cara
selve, ombre beate*' " (Woodland beloved, Come I in quest
of my love). And finally, because his eyes demanded it and,
she hoped, would respond:

> "Drink to me only with thine eyes
> And I will pledge with mine . . ."

As before, she found the answer she sought in his eyes,
and felt a measure of peace, even though his lips never
repeated their message.

Alan and Grey had hired a chaise and pair, and Grey had
agreed to hire Joseph, a young black man Alan had discovered,
to drive and attend him. They would head west on the
metaled turnpike for Lancaster and Harrisburg. Everyone
was up early the next morning to see them off.

Before they departed, Alan took Stephanie into the library
alone for a few minutes.

"Must I still keep silent?" she asked.

"My darling girl." He took her hands and looked as though he wanted to kiss her, but did not. "I think it's better if you do. I'll be back soon—in two weeks at the most. Then, if you still feel the same way..."

"I shall. The question is, will you?"

"We were both going through emotional turmoil, night before last." His handclasp tightened, but his eyes escaped to the bookcases behind her. "Stephanie, I want only the best for you."

"Alan..."

He bent and kissed her hands, then released them and reached out to touch her cheek. "You must think about this very carefully. I have no inheritance, no steady job. I'm gone much of the time..."

"You are being much too reasonable," she complained. She took the liberty of arranging the heavy, double cape of his carrick over his shoulders. The possessive, intimate gesture was infinitely satisfying.

"One of us has to be," he said. Her eyes glistened with tears. He relented and kissed her after all.

CHAPTER
XVII

"Did you see this, my dear?"

Folding it to an inside page, Morton passed Mr. Lewis's newspaper, *The Sentinel of Freedom*, over to Stephanie as they sat in the library, he reading the newspapers, she a novel. It was the second Saturday in January. Dorothea, alerted by Clare that her boots and gloves were in a most disgraceful state, had taken her younger daughter shopping. Hugh had left the day before for Washington, to work on Senator Hamlin's staff.

Stephanie put aside her book and took the paper with an inquiring glance. Morton beamed and pointed, and she followed his finger.

"A Visitor from England Tells Us about Ourselves," read the headline, followed by a chatty introduction from Mr. Lewis:

"Mr. Alan Dunstable of the London *Times*, being on an extended visit to the United States, has spent some time in our fair city and herewith offers his impressions."

She glanced up and saw her father's eyes on her face.

"Oh, yes, he said Mr. Lewis had asked him to write something for his paper." She bent her head to the article, evading Morton's gaze, but a hot flush settled on her cheeks anyway. Seeing his name on the printed page thrilled her so much that she could not follow the sense of the words for several moments. Alan—his face, his hands—were vividly before her, and her body responded with a ripple of excitement. Such a sensation had become more and more familiar this past week. It both embarrassed and interested her. It challenged all the dictates her mother had ever set before her, and sent her, somehow, beyond the boundaries of acceptable behavior, but to what, she did not know.

When she did finally manage to concentrate, she read Alan's description of Philadelphia with an eager pride in both writer and city. *Her* city.

"From its attractive waterworks station on the Schuylkill to its book publishers, Philadelphia exhibits the ingenuity and purposefulness of this new dynamic nation," Alan wrote. "There is no doubt the inventive genius of Benjamin Franklin lives on in its citizens. If one is not of a temperament to be awestruck by the engineering genius of Oliver Evans, the first American to build steam engines commercially, one cannot help but be impressed by the statuary of sculptor William Rush (no kin to the American Minister in London), who has carved everything from wooden figureheads on ships to the impressive marble *Nymph of the Schuylkill* which adorns the fountain at the Columbian Gardens.

"A typical representative . . ."

"Oh, did you see, Papa, he's talking about you," Stephanie exclaimed. And she began to read aloud.

" 'A typical representative of the enterprising spirit of this new nation is Mr. Morton Endicott, owner of Endicott Shipping, with whom I have had the good fortune to reside while in Philadelphia. Keen-minded, energetic, and totally committed to all things American, he is ever attracted to new inventions and eager to try them. One example of this is his installation of water into his home. It is piped into the kitchen, where it may be pumped into a large, cast-iron sink, and also into a tub in the upstairs bathing room. He speaks of lighting his home with gas in some future year, although only a very few public buildings in Philadelphia are presently so equipped.

" 'Away from home, Mr. Endicott is committed to greater facility in travel. He dreams of steamships crossing the ocean in half the time it takes to sail, and is presently involved in planning one canal and helping to finance another, to promote Philadelphia's inland waterways, by which anthracite coal may be brought down the river to the city and used for steam-powered machines. His newly established mail packets, which have begun service to and from New York, proved to this wanderer to be all anyone could wish in ocean travel.' ''

"Well, well," Morton said with a gratified smile. "I wondered why he was quizzing me last week." He placed his hands comfortably over the broad expanse of his corded waistcoat. "I hadn't read it to the end. That's kind of him."

"It's very true, too," Stephanie said.

"You don't think he's trying to curry favor, do you?"

"Alan wouldn't do that kind of thing."

"Wouldn't he? You know him pretty well by now, do you?"

"I think I do." The blush returned. She looked at him earnestly. He seemed uncertain whether to continue the topic. He very rarely spoke to his daughters of personal matters.

"I thought, perhaps . . . at the New Year's Eve ball . . . Have you an understanding with him?"

"I hope so."

He frowned. "He's said nothing to me. You're not entertaining a false hope, are you?"

"N-no, we . . . Papa, may I speak frankly?"

He spread out his hands, welcoming her frankness.

"We have confessed love for each other, but he holds back from a true proposal. He says I must think it over. He's not well-off, his income is uncertain . . ."

Morton nodded. "He doesn't want to live on your income, is that it?"

"*My* income?"

"When you marry, I shall certainly see that you have a comfortable income. It's common enough, and most men would be delighted to have a wife with money of her own. Is he too proud, too independent to accept that?"

"Perhaps. We never discussed that. I believe he feels there's some social barrier, but I don't agree. He said that I must think about my future carefully while he is gone, and so I have. I only hope there is not something else.''

"What else would it be? My dear, you mustn't borrow trouble. I should be delighted to welcome Mr. Dunstable into our family. He seems to me to be intelligent, possessed of drive and ambition, and with many kindly instincts.''

"Yes, Papa, all that is exactly what I so admire in him. But he hasn't written a word to me since he left and . . . What do you suppose Mama will say?''

"You may safely leave your mama to me, I think.''

And then Dorothea herself walked through the door. They hadn't heard her arrival and looked up, startled.

"Oh, here you both are,'' she greeted them. Her manner was distracted, without the enthusiasm she usually brought back from a shopping expedition. She peeled off her gloves, dropped them onto a table with her reticule, and walked to the fire, holding her hands out to the warming blaze.

"Where's Clare?'' Stephanie asked. "Did she find boots to suit?''

"Yes, and a myriad of other things she absolutely required, of course. She and Jenny took them up to her room. Stephanie, dear . . .''

Her mother's voice turned solemn. Stephanie felt a lump form in her chest. "Yes, Mama?''

"A terrible thing.'' She untied her bonnet and sank into a chair across from her daughter. "You must be prepared for a shock.'' She glanced up at Morton, who had risen at her entrance. "You both must be. I met Mrs. Eddy at the bootmaker's. She had the news from the sheriff's wife. It seems Dick Harlow has been found.''

"Found?'' Morton asked, puzzled. "Was he missing?''

"No one had seen him since the night of the ball.'' She looked up at their silent, suspense-filled faces. "He apparently died of exposure. His body was covered with snow. He must have lain there—in the woods, near the Delaware . . .'' She shuddered and reached for her pocket handkerchief and buried her face in it a moment, sniffing. "They say he was there nearly two weeks, before deer hunters came upon his body this morning. Oh, it's all so horrible!''

Morton hurried to put an arm around her shoulders and

lean his face against her brown curls. "There, there, Dorothea. It's certainly a shock and a shame, bu you mustn't . . ."

"Nearly two weeks!" Stephanie echoed, horrified. "The ball . . ."

"Was two weeks ago tomorrow," Dorothea said, raising her face again. "He—he still wore that harlequin costume." She dabbed her moist eyes.

"Oh, no!" Stephanie's hand went to her lips. "Then he never went home that night. Everyone thought he'd just locked himself in his house, but he didn't. He just started walking. He walked and walked . . ."

"Pru's right, of course," Morton reflected. He stood erect, and his gaze went to Stephanie but he kept a hand on his wife's shoulder. "He was more than a little mad."

"It's simply dreadful," Dorothea moaned. "And to think he was nearly our son-in-law."

"Such talk doesn't help," Morton said shortly. "We can be grateful he wasn't."

Stephanie arose slowly. She still held her novel, but the newspaper slipped to the floor from her lap, unheeded. She ought to feel something—a terrible sorrow and regret. Instead, her mother's careless observation had brought a stab of resentment. *He was nearly our son-in-law.* This somehow suggested that if he had been, things would have been all right. Consequently, Dick Harlow's death had, somehow, been her fault.

"I . . . pray excuse me, Mama, I'm going to my room," she said. "Does Clare know?"

"She was with me when Mrs. Eddy told us."

Stephanie left them, moving like a sleepwalker down the hall to the stairway. She thought of cold and wind and snow. And a man, possessed of an inconsolable grief, walking, walking, walking. Not seeing where he was going, not caring, heedless of the weather until it had overcome him. Was it, indeed, all her fault?

Before Christmas Mr. Carr, who had conducted the Handelian Society's concert, invited Stephanie to join a new organization formed while she was in England called the Musical Fund Society. She had agreed, flattered to be among the few females proposed for membership and enthusiastic about its aims. They would sponsor frequent concerts throughout the winter season, both to raise money for the relief of distressed musicians and their families, and to cultivate good taste and proficiency in the musical art among its members.

When Mr. Carr offered to take her to the first meeting of the new year, Stephanie was grateful for the distraction. It took her mind from the shocking news about Dick Harlow and her suspicion that everyone in town who had known of her engagement to him held her responsible for his death. It also stopped her from dwelling on the emptiness she felt during Alan's absence. He had not promised a letter, but she began to look for one anyway as early as a week after he and Grey had left. None came. But what she needed more than letters were Alan's presence, his support and love, the only things that could absolve her from the guilt she felt over Dick's death.

As she donned her warm mantle and bonnet for the meeting at Carpenter's Hall, she said over and over to herself, *Two weeks. He promised to be back in two weeks. That's tomorrow. Even if they are delayed a few days, by weather or by his interest in something, it won't be long now. And I'll be ready. I've thought everything over very carefully. No matter where he goes or what he does, I can't live without him.*

She could not help wondering, as she met new people and greeted acquaintances that evening at the meeting, if people who knew about her and Dick would be cold to her. But no one was, and she soon became too engrossed in the Society's plans for future concerts to be morbid. They set a tentative date for their first concert, toward the end of April. Mr. Carr asked her to sing at it. Surprised and pleased—for he was one of the most knowledgeable musicians in Philadelphia—she agreed.

Taking her home afterward, Mr. Carr said, "By the way, I saw your English friend, Lord Talbot, this afternoon. He was checking into Judd's Hotel."

"Oh, you must have been mistaken," Stephanie said. "He's gone west with Mr. Dunstable."

"No, it was him all right. If you recall, I talked to him quite awhile after our *Messiah* performance. He's a singer himself, isn't he?"

"I can't imagine he'd return without telling us."

"Well, he was looking a bit peaked. He said he'd been under the weather and needed a rest."

When she said good night to Mr. Carr, Stephanie still believed he had been mistaken. Nevertheless she told her mother who, ever alert to Lord Talbot's name, told Morton, who investigated Mr. Carr's statement the next morning on the way to his office. From there, he sent a boy back to the house with a message that it was true; Lord Talbot had engaged a room at the hotel and had retired to his bed. He was very sick and did not wish to impose himself on them. Joseph had returned with him and was running his errands. A doctor had seen him and prescribed medicines, and told him to stay in bed.

"Medicines!" Dorothea gave a disdainful snort. "What he needs is some of Mrs. Buxton's good broth and a woman's loving care. Girls, we must persuade him to come back here, where he belongs."

Stephanie and Clare agreed, and Mrs. Buxton made up a pot of soup. Since it would not have been proper for her unmarried daughters to visit a sick man, Dorothea had Harry drive her and Jenny to Judd's Hotel to deliver it.

As Stephanie and Clare anticipated, Grey stood no chance against their mother's persuasive tongue. By mid-afternoon, he was ensconced in his former bedchamber on the second floor. Elsa had made the bed afresh and started a charcoal fire to make the room cosy. Grey, coughing and blowing his nose at frequent intervals, said hoarsely that all he wanted was sleep. Stephanie and Clare were allowed to smile and wave at him from the door, while Joseph unpacked his belongings. Then he fell into a deep sleep, induced by the laudanum the doctor had prescribed and lulled by the comfortable surroundings. They did not see him until the next day.

Even had he remained awake, Stephanie knew it would not have done to bother him about Alan, his plans or his whereabouts, but she grew more and more curious as the day passed into evening. When Morton returned home, he was not much help.

"All Grey told me when I stopped at the hotel this morning was that he'd taken cold in a snowstorm they encountered the day they left. They lost their way at one point, and one of the horses went lame, so they were out in cold and snow for quite some time. Grey thought to recover in Lancaster, but only got worse, so when Alan wanted to go on to Pittsburgh, he decided to return here. He seems to feel Philadelphia is more civilized."

"But I thought Alan was coming back here in two weeks' time," Stephanie said. "He promised me . . ."

Morton, shrugging his shoulders, said, "That's all I know. Doubtless you can ask Grey yourself in a day or so."

She didn't have to wait that long. They had just finished supper when Joseph approached her and handed her a letter. "Mistuh Talbot says to give you this, ma'am. He forgot it when we first come."

Stephanie retired to the music room, often her private sanctum, for no one else used it very much. She was not familiar with Alan's handwriting, but she knew instinctively that it must be from him, and tore the seal open eagerly.

The writing was a bold scrawl, difficult to read. For a moment, glancing at the greeting, she doubted it was from Alan after all.

> *My dear Miss Endicott,*
> *By the time you receive this, I shall be well on my way to Pittsburgh. After that, I intend to travel to Frederick, Maryland, and, from there, to Charlottesville, where I hope to meet President Jefferson.*
> *My reason for not returning first to Philadelphia, as I had promised, is simple. Seen at a distance, the last days I spent in your company can only be termed an anomaly. Perhaps a better word is dream: a wonderful, ineffable dream, but totally alien to the true state of things.*
> *In short, I cannot marry you, and I would not accept your love on any other terms. I will turn*

*thirty on my next birthday. I am no longer en-
tranced by Shelley's eloquent arguments for free
love. I have learned, by painful experiences, that
such precepts provide a marvelous rationale for a
man, but they ultimately cause women only suffering and disgrace.*

*Forgive me for all I have done to hurt you.
Forget me if you can. Perhaps Lady Burleigh and
your mother are right: You will be happiest, down
the years (and I doubt not there will be many
ahead for you) with Grey Talbot.*

Alan.

Stephanie read it over twice before the true import of the
letter sank in. The second reading only confirmed her first
impression. It was a cruel letter, granting her nothing, not
even the satisfaction of knowing she had touched his heart.
It was obvious he wanted a complete, irrevocable break.

A dream only. A fantastical, foolish, futile dream. A kind
of insanity, if one interpreted his words correctly. Was he
right?

The tears came slowly, but, once begun, they would not
stop. Sometime later Dorothea found her still seated in the
chair by the window, sobbing inconsolably, no longer trying
to hide the sound.

"Why, my dear!" She came over and laid gentle proprietary hands about Stephanie's shoulders, caressing and gathering up the folds of her daughter's cashmere shawl closer
around her neck, as if its warmth must comfort her. Stephanie
tried to speak but could only shake her head. Halting her
caresses, Dorothea handed her a handkerchief and picked up
the sheet of paper lying in Stephanie's lap. The ink was
spotted and blurred with tears. As she read the letter,
Dorothea's eyes grew steely, and her mouth firmed into an
angry line.

"Oh, Stephanie," she said sadly at the end. Stephanie,
blotting her eyes, took a deep breath, but it only ended in a
sob. "I had no idea," her mother continued softly. "You
poor darling. I never trusted that man from the time I set
eyes on him."

"Don't, I pray you, Mama."

"What did he do that he must tell you he cannot marry you? He never said a word to your father or myself. Any gentleman goes to a girl's parents first before approaching..."

"Nothing," Stephanie said weakly. "Nothing, really. It was only a kiss."

"Only a kiss? How long were you here with him, alone, on New Year's Eve? It was so foolish of Morton not to tell me everything right away. I sensed something was wrong, and I had to pry it out of him. Whatever was he thinking of, letting Mr. Dunstable take you home? He ought to have taken you himself. In the middle of his whist game, I doubt not, and didn't want to leave it. Oh, that man!"

"It's not Papa's fault," Stephanie protested, her voice stronger in her indignation. "It was mine, only mine."

Dorothea stared at her a long moment, startled by her vehemence. Stephanie blotted her eyes—they would keep watering—and blew her nose. Dorothea looked down at the letter again. Finally she said, in a mildest tone, "He does show some sense, I'll grant him that. He even recommends that you forget him and marry Lord Talbot."

Stephanie looked up with stricken eyes. "Oh, Mama, don't!"

Dorothea turned tender again. She bent and kissed her daughter's forehead and smoothed away her damp, disheveled curls. "My dear child, I'm only angry for your sake. I know this is very painful for you. But you will recover, I promise you. I know. And remember, I want only the best for you."

Stephanie arose and returned her mother's warm hug. That was the trouble; everyone wanted the best for her, and everyone, apparently, knew what that best was except she, herself. Was she really so stupid, or were the others all wrong?

CHAPTER
XVIII

"Uncle Perry's here," Clare announced from the doorway of Stephanie's bedchamber. "Do come down. He wants to go over our duet."

"I'm busy now, Clare."

"Doing what?" Clare advanced so quickly that Stephanie barely had time to shove the letter she was writing under her stationery box. She turned swiftly on her desk chair to confront her sister.

"None of your business."

"You've been 'busy' for days, Steph. I know you're just plain moping."

"I am not moping."

"Have you forgotten the duet we're doing for Mrs. Bingham's tea? It's only a week off, and I need the practice most desperately. I know you must find me a poor partner. I'm not at all as good . . ."

"Nothing of the kind," Stephanie said. She fingered the edge of the hidden paper as though she longed to return to it, but in truth she would as soon have ripped it up. "We'll disturb Grey," she said.

"Mama said he enjoys hearing us. He is feeling much better."

"In—in a minute, then."

Stephanie turned toward her desk again, hoping that

would settle the matter. She began moving the inkwell and a clutter of papers purposefully, and rubbed off a smudge of ink that had escaped her pen to glisten on the finish of the polished rosewood desk. She heard Clare sigh and walk toward the door, and glanced around, hoping her sister had gone. But instead Clare had turned in the doorway and was contemplating her, head tilted to one side.

"I do hope you're not going to turn into an old gloomy Gus like Grey was," she said.

"Clare!"

"Oh, I know you think you're hiding it, but you're not."

"Fudge."

"Fudge, nothing. It's moping, pure and simple. And I know what it's about, too. It's Alan, isn't it? He's the one you fell in love with."

"I can't imagine where you get such ideas."

"I knew it when you two disappeared around the bend the day we went skating, and then, afterward, when you pretended to ignore each other up at the house."

Clare's face remained serious, and Stephanie realized she was not trying to be provoking or show how clever she was. She shrugged, unwilling to admit to anything.

"Besides, I overheard Mama telling Papa about it."

"What did you hear?"

"That he—Alan—had sent you back a letter by Grey. Not a nice letter. And then Mama was scolding Papa for letting it go so far, for trusting you with him the night of the ball. Did he do something he shouldn't have, Steph?"

"He was a perfect gentleman," Stephanie said. She added thoughtfully, "Yet, Mama did trust me with Dick, all last year."

"That was before he went queer."

Stephanie looked up quickly. "Do you think it was my fault, Clare?"

"What was your fault?"

"Dick's dying that way."

"My stars, no!"

"Still . . ." Stephanie's eyes returned to the floor and her shoulders drooped. It had become a familiar position the past few days. Every time she assumed it, she felt a sensation of hopelessness.

"Come down and sing, Steph. I know it will make you feel better." Clare was at her side again, a hand on her shoulder. "I do sympathize, honey. I guess being in love must be the most miserable condition in the world. I almost hope it never happens to me."

A reluctant smile touched Stephanie lips. "Almost?"

"Well, it would be interesting, too. And exciting. But why does it always end up in misery?"

"Does it, always?"

"It seems to. I knew something had happened between you and Alan, even if he didn't kiss you under the mistletoe. I watched you, you know. First you were happy, and then, after he'd gone, you were on tenterhooks, and now, since the letter . . ." She stopped and waited to be filled in.

Stephanie was flooded with affection for her sister. She looked up and put her hand over Clare's. "He says he can't marry me, and he won't even say why. I keep writing answers to him. Horrid answers, reasonable ones, pleading ones. I always end by tearing them up. Besides, I don't know where to send them."

"Come and sing with me."

"Oh, all right." Stephanie managed another faint smile. "For your sake." She stood and hugged Clare impulsively. Together they went down the stairs to the music room.

The girls were nearly through singing "Grace Thy Fair Brow with Contentment" for the second time when Stephanie caught a movement in the corner of her eye and turned to see Grey standing there, one hand on the doorjamb, a tentative smile on his lips. He wore a dark blue velvet dressing gown with satin collar and cuffs over his long, high-necked nightshirt. Though he looked pale and his hair had lost its healthy sheen, his eyes were bright and interested.

"That was nice, but so faint that I had to come down to hear it better," he said in a hoarse voice.

"You're better, Grey," Stephanie said. "That's marvelous."

"Come in and sit down," Perry invited. "These girls need an audience."

"Perhaps Mrs. Endicott won't approve." But he came in anyway and sat in the chair by the fire, coughing into his handkerchief.

"Are you sure you're all right?" Clare asked.

"Much better, thank you. I took to walking about my room yesterday. Dr. Ruggles said this morning the infection is much reduced." As both girls continued to gaze at him with concern, he waved an imperious hand at them. "Pray continue. I didn't intend to disturb you."

They did so, this time facing him and singing from memory. Clare's voice, though equally high and sweet, was less strong and sure than Stephanie's, so Stephanie always toned hers down when they sang harmony. Clare tried to make up for her weaker voice by her expressive face and delicate phrasing. This time she began adding extravagant gestures, turning Handel's sentimental song into a parody.

" 'All thought of danger banish,' " Clare sang, casting a worried look over her shoulder and clutching her hands to her breast. " 'How canst thou fear today?' " With " 'Mother, Oh! Weep no more, Oh! Weep no more, No!' " she flung out her hands in an agonized plea. Grey started to smile. Before she was done he had broken into laughter, and Stephanie, catching his mirth, abandoned singing to join in. Uncle Perry stopped playing and turned on them with feigned indignation. "What is going on here?"

Clare looked at them all with wide-eyed seriousness. "I have no idea. I was simply trying to put some expression into it, the way you're always telling me to."

This drove Grey into a new paroxysm of laughter that ended in a coughing spell. Rather than ring a servant, Clare ran to get him water from the kitchen. By the time she returned and handed it to him, the cough was subsided. "I'm sorry," she said.

He took the glass with a smile. "No matter. Thank you."

Stephanie thought she caught a gleam of satisfaction in her sister's eye. At last Clare had made Grey laugh.

For ten days Dorothea had watched over Grey as if he were her own son, leaving only the most personal care to Joseph and Sally. Now that he was on his feet, she returned to her social duties. As the wife of a Philadelphia selectman, secretary of the Orphan's Society, and board member of Christ Church's hospital for distressed women, Dorothea's responsibilities were numerous and taxing. She was frequently away, leaving the entertainment and spiritual restoration of their guest to her daughters. She apparently had no qualms about leaving them, either together or singly, in *his* company.

Grey's cough lingered, and Dr. Ruggles advised him not to go outdoors in the cold unless it was absolutely necessary. Stephanie and Clare helped him pass the time by reading aloud, swapping riddles and conundrums, and playing card games. Clare plied Grey with questions about England. He told her about Enderlin Abbey in Bedfordshire, ceded to the first Earl of Woodworth by Charles II for services rendered to the royal forces during the Civil War. Through the years, Enderlin Abbey had become Enderlin Hall, "a big overgrown fortress of a place," Grey called it, with two hundred rooms and twelve hundred acres of grounds, including a village. "It also has a fairly extensive conservatory that Uncle Lucien installed," he added, having noted Clare's preoccupation with her plants.

This last piece of information seemed to impress Clare most. "And you'll inherit it?"

"Someday." Grey shrugged. "Not very soon, I hope. For the most part, my uncle has always been in prime health."

"Well, someday, when you have, I shall come over and visit you," Clare promised. "I should so love to go to England." She cast an envious eye toward Stephanie. "I would have gone last year, but I was getting over an illness."

"What a shame," Grey said.

"Of course, I would have been in the way, too. Mama wanted to concentrate her attentions on Stephanie."

"Sometimes," Stephanie said, dealing the cards with a vicious little flip to them, "your tongue is much too frank, Clarinda Sue."

She was not really angry. Both Clare and Grey were helping her keep her mind off Alan. If she did only go through the motions, at times, she had ceased writing letters that Alan would never see. Music didn't help. Because she

had been singing the first time she ever saw him, she would
be reminded of him whenever she sang. She had put her copy
of "Drink to Me Only with Thine Eyes" at the bottom of
her pile of songs. She doubted she would ever take it out
again.

Then a letter came from Kate in Washington.

"Papa has decided to buy a house in Georgetown," she
wrote. "It is much better than trying to live in a cramped
lodging house near the Capitol, even though it is considerably farther from his office. Despite whatever rumors you
may have heard of Washington being a literal slough of
despond, I do not think it is really that bad. A goodly
number of very nice brick residences continue to be built,
and the public buildings are very impressive. The trouble is,
they are separated by these vast spaces that look like
swampland or wilderness.

"As for Hugh and myself, our paths don't cross too often,
but when they do (all in the course of our duties, you
know), I am very reserved and polite and try not to look
sheep's eyes at him. So I believe he is beginning to feel he
needn't be on his guard anymore. How long do you suppose
it will take him to come round? (There I go, the eternal
optimist!)

"How is your own romance progressing? Don't tell me
there is none—I know better. All the time Alan danced with
me at that infamous ball, he was trying to steer us so he
could see *you*, as you danced with Dick. He reminded me of
a watchful, concerned English sheepdog, ready to tear into
the fellow at the first sign of distress on your part. How
lucky for you he behaved so—and thus was around to help
you when you really needed him. So don't worry, my dear
friend, if he hasn't said anything to you yet, I am most
confident that he will. Trust Kate."

Stephanie wanted to tear the letter up and throw it away,
but because it was from Kate, she did not. She would have
to answer it, somehow. She would have to tell her friend
just what had happened. Better that than continue to receive
references to a "romance" that would never be.

After Kate's signature was a notation. "P.S. See other
side." Turning the page over, she read, "I nearly forgot a

matter of vital importance. I have been asked to put out a certain hint to you. How would you like to sing at President Monroe's inaugural ball in March? A number of people on the committee here heard you sing when they were in Philadelphia, and are convinced a song or two from you would be just the thing to put a cap on the evening. I understand it's not even required that you sing "Hail Columbia," although I suppose something patriotic would be in order. Anyway, you are hereby forewarned. I believe you will get a formal invitation very soon. Ever, Your loving K."

Stephanie was standing beside the parlor fireplace, still regarding this astonishing postscript, when Grey entered the room.

"May I ask what is making you frown so?" he asked.

She told him about the invitation. He raised his eyebrows. "And will you?"

"I hardly feel I should. There are bound to be so many important—and worldly-wise—people present."

"Would your parents even allow it? At so public an occasion?"

"I hadn't thought of it that way. I thought only of all the people who will attend such an event. Ambassadors from other nations, even heads of state. People who have heard the best, most famous singers in the world."

"Yes, exactly. There are many excellent professional singers . . ."

Stephanie moved to one of the chairs that faced each other next to the fireplace. "*You* don't think I'm good enough, either," she noted with a little grin.

"Oh, it's not that. You have a tremendous voice. It's just—the fitness of the thing."

"I see," Stephanie said, but she didn't, not really. She laid the letter aside and took up the piece of embroidery she had been working on before the mail arrived. "Won't you sit down?" she asked. "You really are recovered, aren't you?"

"Yes, quite." He sat in the chair opposite her with his usual attentive smile. "And I shall enjoy celebrating my recovery at the theater tonight. What is the play?"

"*Damon and Pythias*. I'm sorry you missed Kean."

"No matter. I saw him often enough in London. And he's not so good anymore, is he?"

"The local papers did question the adulation he has received in England. I thought perhaps American tastes . . ."

"No, he just drinks too much, and he can be very erratic at times. He used to be a genius, though." His eyes grew thoughtful as he looked into the fire.

More memories, Stephanie thought, watching him. And yet, not always sad ones, for a flicker of a smile showed around his finely chiseled lips. She wished he would share the memory.

"Have you received any letters from home?" she asked.

He glanced up as though startled she was still there. "As a matter of fact, I have. Your mother had kindly suggested I give Valeria—Lady Burleigh—your address."

He brought a letter out of his vest pocket and handed it to her. "You might like to see it."

She unfolded the sheet and saw large, wobbly letters printed in pencil.

> *Dear Papa,*
> *I miss you very much. My pony went lame. Will you be home for my birthday?*
> *Your loving son,*
> *Kevin*

She smiled as she handed it back to him. "How sweet. How old is he?"

"He will be six in April. I was amazed to receive this. He could barely print his name when I left."

"He must have worked at it very hard."

"You don't seem surprised to learn I have a son."

"I . . . knew," Stephanie said hesitantly.

Grey reread the letter himself and refolded it but did not put it away. "Did you not wonder why I never spoke of him?"

"Well, I . . . yes, I suppose I did."

"It was because . . . he reminded me too much of Polly.

At times, right after she died, I could hardly bear to look at him.''

He waited, expecting—what? A condemnation? Stephanie remembered Kevin was not really Grey's son. Would he confess to that, too?

"You must think I'm rather awful," he said sheepishly.

"Oh, no, I . . . think I understand."

"Do you?" His blue eyes searched hers. The moment became more intimate than she wanted.

"When did you see him last?" she asked.

"In September. I was at Enderlin Hall when Alan stopped by so that we could go to Liverpool together."

"Do you still think it only a coincidence that you and Alan took *The Good News*? Did you ever really think that?"

He frowned in surprise. "What are you talking about? I told you, Alan had heard of the new packet service . . .?"

She shook her head, smiling. "That's what he told *you*. So, you weren't in on the scheme."

"What scheme?"

"To bring the two of us together—in the holy bonds of matrimony, of course." He looked so shocked that she added, "No, of course you weren't. But it appears that everyone else was."

"Everyone?"

She nodded. "Lady Burleigh, my mother, Alan. He told me himself, on New Year's Eve. I'm not sure about Papa."

"Alan, *too*? Oh . . . of course." His expression turned thoughtful. "That's why he invited me along. I guess I knew his reason was a ruse. He doesn't need another viewpoint for his articles. But I thought it merely a scheme to help me back to health. My aunt . . ."

"She and Alan are 'old friends,' according to Alan."

"They were also lovers," Grey said. "But I very much doubt he told you that."

His bold words, so foreign to his usual gentlemanly manner, were like a slap across the mouth. Seeing her stricken face, Grey's chivalrous instincts immediately came to the fore. "Forgive me. I only thought you should know, should . . . see him more clearly. Since I've returned—well, I would guess he's dealt you some sort of blow."

"Of which you warned me." She took a deep breath, managed a faint smile, then spread her hands helplessly. "Warnings don't help, do they?"

He shook his head sadly. "My dear Stephanie."

"What...other things don't I know about Mr. Dunstable?"

He drew back just the least bit, settling his elbows on the chair's arms, clasping his fingers together before him. "I'm not sure I should tell you."

"Yes, indeed, you should. If I am to recover, I need strong medicine. And it looks as if I have no choice but to recover."

Still he hesitated, his eyes evading hers.

"Was Lady Burleigh one of those whose heart he broke?" she asked, trying to make it easier for him. "It seems an odd sort of attachment. She's considerably older."

"No, nothing like that. Valeria was trying, I think, to recover from my uncle, at a time when she thought he was lost to her forever. Alan was...a convenient interlude."

"And he...?"

"I doubt he really loved her. But she had the money to finance publication of his poems."

"Oh!" Stephanie put her hands to heated cheeks. "That sounds dreadfully self-serving."

"I don't think he thought of it that way. It was—is—an accepted way for new authors to get recognition. I mean, to find a patron, not to..." His voice faded, as though he could not bring himself to repeat his accusation.

The shadows were lengthening. It was teatime, but neither Dorothea nor Clare were home yet. Her father would dine with the Philosophical Society. Stephanie rose and attacked the bellpull as though it were a living thing, a symbol of her illusions about Alan Dunstable.

"I kept pondering it on the boat," she went on, trying to make her tone merely conversational. "Why it was that, for two supposedly good friends, you didn't seem to like him very much."

"Alan has always been very friendly to me. I've been the standoffish one. Call it snobbery, if you like." Turning back to him, she raised her eyebrows and shook her head in protest. "No," he conceded, "I didn't think it was snobbery, either. I just always felt he . . . wanted something from me; wanted to use me in some way. I suppose you could say he's still doing that, isn't he, inviting me on the trip.''

"But for *your* good, not his.''

"Well, that's what we suppose, isn't it? And I admit it has been good for me." His smile this time was wholehearted.

Elsa appeared in the doorway. "We'd like some tea, Elsa," Stephanie said.

"*Ja*, miss," Elsa replied, and disappeared.

Stephanie returned to the chair. "You'd think she might have learned to say 'yes,' by now," she complained, as though a servant's speech was the foremost thought in her head. Her fingers worked nervously in her lap. She wanted to ask more, but would revelations help? Grey, it was clear now, saw Alan as a bumptious, aggressive social climber, willing to use a woman any way he could to progress in his career. She could not quite believe it was true.

Yet even her father had said, "Do you think he's trying to curry favor?''

"May I ask you what—who—were the girls Alan hurt? Did you know any of them?''

She spoke in a low voice, looking at her hands and forcing them to be still. She wished the words back almost as soon as they were out. When she glanced up, she was arrested by the expresssion on Grey's face. His jaw had tightened and his clear blue eyes, gazing past her out the parlor window, were dark with pain.

"It was Stella," she guessed. "You sister Stella.''

"Yes," he said. The word was crisp, stark, angry.

"Wha-what did she die of? Oh, I'm sorry, I oughtn't to ask.''

His gaze swung back to her slowly. The rest of his body remained motionless. "She killed herself. Took an overdose of laudanum.''

"Oh, Grey!" It was worse than she had thought. Accident, disease—both were unavoidable, even if pitiful in one so young. But suicide!

"Because A-Alan abandoned her?''

"No." Grey's lips twisted in a bitter smile. "Because he made love to her.''

Elsa arrived at that moment with the tea and set it on the table between them. "Anyt'ing else, miss?"

"No, this is fine, Elsa. Thank you."

The interruption helped settle her thoughts, which had turned into an angry, despairing whirlwind. She blinked back tears. At the same time, the logic of his statement was not clear to her. She took a deep breath, trying to restore her equanimity.

"Sugar? Milk?"

"Both, please. Not much sugar. Yes, that's exactly right." She handed him the cup. "I ought not to ask..."

"Perhaps you ought," he said curtly. "You *do* need to know it all."

"Did he . . . abandon her, then?"

"No, it wasn't like that. It had to do with Stella herself. She loved him, but she was very religious. It was at a time when she needed someone, and Alan . . . was there. I wasn't, I'd gone to Europe." His voice took on an even harsher edge, as though he blamed himself for not having been there. "He thought—I didn't speak to him about it, naturally, but he told Polly, afterward—he thought his love would help her, free her. Stella only thought, after it was over, that she had damned herself."

"Oh, the poor girl!" Stephanie cried out.

"She was very much the innocent," Grey said, his eyes appreciating her sympathy. "Alan ought to have recognized..."

I will not shame you, Alan had said when she offered herself, without shame, to him. Stella had had what she, Stephanie, wanted (what she *had* wanted, she corrected). But Alan had refused to take advantage of her wantonness. What had he written about Shelley's beliefs on free love? A wonderful rationale for a man, but they cause women only suffering and disgrace.

No. Her head jerked up. *I won't tell myself he's changed. I will not excuse such a despicable act.*

She put the teacup to her lips and took two large swallows, burning her tongue. *I'll burn him out of my brain, out of my heart*, she thought. *Mama was quite right not to trust him.*

"I don't see how you could travel with him," she marveled.

"It was six years ago, even more..."

"Even so."

"We're all entitled to a mistake or two. I've made my own."

"A mistake! You speak very mildly about your sister's death, I must say."

He shook his head. "The guilt wasn't wholly his, and I know that. I don't hate him anymore."

"You should have told me earlier."

"Would it have helped? But that's a poor way to treat someone who's trying to help you, talking about his past behind his back. I... almost regret telling you. And yet, I felt you ought to know."

Stephanie drained her cup and set it down with a clatter. "And I thank you for being so frank. Now I can burn that letter he wrote me. And start to live again."

CHAPTER
XIX

The evening of February second was astonishingly mild, leading Clare to plead with her mother that they might walk rather than take the carriage to attend the theater.

"It's such a tiny little way," she pleaded. "I promise to be careful to lift my skirts over the mud."

Dorothea, herself seduced by the springlike weather, agreed, but with all due pessimism. "I hope this won't prove to you that, with all the slush and mud that's underfoot, you cannot help but ruin your hems. And we might all come down with colds."

Stephanie, joining in Clare's plea, promised to wear boots and extra stockings. It was always chilly in the theater, anyway.

So now Clare and Stephanie, in their fur-trimmed mantles and plumed bonnets, walked behind their parents on either side of Grey as they went north from Locust to Walnut Street. Because of the thaw the men had left off their carricks.

In places their path grew narrow because of melting snow or the rivulets of water that settled in the uneven depressions of the brick walk, and the trio had to break up, one or the other of them walking ahead. Grey was equally attentive to both girls, helping them over the treacherous places. Stephanie wondered if he had a preference for herself or her sister. If so, he did not show it.

Clare took care of the conversation, an obligation Stephanie could not seem to manage tonight. Wonderingly, she observed that the stars were so bright that it seemed one might, with only a little effort, touch them. She mourned that the beautiful theater on Chestnut Street had burned down the previous April, so they would be attending the old Olympic, rechristened the Walnut Street Theater, where circuses and equestrian shows had formerly been performed.

"I hope it won't be too drab and simple for your English tastes," she said to Grey.

"You ladies must stop apologizing for your local offerings," Grey said, taking one, then the other, into his glance. "I am quite convinced I shall enjoy it, if only for the company."

"How gallant," Stephanie remarked. Her tone was dry. Then she feared she had sounded sarcastic. Would Alan have paid them such a compliment? No, she would not think of him tonight.

A large phaeton pulled by matched blacks came abreast, then passed them, its high wheels splattering water and slush, its lanterns shedding a yellow reflection on the glistening road. Even in the light of a street lamp, Stephanie could not see who was within, but Dorothea called out, "I do believe that was Mr. Dickinson and his wife. Oh, dear, I shall feel foolish, arriving in this manner."

"Just keep your head high and smile," Morton advised.

Good advice, Stephanie thought, unconsciously raising her chin. *And keep your mind on the present, not the past.*

That was not so easy. They had taken box seats in the first tier on the side, where they had an excellent view of the stage. The footlights—Argand burner lamps whose glare was screened from the audience in the pit by green baffles—bathed the center forestage in light, but the wings remained in shadow. Somehow, despite the histrionics on stage, it was far too easy for Stephanie's eyes to drift to those shadows or to the tallow-candle chandelier hanging from an ornate ceiling, and settle into gloomy memory. Stephanie was grateful that the play's central theme was the friendship between two men, not the romance between a man and a woman. It should not be difficult to forget Alan; there were not that many memories. If she never had occasion to see him again. . . .

A chill invaded the very marrow of her bones at such a thought.

A man sang a comic song in front of the curtain during the intermission between *Damon and Pythias* and the second presentation, a farce called *The Apprentice*. This time, Stephanie's mind returned to Kate's letter and the forthcoming invitation to sing at the President's inaugural ball. A little seed of excitement blossomed within her, chasing away her bleak thoughts. The prospect was frightening but also quite intriguing. She had never been to Washington, and with Kate and Hugh there, it would be enjoyable to see it. Doubtless Grey would welcome a chance to see their new capital, slowly emerging from a marshly wasteland on the banks of the Potomac. He had not seemed to like the idea of her singing at such a public function, but that might be an excellent reason to do it—to show an Englishman that young American ladies were not—and need not be—so restricted.

After all, why should she not sing? She had heard professional singers, even in London, who could sing no better than she, and some who were worse. By the time the curtain opened on *The Apprentice*, she had decided to accept the invitation.

It was late when the play ended. A number of friends, waiting in the lobby for their carriages, stopped the Endicott party to chat, to express their reaction to the performances. Everyone seemed delighted to meet Lord Talbot, or to greet him again if they had already met him. He laughed and joked with them without a trace of the old melancholy, parried questions and put forth comments about his impressions of America with good-natured grace. How handsome he was, how at ease with everyone. The ladies frequently cast knowing, speculative glances from Grey to Stephanie.

It occurred to her that everyone believed she would marry Lord Talbot. A minute later came the question, well, why not? She had to marry someone, someday. She did not really want to be an "old maid." And if it could never be Alan, it might as well be Grey Talbot. She could not think of anyone she liked better.

Of course he might not ask her, and she would never push him to do so, as she had Alan. She, as well as Kate, had learned her lesson.

She had told Grey quite frankly of the plot to bring them together. Had it put the idea in his head, or only made it distasteful to him? She wished now she had never said anything about it.

Outside, the street was alive with carriages and horses driven by servants who had returned to pick up their masters and mistresses after the theater. They were lined up far down Walnut Street, the horses occasionally whinneying and stamping their feet, their breath steaming in the damp air. The theater crowd streamed out the doors, chattering and laughing, then breaking up to find their particular vehicle.

"Aren't you relieved we don't need to stand and wait for our carriage?" Clare asked her mother, pointing to the long line. "We'll be home before they get a start."

Dorothea shivered and turned up her fur collar. "That's all very well, but my feet are cold. And I trust you have no muddy spots on your flounces."

They looked for a place to cross the street at the corner of Walnut and Ninth. Some vehicles had moved out from the walkway already, and it was difficult to see around a standing carriage to watch for an approaching one.

"I believe we can cross now," Morton told them, and gave Dorothea his arm.

"You take Clare, I'll follow," Stephanie told Grey. "It will be easier that way."

Clare, remarking laughingly that what they really needed was a bridge, took Grey's arm and followed.

"Yoohoo, Stephanie!" a voice nearby called out. She looked up to see Mary Foster, now Mary Coxe, settled beside her husband in a little two-seated tilbury next to the crossing. Stephanie smiled and waved, and moved out in front of their horse, her eyes on Grey and Clare who were nearly across the street.

A curricle with a single trotting horse came out of

nowhere, past the waiting carriages. She looked up in alarm, slipped on the slush, and fell to her knees, then onto her hands and elbows.

"What the devil!" the driver yelled, jerking his horse to avoid her. Someone screamed. The horse's hooves and the high wheels of the chariot splattered past, only inches from her head, hitting the brim of her bonnet, showering her with muddy water, whipping her face with wind. She found herself kneeling in the street in damp, cold, disagreeable slush that promptly penetrated her skirts and stockings, slipped up her sleeves, and invaded the tops of her boots. Her knees and elbows and the palms of her hands throbbed and stung.

People were at her side almost immediately. "Oh, ma'am, are you hurt?" "What happened?" "That foolish driver!" "Oh, your lovely mantle!"

Someone helped her rise. She looked up, feeling dazed and disoriented. It was Grey, holding her arm tightly with one hand, his other hand about her waist.

"Stephanie!" His voice was husky with fright, his face strained and white in the light of the corner street lamp.

"I'm all right," she managed.

The little crowd fell away as he led her across the street to safety. Her mother scowled her concern. "Stephanie, dear!"

"I'm all right," she repeated.

Morton put a hand on her shoulder to assure himself she was in one piece. Clare cried out, "That driver came down the street so fast, and just kept going!"

"You mantle is ruined," Dorothea said in her best "I told you so" voice. Stephanie looked down but couldn't see the damage. She brushed away grit and wetness with a ravaged glove. "My muff?" she asked. As though he had guessed her thoughts, Grey handed it to her. The silver fox muff that had once been Clarinda's was limp and sodden, like a very wet lap dog. She took it gingerly, with some disgust, but did not dare say anything about its state to either her sister or her mother.

"I'm much obliged to you," she said, looking up at Grey.

He pressed a gloved hand against the one she had placed

on his arm. "What a scare you gave us," he returned. His voice dropped as he leaned closer and added in her ear, "You are very dear to me, you know."

After that, the atmosphere in the big house on Locust Street became charged with expectation. Dorothea redoubled her efforts to be hospitable to Grey, inviting friends—many of them prominent citizens—to dine with them each evening. Morton took Grey down to Front Street and introduced him to his business associates—wealthy merchants like himself, lawyers who dealt with the trade laws, sea captains, selectmen, and members of the Philosophical Society.

Now that Grey was well again, his energy seemed boundless and his melancholy had completely vanished. "What can we do today?" he would ask at the late breakfast he shared with his hostess and her daughters. Clarinda, usually the first to plan expeditions, began to excuse herself from participation. She was planning to visit her friend, Elizabeth Carpenter, or go shopping with Aunt Pru, or help quiz Tim on his history lesson. Dorothea would also have duties—a new gown she must finish for a tea at the mayor's house, a committee meeting concerning Christ Church hospital, and always numerous social calls to make.

So it was Grey and Stephanie who viewed the lifelike scenes at the Wax Museum (from the Birth of Jesus to the Battle of Waterloo). Or argued about the significance of the steam-driven, self-moving machines at the Mechanical Museum on Front Street, or stood entranced before Mr. Tilley's fancy glassblowing exhibition. When the Lenni Lenape Indians came to town, as they did periodically, Grey and Stephanie watched the war dances at Warwick's Tavern, and Grey bought a birchbark basket to take back to Lady Burleigh.

Now that illness and melancholy had vanished, Grey was turning out to be a delightful companion. Occasionally he would say, in passing, "Polly and I used to . . ." in a tone that confirmed Stephanie's guess that he had, at last, managed to place his wife's part in his life firmly in the past. Stephanie no longer wondered if her revelation about the "plot" had taken its effect. The glances of his bright eyes and the pressure of his hand when he helped her into or out of a carriage or across a muddy street told her that he was taking it very seriously, indeed.

At times, knowing what was surely to come, she felt poised and ready to give the answer everyone (even Alan) wanted her to give. But when she was alone in her bed at night, she would feel a deep desolation, a need to hide her face in the pillow and moan Alan's name over and over. Then waves of hot desire would chase each other through her body and leave her weak and wretched, as if in the grip of a physical illness. And she would think, *There has to be a way to win him back, there has to be. How can I live the rest of my life, never having known what it was like to be held in his arms, all the vague, fanciful longings satisfied, the promised ecstasy of his kisses, fulfilled?* Even if they didn't marry, even if it only happened once.

How could Stella, having been loved by him, feel so damned as to take her own life? Stephanie could not imagine it, knowing Alan and not having known Stella.

But whenever rationality raised its head, Stephanie's whole perspective changed. What he had done was unconscionable, totally wrong. He had ravished a trusting, innocent maiden. He had had a loveless affair with Lady Burleigh. He must have had affairs with other women all over Europe. Recalling his vital masculinity, the excitement of his glances, she could not doubt it. No, she could never marry a man who had played with love the way he had done.

After a week of springlike weather, when the snow nearly disappeared under a benevolent sun, winter struck again. Faced with heavy snow and disagreeable winds, the expeditions ceased. One afternoon Stephanie found herself alone in the parlor with Grey. Dorothea, in the sewing room next door, was putting the finishing touches on her new gown, and Clare had rejected a game of cards with them for the pleasures of reading Goldsmith's *History of England* in her room.

The cribbage game was not going well. Grey seemed distracted. As Stephanie placed her last peg in the winning hole for the second time in a row, she said, "Why don't we try some duets? Your voice is restored, isn't it?"

"Maybe later," he said, smiling. His eyes were collecting light from the fire's flames, from the candle lamp she had lit against the dull gray day. His hand went out to cover hers as she gathered the cards together. "Stephanie, I've spoken to your father, and . . ."

She looked up and realized, with a little shock, that the moment was at hand, and she had no excuse not to make a decision.

His proposal was a little like a dream. He said all the right words, and she heard them. Yet there was no emotional response in her as she gazed back into his warm, earnest blue eyes. The room around them seemed to sway as if she only saw its image reflected in water. The dark blue of the velvet draperies ran into the pale blue-and-ivory design in the wallpaper. The scene embroidered on the fireplace screen was a jumble of meaningless color, and the picture on the wall of Josiah Endicott in his best lace-ruffled shirt and powdered wig took on a slightly menacing aura.

"I . . . am truly honored by your proposal, Grey," she heard herself saying, "I-I only wonder if, before I answer you, you have told me everything I ought to know about yourself."

"Why? What do you want to know?"

She had hoped for his acknowlegment of Polly's origins. Or his acknowledgement that the child, Kevin, was not really his. When no confession seemed forthcoming, she realized she could not ask such questions. She took refuge in the mundane.

"Would we live with Lord and Lady Burleigh, then, at Enderlin Hall?"

"We wouldn't have to. We could take a house in London, if you like. In fact, we probably should. Then we could attend as many concerts and operas as we have time for. Polly preferred the country, but I find it dull after awhile."

"And . . . do you suppose Kevin will like having a stepmother?"

Grey smiled reassuringly and patted her hand. "He will love you. But English boys go away to boarding school, you know, sometimes when they're only seven or eight."

She withdrew her hands from his gently. "And what will you do with your life, Grey? How will you occupy yourself?"

She wondered if he would think it odd of her to suggest that he declare some purpose to his life.

"Sing duets with you?" He was smiling, as if she had made some kind of joke, but his eyes were questioning. Her disappointment must have showed, for the smile quickly vanished. "Seriously, I shall probably get more involved in Parliament. Once I inherit the title, I'm automatically in the House of Lords, you know. I believe I could be interested in politics if I took the trouble."

"Is that all?"

"All?" he repeated. He rose and moved around the end of the card table to stand by her seat. "I'm not another Morton Endicott, you know," he said.

She looked up at him with a little frown. He offered her his hands and she put hers in them hesitantly, allowing him to pull her to her feet. His eyes grew searching. "I know you were in love with Alan. I daresay you still are. But might I hope that, someday, if you are properly swept off your feet . . . ?"

Could one be swept off one's feet, loving another? And how would he go about it? Her smile was tremulous. But the room had stopped shimmering, and that gave her courage.

"Grey, I can't think of any man I'm fonder of than you."

"We could have tremendous times together. And we could come back and visit Philadelphia often. And invite Clare to England as often as she likes."

"You wouldn't want to settle here?"

"I might, for a while. I do like Philadelphia. The people have been very cordial. But I have family obligations, and eventually I'll have to return."

"Of course. The inheritance."

"London is the center of the world, you know. You'll find it an exciting place to live. And Enderlin Hall is beautiful. You'll love it, once you get used to it."

But these are not the important things, she wanted to cry out.

"I love you, Stephanie. Do say yes." His arms went around her, and his face was very close. She felt protected

and desired, her wounded pride restored, her guilt over
Dick's death dissolved. She returned his warm gaze and
nodded. As his eyes lit up, she said, "Yes, Grey, I'll marry
you. I think . . . it will be easy to love you."

His kiss was gentle at first, but as she responded, his lips
sought more with a hungry eagerness and his arms tightened
around her. Then she remembered he was a man who had
been without his wife—his dearest love—for over a year.
She responded to him out of affection and pity, but not out
of love.

CHAPTER
XX

"What you must do," Kate said, as she offered Alan his choice of drinks, "is attend one of President Monroe's evening levees. You don't need a ticket or anything. All you need to do is go. You'll see an amazing cross-section of the country, come to pay their respects."

"How often does he hold such egalitarian affairs?" Alan asked, pointing to the bourbon. "I'll take that, thanks. It's quite good, nearly as good as Scotch."

"Indeed? I must tell Father. I've never tried it msyelf; it's supposed to be too strong for women. The receptions are once a week, on Monday, I think. I'll find out for sure. Do sit down, Alan. You came at a good time, and I'm most eager to hear about your travels."

Alan sat down, the whiskey glass in his hand, and looked around. Senator Hamlin's Georgetown house, built to overlook the Potomac about ten years ago, was of neat red brick, in the Georgian style—no, he must remember to call it Federal. Not too large but, as Kate had pointed out, spacious enough for her father to entertain a dozen guests to dinner comfortably, and to hold important but unofficial conferences with colleagues. Alan liked the neat geometrical design painted in blue and tan and orange on the canvas floor covering, the unpretentious muslin curtains, and the slender-legged simplicity of the Adam furniture. He was beginning to feel at home, despite Kate's initial greeting, which had combined surprise at seeing him with a hesitation to invite him inside. For a moment he had sensed a reserve that was almost hostile.

But now she was her cordial self, her relaxed, composed bearing comfortably unfeminine. He now understood why Hugh did not consider Kate for a prospective wife. Her frank gaze did not distinguish between male or female. She displayed no feminine softness nor any of the tricks of adoration and helplessness with which women sought to ensnare a man. Despite her muslin gown and the lace at her throat, she behaved more like another man than a woman, and consequently was not the sort designed to make most men's hearts beat faster.

Kate poured herself a small glass of white wine and sat opposite Alan in a blue-and-tan-striped satin settee. The fire leaped hospitably in the hearth, and its reflection gleamed on their glasses.

"Of course," she added, "if you have a letter of introduction from Mr. Jefferson himself, you needn't mingle with the hoi polloi."

"What amazes me is that your president does this. Although I don't know what I expected. He's not a king, after all."

"He's not democratic enough for some tastes. People call him "James the Second" behind his back. Because President Madison's name was James, too, of course, but also because he's perceived as putting on aristocratic airs. Mrs. Monroe has established certain rules for Washington social life. For one thing, she doesn't return the calls of the Congressional wives who leave their cards at the White House. Dolly Madison returned them all—and loved it. You can imagine the hurt feelings. And the Monroes use gold tableware at their state dinners. They even use forks. One of those showy royalist notions they picked up in France, no doubt."

Alan laughed. "Yes, I've noticed that in most ordinaries, forks are not part of the tableware. They're not used among the common people in England, either. I think your idea is a very good one, Kate. I should like to see the sorts of people, from all over, who come to call on the President. Then I may get a chance to size him up before I meet him in a more personal fashion.''

"Now tell me about your visit to Monticello, Alan. I saw Mr. Jefferson years ago, when I was just a child and he was visiting in Philadelphia, but I don't believe he travels much anymore.''

"He seems in good health, but I suspect he hasn't so much energy as before—he is seventy-seven. I was—well, overwhelmed wouldn't be too strong a word. By his hospitality, his charm, his knowledgeability. Do you know there were a dozen guests beside me, at Monticello? I had sent him a note from my hotel in Charlottesville, only asking for an interview, and I ended up spending four nights there. He told me he likes Englishmen, it's just the British government he can't abide.''

Kate laughed. "You must have been relieved to hear that. Tell me what Monticello is like.''

He told her about its Greek architecture, its mountaintop view of Albemarle County and the mountains in the distance, the many conveniences and inventions its owner had installed. And his own feelings of uneasiness as Jefferson took him around its five thousand acres on horseback.

"Even as I admired him, I could not but compare his opulent way of life with that of the plain folk I had stayed with in western Pennsylvania.'' He shrugged off the incongruity. "Of course, he pointed out that the estate is nearly self-sufficient. Most of the two hundred slaves are skilled at some craft, and I could readily believe he is truly concerned for their welfare. Yet, they *are* slaves, aren't they?''

"He favors their freedom but cannot decide how it should be accomplished,'' Kate said. "That's what I've heard. It's very complex. I should think they will need to be educated first. Not all owners are as enlightened as Mr. Jefferson.''

She went into a surprisingly deep assessment of the situation. Alan sat back and listened, and became aware of little pauses, of covert glances, of occasional gestures of uncertainty, and decided she was talking about slavery to avoid talking about something else.

"I'm sorry, I've bored you,'' she said when he didn't

respond to a comment she made. "I tend to get carried away. That's why most men find me unacceptable."

He shook his head. "I'm not one whit bored, Miss Hamlin. But I've begun to suspect that you're really thinking about something else."

She avoided his glance. "May I fill your glass?"

"Thank you." He handed it to her and she returned to the small liquor cabinet in a corner of the parlor. Despite her height and thinness, she walked with grace. Her straight blond hair was done in a bun at the back of her neck, but newly cut and crimped fringes around her face had softened its angularity. He wondered if the improvement was for Hugh's sake and if it had helped.

"Are you planning to stay in Washington through the inauguration on March fifth?" she asked over her shoulder.

"Yes, I probably shall. Before that happens, I want to watch Congress in action. And talk to some people."

"Would you like to stay with us?"

"That's very kind of you, but no, I'm quite comfortable at the boardinghouse."

She returned with his glass one-third full. "Did you know that the Endicotts are coming?"

His gaze leaped from the amber liquid in his glass to Kate's face. "For the inauguration?"

"Yes. Stephanie has been asked to sing at the President's ball."

He tried to still the shock that flashed through him from head to toe, and hoped it didn't show in his face. He took a sip of his drink.

Kate was looking at him with candid, questioning eyes as she reseated herself opposite him. "What happened, Alan, if you don't mind my asking?"

"What happened to what?"

She made an impatient gesture with her hands. "You know perfectly well what I mean. I was sure you and Stephanie had an understanding of some kind before you left Philadelphia. It was quite obvious the both of you were in love. So what happened? Did her family object?"

All at once he realized she was speaking out of some

particular knowledge that went beyond her assumption of "an understanding."

"Has she written you?"

"Yes. More than once, as a matter of fact. In the first letter I received, she asked me not to mention your name in my letters to her. In the last one, which came only yesterday, she informed me that she is to be married to Lord Talbot."

This time the shock left him feeling weak and sick. Even a gulp of bourbon didn't help. He nearly dropped his glass and found it impossible to look her in the eye.

"That's fine," he said at last, harshly. "That's exactly what I had hoped would happen."

And what does the word "hope" mean? taunted his writer's mind. A verb used as a cultivated mask, stating the obvious, as in "I hope you are well at this time?" Or a genuine, deep-seated desire? If the latter meaning, he had just perjured himself.

"You did!" Kate exclaimed. "*You* hoped? Does that mean you're the one who wrecked Stephanie's dreams, her joy, her..."

"Oh, come now, Miss Hamlin. It's not like you to speak so extravagantly."

His accusation was met with a cold stare and absolute silence. "We are not at all suited, Miss Endicott and I," he added firmly.

Kate sipped her wine once, twice, then downed the rest of it like a man preparing to do battle, and set her glass on the teatable. "I would expect such talk from a father or mother. Even, perhaps, from a brother. But not from a lover. Not from you, Alan."

"Am I not allowed to be sensible?"

"Yes. By all means, be sensible. But not stupid."

He tried to smile. He watched the whiskey as, for no particular reason, he twirled his tall glass and made it leap partway up the sides. "You don't really know me, Miss Hamlin."

"Stephanie knows you. She loves you. I'm not speaking of a passing fancy, Mr. Dunstable. I'm not speaking of polite accommodation, a wish to do what society requires.

I'm speaking of *love*, of a—a physical bonding, of . . . almost, an obsession. That's the way she loves you.''

His mouth went dry. He put the whiskey on the little end table beside him and rose restlessly. He walked the length of the room, hands in his frock coat pockets, to windows that overlooked the Potomac. His eyes caught sight of a barge loaded with canvas-covered produce, moving slowly through the cold, winter-white waters.

"How do you know?" he asked huskily.

"I know Stephanie. We've read each other's minds since we were twelve. I *know* her, Alan. I know that no man has ever touched her heart the way you have."

He would not have imagined Kate could speak so passionately or that he would be so moved by her words. Tears formed in his eyes, and he had not cried since he was a child. It was a stupid reaction, too trite, really, for what he was feeling. He blinked them back and searched out his handkerchief.

"Well, it's too late now, isn't it?" he said. After a long silence, while he pretended to blow his nose, he turned to face her again.

She spaced her words evenly for emphasis. "It's not too late, Alan, not so long as the two of you are still alive."

Her use of his given name was another assault on his defenses. But he rallied them, anyway. "You assume she loves me. I assure you, Grey has probably told her things that . . . Well, by now she must detest me.''

"Why should she?" Kate's voice was only a murmur. She stood up and brought his drink to him. "Come, now. I find you a charming, articulate, interesting person. Much more interesting than your friend Lord Talbot. You've done a great deal in your life. I'd vouchsafe that you have within you a certain integrity that not many could match . . .''

"Oh, stop it, Kate!" He turned away from the drink she still proffered. Evading her gaze, he strode across the room to the door that led to the front entry hall. Then he whirled back to face her. "I have not led an admirable life. I have used women for my own pleasure and avoided all forms of responsibility. In some cases I've compromised my own soul. In one particular case, I compromised the soul of another, a young girl. She committed suicide. I might as well have dealt the death blow myself. Now, where's my hat?"

"Alan, don't go." Her frank appraising eyes stared straight at him, not flinching from what he had told her. She put the rejected glass on the windowsill and moved toward him. He could not understand her motives and stood there, riveted.

"Come back and sit down," she said, gesturing to his seat.

He stared back a long time, angry at first, wondering why he didn't just turn around and leave, hat or no hat. He was not used to baring his soul like this and was disgusted that he had done so. But something about her gaze—softening, inviting, forgiving—offered him a kind of balm, a release.

"There are not many men who would admit to moral wrongdoing," she said softly. "Don't you know that? They would excuse themselves, blame someone else. They would try to justify..."

"I've always tried to see things as they really are." His voice was still angry.

"Yes. And so do I. I try. But in this case, my friend, I doubt you have succeeded."

"You ought not waste your time with me."

She gestured again to the chair, this time impatiently. He returned, a faint smile on his lips. "Haven't you heard enough? Do you want details?"

"No." She waited until he had reseated himself, then settled against the back of the settee. "But I think there's something else you ought to know. Tell me, have you heard from anyone back in Philadelphia since you left?"

"No, I've been too much on the move. I had no idea where I would be, so I couldn't even give Grey an address."

"You didn't know if Grey had returned safely, or if he recovered from his illness?"

"I assumed he had. There was no reason why he ought not to have done."

"Such indifference! I thought you were the best of friends. Or is that jealousy speaking?"

"Neither. Grey and I have never been the best of friends."

"But you asked him on this trip."

"An act of atonement. For the sake of his health. And because Lady Burleigh—Grey's aunt by marriage—had decided Grey and Stephanie would make a perfect match."

He waited for her shock. She only looked puzzled. "Atonement?"

"It was Grey's sister who committed suicide. And if he hasn't told Stephanie why by now, he has more restraint than I gave him credit for."

"Oh." It took Kate some time to absorb this. Her face turned thoughtful, her eyes looked toward the fire, her hands clasped across one knee. She showed neither surprise nor condemnation.

"What did you think I ought to know?" he asked, his voice now gentle.

She looked back at him and returned her legs to a properly genteel position, ankles crossed, skirts smooth across her lap, hands folded before her. "Strange. There's a kind of parallel, isn't there? Alan, you remember Dick Harlow?"

"How could I forget him?"

"He was found—his body was found—covered with snow, some two weeks after the ball. He had died of exposure."

"My God!" And then, after a moment, "You're sure of this?"

She nodded. "Stephanie blames herself."

"She needn't. He was a fool. Poor girl . . ."

"I agree with all you say. So, can you not consider that the case is not very different from your own?" She leaned forward, and her blue eyes gleamed with earnestness, imprisoning his gaze. "Perhaps, Alan, Stephanie could see it, too. Because I don't believe you're any more responsible for that poor girl's death than Stephanie is for Dick's. People have to be responsible for themselves."

He might have objected. He could have claimed the difference in circumstances. He might have denied that Stephanie could—or needed to—feel the same responsibility that he did, or rejected the implication that she carried as searing a burden of guilt as he had, the past six years. But

Kate's words resurrected a tiny flicker of hope, and so he allowed them life, unchallenged.

What Alan had thought was over—what he had sworn to put behind him, even if it meant a gaping wound in his life—was not over, after all. The pictures he had consigned to an unvisited part of his brain, marked OUT OF BOUNDS, where they must fade and die for want of nourishment, now threatened to break the walls he had built around them.

Stephanie, tumbling into the snowbank, laughing and breathless, snow clinging to her forehead and nose, her cheeks bright, bronze tendrils escaping from under her brown fur bonnet. Stephanie in ivory lace and green silk that matched the light in her green eyes, hesitating under the mistletoe, waiting for the kiss that he refused her. Stephanie in his arms, snuggling against him on a cold, starry night, her breath warm against his cheek, making him invulnerable to cold or the slippery ice beneath his feet. Stephanie, sitting on a blue tapestried chair, the fire painting her face and hair rose and gold, looking up with her oblique gaze, offering herself to him *without shame*. . . .

He barely noticed the long rows of lombardy poplars that lined Pennsylvania Avenue as he paid the hackney driver and turned to walk toward the newly restored Capitol. He, with his reporter's eye that usually viewed his surroundings with written words constantly forming in his head, had paid no attention to them for—how long a distance?

"The Capitol building in Washington has been completely restored to the state it enjoyed before the invading British Army shamefully burned it in 1814 . . ." (Would the *Times* delete the word "shamefully"?) "The two white-painted stone wings, one housing the Senate, the other, the Hall of Representatives, rise splendidly above a screen of small trees on an impressive hill. They are connected at present by a long, arcaded walkway. The proposed central dome has yet to be begun."

At the entrance to the Hall of Representatives, he presented his card. Newly printed for his trip to the United States, it read:

Mr. Alan Dunstable, Journalist-at-Large
THE TIMES of London

He was admitted to a half-empty visitor's gallery and took a seat in the first row. From there he could peer out between the marble columns that supported the ornate semicircular ceiling. Overhead, crimson curtains hung in graceful drapings from one column to the next. Across the expanse of desks and seats, two huge brass candlesticks guarded the speaker's desk on its raised platform. Above it a round gilded dome rained more crimson silk, providing the backdrop for an enormous gilded eagle.

"Our simple republican tastes," some American had told Alan. He smiled to himself and mentally wrote a sarcastic comparison of this room to the Chamber of Deputies in Paris, one of the most ornate assembly halls he had visited. Stephanie would have appreciated the satire.

The business at hand was to tally the electoral votes, cast in December for president, and announce the results. Men in frock coats, white neck cloths, and dark cravats moved up and down the aisles, saluted colleagues, assembled in twos and threes, and took their seats. Alan drew out his black notebook, bumped elbows with another man sitting next to him, apologized, and settled back in his seat.

Again Alan's thoughts turned to Stephanie, saying good-bye that last day, straightening the capes of his greatcoat. "Must I still keep quiet?" she had asked. *Oh, my darling, if only I had allowed you to speak; had spoken myself to your father. . .* "It's not too late, so long as you both are alive." *Shall I bless you, Kate Hamlin, or curse you, for resurrecting this dream?*

Today the senators were joining the representatives for the formal count. They marched into the chamber in a body, following the President of the Senate, attended by the Secretary of the Senate and a Sergeant-at-Arms. ("Quite a royal procession," Alan wrote, not sure he would include that phrase in his article.)

The Speaker of the House offered his chair to the President of the Senate and retired to a chair on the left. The procedure, Alan had been told, would be for the President of the Senate to open the ballots of the states and hand them one by one to the tellers. It was a mere formality. Everyone knew James Monroe had won, had received every electoral vote save one, withheld by a New York elector who wanted to reserve the honor of a unanimous ballot for George Washington alone.

"A tedious business," Kate had warned. "Why not wait for a real debate?"

After considerable searching, Alan spotted Senator Hamlin's bushy blond hair and sideburns. The Senator, seated beside his colleague from Pennsylvania, was dressed soberly in black, and wore a single diamond stick-pin in his cravat. There might be some problem about Missouri, the senator had told him, since its constitution had not been formally approved by the Congress, but there were plans to smooth that over.

"Alabama," intoned the President of the Senate, handing the ballot to the teller. Alabama's votes went to James Monroe. Sedately, the other states were announced alphabetically. Twenty-four states—or would it be twenty-five?

"Missouri," the President of the Senate announced.

"Objection, objection!" a voice yelled from among the seated representatives. "Missouri is not yet a state."

Alan was amazed to hear a multitude of responses, all sounding at once. The presiding officer banged his gavel. No one heard. Someone called for the senators to withdraw. A motion for order was seconded and declared carried without a vote. No one paid attention.

"*Qu'est-que c'est que ça?*" the man next to Alan asked in bewilderment. Alan, understanding the question but uncertain of the answer, merely shrugged his shoulders and kept his eyes on the tumult below. Not much different, he thought, from a verbal battle in the House of Commons.

The Maine-Missouri Bill, Senator Hamlin had explained to him at Christmastime, had to do with the admission of those two states either allowing slaves or forbidding them. Senator Clay had engineered a compromise: Slavery would be allowed in Missouri but not in either Maine or any other state created out of the Louisiana purchase.

Jefferson, who owned two hundred slaves and deplored it,

said the slavery issue reminded him of holding a wolf by the ears. It was too dangerous to hold on, but equally dangerous to let go. Somehow, emancipation had to be coupled with expatriation to Africa. There was a colony now, Liberia; its capital, Monrovia, had been named after the United States President.

The senators had arisen in a body and were walking out. Alan took notes, both on the pandemonium ruling the floor below, and on his memory of the complex political situation that had caused it. He became so absorbed in his writing that he hardly noticed the noise was abating until he heard a clear call that Missouri be considered one of the states and its vote counted. The motion was tabled. Two black servants marched down the aisles, lit the candles on the speaker's desk, then lowered the central three-tiered chandelier and lit that also. The ceremony corresponded to growing hunger pangs in Alan's stomach.

"It is a curious fact," he wrote, "that an interruption of protocol can upset the most routine of procedures. In such cases, men acknowledged and elected for their intelligence and faculty for deliberation become as wayward as misdirected donkeys." He didn't know if he would keep that sentence, either.

Finally, decorum returned. The forty-eight senators again marched in and took their places.

"Missouri," the President of the Senate announced. This time no one interfered with the teller's announcement. The tally continued without incident, on to Virginia, the last state. The President of the Senate, with a dignified squaring of his shoulders, read off the paper handed to him. "With Missouri, James Monroe has received two hundred thirty-one votes. Without Missouri, James Monroe has received two hundred twenty-eight votes. I therefore declare that, in either case, James Monroe is elected President of the United States."

Alan breathed a sigh of relief, returned his notebook and pencil to his writing case, and stood up to don his carrick. Only two other men had remained in the visitors' gallery. The confused Frenchman next to him had long since left.

"Point of order," a voice called. "Is the vote of Missouri part of the official tally or not?"

"Order, order!" several voices shouted. A vain hope,

Alan thought as he escaped up the aisle and quitted the chamber by a side door, nodding to a Negro doorman. The fresh, cold night air hit him in the face, and he breathed deeply in his relief at being free of the useless proceedings. He looked for a hackney cab to take him to his boarding-house, and hoped he would not be too late for dinner. As he climbed into one and received the black driver's salute, he considered a title for his article. "Even in America: Much Ado About Nothing."

CHAPTER
XXI

"My dear girl, I'm so pleased for you," Dorothea exclaimed, rising from her dressing table to run over and hug her daughter.

Stephanie withstood her approving embrace, the soft, powdered cheek pressed several long moments against her own, with admirable fortitude. Her mind whirled. *I must show enthusiasm, excitement, anticipation. I must show them I really want to marry Grey.*

Her mother backed away and looked up into Stephanie's green eyes. "Are you quite sure, my dear?"

"Mama, how can you ask such a thing? It must be nigh onto eight months since you first picked Lord Talbot out for me."

Dorothea uttered a little shamefaced laugh. "Well, of course." She backed away, keeping a grip on Stephanie's hand, drawing her farther into the room. "But at that time, you had not yet met Mr. Dunstable. What I mean is, have you given yourself enough time . . . ?"

Stephanie's slender jaw tightened. "As much as I need, Mama, you can rest assured. I do not think I shall ever again be tempted by Mr. Dunstable."

"Well, then, we must think about putting a notice in *The Aurora*. And of course you will have to write Lord and Lady Burleigh, once Grey has done so. And then . . ."

"No, Mama, not yet," Stephanie said sharply.

Dorothea raised startled eyebrows. "What do you mean?"

Stephanie smiled, trying to soften her impulsive words. "He only asked me this past hour. How can you rush ahead so? We've made no arrrangements, nothing." Her mother's gaze remained fixed on her.

"It's . . . too soon since Dick died," she said. "I'm sure people think my heartlessness is directly responsible . . ."

"Not at all, my dear."

Stephanie shook her head. "No, really, Mama, I do believe that. And if I announce a new engagement so soon . . . Let's at least wait until after our return from Washington. Let's wait until spring. Then we'll have made some plans to include in the announcement."

"Oh, yes, I see what you mean." Dorothea's shoulders relaxed and she smiled in relief at Stephanie's reasoning. "I suppose I did go off a little, didn't I?"

She returned to her dressing table and picked up the necklace she had been about to put on. "Do you suppose you might fasten this? I sent Jenny in to your sister, to help her dress for dinner. Clare's far too likely to forget entirely that we're having guests for supper once she gets into a book."

Stephanie placed the large pearl-and-diamond pendant against her mother's throat, then drew the chain to the back of her neck and fastened it. "Having two Englishmen for guests has really stimulated Clare's interest in English history."

"Still, it does make her a bit quaint, don't you think? Reading history is scarcely good preparation for marriage. Besides, it's bad for the eyes."

"I suppose that now you have my future assured, you must immediately begin to concentrate on Clare," Stephanie observed.

"And speaking of Clare," Dorothea continued, unperturbed by Stephanie's gentle teasing, "will you tell her of your engagement, or shall I?"

"Oh! Must we . . . tell her, yet?"

"I think we ought to. We've been waiting for this for so long, my dear, and your father will want to announce it at the table tonight, when the Carpenters and Coxes are here."

Stephanie swallowed her dismay. "You tell her, Mama. If—if you think Papa _must_ announce it."

"Is there any reason why he should not, among our very close friends? _They_ surely don't blame you for Mr. Harlow's unfortunate demise."

"No reason, Mama." She lifted her chin. "There is no danger I'll change my mind this time."

No danger, no danger at all, her thoughts mocked her all through supper. Uncle Perry was present, as he frequently was on a Friday night. The Carpenters, dressed fashionably but in muted grays and whites as befit their Quaker simplicity, had, of course, brought their seventeen-year-old daughter Elizabeth, Clare's particular friend. Nineteen-year-old Geoffrey Coxe, who accompanied his parents, was doubtless a prime candidate in Dorothea's mind for a second son-in-law. Stephanie suspected that if her father announced her engagement to these few friends, half of Philadelphia would know by suppertime tomorrow that the Endicotts' eldest daughter had agreed to be the wife of Lord Talbot of England, even if Morton asked them to keep it quiet.

But there was no danger at all that she would change her mind.

Morton made the announcement over the dessert, accompanied by a champagne toast to the happy couple. Stephanie continued to avoid his eyes as she had all evening. She didn't want to know how he had received the news from her mother, but she remembered he had liked Alan better. Yet, even Morton had had his doubts. ("You're not entertaining a false hope, are you?") Now he might well ask, "Are you really sure this is what you want, Princess?"

Oh, had there ever been a more mixed-up person than she was right now? Her gaze clung to Grey's for reassurance. His blue eyes, steady and tender, continued to meet hers confidently. He managed to say all the right things to the company. Stephanie scarcely spoke a word.

Clarinda was uncommonly quiet, too, despite the presence of Elizabeth and Geoffrey. But Stephanie, dealing with her own churning emotions, did not realize this until much later. After the meal the Coxes, encouraged by Dorothea, asked Stephanie and Grey to sing the duet they had heard about, the one that had caused such a sensation aboard ship. "*La ci darem la mano*,"—"Give Me Your Hand."

Grey and Stephanie sang for their guests while Uncle Perry played. Grey now used all his considerable talents to project a teasing, ardent spirit. His eyes were bright, his arms caught her about the waist at the song's climax, and it was easy for Stephanie, for the duration of the duet, to respond in kind. It was easy to take on a musical identity, easy to playact with Grey, to love him. At least for tonight.

When they finished, to enthusiastic applause, Stephanie noticed that Clare was not among the listeners. No one seemed to know how long she had been absent. Jack and Harry began carrying two extra tables into the drawing room, so all twelve could play whist. "We need Clare to complete the third table," Perry said. "I'll go look for her."

"Let me, Uncle, I pray you," Stephanie said with a flash of intuition. Outside the drawing room's double doors, she took a candle from the hall stand and climbed the big front stairs to Clare's bedchamber.

The door was ajar, but the room was nearly in darkness. A single candle glowed in a wall sconce near the door, but no one was on the bed. The little dressing table chair was empty, and so was the daybed at the foot of the four-poster. Finally, she saw Clare standing at her window, which overlooked the front of the house. Her hands held the yellow muslin curtains apart against the frame of the window.

"Clare?" Stephanie called from the doorway.

Clare turned her head. "Oh, hello, Steph." Then she returned her gaze out the window. Sensing something different about her sister's attitude—though her voice sounded normal enough—Stephanie crossed the room, stood beside her, and matched her gaze to Clare's. The lantern above the portico cast light on dwindling mounds of snow. A narrow patch of dun-brown grass now showed on either side of the stone path leading to the street. Beyond the gate, Locust Street gleamed damply with melting snow.

"What are you looking at?" Stephanie asked, slipping an arm around her sister's waist.

"Nothing in particular." Clare let out a sigh.

"We're ready for whist. We need another player."

Clare looked up at her. Her hazel eyes—all gray now, in the room's twilight—were rimmed with red.

"You've been crying. What is it, honey?"

Clare turned away. "Nothing really. I don't know."

"Clare, surely you know."

"No, I . . ." Clare sighed again and shrugged away Stephanie's arm. She let the muslin curtains fall into place and turned back to sit on her daybed. "I've known all along that Grey was for you. I've especially known it recently, since he recovered from his illness, but I thought, after Christmas . . . Steph, I thought it was Alan you loved."

She looked at Stephanie, a little frown wrinkling the brow of her round face."

"It was . . . nothing." Stephanie dismissed Alan with a wave of her hand. "A temporary madness."

"Yes. Well, Mama did discuss her hopes for you. After your accident at the theater, she thought . . . Well, I agreed to stay out of the way so he—so Grey could propose to you. And now he has. It all worked out perfectly, didn't it?" There was a desolate tone in her voice. She turned to plump up a decorative pillow and smooth out the white crocheted spread on the bed.

Stephanie's heart plopped into her throat. "Clare, *you're* not in love with Grey, are you?"

Clare looked up. Her lips were pursed. She looks like Polly, Alan had said. Her coloring, her stature, even her eyes. And though she had never met Polly, Stephanie had a disorienting sense of déjà vu. "Are you?" she asked again, sharply.

Clare shook her head slowly, as if she were puzzled. "In love with Grey? Oh, no, I never meant . . . No, of course, I'm not." She stood up. "I'm just foolish and very selfish. I don't want to lose you. I don't want you to go all the way to England to live."

Stephanie's relief was so great that she almost laughed. "But Clare, you can come visit! And stay and *stay* . . ."

"Of course I can." Clare smiled back tremulously. "It wasn't only that, Steph. It was . . . wanting to be in love, too. Wanting to be happy, like you were tonight. When you sang your duet . . .''

"Oh, honey." Stephanie put her arms about Clare, feeling the moisture coming to her eyes. She was a little surprised at the fierceness of Clare's reciprocal hug. "You will," she promised in a whisper, her cheek against her sister's dark curls. "You've plenty of time."

"I know," Clare sniffed against Stephanie's shoulder. "I'm just a silly." She backed away and reached for her handkerchief, lying atop her dressing table. It was already wrinkled and damp, but she wiped her eyes with it anyway. "Come on," she said briskly, "let's go play whist."

Two days later, having duly returned an acceptance to sing at the inaugural ball on March fifth, Stephanie was ransacking her music for suitable material. Something patriotic, Kate had suggested. The only patriotic songs she owned were "Yankee Doodle" and "The Liberty Song," which seemed far too warlike for the present peaceful era. She would have to ask Uncle Perry for his opinion.

Everyone else was out. Clare had left that morning and would spend the day and night with Elizabeth Carpenter. Morton was at the Northern Liberties shipyard, checking the finishing details of *The Enterprise*, third of the Green Tulip Line, scheduled for christening in April. Dorothea, taking advantage of Grey's new status as prospective son-in-law, had asked him to escort her to the Orphan's Society building on Cherry Street for her monthly inspection, as the Society's secretary, of the facilities and its eighty-odd inhabitants.

It was good to be alone. Stephanie vocalized loudly, not needing to worry about disturbing anyone, then sang over some of her favorites, accompanying herself imperfectly on the pianoforte. Then she rang for Elsa, ordered tea, and sat in the chair near the bookcase while she waited for the refreshments to arrive.

Her eyes moved aimlessly over the titles and stopped at a slender white volume wedged between Byron's *Prisoner of Chillon* and Washington Irving's satirical *History of New York*. She knew, without looking, that it was *Sonnets* by A Gentlewoman.

Softly, unobtrusively at first, the spirit of Stella Talbot began to hover. Stephanie reached for the little book as if directed to it, then hesitated. It had come from Alan's hands. It was Alan who had explained the sad fate of its author, a fate for which he himself had been responsible. How had it made him feel to bring Stella's poems to her? What had he really felt at her death?

A pain stabbed her chest, a sensation so vivid that she put her hand to the place. Then she lifted her chin defiantly. She must learn not to flinch from memories of Alan. And a fresh reading of the poems might give her a new understanding of the poet's brother, the man she was going to marry.

She took the book out, opened it, and began to leaf through the pages. "Windmills on the Downs." "The River in Autumn." "Crushed Blossoms." "Why the Birds Sing." "My Distant Brother." "The Purest Soul." "When Death Lies Waiting."

Even the purely descriptive ones, the ones most bound to nature, had an air of ethereal melancholy about them. She turned for a second time to "My Distant Brother."

> Fate parted us one day long years ago,
>   The lad who sang away my infant tears.
> We shared no common hearth, could never know
> Each others' foibles, strengths, loves, hates, and fears.
> Once grown, our glad reunion seemed near wrought
>   Then, caught in ways I could not understand,
> He spurned the love I offered, worlds sought,
> Entrapped by lures from Pleasure's beckoning hand.
>   A stranger was the instrument who cast
>   Our separate lives together, by love's net.
> Bold sorceress, waif, deceiver, friend at last,
>   A girl, yet woman; 'twas through her we met.
> Restored now, newer than the rising sun,
> Our kinship bonds shall ne'er more be undone.

Grey, the distant brother. Brought up in his uncle's great house, while Stella remained at home with an improvident father. But who was the stranger who had brought them together—the "sorceress, waif, deceiver, girl-yet-woman?"

Polly, echoed in Stephanie's brain. Never referred to as Lady Talbot. A paragon, she had suggested once to Alan. Far from it, he had said, laughing at the idea. Polly— illegitimate waif, mistress ("sorceress, deceiver"). But "friend at last." Certainly an unusual person, a girl who could captivate both a worldly earl and his pleasure-seeking nephew, but also earn the friendship of naive, religious Stella. Polly. So many hints were in the poem of the relationship between the three of them. She was amazed she had not recognized it before.

Elsa arrived with her tea. Stephanie thanked her absently and poured herself a cup as the German girl left. Putting the steaming cup to her lips, she stared toward the drawing room door, pondering. At the very beginning, faced with Grey's melancholy, she had balked at the impossibility of filling the shoes of a dearly beloved deceased wife. How could she have ceased to consider the enormity of that task this past month? Polly was still there in his memory and always would be. Two ghosts hovered now—sister and wife. Two ghosts with whose memory she must compete for the rest of her life. What would Polly think of her, entering into marriage with Grey, only *hoping* she could love him? What would Stella have thought?

Footsteps sounded, approaching down the hall from the front entryway, then were muffled, so she knew someone was walking across the carpet in the drawing room. She looked up and saw Grey in the doorway. "Hello," he said. "You're all alone?"

"Yes." She smiled up at him. "Come in. You're just in time for some tea. Elsa always brings two cups, just in case she heard the order wrong. How was the orphanage?"

He entered and sat across from her in the matching wing chair, shaking his head. "Terrible, in a way. And yet, I know they try to give the little buggers everything they can. Your mother seemed quite exhausted by the visit and said she needed a lie-down."

"Yes, she is always deeply affected by visiting so many children without any family."

He waved his hand at the piles of music still lying on the floor. "What's all this?"

"I've decided to accept the invitation to sing at the President's inaugural ball. I was looking for some appropriate music." She spoke boldly, fearing his reaction, yet not knowing why she should fear it.

"Oh." He looked disconcerted. "Your parents have agreed to this?"

"Indeed, they have. It's a great honor. We shall all have invitations to the inauguration itself and the reception afterward at the President's house, as well as the ball. Even Uncle Perry and Aunt Pru are invited."

"I . . . thought you had decided against it."

"That was my first reaction. I was being a nervous Nelly. But then I thought, why not?"

"Why not, indeed?" He gave her a cold little smile. "American girls are bold. But I shouldn't think your mother would care to have strangers gaping at her daughter in such a fashion."

"Gape . . ." She did not finished the word for she understood, all at once, his perception of her appearing in public, seeking applause for what should be a modestly held talent. Courting approval from an audience of strangers was, by his standards, vulgar.

"You don't approve."

"Apparently whether I do or not is beside the point. You didn't consult me."

"I didn't think it necessary."

"And will you also think it unneccessary after we are married?"

"Oh, Grey!" She rose impulsively and leaned over to kiss his cheek, her hands on his shoulders. "I'm sorry," she said as she straightened. "I'm not used to being engaged. Besides, I decided on this even before you proposed. Once we are married, I shall, of course, consult you in everything."

It was an approved speech, but even as she said it, she rebelled against it just a little.

He smiled up at her and caught and squeezed her hands. "Forgive me. I was startled, that's all. I'm not used to ladies displaying themselves in public."

"I have something else," she said, seeking to change the subject before she started to argue with him. "Something I want to show you. I was just reading this when you came in."

She turned away to pick up the white volume of Stella's verse. Opening it to "My Distant Brother," she handed it to him, then resettled herself in the chair.

He glanced at it, then back to her. "Poetry?"

"Your sister's poems. I'm sure this one is about you."

He bent his head to the book and read the poem, sitting perfectly still. She watched his face—the perfectly shaped nose, the way his hair sprang up from his forehead with a slight wave, the graying at the temples. *This is the man I'm going to marry.* But her heart was uncomprehending, neither heavy nor light.

All at once she saw a tear course down his cheek. He handed the book back to her and wiped it away, blinking.

"Polly," Stephanie said softly. "Polly is the 'girl, yet woman.' "

"Yes, you must be right. How did you know?"

She shook her head, not wanting to give away Alan's clues that had made it all logical. "I . . . guessed. Didn't you remember the poem?"

"I—I guess I'd forgotten." But then he shook his head angrily, gesturing toward the book. "No, I didn't forget. I've never read these poems. I . . . couldn't, at first. And after awhile, I suppose I forgot about them."

She put a hand out toward him in a gesture of sympathy. "I-I'm sorry, Grey. I feel I've been prying into something I shouldn't. But it seems strange to hear you say you never read them. I just assumed you carried the book with you everywhere so you *could* read them."

He gazed at her with an uncomprehending frown. "Why should you think that?"

"Else why would you have this copy, to send me when we were on the ship?"

His expression continued puzzled only for a moment. Then suddenly he rose and knelt before her, arms enfolding her waist, his head against her breasts. Surprised, she laid her cheek on his hair and her hands, one still holding the book, against his back. She wondered at his reaction, which seemed more from a need for comfort than from passion.

"What a devilish connivance," he muttered.

"I don't understand, Grey."

He moved back, resting on his haunches, took her free hand in both of his, and gazed up at her earnestly. "I never gave you that book, Stephanie. I never had it with me. It was all Alan's doing. It's *his* book. *He* had her poems published after she died. I was opposed to it. He thought I'd want them to remember her by, but I didn't want that memory of her. Don't you see? The poetry was *his* memory of her, not mine."

"But he said *you'd* sent me the book."

"I didn't. I didn't even know he had it."

She still would not believe it. "But he visited me after we'd all been so sick, after the storm . . ."

"I know, I know," he broke in impatiently. He rose and flung out his hands. "But you see, it was all Alan's idea. And when you—you thanked me for them, I didn't know what the deuce you meant. I only pretended I did. Then later, when you started talking about Stella, I figured it out."

She drew a deep breath and leaned back on the chair. "He was trying, even then, to promote your suit. . . ."

"Was that it? Well, I never asked him to." He was still angry. She hated his anger and wanted to defend Alan. Yet she must not defend him.

"He's the one, then, who carries her poems around with him," she murmured after a moment.

"Or did, until he met you." He fell heavily into his chair.

"Oh, Grey, I beg you . . ."

"Polly, I'm sick of Alan. I'm sick of his manipulation, of his . . ." He stopped, responding to the shock she could not keep out of her eyes. "What . . . is it?"

"You called me Polly."

"No, I . . ." His eyes locked with hers. "I did?"

"Yes."

He shook his head, rubbed his forehead with both hands. "My darling Stephanie, it—it doesn't mean . . ."

"I know." She laid her head against the chair back and closed her eyes. She was suddenly tired of the whole situation. "It was just a slip of the tongue. I understand."

She opened her eyes. "You're quite sure you're ready to marry again?"

"I might ask the same of you," he countered. "Is not your loss much more recent?"

"I have no 'loss.'"

"I'm happy to hear it. Then it won't disturb you to know that Alan Dunstable is sure to be one of the people who attend President Monroe's inauguration."

CHAPTER
XXII

"The American Secretary of State, Mr. John Quincy Adams, is a short, stout man in his mid-fifties, with a bald head and a countenance not readily given to smiles. He greets a person as if he distrusts that individual's motives for speaking with him, and hopes the encounter will be brief. However, once he condescends to talk—of his long periods of public service, about which he is humble, and of his famous father, of whom he is proud—one comes to admire the wide range of his learning and to overlook his awkward, antagonistic manners.

"Senator Henry Clay of Kentucky, on the other hand, is, at forty-three, a tall, lanky, vigorous man with a plentiful supply of pale hair and the kind of blue-gray eyes the ladies love to look into. He greets you with an over-elaborate welcome, then charms you with his frank, effusive conversation. Never retiring or humble, he does not mind admitting to an ambition to serve in his country's highest office. He has long been the most famous man west of the Alleghenies, a fame now enhanced by his recent devising of the so-called Missouri Compromise.

"Confronted with the diversity of these two men, both respected public servants, one may well ask: What qualities make a man a politician or a statesman?"

Hugh handed the closely written sheet of foolscap back to

Alan with a nod that was meant to appear judicious and wise. He had just turned twenty-one. "Fair enough evaluation," he said. "I've met both men, and I must admit to preferring Senator Clay's company." He rose and went to the small sitting room's fireplace and stirred up the embers in the grate, then added more coals from the hopper. They were in Mrs. Bundy's lodging house on D Street, where Hugh shared two rooms with another senatorial aide.

"I shall probably rewrite it," Alan said.

"Why would you do that?"

"My first impressions are not always publishable. I've learned to tread softly where public personages are concerned. Too many English journalists languish in jail for taking liberties with certain royal figures."

"But this is America. The Sedition Laws are a thing of the past."

Alan shrugged. "Well, let's just say I have no wish to start an international incident."

Hugh returned to his seat with a world-weary sigh. "Politics is all hugger-mugger, anyway. It's a moot question, what makes a politician."

"Why do you say that?"

"It's all like a very thick pea soup. You can never see your way to the bottom."

Alan gave him a keen glance. "Are you becoming disillusioned?"

"You might say so. No matter how pure a man's motives when he is elected to Congress, no matter how passionately he believes in some principle or other, he ends up compromising it."

"Good men can passionately hold opposing sides. You have to compromise to run a government."

"It all depends on what that principle is."

"Oh! Senator Hamlin . . . ?"

Hugh shrugged. "He does better than most. But I'm finding that the pragmatic approach sometimes sticks in my craw. I'm beginning to doubt if I'm cut out for politics. Or law, either."

"Perhaps you haven't given it enough of a chance," Alan

suggested, rising. "Well, I had better get back. Thank you
for the tour of the Navy Yard. It was most impressive."

Hugh rose and followed him. "My pleasure. I may have
disappointed Father by not going into the mercantile trade,
but I take a great deal of interest in naval affairs. Shall I see
you this evening, then, at the Hamlins'?"

"Yes," Alan said after a moment's hesitation. "It would
be rude of me not to go."

Hugh grinned. "I don't believe you welcome a reunion
with the Endicott family."

Alan protested that this was not at all the case, and left
Hugh with a good-natured farewell. If Stephanie's own
brother had no idea why he should be reluctant to see the
Endicotts again, Alan was not ready to enlighten him.

Walking back to his hotel through the muddy streets, he
felt the same lump of nervousness in his stomach that
always developed when he considered seeing Stephanie
again. It was all very well for Kate to urge him to reconsid-
er, to admit his mistake, to try to win her back. It was quite
another thing to figure out how to go about it. Kate was
making it easy for him to meet Stephanie in the relative
informality of the Hamlin home, but what could he accomplish in the midst of a festive dinner party to celebrate
Hugh's twenty-first birthday? And was he quite certain he
wanted to accomplish anything?

Alan marshaled together the pros and cons in his mind as
he walked around late winter's puddles, avoided horses'
feces, and stepped back so that lumbering, mule-driven
wagons or fine cariages could pass in front of him without
splattering his clothes with mud. Despite the soggy streets
underfoot, the sun warmed him, and the breeze off the river
was balmy, promising spring.

The reasons he should do nothing at all seemed far too
sound to be ignored, much less questioned. One: Stephanie
was now betrothed to another, to the very man whose suit
Alan had promised to promote. It would be very poor
sportsmanship to interfere now. Two: Stephanie would, in
all likelihood, be happier with Grey in the long run. When
passion died, Grey would still have his charm, his manners,
his money, and his title. If passion were never there to begin

with, perhaps she would not miss it. Taken as a whole, women were less passionate than men. Alan had plenty of experience with women whose come-hither looks promised the world but whose response proved chill or indifferent or downright hostile in bed. It was the game they enjoyed, the flirtation, the little favors, the courtship, not what it all led to.

Three: Was Stephanie, after all, so different from those other women whose names he could barely recall? Would he himself grow indifferent and yearn to break out of wedlock's restrictions? Would he become attracted to another woman and betray Stephanie's love? Somehow this prospect gave him more qualms than the others. Hurting Stephanie in the future, making her life a misery, marrying her knowing he might hurt her in that way, seemed a far greater sin than those he had already committed. Far better to abide by his letter to her and by the evident acceptance of it. Far better to remain outside marriage, as he had always intended, and thus not risk ruining her life.

But . . .

Stephanie was different. Her very glance sent him into a rarified state of bemused expectation. Her laughter, her graceful gestures, her little airs of propriety, which seemed to mask a deep-rooted, exciting sensuality, seemed to him unique in the history of womankind. Would she ever kiss Grey the way she had kissed him—a kiss that had plumbed his very soul? Was it not a perversion of the true order of things to allow her to marry a man who had already experienced his great passion; a man who, Alan had some-times thought, was a living personification of that rarity, the one-woman man? Might not he, Alan Dunstable, be able to give her the greater happiness after all?

The basic substance of his arguments, the one he spent the most time on, centered on this: With which man would Stephanie be happiest? His complete lack of selfishness always surprised him. It encouraged him more than a little. If he truly put her welfare first, if he truly loved her, then his fears about his own future conduct might very well be groundless.

The least he could do, he thought as he climbed to his

room on worn wooden steps soiled with the muddy boots of many lodgers, was to give her a choice. The difficult part was to be understanding if her choice was not the one he wanted.

Seeing Alan shed his coat and give it to the black butler in the Hamlin's entry hall that evening, Annie and Tim ran to him, each grasping one of his hands.

"Cousin Stephanie said you wouldn't come, but I knew you would," Tim said. "I say, Mr. Dunstable, did you know Uncle Morton is going to take me in a skiff all the way down the Delaware when spring comes?"

"Mr. Dunstable, why didn't you come back to Philadelphia when Mr. Talbot did?" Annie asked. "You know you promised to bring me something from your trip."

"And what would I bring you, gentle Annie?" Alan asked with a smile. "It was too early for maple sugar candy and the wrong season for pippins."

"Annie, where are . . . oh!" came a voice from the parlor entryway. He looked up and saw Stephanie.

Her changeable maple-brown hair seemed darker, her golden complexion more golden than he remembered in the half-light of the hall's triple-branched wall candles. Her long lashes flickered in surprised recognition, and one hand went to the large jeweled medallion that hung just above the finishing lace of her peach-and-white-striped bodice.

"Hello, Alan." Her tone was as cool and composed as ever.

He bowed, unable for a moment to find his voice.

"Come on, come on," Annie insisted, tugging on his arm. "Come see what Kate has over her mantle."

"Give Mr. Dunstable a moment to catch his breath, Annie," Stephanie said. Her smile reached him belatedly and turned impersonal. "I believe we're ready to go in to dinner."

He cleared his throat. "Yes. I regret that I'm late."

She moved aside, and he passed her with a little bow and went into the parlor, escorted by the children. Tim was asking him if he had seen the President yet. Annie pointed to the picture over the fireplace—an Indian chief in full war bonnet—while everyone else chorused greetings to him.

Kate took his arm and said, laughing, "An Indian chief? No, it isn't really. Look again." And he saw that it was Senator Hamlin, who had received a delegation of Indians from western Pennsylvania the previous year, and had had his picture painted in the feathered bonnet they presented to him.

Everyone greeted him warmly. Mr. and Mrs. Endicott—he hearty and welcoming as always, she extra cordial, now that she believed her daughter was safe from him. Aunt Pru (he could never think of her as Mrs. Sanford), her manner fluttery, her eyes bright as they sought the senator—was another romance under way? Perry Endicott, proudly asking what Alan thought of their capital city. Senator Hamlin, his bushy hair flying, offering him a drink. Clarinda, calling him "dear Alan" in her friendly, breezy manner. Hugh, saluting him with his glass from a corner. It suddenly occurred to Alan to think of these people as family—a close-knit family with much love among them, enough to share with strangers. A family such as he had never had.

And Grey, coming up with a drink in his hand. "Glad to see you survived the wilds of western Pennsylvania."

"And Virginia," Alan reminded him. "And you recovered from *la grippe*?"

"Most satisfactorily," Grey said. "It was a most salutary arrangement for me to return to Philadelphia—in every way." He smiled down at Stephanie, who had joined them, and slipped a hand about her waist.

She lifted her face toward Grey's with an answering smile and a flutter of her eyelashes. It was an obvious gesture of belonging, but it struck Alan as entirely uncharacteristic of Stephanie to proclaim her attachment in such a way. The flirtatious flutter of her lashes was also unlike her. The smile was a performance smile, reminding Alan of their famous duet aboard ship. At the same time, he noticed the knuckles of her left hand as she gripped a fold of her silk dress. They were white.

Despite Grey's veiled invitation to do so, Alan did not congratulate him on his betrothal.

*   *   *

Brown's Indian Queen Hotel rose five tall stories at its
center and spread out in two wings of four stories each
along Pennsylvania Avenue. Atop the central roof, a whitewashed promenade fence stretched from chimney to chimney, but no one was using the walkway today. The weather
had turned chill again, and very windy. Stephanie shivered
in her fur-trimmed pelisse as she descended from the carriage onto the walkway before the hotel and took Uncle
Perry's arm. The multi-paned floor-to-ceiling windows that
marched along the hotel's ground level caught the morning
sun, dazzling her eyes. They walked under the big entryway
arch, between two marble pillars, and up three steps. A
doorman in a red-and-blue uniform obligingly held one of
the heavy doors open for them.

"Are you sure we need to do this, Uncle Perry?" she
murmured.

"Even if you don't, my dear, I confess to a strong desire
to see where we are to perform Monday eve. And, if
possible, I want to try their pianoforte."

The hotel lobby was big and ornate, with a crystal
chandelier overhead and a thick carpet with Indian designs
underfoot. Elegantly dressed people came and went, servants
carried luggage up a wide staircase, men gathered in the
saloon just off the entryway, hailing each other, buying drinks.
Perry explained their mission to the hotel clerk at the desk.

"This young lady, my niece, is to sing at the inaugural
ball Monday evening. Could we possible see the ballroom,
and try out the piano I'll use to accompany her?"

They might look into the ballroom, the clerk told them,
but it was being readied for the ball and they could not go
in. As for the piano, it has been placed temporarily in a
room across the hall. They were welcome to try it, but it
wouldn't be tuned until it was set in place Monday morning.

"If someone would be so kind as to show us the way,"
Perry suggested.

"Certainly." The clerk signaled to a bellboy, sitting on a
bench with two other youths.

"Come along, my dear," Perry said, taking Stephanie's arm. They followed the boy up the wide, curving stairway.

Stephanie's head was swimming. She felt as if she had not slept all night. The little sleep granted her had been too dream-laden to be restful, and this morning her mind seemed to have only a tenuous hold on reality. Her thoughts were still with the previous evening, which had been a kind of nightmare. Covering up her internal tumult had become increasingly difficult as the evening progressed. At supper—had it only been because it was his birthday that Hugh had responded to Kate's presence so warmly, laughing at her witticisms (the only way, Kate had confided to her, she dared to speak to him), thanking her profusely for her little gift, sending her approving glances even when she spoke to someone else? And Aunt Pru, hanging on Senator Hamlin's every word. Stephanie had been astonished. Love was in the very atmosphere, this night of all nights, when she must face Alan again and prove to him she no longer cared.

Understanding her dilemma, both her parents, as well as Grey, kept her occupied and away from him. She became animated and overly gay. There were plenty of people to talk to, to laugh with, and much to say about a wide variety of topics, without directing any conversation to Alan Dunstable. But whenever an allusion was made to her coming union with Grey, the glances he cast her way were distinctly sardonic. And then, in an unguarded moment, he was at her side, and she was shocked to hear his voice low in her ear. "Is there any way we might have a private conversation?"

She did not look at him as she said, "I can't think of a thing we need to say to each other, Mr. Dunstable." She thanked heaven he had not approached her again.

At the end of a wide, polished hallway, the bellboy opened one of two sets of double doors and gestured inside. "Here's where it's to be, sir, but they're workin' on the floor."

Stephanie looked inside. The room was huge and bare. At the opposite end, she saw a raised platform framed with red velvet curtains. "Doubtless you'll stand there, to sing," Uncle Perry guessed. Along one side were tall crimson-curtained windows. Three men were sweeping the floor, and two more were replacing tapers in the two chandeliers, which had been lowered from the ceiling.

"Think you can sing loud enough for so large a place?" Perry asked jovially. She didn't bother to answer. Uncle Perry knew that being heard had never been one of her problems.

"The pianer's in here," the boy said, leading them to a small room across the hall. "You want to try it, go ahead."

"Thank you," Perry said, handing him a coin. The boy saluted and left. Perry waved Stephanie in ahead of him.

A beautifully grained walnut piano stood just beyond the door. She walked up to it and played a tentative chord, thinking that practicing wouldn't accomplish much if it was badly out of tune. She tried another, adjacent chord. Well, it wasn't too bad. . . .

From the doorway Perry said, "Oh, dear, there's nothing for me to sit on, is there? Wait here, Stephanie, and I'll try to find a chair."

She nodded, not looking back, played another chord and tried a light scale on "la." When she heard the door click shut she turned around, expecting to see Uncle Perry with a chair.

But it was Alan, standing just inside, his hand on the doorknob, his face hopeful.

All the blood seemed to rush from her head. For a moment she feared she would faint. She reached behind her with both hands for support, and a jarring dissonance leaped from the keys she had leaned on.

"What are *you* doing here?"

"I . . . understood you would be coming here to practice, and so . . ." His husky voice seemed all too casual.

"Who told you that?" She almost shouted it. Her momentary dizziness receded and was replaced by anger.

"Kate sent me word." Stephanie thought she saw a hint of a smile on his lips and grew even angrier. She wanted to slap his face for frightening her so. Instead she took a deep breath and, moving to the side of the instrument, laid her gloves behind the music rack. Her fingers were trembling. She felt, rather than saw, him come up behind her.

"I don't appreciate this, Alan," she said in a low voice,

keeping her eyes on the pianoforte and the gloves. "You wrote me a most heartbreaking letter."

"It was wrong of me." His voice was in her ear. He laid a caressing hand on each shoulder.

"Don't touch me!" She whirled to face him and pushed at his chest. He dropped his arms and backed off two steps. "I don't know what you think you're doing, but whatever it is, you are too late. In case you didn't realize it, Grey and I are betrothed."

"I know that."

"Then what in God's name are you after? That was what you've wanted all along, wasn't it?"

"No, no." He shook his head, his eyes never leaving hers. "I said so, but I was wrong. My letter was wrong, my excuses were stupid." His voice was full of self-hatred. He lifted his arms toward her, an embracing gesture, yet he didn't quite touch her. "I love you, Stephanie. I love you, I need you. I'll take care of you. I'll find some way to—to give you the world. Or at least as much of it as . . ."

"Oh!" she cried out, pressing a fist against her lips. "Stop! I can't bear it. You mustn't. It's too *late*!"

His hand finally alighted urgently on her sleeve. "Do you love him?"

She pulled away. "That's not the point; you rejected me."

"I was a fool."

"Do you expect me to break my engagement? Is that what you want of me?"

"Yes." He took a deep breath but made no further move, as if he feared the least gesture would alarm her. "I—I would ask you to marry me. I was too woolly-headed before to see . . . I thought I had no right to what you offered me."

Anger flooded her again—and shame at the memory of her offer. Her body grew taut and hard and her face turned to flame. She raised her chin proudly. "You missed your chance, Alan. It's too late. I will not abandon Grey. Do you want me to destroy him, too?"

She felt suddenly imprisoned by his gaze, by his nearness. She grabbed wildly for her gloves and turned to avoid his figure as she made for the door. He stepped into her path.

"If you'll kindly let me pass..."

She tried again to go around him, but he grabbed her arm. "Stephanie, you've got to listen to me."

"I did. Oh, indeed, I did! And I cannot fathom why you believe I could consent to anything so dishonorable."

"Is it more honorable to marry a man you don't love?" He pulled her to him so quickly she had no resistance. But before their lips met, she slapped his face as hard as she could with her free hand.

He back away immediately, his hands falling to his sides. The white mark of her blow gradually turned red on his cheek. She stared at him—at the mark—for a long moment.

"Don't you dare force yourself on me, sir," she said in a low, intense voice. "If—if I were betrothed to no one at all, I still would not marry *you*!" This time, when she walked to the door, he made no move to stop her.

Outside, in the corridor, Perry stood by the far wall, holding the back of a chair.

"You knew, didn't you?" she muttered under her breath. "You knew he would be here."

"Now, Stephanie, don't get all..."

"Well, you can take me back right now, back to Georgetown. We'll do perfectly well without that rehearsal."

In the carriage, Uncle Perry kept apologizing. "I'm truly sorry, my dear. I only agreed with Kate that the young man deserved a chance to make amends."

Stephanie had drawn herself up stiffly into one corner of the carriage, pretending to look out the window. She did not respond to his protestations for nearly half the drive. Finally, tight-lipped, she said, "Pardon my saying it, Uncle Perry, but it was none of your business." She put a hand to her pounding forehead. As an afterthought she added, "Mama will be furious."

"With all due respect," Perry returned, "your mama has no more sense when it comes to affairs of the heart than a—a tadpole."

She jerked her head toward him. "And you do?" He flushed. She turned toward the window again, her shoulders stiff with outrage.

"Am I to assume, from that little remark, that it was on

your mother's recommendation you became engaged to Lord Talbot?"

"Not at all. It was strictly my own decision."

"I see." Perry made several futile jabbing movements into the floor of the carriage with his walking stick. "In that case, I can say no more."

CHAPTER
XXIII

Kate refused to apologize. "Darling Stephanie, you're being foolish. Alan loves you, and you love him. Your engagement to Grey hasn't been announced yet. What better time to back out gracefully?"

"I can't, Kate. I can't go up to Grey and reject him without any reason. What if he ended up like—like Dick?"

"Why should he?"

"It was my fault that . . ."

"It was not your fault. Dick was always a little odd."

"That's no excuse, especially with Grey. He's not the least bit odd."

"No, and chances are he'll recover nicely."

"But he has only just recovered from his wife's death. Another blow like this, and . . ."

"A temporary blow now, or a lifetime of regrets. Which do you want, Steph?"

Stephanie only shook her head, her eyes avoiding Kate's.

"Where's the girl who vowed to marry for—what was it?—'wild, incredible, irresistible' love?"

Stephanie pursed her mouth in disgust. "I was a silly infant."

"And you're wise now? That was only three months ago."

"Oh, do be quiet!"

Kate left her alone. She was busy these days, with a houseful of guests and new servants to manage. Since they had bought the house, Kate no longer worked in Senator Hamlin's office. He had hired a male secretary, so she would have time to run the household. Stephanie knew that, having once spoken her thoughts on the topic, Kate would not repeat them. This was a vast relief. She certainly did not want to tell Kate her more compelling reasons for rejecting Alan, all the things Grey had told her about his past. She would not look back, but forward, only forward.

Although the Endicotts were staying with Kate and her father, Grey, Perry, Pru, and the children had put up at Long's Hotel because of the Hamlins' limited bedchamber space. Stephanie was relieved that Grey had not been at the house when she arrived after the disastrous encounter with Alan. She did not ask herself why she was relieved.

After a quick lunch, of which she ate little, Stephanie retired to the bedchamber she shared with Clare. Once alone, she was unable to keep back a few tears. By the time her sister arrived to change her outfit for an expedition with her aunt and the children, she was still red-eyed and braced for questions. But Clare, if she noticed, did not ask what was the matter. Stephanie was surprised and grateful. Perhaps Clare was growing up and realized people liked to keep some things to themselves. Thinking back to the previous evening, she realized Clare had not even offered her opinion on the current relationship between Kate and Hugh, or discussed Uncle Pru's possible infatuation with the senator, situations that would have been irresistible to her not so long ago.

Just before they had come to Washington, Stephanie had tried, partly out of curiosity, partly out of sympathy, to learn more from Grey about his first wife.

"You're wondering about all those contradictory references in Stella's poem," Grey said in answer to her question. "You have to remember, Stell was a poet. She wrote in metaphors a lot."

Stephanie shook her head and tried to put out of her head what Alan had told her about Polly. Would Grey ever admit the truth of his relationship to the boy, or of Polly's relationship to his uncle? She could not imagine having the knowledge of what he had withheld from her hanging over her head for the rest of their married lives.

"I just wondered how *you* saw her," she said.

Grey frowned a little. "I don't know if I can . . . tell you."

"Oh, I'm sorry, I . . ."

"Not because I can't speak of her. I think now I could. But . . ." She waited, letting him gather his thoughts. Finally he said, "She made life jolly, somehow. She laughed about things most women would consider hardships. She had a—a vast disdain for the 'nobs,' as she called them— the nobility. But she loved me anyway."

"Why did she feel that way?"

"Oh, she thought that most of the time they did nothing useful." He grinned at her. "I received an impression you shared that attitude, my dear Stephanie, when you asked me what I plan to do with my life."

Stephanie smiled back. "Oh, yes, I suppose I do admire a man who *does* things, like my father. Because that's what I'm used to."

"There, you see? I suppose, in that way, you remind me of her."

"And she never made you . . . *un*happy?"

"Oh, we used to argue. We didn't always see eye to eye. But the only time she ever made me really unhappy . . ." He stopped and frowned out the parlor window.

"You don't have to tell me," Stephanie said softly.

He didn't seem to hear her. "She left me for a while. She thought I'd be happier without her. It wasn't because she didn't love me, and I knew that, so her leaving made me all the more miserable. Because I knew it was, somehow, my fault. God!" He shook his head and shuddered. "I hope I never have to go through something like that again."

Stephanie made a sympathetic sound. Grey turned and covered her hand with his. "You'd never do anything like that, would you, Stephanie? Leave me for 'my own good'?"

"Of course not, Grey," she assured him warmly.

And that, she reflected (sending a silent message to Kate and Alan and Uncle Perry and anyone else who might think her mad to go ahead with her decision to marry Grey) is why I can't back out now. And if there are regrets, I'll have to learn to live with them. Maybe, eventually, I'll forget them.

The household awoke the morning of Monday, March fifth, to an unpleasant surprise. A heavy rain the evening before had turned into a wet, heavy snow which, though now over, clogged the already muddy streets. The unpleasantness underfoot was compounded by cloudy skies and a brisk wind.

"That settles it," said Dorothea, who had been arguing with Pru and the children, as well as with Clare and Hugh, about the advisability of watching the presidential procession from White House to Capitol. "We cannot possibly stand out in this weather just to watch President Monroe drive in his carriage down Pennsylvania Avenue. And now, since the ceremony will have to take place indoors, the Capitol is bound to be too crowded for us to even get in. We should only get crushed for our pains. We shall wait and go to the White House, after it is all over, when the Monroes are receiving. After all, we are invited to the ball in the evening. That is by invitation only, and will be much more pleasant."

But Morton had gone out early that morning with Senator Hamlin and returned home with the notion that if everyone went to the Capitol two hours early, before the crush, they might easily find adequate seating in the Hall of Representatives.

Dorothea did not find the idea of waiting so long or of going out in such inclement weather either attractive or necessary. She had little patience with Morton's reiteration that this was the chance of a lifetime to take in all the inaugural activities.

After listening in dismay for several minutes, Stephanie reluctantly entered into the debate, which was becoming increasingly acrimonious. "Mama's right, I'm afraid," she said to her father. "I must be careful of my voice, and we have much to do to get ready. I don't really care that much about the inauguration itself. We can read in the newspapers what the President said." She was also thinking that, judg-

ing from the way things were going for her, she would be
sure to meet Alan Dunstable. No matter how many thou-
sands jammed the Capitol, he would not fail to be there.

To Stephanie's surprise, Clare also declined to go with
her father. She appeared listless, her eyes dull. Dorothea felt
her younger daughter's forehead with an anxious hand.
"Are you feverish, darling?"

"No, Mama, nothing like that. Just tired. I didn't sleep
well."

In the end, Morton arranged to pick up Pru and the
children at their hotel and take them to the Capitol, forego-
ing watching the procession. Grey and Perry would meet
them and Hugh there. By then Dorothea and her daughters
were in the midst of the tedious process of shampooing,
curling, and arranging their hair, with the help of Jenny.

While the maid worked with Dorothea, Stephanie and Clare,
in shifts and velvet wrappers, were combing and drying
each other's hair before the fireplace in their bedchamber.

"I wish my hair would grow out," Clare said as she
stood behind Stephanie's chair, one side of her toasting in
the fire's heat, and combed the tangles out of her sister's
maple-colored locks.

Stephanie had her eyes closed, enjoying the soothing
sensation of the comb, for Clare was always very careful not
to pull when she came to a tangle.

"It's getting longer," she said, keeping her eyes shut.
"It's below your ears now, and quite long in back."

"I want it *long* again, like yours."

"Why? Yours is much easier to manage. See how quickly
it dried. And it never gets as hopelessly tangled as mine. I
thought you liked it."

"I used to." Clare gave a discontented little sigh. "Until
you told me I looked like Grey's wife. I think I'd look less
like her with my hair long."

Stephanie opened her eyes and turned to look at Clare in
surprise. Her tone had been almost—well, jealous. "Does it
bother you to be told you look like her?"

"In a way. Do turn back, Steph, I can't comb this part
unless you're quiet." Stephanie turned back obediently. "I
wonder, though, what she was really like," Clare contin-

ued. "I can't imagine Grey marrying someone like that, someone who wasn't a lady. He's so fastidious."

"How did you know she wasn't a lady?" Stephanie asked.

"Why, he told me one time. He said she'd started out as a servant in a London inn. She didn't even know how to speak properly. She spoke—what do they call it?—cockney. Lord Burleigh took her in and educated her, and that's how Grey met her. But still . . ."

Stephanie's mind was whirling, and she ceased to hear what Clare was saying. "He told you?" she interrupted. "When?"

"Oh, not long ago. Something I said or did reminded him of her—of Polly." Again, that queer note of jealousy. She stopped working on Stephanie's hair. "You knew, didn't you? I mentioned it to Papa, and he said he found out in London, last summer, but he and Mama didn't want to tell you then, for fear it would give you the wrong impression of Grey. I mean, if you knew the truth about his first wife, you might think . . ."

"Wh-what?" Stephanie jerked her head about to stare at Clare, knocking the comb out of her sister's hand.

"Steph!" Clare cried out. She bent to pick up the comb.

"Both Mama and Papa knew?" Stephanie repeated incredulously.

"Why, yes, and about Polly's son, too."

Stephanie clapped her hand to her forehead.

"You *did* know about Kevin, didn't you?" Clare asked, staring at her in concern. "If you're going to marry him . . ."

"Yes, I knew, but only after Grey showed me a letter . . . Clare, how did you find *that* out?"

"How? Oh, from Grey, the same time he told me about Polly. He said Kevin is Polly's son by a former marriage. It was very good of him to adopt the boy, wasn't it. I think Grey is a very good sort of person, Steph. Do you know how lucky you are?"

Now her voice was wistful. A shiver leaped through Stephanie, cutting through her astonishment that her parents had known of Grey's past, even if the story had been cleaned up, so to speak. Did Clare love Grey, despite what

she had said before? If so, that was awful enough. But it
seemed even worse to realize that Grey found it easier to
confide the secrets of his past life to Clare than to her, his
future wife.

Returning to his hotel early that afternoon, Alan wrote the
following paragraphs, which he intended to elaborate on at
his leisure.

"James Monroe began his second term as President of the
United States of America today. The weather was not at all
cooperative, and there were virtually no spectators lining the
mile-long Pennsylvania Avenue when the President rode to
the Capitol for the ceremony.

"Three-fourths of our nobility would have disdained his
plain carriage as too humble. It was pulled by four excellent
horses, but only a single footman stood behind. The secretaries of State, Treasury, War, and the Navy, each in a
carriage drawn by a pair of horses, came next. There was no
band, no cheering, no celebration.

"Not, that is, until they reached the Capitol, which was
already choked with people. The President and his Cabinet
had to squeeze their way through the crowd to reach the
Hall of Representatives, where the oath of office was to be
administered. Our own Minister, Sir Stratford Canning, despite his credentials and the splendor of his court dress, was
unable to get into the hall. Neither, unfortunately, was this
reporter. I have it on good authority, however, that the Chief
Justice of the Supreme Court, Mr. John Marshall, swore in
the President as planned, and Mr. Monroe gave a fine
speech, and the Marine Band played some fine tunes, after
which cheers went up from the gallery.

"At present, the President and Mrs. Monroe are receiving
congratulations at the presidential mansion, which has been
dubbed the White House since its restoration. Tonight, there
will be a gala inaugural ball at Brown's Indian Queen Hotel
where, one can hope, it will not be too crowded for the
participants to dance and enjoy themselves."

And so it was over, he thought as he carefully wiped his
pen, put it back in his writing case, and sprinkled sand over
the sheet of foolscap. It was the end of the line, so far as his

assignment was concerned. He could begin the return jour-, ney to England tomorrow, or he could stay in the United States, travel as far south as Florida or as far west as the Mississippi. He could, if he wished, even lose himself in the vastness of this land that now stretched to the Pacific Ocean, a land with limitless dangers, seemingly limitless miles, and, probably, limitless possibilities. Or he could go to Mexico, Colombia, Argentina, and look for an uprising, a revolution, to report.

But he liked the United States. He had particularly liked its microcosm, Philadelphia, for the energy and inventiveness of its citizens and the integrity of its institutions. He could have settled quite happily in Philadelphia.

In any event, he did not really want to return to England, and, with his unofficial mission from Lady Burleigh satis-factorily concluded, he did not need to. He could write her and say, "As Grey has doubtless written you already, my commission from you has been carried out. . . ."

Had Grey written to his aunt and uncle yet? Was he planning to return to England with his bride, or would he stay in the United States for a while? How would Stephanie adjust to life in England? Would she enjoy being the wife of a peer, being a countess? Would she be content to take up the duties of that position, or would she rebel, as he understood Polly had sometimes done? And would she be happy . . . ?

Desolation descended on him like a great, gray blanket. He rose and went to his liquor cabinet and found the bottle of bourbon that Kate had given him. Pouring himself a shot, he raised the glass in mock salute. *Cheers to you, Kate Hamlin, and here's to your marvelous advice. Much good it did me—or Stephanie, either, for that matter. So I strip myself of pride, bare my very soul, speak plainly and passionately—and receive a resounding refusal. Is there some way I could have gone about it that would have gotten a different result? Some way that would not have angered her, turned her against me? To propose that she marry me instead of Grey has been labeled "dishonorable." Yet, it is, without doubt, one of the least dishonorable things I have ever done.*

Oh, well, the devil take her! The devil take all women!

He drank the whiskey down in one swallow, like a victory toast, and took satisfaction in the way it burned a path down his gullet.

CHAPTER XXIV

The ballroom, sparkling with polish, gay with flags and red, white and blue bunting, brilliant with the lights of two large chandeliers, was already crowded with dancers when Stephanie arrived on Grey's arm. She wore her favorite dress, the green silk Morton had paid a small ransom for in London, the one she had worn when singing at the American Minister's home. Instead of daisies above her ears, she now wore pale green-and-white feathers nestled among the curls at the back of her head.

She was trying to appear as bright and excited about this gala occasion as everyone else seemed to be, to not think of opportunities bungled, of decisions too hastily made. Besides, she must perform her solo, which would occur later in the evening, during an intermission. She had been told it would follow a reading of poetry by Mr. William Cullen Bryant. When she saw the pianoforte sitting on the platform at the end of the long room, she felt her mouth go dry and wished she and Uncle Perry had rehearsed her numbers here after all.

She and Grey followed Morton and Dorothea into the hall and joined the line that greeted President and Mrs. Monroe, along with the Vice-President, Cabinet Secretaries, and their wives. Behind them came Uncle Perry, escorting Pru, who had left the children at the hotel with a nurse. Then Hugh,

escorting Clare, and Senator Hamlin with Kate. "The Philadelphia contingent," Morton had laughingly dubbed them,
although there must be other Philadelphians present.

President Monroe, tall and slender in his black broadcloth
cutaway, wore a lace stock at his neck, knee breeches and
hose, and buckled shoes. In his elegant but old-fashioned
clothes, he seemed to Stephanie a figure straight out of the
past. His abundant brushed-back hair was white along its
receding widow's peak. His frank blue eyes met hers with a
smile. "Miss Endicott. I understand you will favor us with
some songs later."

She was surprised and impressed that he remembered her,
after all the people he had doubtless encountered today.
"Yes, Mr. President," she said. "For your sake, I shall
endeavor to do my best."

She hoped Grey, just behind her, had heard the President's words. Surely there was no cause, now, to feel that
she was doing something not quite *comme il faut* by singing
tonight.

The President's greeting, and the equally cordial handshake by his First Lady, restored Stephanie's confidence.
The delightful leaps and runs and trills of Mozart's "Allelujah"
and Bach's "My Heart Ever Faithful" had always been easy
for her. Uncle Perry had been right to select such joyous,
religious numbers for this occasion. Since her voice had
shown no signs of going hoarse, she had nothing to worry
about.

The music—spirited waltzes and reels and stately cotillions and minuets, played by the small orchestra—helped
her retain a sense of anticipation and gaiety for much of the
evening. There was no danger of encountering a certain
English journalist tonight, although the crowd was alive
with foreign dignitaries—stiff English ministers, glittering
French aristocrats, bemedaled Prussian generals. Stephanie
danced with a number of these men, and their faces passed
before her in a daze. Dorothea, hovering in her characteristic way to make sure Stephanie did not overtire herself,
insisted she sit out a dance every once in a while and drink
some punch.

She was doing just that, seated near the orchestra between

Aunt Pru and Uncle Perry, when she saw Clare and Grey dance by. It was a waltz, a dance at which Grey seemed to excel. His tall, lithe figure in the tight, perfectly fitted black pantaloons, gleaming satin waistcoat, and velvet-collared coat was a perfect complement to his youthful, handsome face with its intriguing, melancholy hint of gray at the temples.

Clare's dark curls sparkled with diamond-studded combs. The firm young flesh of her white neck and shoulders were lovely above her ivory silk gown. The low neckline had been a source of contention between Clare and Dorothea, who was not ready to admit to such sophistication for her youngest child. Clare had won the battle, and was attracting many male eyes, as she had doubtless intended to do. But Clare's eyes were fixed on the face of the man who held her in his arms. Adoringly, without reservations, so that there was no doubt in Stephanie's mind that she had guessed right that morning after all.

And Grey? For a long while Stephanie could not guess his attitude. His head was inclined toward his partner, but they did not seem to be speaking to each other. Then they whirled by, right in front of her, and Stephanie saw Grey's eyes return Clare's adoring gaze, yet with an odd cast to them, as if they saw her through a veil. It reminded her of the way he had stared at her sister when they had first met, but this time the gaze was not antagonistic. Rather, it accepted and welcomed her, almost as if he believed he danced with Polly again, in a different ballroom, in a different time.

Was he only pretending or was he really so caught up in the past, or did he only want to be? Was she really seeing what she thought she saw in his face? Polly and Grey, Grey and Polly. *I have never seen two people more in love.*

She shook her head angrily as Alan's words rang in her mind. Aunt Pru, who had been deep in conversation with her brother, looked at Stephanie inquiringly.

"It's nothing," Stephanie said.

"Perry and I were just commenting on how handsome Grey is."

"And how nicely he and Clare dance together?" Stephanie asked, her voice astringent.

Pru frowned. "Why would you say that, honey?"

"Because . . . because they do," Stephanie said more gently, smiling. Her heart beat wildly. She feared Pru could read her mind, that her aunt must know she had nearly said, "Because Grey and Clare are in love."

Mr. Bryant's reading of his own poetry was not heeded by everyone. Some on the fringes of the large crowd continued to wander to the punch table and murmur asides to a neighbor. Stephanie, standing next to Grey close to the platform, suspected the same would be true when she sang. She was both irritated and amused, and relieved of a certain nervousness that had crept upon her as the time for her performance neared. As for Grey, once he had returned to her, he seemed as attentive as ever, and she could not help wondering if what she had seen had been only a figment of her imagination.

> ". . . The cool wind
> That stirs the stream in play, shall come to thee,
> Like one that loves thee nor will let thee pass
> Ungreeted, and shall give its light embrace."

The poet finished in his sonorous voice to polite applause. The chairman of the inaugural committee announced "Miss Stephanie Endicott, one of the fairest songsters ever to come out of Philadelphia." She smiled and wrinkled her nose at Grey at the extravagant introduction as everyone applauded again. He did not return her smile. Then Uncle Perry escorted her up the two steps onto the platform, and she took her place along the piano's gleaming side. Clasping her hands before her, the way a voice coach had taught her years before, she nodded for him to begin.

Her gaze was fixed on lights and bunting, not on faces, as her voice floated out pure and strong. "My heart ever faithful, sing praises, be joyful . . ."

Ever faithful, ever faithful, the words mocked her. *How faithful you are, Stephanie Endicott, breaking one engage-*

ment, wanting to break the second. Grey did not approve her singing tonight, but that did not matter. Alan, who would have approved, was not here, but she would not let that matter either.

She bowed her head at the end of "My Heart," and curtseyed low at the end of "Allelujah." Everyone was smiling, nodding, clapping. She returned to Grey's side. Her parents hugged her, and then Grey said, "You sang those runs so effortlessly, Stephanie." It was his only comment before she was flooded with congratulations from others.

"When we were in France," Mrs. Monroe said, "we heard Madame Catalani. Perhaps I am not a true judge, but I believe you sing just as well."

Two rosy spots appeared on Stephanie's cheeks as she expressed her gratitude for the First Lady's praise. To be compared to Europe's greatest operatic soprano! She glanced up at Grey, thinking, *There, you see? I do have a right to share my gift, even with strangers.*

The Monroes left soon after, before the supper that was held in an adjoining room. As he escorted her to it, Grey said in her ear, "There was a fellow near me as you sang. I didn't like the way he looked at you."

"What fellow?"

"I don't know. A Frenchman, I think."

"Looking at me how? I didn't notice."

He shrugged. "I'd rather not say, in polite company. Anyway, I thanked God that this is the last time you'll be doing this sort of thing."

She turned to him quickly. "Oh, but it isn't, Grey. I've agreed to sing at the first concert of the Musical Fund Society, in April. Didn't I tell you?"

His face showed a mortified anger, but, because of the crowd around them, he said no more. If he married Clare, Stephanie thought, there would be no such stupid argument. If he married Clare ... Was there any possibility? Her heart leaped with a wild joy, which she immediately tried to quell. *Tomorrow*, she thought wearily. *Tomorrow, I shall think about it*. But she hadn't an idea in the world what she intended to do.

* * *

The Endicotts took a day to rest before embarking on the return trip to Philadelphia. Because Dorothea insisted they stop at good inns and not travel too long at a time, this would take four days. Stephanie thought the idea of a rest day was ironic. She had not been able to rest for what remained of the night after they returned home from the ball. She had heard servants stirring below in the kitchen and heard the early morning cries of a muffin man and the jangle of a milk cart in the streets before her tired brain finally gave up and allowed her sleep.

It was nearly noon when she awoke and became too restless to stay in bed. Beside her, Clare still slept soundly, rosy-cheeked and childlike. Stephanie slipped out of the four-poster carefully, donned her wrapper, and tucked her braided hair under her morning cap of lace and satin ribbons. The mirror told her she looked as wan and tired as she felt, but for lack of anything better to do, she wandered down the stairs and into the dining room, where a black maid was clearing away a place from the table set for six.

"Only Massa Endicott and Massa Hamlin been up and gone," she said. "To see some man at de Treasury buildin'. No one else astir. You wants breakfast?"

"Just coffee and toast, if I may," Stephanie said. She went to the window and looked out onto a bleak backyard, still winter-bare, with mud and puddles left from the recent snow. The day was sunless, and the room was full of shadows. Her thoughts were no less muddled than they had been last night.

Even supposing she broke her engagement to Grey (for the sake of Clarinda, not for her own sake), could it mean anything for her and Alan? She could not dwell on the thought, for it started her heart to beating in a most frightening way and sent the blood leaping to her temples. No, she could not think about that at all.

When the maid returned with her toast and a small china pot of coffee, she doubted she could eat a thing, but she sat down anyway and poured herself a cup of coffee. She was spreading currant jam on the toast when the maid reappeared in the room.

"Lord Talbot to see you, ma'am. You want I should send him in, or ask him to wait in de parlor?"

"Send him in," Stephanie said.

Apparently Grey, too, had had difficulty sleeping. Despite his usual faultless dress, his face looked haggard.

"Won't you sit down?" She gestured to a chair opposite her as he entered. "Will you have something to eat?"

"No, thank you, I've breakfasted." He sat in the chair and began to twiddle with a knife, not looking at her. She thought she should say something, perhaps make a reference to last night's affair, but could not bring herself to do so.

"I didn't mean to appear indifferent toward your singing last evening," he said at last. "You gave a capital performance. But I must earnestly beg you not to consider future appearances in public. As my fiancée..."

She laid down her toast and stared at him. "How can you make such an issue of this, Grey?"

He put the knife down and leaned forward with his hands clasped together above the plate. "The whole point," he said earnestly, "is that by singing in public places you expose yourself to the eyes of anyone, men with gross appetites who, because you are doing something in public, may take you for a different kind of woman than—than you are."

"Not a lady, you mean."

"Precisely." He leaned back as if relieved she understood so easily.

"But I still am a lady, I hope. I can't help what others may think."

"What if someone accosted you?"

"I should very quickly discourage him."

"Would it be that simple?"

She looked down and traced the edge of her plate with her finger, as if trying to chart her course in this argument. "Grey, the Musical Fund Society is hoping to establish a series of concerts each year, both to bring noted artists to Philadelphia, and to raise money to help elderly musicians who can no longer perform, or to help their widows and orphans. We plan to use local musicians for the benefits, and I feel honored to have been selected to sing at our first concert. Our audience will certainly be genteel in the truest sense. I shall not be displaying myself unduly. After all, I shall still wear acceptable clothing.''

He met her little sally with a stony face. "Stephanie, you have no way of insuring who will appear at a public concert. But that isn't the point, really.''

"What is the point?''

"When we marry, I should much prefer you don't do this sort of thing. When we return to England . . . Well, in England, once you're the wife of a peer . . .''

"The point is," Stephanie broke in, "that you are not really sure you want to marry me. Wouldn't you really rather marry my sister Clarinda?''

His body hit the back of the chair's curved frame as if he had been struck. His hands fell to his lap and his face went perfectly still. After a long moment he said, "Clare! What do you mean?''

"You danced with her last night.''

"I danced with a number of ladies.''

"I happened to see the two of you, dancing together. Grey, Clare is in love with you.'' She tried to hold her gaze to his, to impress her words on him.

He looked away almost immediately, then sprang up, spreading out his hands in a kind of shrug. "What do you expect me to do? Stephanie, if you're trying to get out of a marriage you don't really want, you have only to say so.''

His expression turned forlorn. She bit her lips and, retreating in confusion, took another sip of coffee for want of something to do.

"I—I just thought . . . It looked to me, as I saw you dance with her . . . Grey, I'm not sure you are really recovered from your wife's death.''

He turned away impatiently and strode to the room's only window, still avoiding her eyes. "I don't think that's the point, either.'' He gazed out the window a long moment, then turned back, resolution on his face. "The real point is you have seen Alan Dunstable again, and he's the one you really want. But what good is it going to do you?''

"I-it has nothing to do with Alan. I don't want to be unfair to you.''

"And what does that mean—being 'unfair' to me?"

"To marry you and not give you . . . everything Polly did."

"I wouldn't expect . . ."

"I think you would. There would be a constant, inevitable comparison. I—I can't give you that kind of love, at least not now. Maybe not ever."

He folded his arms and stared at her.

"I think Clare could," she added, her tone now less certain.

"So you are refusing me? Breaking it off?"

"I—yes, I am. I'm so sorry, Grey. I feel so stupid for breaking a second engagement, but . . ." She shook her head and toyed with the handle of her cup. The toast and coffee were cold now. She was cold, too.

He returned to his chair, took hold of the back with both hands and leaned toward her. "You needn't feel that way," he said gently. "But I'm concerned . . . for your sake."

Her eyes flew to his. "You're not shattered, I hope."

"I'm not pleased. Or happy. Or relieved. I did most earnestly look forward to marrying you, Stephanie. I've come to admire you a great deal. But I shall recover. The question is, will you?"

She started to reassure him, knowing he referred to Alan, when Clare entered the room unexpectedly. They had not heard her footsteps—had not noticed them at all.

"Good morning!" she sang out gaily. Then something about the expression on Stephanie's face, about the way Grey turned slowly to look at her, must have given her pause. "I'm sorry, I'm interrupting something, aren't I?"

Stephanie made herself smile, even though the expression seemed difficult and artificial. She half-rose in her chair. "No, no, it's all right. Come on in, Clare."

Grey pulled out the chair he still held. "Your place is ready and waiting, ma'am. I was just leaving."

Clare moved toward the chair slowly. "Leaving!" She looked from one to the other. "But why? Didn't you just get here?"

"I only . . ." Grey began, but Stephanie, sure he was about to deflect the question, cut in decisively.

"Grey and I have decided not to marry after all," she said. "It was a mutual decision."

Grey had no chance to depart before Dorothea appeared in the dining room and, almost immediately after, so did Kate. Clare blurted out the news, and her mother sank into a chair and held her head with both hands, as if someone had died. Kate came to Stephanie, put her hands on her shoulders from behind her chair, and leaned over to whisper in her ear, "Shall I send someone to Alan with a message?"

Stephanie managed to shake her head. Kate pulled up a chair next to her and held her hand supportively as Dorothea began a long, plaintive account of the embarrassment, shame, and perplexity her eldest daughter continued to cause her. Stephanie heard her through ringing ears. The words made no sense, though she tried to pay attention. Why was everyone here, all of a sudden? Worse, why must all this be discussed? She only wanted to go back to bed and sleep.

"You seemed so well suited," Dorothea mourned, and raised her eyes to Grey, who had remained standing by the chair Clare now occupied.

"I very much regret having caused you such distress, Mrs. Endicott," Grey said gravely, taking all the onus for the deed on himself.

"It's not Grey's fault, it's mine," Stephanie said. "You were right, Mama. I wasn't ready to engage myself again, so soon . . ."

"I think you are all missing the main consideration," Kate said, her clasp on Stephanie's hand tightening. "And that is, Stephanie and Alan Dunstable are in love. Stephanie became engaged to Grey because of a disagreement with Alan, but now that an opportunity has opened . . ."

Stephanie began to shake her head vehemently. "No, Kate, no, you mustn't!" She pulled her hand away from Kate's clasp.

"Why are you being obstinate? I know perfectly well that's why you've broken off with Grey."

"No, Kate! It wasn't that."

"Stephanie and I disagree about her singing in public," Grey put in, coming to her assistance.

Stephanie stared up at him in dismay. Then she looked at Clare, whose chin was set, her eyes angry and bewildered. "That's the most stupid reason I ever heard, if you truly love each other," Clare cried out.

Total silence fell. Grey finally shurgged. "You're right," he admitted. "So is Kate, for that matter. The real reason is that Stephanie loves Alan."

"And *you* still love Polly," Stephanie retorted.

"Perhaps." He abandoned his hold on the back of Clare's chair and moved to the far corner of the room, behind Kate and Stephanie. "We were both trying to find . . . consolation, I suppose."

"But Mr. Dunstable!" Dorothea broke in. She had never called him by his given name. "After he hurt you so, Stephanie, surely you would never . . . You must not marry him."

"There's little danger of that," Grey said dryly.

Kate turned to him. "That's not true, Grey. Alan very much wants to marry Stephanie. But she refused him because of her commitment to you. Now . . ." she swung her head back to Stephanie and put a hand on her arm. "Do let me send a message to him, dear."

"Oh!" Stephanie cried out, putting a hand to each ear. "I wish you would all be quiet and leave me alone!"

The room became immediately still, but no one moved to vacate it, and she realized all eyes were again riveted on her.

"Not Mr. Dunstable, Stephanie, I pray you," Dorothea murmured at last.

"Why not, Mama?" Clare asked. "What is wrong with Mr. Dunstable?" She looked at Grey, who was now across the room from her. "Let's ask Lord Talbot, whose judgment we all trust. Tell us, Grey, why not Mr. Dunstable for our Stephanie?"

Grey returned her gaze for a long time. Stephanie, who could see Clare from where she sat, watched her sister's eyes soften perceptibly, and wondered what she had seen in his face.

Finally he said, "Stephanie knows. The decision should be hers."

"Knows what?" Dorothea asked.

Stephanie shook her head and lowered her face to her hands. Why did everyone insist on cornering her this way?

"I suppose you could say Alan Dunstable has led a checkered career," Kate said, "but he is an honorable man."

Dorothea's eyes were still on Grey. "You must answer Clare's question, Lord Talbot," she said. "You know him, you've traveled with him."

Grey moved again, this time toward the door, as if he wanted to escape. Stephanie saw him run his fingers through his hair. He was fidgeting. Normally, Grey never fidgeted.

"I understand your concern, ma'am," he said finally, speaking directly to Dorothea. "I even shared it, not so long ago. But I suspect things have changed. Alan has changed. And if I've learned anything, it is that . . . one must forgive past wrongs. I would never have married Polly if I had considered only her past. And she gave me more joy in five short years . . ." He broke off, and his gaze returned to Stephanie. "Kate is right. Alan is an honorable man. If he wants to marry you, I think you should accept him."

Everyone but Stephanie tried to speak at once. Dorothea's eyes lost their outraged look. "I suppose, since you know him so well . . ."

"Bravo, Grey," Clare said, clapping her hands. "I agree most heartily."

Kate leaned toward Stephanie. "*Now* may I send for Alan?"

Tears filled Stephanie's eyes. She felt, suddenly, a thousand pounds lighter. If Grey could forgive Alan, what had she to hold against him? "Yes," she whispered to Kate. "Oh, yes!"

They had barely noticed the commotion in the front hall. Now, Annie and Tim burst in on them with their usual enthusiasm, followed closely by Pru and Perry. Kate rose to greet them, and took Perry aside to speak to him in a low voice. Stephanie, warding off a bear hug from Annie, looked up to see Perry glance in her direction with a frown.

'Sshh! Wait a minute, Annie,'' she cautioned, and gave her full attention to his word.

"I already stopped by Alan's boardinghouse this morning," he was telling Kate. "I'm afraid he paid his bill and departed early. The landlord had no idea where he went."

CHAPTER
XXV

Dorothea's wedding gown, with its 1790's-styled tight-fitted bodice, low waistline, and paniers over a gathered skirt, was a perfect fit for Clarinda. Jenny repaired the hem of the pale blue satin skirt, restored some of the silver Brussels lace at the neck, and sewed on new buttons in the back, but that was all. In it, Clare looked like an old-fashioned China doll, her pale complexion heightened by a becoming blush.

"I can't believe it," she said, watching herself in the cheval glass as Stephanie experimented with the exact positioning of the wreath of forget-me-nots and stephanotis that would hold her veil in place. "I just can't believe, Steph, that on this twenty-ninth day of April, in the year of Our Lord eighteen-twenty-one, I am really going to become Lady Talbot. Or that I'm going to England to live."

"You won't be Lady Talbot," Stephanie reminded her. "You'll be Lady Burleigh, Countess of Woodworth, now that Grey is the Earl."

"Then what happens to the present Lady Burleigh?"

"She becomes the Dowager Countess, I believe—a title she will hate because it will make her sound old." Stephanie grimaced, remembering Lady Valeria Burleigh. "There. Isn't it better to have the wreath forward on your head?"

"Yes, perfect." Clare arranged the short veil over her hair

and turned to look at her profile. "Do you think I'll like her? I mean, Lady Burleigh."

"You and she will get on famously."

Clare turned around to face Stephanie. "I was so sorry for Grey when he got word his uncle had died so suddenly. But I do believe he would never have gotten to the point of proposing if he hadn't needed to return to England right away."

"And you didn't help make up his mind, just the least bit?" Stephanie asked with a teasing grin.

"Oh, maybe just a bit." Clare's small returning grin disappeared as she gave Stephanie a hearty hug. "Thank you, big sister," she murmured. "Thanks for making it possible. I only wish things had gone as well for you."

Stephanie returned her hug warmly, even though Clare's words had brought back the familiar leaden lump that so frequently dwelt in her middle.

"Don't forget to take my seedlings up to Tulip Hill when you go next week," Clare said.

"I'll remember. I'll plant them myself," Stephanie promised. They separated, smiling. "Are you quite sure you're prepared for everything?"

"What things?"

"Well, Polly's ghost, for one."

"Oh, that." Clare turned back and looked at herself in the mirror. She rearranged a lock of hair under the veil. "Maybe I should dye my hair blond."

"Oh, no, you mustn't. Anyway, it wouldn't help."

"I know." Clare sighed. "I can only take Grey on faith right now. But I'm determined that someday he'll love me for myself, not because I look like *her*. And I love him so, Stephanie. It seemed I couldn't bear it if he'd gone back to England without me."

"Has he ever called you Polly by mistake?"

"No," Clare said. "Is that significant?"

"It's a good start," Stephanie assured her.

The wedding, held in Christ Church and presided over by Bishop White, a friend of the family, was a quiet one, both because of Lord Burleigh's death and because it had needed

to be arranged quickly. Since Congress had recessed for
Easter vacation, Kate and her father were among the small
crowd of close friends who filled the pews. Hugh attended
Grey, and Stephanie and Elizabeth Carpenter were Clare's
attendants.

Standing in the reception line at home afterward, Stephanie
kept a smile on her lips and her chin high, Morton's
recommended behavior for difficult occasions. She guessed
at the question in everyone's mind: Why Clare and not her?
When, if ever, was Stephanie Endicott going to be married?
All the girlfriends she had grown up with, save Kate, now
experienced "wedded bliss" and most of them had one or
two children.

Sometime during the reception Kate told her, without
preface, that she still had no idea where Alan had gone
when he left Washington. He apparently had confided his
plans to no one, and he had not written to her. Stephanie
wondered why she would have expected him to do so. She
changed the subject, trying to forgive Kate for keeping
Alan's image before her mind. Not that it needed Kate to
remind her. After more than six weeks, the yearning and
sadness that came over her, especially at night, had not
diminished. Most of all there was regret that she had let
pride and anger and her mother's sense of propriety come
between them when Alan had pleaded with her at the hotel.
But at least she had done one thing right, and now Clare
would have Grey.

When the Musical Fund Society had given its first benefit
concert the previous Tuesday, Stephanie had thought she
saw Alan in the audience. The affair had been well advertised, and Washington Hall was filled to capacity. As
Stephanie sang *"Una voce poco fa"* from *The Barber of
Seville*, she had allowed her eyes to wander over the faces in
the audience. It was while she waited for the orchestra to
play a few bars alone that she saw a head of black curls
several rows back. She felt a rush of fright, then of elation.
Her heart raced, and her head began to swim. Only by
clenching her fists until her fingernails dug into the palms of
her hands did she recover in time to begin *"Io sono
docile . . ."* on cue. By force of will she kept her mind on

the aria to the end, not missing a twist or turn of the runs, or any of the complex Italian words. She did not look in that direction again.

Two days after the wedding, Clare and Grey traveled to New York where they would board *The Enterprise* on its maiden voyage to England. Stephanie thought it was more difficult for her to say good-bye to Clare than it was for their mother. She had lost Kate to Washington; now she was losing Clare to England. Would there ever be a confidante she could turn to in their place? The future was a bleak void. Only the prospect of going to Tulip Hill for a week cheered her.

The whole family and several servants went to the farm— Morton to get away from the constant pressure of his business, Dorothea to oversee the airing and cleaning of the house in anticipation of their frequent occupancy during the summer, Hugh because he decided not to go back to Washington with the Hamlins. He had made clear to Morton his disillusionment with politics, and was not sure, at this point, whether he even wanted to continue his law studies. Morton said acidly that perhaps he'd like to apprentice himself to Ned Nickerson at Tulip Hill and learn how to train racehorses. Hugh was not at all offended by the possibility.

The countryside was soothing. On the day after their arrival, Stephanie fulfilled her promise to plant the seedlings of marigold, petunia, and impatiens that Clare had started late in March. The sky was a serene blue. Standing in the sun, she could almost believe it was midsummer. The breeze playfully lifted strands of her hair and soothed her warm cheek as she dug in the moist dirt with her trowel, set the plants in their place, packed the dirt about the tender roots, and watered them with the watering can. With all the seedlings planted, she stood up, stripped off her muddy gloves, and gazed with satisfaction at the results. The tiny green leaves on their delicate stems stood like proud little soldiers in their precise rows. They were just starting out in life. She wished them good health and understood why Clare loved gardening so. Now she would have a whole conservatory at Enderlin Hall.

Ned Nickerson was in the potting shed, taking inventory of what supplies would be needed for the planting season. Stephanie put away her trowel, gloves and can, and told him, "If anyone should ask, Ned, I'm going to the summerhouse. The day is so glorious, I want to enjoy it outdoors."

She washed her hands at the pump and let them dry in the breeze as she climbed the little hill to the vine-shaded arbor and summerhouse. Her printed calico and apron were both smudged with dirt, her hair was disheveled, her cheeks overheated and, probably, none too clean, but it was unlikely anyone would see her before she returned to the house to clean up.

She settled into the white slatted chair swing in the west opening of the octagonal, open-sided summerhouse—the same swing where Annie often rocked her dolls to sleep. Swinging herself, Stephanie gazed drowsily down the wooded slope and caught glimpses of the river shining through the trees. The inlet where they had skated the previous winter was not visible from here. Even so, she thought about it, jealous memory forcing her to recall that wonderful day in all its detail, that day when she had been so certain where her future lay.

Happy endings were wonderful and sometimes so simply achieved. Why did her own always seem to elude her? Even Pru, whose first marriage had probably been a disaster, seemed about to reach her nirvana, for Hugh had told them on the way to the farm that he had noticed the senator hovering in attendance on her during the wedding festivities. "What about you and Kate?" Stephanie had asked. That was an altogether different matter, Hugh said. Kate was angry with him now because he had decided to abandon Washington for good. The fact that he was despondent about her anger seemed to be a good sign in Stephanie's opinion. Given the chance to pursue the lady of his choice, Hugh might just do that some day. But first he would have to decide what direction he wanted his life to take.

As for her own life, Stephanie could not even begin to think ahead. One day at a time was all she could manage.

She closed her eyes, frowning against the pain of memory. The chain that held the chair swing squeaked rhythmical-

ly. The birds chirped and twittered in the trees. Squirrels
scolded each other and dashed up and down the trunk of the
nearest tree. She could even hear the rustling of small
animals frisking in the underbrush. Life was peaceful all
about, but not within her own heart. Would there ever come
a time when pain was replaced by a bittersweet nostalgia?
And was that the best she could hope for?

"You *are* here, just as I was told."

That voice. . . .

Her eyes flew open and she jerked upright, making the
swing careen violently. Sun dazzled her eyes; she saw no
one. Then a hand settled on each shoulder, halting the
swing's motion.

She twisted her head backward and looked up. "Stephanie,"
he said, smiling down at her.

"Alan! You gave me such a scare!"

"No doubt the worst of all the sins I've committed
against you." He moved around the swing to face her, one
hand on the chain that fastened it to the ceiling of the
summerhouse. "You looked so peaceful sitting here that I
was loath to wake you."

"I—I wasn't asleep."

Every emotion he had ever aroused in her now awoke and
clamored for primacy somewhere in her breast. Still, her
eyes feasted on his appearance. How wonderful to see again
those thick black curls, the long, vivid brown eyes awaiting
her welcome, the white teeth between slightly parted lips,
the square hard line of his jaw. He wore a plain white shirt
and muslin neck cloth without a cravat, a brown hunting
jacket, and no hat. She noticed a tiny muscle twitch in the
cords of his neck, all that betrayed his tension.

"Where did you come from? How did you know I was
here?"

"I spoke to your father at his office, day before yesterday." His face was solemn, awaiting her response.

"Papa? He never said a word."

"He suggested I wait until today to give you a chance to
settle in here. I wanted to pick an occasion that would be
just right." He knelt before her, one hand on the arm of the
swing to steady himself, his eyes anxious. "Do you wel-

come me, Stephanie? Shall I stay or go back down the hill and disappear from your life forever?''

She caught her breath. Her lips refused to form words.

"Stephanie, why didn't you tell me?"

"T-tell you what?"

"That you weren't going to marry Grey?"

"By the time it was decided, you had left. No one knew where you had gone."

His hands gripped her passive ones. She did not withdraw them, nor could she withdraw her gaze from his. "I was in Baltimore last week," he said, "awaiting a ship to take me to New Orleans. The man who had just vacated the room I took left behind a week-old copy of *The Aurora*. In it I saw the announcement of the wedding of Lord Greycliff Talbot, Earl of Woodworth, to Miss Clarinda Sue Endicott. I must confess I thought they had the names wrong. I gazed at it, read it over and over, for at least ten minutes before I was convinced."

She began to smile, but he went on, speaking rapidly, "Then I saw an announcement for the Musical Fund Society's benefit concert. It had taken place just a night or two before I saw the paper. And there was your name. 'Miss Stephanie Endicott, soprano, will sing, in Italian, an aria from the opera . . . ' I decided right then that I had no use for New Orleans after all." His clasp on her hands grew tighter. "I knew only that I needed you."

"I'm . . . very flattered," she said with an automatic politeness.

He jumped to his feet as though she had insulted him. "Flattery be damned! It's obsession, desperation. It's 'the world well lost for love.' Wake up, Stephanie, we've lost so much time!" He pulled her up and against him in one of those swift, energetic motions that she found so exciting— and so disturbing. She laughed nervously.

"Alan! I pray you!"

"You cannot say again that it's too late."

"No. But would I find my life with you, or forfeit it? I thought it all a delusion. I thought you never really wanted marriage. There were things Grey told me . . ."

"My past sins returned with a vengeance, is that it? He told you about . . . Stella?"

His gaze had become too intense for her to face. She nodded, looking away over his shoulder.

"Would it help you to know I've been atoning for her death for years?"

She began to shake her head, but he stopped her, imprisoning her face between his big, strong hands. "Stephanie!" He drawled out her name, in reproach, amusement, distress. "Stephanie," he whispered, and brought his lips gently against hers. Even the gentleness burned, sent currents in every direction. She trembled, but still she faced him with her eyes open, her arms passive at her sides.

"I always talk too much," he whispered against her cheek. Then he closed her eyes with kisses and began to memorize her face with his lips, letting his hands slip back from her temples, one delving deep into her hair at the back of her head, the other sliding down her throat and shoulders and arm.

In unconscious response, her arms encircled his waist. His embrace became stronger, his lips returning to hers with new demands, asking more than a token, even more than the promise she had given on a cold New Year's Eve. Helpless, she returned all he asked.

"You *do* belong to me—we belong to each other," he murmured against her cheek. "Must I remind you that once you offered yourself to me . . ."

"What a wretch you are, Alan Dunstable, to speak of that again!"

"What other ammunition can I marshal?"

"All those other women . . ."

"None but you," he said. "The past is dead. None but you from now until my dying breath."

"Don't hoax me, Alan, I couldn't bear it."

"I have never played false with you, Stephanie."

"Stella was an innocent . . ."

"Dammit!" He stood apart from her and his face blazed with anger. "Yes, that's true. But when I tried to tell you I was not a suitable husband, you dismissed it. Has what you learned about me changed me so much, just since January? I'm still the same person you said you loved then."

I would never have married Polly if I had only considered her past. She could almost hear Grey's voice now. She trembled, gazing into Alan's eyes. How easy it was to lose herself in those eyes. How easy to find her world in his glance.

"I told Kate about Stella, and she was not dismayed. She said—forgive me, Stephanie—she said I was no more responsible for Stella's death than you were for Dick's. If you think otherwise, I'll leave. This is my final plea. Your final choice."

Still she stood there, caught in the throes of the last four months' angers, resentments, and guilts. Dick. Alan was saying she needn't consider herself responsible for Dick.

"Mordecai Lewis is looking for a partner," he said casually. "Someone who, someday, will be able to take over the paper and publish books. Apparently he isn't in good health. He coughs a lot, and . . ."

She back-stepped. *"You?"*

"Yes, he's asked me. We think alike in a number of ways."

"You'd settle in Philadelphia?"

"Only if we marry, Stephanie. Otherwise I couldn't bear it."

"A-and you'd quit your travels?"

"Well, not right away. There is so much to see of the world."

"I've always felt that way, too," she confessed. "Would you . . . take me with you on those dangerous journeys of yours?"

His eyes lit up. "Would you come?"

"Would I come? Would I *come*?" She took a step toward him.

He reached out to brush her cheek with possessive, impudent fingers. "It's good to know you don't mind getting a bit dirty."

"Dirty? Oh!" She pressed her hands to her cheeks in embarrassment. "I—I forgot."

"I like it." He pulled her hands away, bent toward her

and kissed the dirt-smudged cheek. The brief sensation lingered and radiated. She smiled at him tremulously, awash in a sudden weakness. He opened his arms, and she went into them, welcoming him as a lost traveler might welcome a shelter for the night. His cheek pressed against hers.

"I could never leave you behind, Stephanie," he whispered in her ear.

"I wouldn't *stay* behind," she breathed.

"There's just one problem." He backed away just enough for her to see the solemnity of his expression.

"Y-yes?" she asked, startled.

"I shall never be able to sing duets with you."

"Alan, you rogue!" She broke his hold and stood back in mock exasperation. His eyes began to twinkle, and she felt a surge of joy within her. "There are all sorts of duets," she said.

His eyes widened in surprise. He grabbed her hands and whirled her in a semicircle on the rough ground in front of the summerhouse. "So there are, so there are!" His laugh rang out.

Breathless, exhilarated, Stephanie joined him. For several long moments the woods resounded with laughter. The birds chirped their alarm and circled up and away. Below, the Schuylkill, sparkling in the sunlight, rushed south to join the Delaware and the sea.